"ABOUT THE LITTLE MATTER OF WHERE I'M GOING TO SPEND THE NIGHT . . ."
Nick's voice was rough around the edges, but otherwise as calm as ever.

"Use your Lightfoot pull to get yourself a motel room in town." Phila spun around to confront him.

He reached out and gently caught hold of the lapels of her robe, drawing her close. "I'd rather stay here."

Phila tried to tamp down the energy that was beginning to sizzle through her. "Going to bed with you would be a very stupid thing for me to do."

"You think I'm one of the enemy."

"Aren't you?"

"Phila, the shares belong in the family and sooner or later I'll get them back. But that fact has nothing to do with you and me."

"How can you say that?" She searched his face. "Damn it, Nick, how can you *say* that?"

"It's easy because it's the truth. I can say it loud or soft or anywhere in between." His thumb moved along the angle of her jaw. "Take your pick."

"I could never really trust you," she pointed out, feeling desperate. A heady sense of awareness, a feeling of being gloriously, recklessly alive was kicking in for the first time in months . . .

"Will you kiss me?" Nick asked softly. "I've been going out of my head wondering what it would be like."

Impulsively, Phila brushed her mouth quickly, awkwardly against his, tasting brandy and desire . . . She was shaking with need, longing to know more about the tantalizing feelings flowing through her . . .

"Jayne Ann Krentz has taken the powerful themes of family loyalty, the struggle for power, and sex, and woven them into a suspenseful and satisfying story that strikes a deep, human chord."

—Patricia Matthews, author of *Oasis* and *Sapphire*

Books by Jayne Ann Krentz

The Golden Chance
Silver Linings
Sweet Fortune
Perfect Partners
Family Man
Wildest Hearts
Hidden Talents
Grand Passion
Trust Me
Absolutely, Positively
Deep Waters
Sharp Edges
Flash
Eye of the Beholder

By Jayne Ann Krentz writing as Jayne Castle

Amaryllis
Zinnia
Orchid

Published by POCKET BOOKS

THE GOLDEN CHANCE

JAYNE ANN KRENTZ

POCKET BOOKS

New York   London   Toronto   Sydney   Tokyo   Singapore

This book is a work of fiction. Names, characters, places and incidents are either the product of the author's imagination or are used fictitiously. Any resemblance to actual events or locales or persons, living or dead, is entirely coincidental.

An *Original* Publication of POCKET BOOKS

POCKET BOOKS, a division of Simon & Schuster Inc.
1230 Avenue of the Americas, New York, NY 10020

Copyright © 1990 by Jayne Ann Krentz
Cover art copyright © 1990 Morgan Kane

ISBN: 0-671-01964-3

First Pocket Books printing March 1990

20 19 18 17 16 15 14 13

POCKET and colophon are registered trademarks of Simon & Schuster Inc.

Printed in the U.S.A.

CHAPTER ONE

Something in Nicodemus Lightfoot understood and respected small towns and the kind of people who lived in them. He did not wax nostalgic about them, nor did he believe in the myth that small towns were somehow best at incubating American values and right thinking. He did not even particularly like small towns, especially small farm towns in the summer. They tended to be hot and slow. Every kid who had just graduated from the local high school was probably desperate to get out of town as soon as possible, and Nick understood their desire.

He was afraid that his intuitive knowledge of towns such as Holloway, Washington, was in his blood. Nick himself was only one generation away from jobs like working cattle or driving a combine, and he knew it. He accepted it. He had no problem with it. And that was what gave him the edge over everyone else in the families. The other members of the Lightfoot and Castleton clans were still trying to forget how close their roots ran to towns such as this one in eastern Washington.

Nick took another swallow of beer and shifted into a more comfortable position. He was leaning against the trunk of an aging apple tree that dominated the front yard of a little white clapboard house. The grass in the yard was rapidly turning brown. By August it would be dead.

Nick had been sitting in the shade of the tree for almost an hour. The beer was warm, the street of small, neat houses was empty and Nick was getting bored. That took some doing, because he was good at waiting.

Hearing a clatter in the distance, Nick turned to watch two lanky youngsters hurtle down the street on beat-up skateboards. Faithful dogs, tongues lolling, jogged behind. The boys seemed oblivious, as only kids can be, of the late June heat. Nick watched the foursome until they disappeared around the corner, and then he finished the beer.

None of the neighbors had come out to ask him what he was doing sitting under the apple tree, although Nick had seen a few curtains twitch in the houses across the street.

Earlier a couple of teenagers had checked out his Porsche with shining eyes. One of them had worked up the courage to ask if the car was Nick's. He'd admitted it was and tossed them the keys so that they could sit in the front seat and dream for a while. They'd finally left reluctantly when a curly-haired woman down the street had waved them home. That had been the end of Nick's social interaction with the neighbors of Miss Philadelphia Fox.

He was beginning to wonder if the Fox was ever going to return to her lair when the insistent whine of a small-car engine made him glance down the street.

A candy-apple–red mosquito-sized compact darted around the corner and homed in on the one open space left at the curb. With the unerring instinct of a small, annoying insect spotting bare skin, the little red car zipped around a battered pickup truck and dove headfirst into the parking space behind the Porsche.

Nick watched in fascination as the driver of the mosquito realized she was not going to be able to wedge the vehicle into the limited space from such an angle. The compact whined furiously, jerking back and forth in several short, convulsive movements before abandoning its attack.

Nick held his breath as the thwarted mosquito maneuvered its way back out of the parking space and reluctantly pulled forward alongside the Porsche so that it could back properly into the slot. The Porsche survived unscathed, but Nick had the impression the mosquito was defiant in defeat.

He guessed then that the driver of the red insect was Philadelphia Fox. He watched her turn off the engine and climb out of the car holding two paper bags of groceries that were so full they effectively blocked her vision.

His first impression was that he was watching an entity of condensed, restless energy. Her movements were quick, sharp, impulsive. With a flash of insight Nick realized that he was looking at a woman who did not wait for things to fall into place in their own time and in their own way. She pushed them into place.

So this was his ticket home. He did not know whether to be dismayed or delighted.

He had been in exile for three long years and was not yet certain what to make of Philadelphia Fox, but if he played his cards right he might be able to use her to do what had to be done. It wasn't as if he had a lot of choice, he reminded himself. It was Phila Fox or nothing. He had no other options, and time was running out.

The real question, of course, was whether he really wanted to go home. He told himself he was still ambivalent, but he knew that in his heart he had already made the decision. He would not be sitting in the heat and boredom of Holloway, Washington, if he didn't know what he wanted to do.

Nick smiled faintly as he watched Philadelphia struggle with the grocery bags and her keys. From this distance she looked neither sufficiently powerful nor beautiful enough to be capable of tearing the families apart. But that only went to show that dynamite could be packaged in raspberry-pink jeans and an orange, green and black jungle-print camp shirt.

Fox. She suited her name, Nick decided. There was something vixenish about her, something that was both keen and delicate. Her eyes were large in her triangularly shaped face, and they tilted slightly upward at the corners. They were watchful, wary eyes.

She was not very tall, probably only about five-four, and she was slender, with small, high breasts and a narrow waist. Her tawny brown hair was cut in a smooth, shining bob that hugged her jawline. He knew she was twenty-six years old and that she was unmarried. That and the fact that she had apparently had close ties to Crissie Masters was about all he knew.

Yesterday morning's phone call from Eleanor Castleton replayed itself in his head.

"She's a problem, Nick. A terrible problem."

"Yeah, I can see that. But she's not my problem."

"That's not true and you know it, dear. She's a serious threat to the families, and you're family. What happened three years ago doesn't change that fact, and deep down inside I'm sure you realize it."

"Eleanor, I don't give a damn what happens to the families."

"I don't believe that for one minute, dear. You're a Lightfoot. You would never abandon your heritage when the chips are down. Go and see her, Nick. Talk to her. Someone has to deal with her."

"Send Darren. He's the one with charm, remember?"

"Hilary and Darren both tried to talk to her. She refused to listen to either of them. She's biding her time, looking for a way to turn the situation to her advantage. I know that's what she's doing. What can you expect from someone of her background? She's just another mischief-making little tramp like that Masters creature who descended on us last fall. That horrid little tart started all this. If it hadn't been for her—"

"What makes you think this, uh, other little tart will talk to me?"

"You'll find a way to deal with her, dear." Eleanor Castleton spoke with serene confidence. "I know you will. I have complete faith in you. And you're family, dear. You simply must do something about Philadelphia Fox."

"I'll think about it, Eleanor."

"I knew you wouldn't let us down. Family is family when all is said and done, isn't it?"

To his chagrin, Nick had discovered Eleanor was right. When all was said and done, family *was* family. So here he sat under an apple tree contemplating possible methods of manipulating a mischief-making little tramp.

Philadelphia Fox walked right past him up the sidewalk to the front door of the little white house. The screen door banged as she opened it, caught it with her toe and shoved her key into the lock of the main door. The paper bags wobbled.

Nick got slowly to his feet, removing his glasses to rub the bridge of his nose as he strolled up the cracked walk behind her.

The key seemed to have gotten stuck in the old lock and refused to turn. The grocery bags jiggled precariously. The screen door escaped the restraining toe, and Nick heard a softly uttered curse as Philadelphia tried to force the issue.

Nick nodded to himself and replaced his glasses on his nose, satisfied with this confirmation of his suspicion that Miss Fox did everything the fast way and, therefore, sometimes wound up doing things the hard way. This was the kind of woman who, once she made up her mind, would charge straight toward her goal. The eager, zealous, reckless type. Nick contemplated that tantalizing tidbit of information. One didn't run across eager, zealous, reckless, mischief-making little tramps every day.

He wondered suddenly if the little Fox made love at a hundred miles an hour, the way she appeared to do everything else.

Nick scowled at that errant thought and slid his glasses back onto his nose. It was not like him to let such thoughts get in the way of business. Besides, Philadelphia Fox was not his type. At least, he didn't think she was.

Still, perhaps he shouldn't blame himself for the brief fancy. After all, he had never had a woman make love to him at a hundred miles an hour. It sounded exciting.

But maybe that was because it had been so damned long since he had had a woman make love to him at all.

Moving up very close behind the struggling Phila, he asked politely, "Can I give you a hand with those bags?"

He had expected to startle her. He was not expecting the truly frightened gasp and the flash of raw terror in her huge eyes when she swung around to face him. He barely managed to catch one of the grocery bags as it fell from her arms. The other hit the steps, spilling out a loaf of bread, a can of tuna fish and a bunch of carrots.

"Who the hell are you?" Philadelphia Fox demanded.

"Nicodemus Lightfoot."

The fear vanished from her gaze, replaced first by an odd relief and then by disgust. She glanced morosely down at the spilled groceries and then looked up again, her eyes narrowed.

"So you're a Lightfoot. I wondered what one would look like. Tell me, are the Castletons any better-looking? They must be or Crissie wouldn't have turned out so lovely." She crouched and began to retrieve her groceries.

"The Castletons got the looks and charm. The Lightfoots got the brains. It's been a profitable partnership." Nick scooped up the tuna fish and reached out to jiggle the key in the frozen lock. He maneuvered it gently, and a second later the door popped open.

"Funny," Philadelphia Fox said, her face grim as she got to her feet and glared at the open door. "That's what Crissie and I used to tell each other. She got the looks and I got the brains. It was supposed to be a profitable partnership for us, too, but it didn't quite work out that way. I expect you want to come inside and browbeat me, right?"

Nick gazed thoughtfully into the colorful, plant-filled interior of the little house. Bare wood floors gleamed beneath red and black throw rugs, and the walls were painted a brilliant sunshine yellow. The sofa was as red as the little car parked out front. Somehow all the vivid hues combined to look very cheerful and welcoming. Apparently Miss Fox's sense of interior design was similar to her taste in clothing. He smiled again.

"Yes," Nick said. "I would very much like to come inside and talk to you."

"Come on, then," Philadelphia muttered as she pushed past him into the house. "We might as well get this over with. I've got some iced tea in the refrigerator."

Nick smiled again with satisfaction as he watched her precede him into the house. "That sounds just fine."

There was a word for what was wrong with her, Phila knew. Several words, in fact. As she slapped the groceries down on the counter and went to the refrigerator, she considered those words. *Burnout* was one. *Stress* was another.

Her grandmother would have brushed aside such contemporary jargon, of course, and gotten right to the point.

Stop feeling sorry for yourself. The trouble with you, my girl, is that you've let yourself wallow around in your own emotions long enough. It's time to pull yourself up by your bootstraps. Get hold of yourself, child. Get up and get going. The world is waiting for you to fix it. If you don't do it, who will?

Matilda Fox had seen everything as a challenge. The prospect of righting the wrongs of the world was what had kept her going, she had frequently claimed. It gave life purpose. Her son, Alan, Phila's father, had followed in his mother's footsteps. He had been passionate about his causes and in due course had married another passionate world-fixer named Linda. The two of them must have shared a few passions other than the political sort because eventually they had produced Phila.

Phila had no real recollection of her parents. They had died when she was very young. She had a picture of them, a faded color photograph of two people dressed in jeans and plaid shirts standing beside a jeep. Behind them was a cluster of huts, a brown river and a wall of jungle. Phila carried the photo in her wallet along with a picture of Crissie Masters and one of her grandmother.

Although she had no clear memory of them, Phila's parents had bequeathed her more than her hazel eyes and tawny brown hair. They had left within her their philosophy of life, which Matilda Fox had in turn nourished into full flower. From the cradle Phila had been inculcated with a healthy dose of skepticism toward established authority, conservative thinking and right-wing institutions. It was an independent, decidedly liberal philosophy. Some might have called it radical. It was the sort of philosophy that thrived on challenge.

But, Phila reflected, lately it had been very hard to get interested in a new challenge. Everything seemed increasingly unimportant. She now felt her parents and grandmother had been wrong. One person could not save the world. In fact, one person could only get hurt trying to fix things.

It was tough trying to carry on the family tradition when there was no family left to support it. She had been doing it alone for years and now she seemed to have run out of steam.

Crissie Masters's philosophy of life, on the other hand, was finally beginning to make more sense to Phila. It could be summed up in five words: *Look out for number one.*

But now Crissie was dead, too. The big difference was that, while they had died young, her parents had died for a cause in which they had believed and to which they had been committed. Matilda Fox had died at her desk. She had been busily penning yet another article for one of the score of strident left-wing newsletters which printed her work. She had been eighty-two years old.

Crissie Masters, however, had died behind the wheel of a car that had plunged off a Washington coast road and buried itself in a deep ravine. She had been twenty-six years old. Her epitaph could have been, *Am I having fun yet?*

Phila dropped ice into two tall glasses and poured the cold tea. She felt no overpowering need to be courteous to a Lightfoot, especially not to one as big as the specimen out in her living room, but it was awkward to drink tea in front of someone else without at least offering a glass. It was, after all, very hot outside and the Lightfoot looked as if he had been sitting under her apple tree for some time.

She picked up the tray of drinks and headed for the living room. An echo of fear rippled through her as she recalled how close he had gotten to her a few minutes before without her even having been aware of him. *That's how it could happen*, she thought uneasily. No warning, no intuitive sense of danger; just *wham*. Someday she would simply turn around and find herself in trouble.

Phila forced herself to relax as she set the tray down on the glass coffee table. Surreptitiously she studied the intruder. He looked big and dark sitting on her bright red sofa. His eyeglasses did nothing to soften the effect.

He really was a large man, she realized, and that alone made her feel hostile. She did not like large males.

"Thanks for the tea. I've been getting by on warm beer for the past hour." Nicodemus Lightfoot reached for a frosty glass.

The vibration of his voice sent a distant, whispered warning through Phila's nerve endings. She told herself she was imagining things. Her nerves had been more than a little frayed lately. But she had always relied on her instincts, and now she couldn't ignore the way his voice disturbed her senses.

Everything about this man was too calm, too still and watchful, as if he could spend hours waiting in darkness.

"Nobody asked you to sit out in front of my house for an hour, Nicodemus Lightfoot." Phila sat down in a yellow canvas director's chair and picked up her own glass of tea.

"Call me Nick."

She didn't respond immediately. Instead she examined him for a few seconds, noting the gold-and-steel watch, the blue oxford-cloth button-down that he wore open at the throat, and the snug, faded jeans. The jeans looked like standard-issue Levi's, but she guessed that the casual shirt had cost a hundred bucks or more. His type would wear hundred-dollar shirts with old jeans.

"Why on earth should I call you Nick?" She took a swallow of cold tea.

Nick Lightfoot didn't rise to the bait. Instead, he studied her in turn, his eyes thoughtful behind the lenses of his glasses. The window air conditioner hummed in the silence.

"You're going to be difficult, aren't you?" he finally observed.

"It's what I'm good at. I've had a lot of practice."

His eyes swept over the glass coffee table, spotted the stack of travel brochures. "Going on a trip?"

"Thinking about it."

"California?" He flipped through a couple of the folders with their scenes of endless beaches and Disneyland.

"Crissie used to say Southern California would be good for me. She always claimed I needed a taste of life in the fast lane."

Lightfoot said nothing for a few minutes, and Phila watched him out of the corner of her eye. He was a predator, she decided. His light gray eyes reflected little . . . only perhaps an unending search for prey and a cold intelligence. The thin lips, bold, aggressive nose and the high, blunt cheekbones made her think of a large animal. The heavy pelt of his dark hair was lightly iced with silver. He was somewhere in his mid-thirties, she guessed. And he'd done some hunting in his time.

There was an unconscious arrogance in the set of his shoulders and a lean but powerful strength in his body. She knew that his must be a smooth, prowling stride that ate up ground as he moved. He could stalk a victim all day if necessary and still have plenty of energy left for making the kill at the end of the hunt.

"You aren't quite what I expected," Nick said finally, looking up from the brochures.

"What did you expect?"

"I don't know. You just aren't it."

"I've had phone calls from someone named Hilary Lightfoot who sounds like she runs around in an English riding habit most of the time. Also, some from a man named Darren Castleton. He sounds like he's running for office. Where do you fit into the scenario, Mr. Lightfoot? Crissie never mentioned you. Frankly, you look like hired muscle."

"I never met Crissie Masters. I moved from Washington to California three years ago."

"How did you find me?"

"It wasn't hard. I made a few phone calls. Your ex-boss gave me your address."

"Thelma told you where I was?" Phila asked sharply.

"Yeah."

"What did you do to her to make her tell?"

"I didn't do anything to her. I just talked to her."

"I'll bet. You say that a little too easily for my taste."

"No accounting for taste."

"You're accustomed to people answering questions when you ask them, aren't you?"

"Why shouldn't she have been willing to cooperate?" he asked with the mildest possible expression of surprise.

"I asked her not to give out my address."

"She did say something about you wanting to dodge reporters but when she found out I wasn't interested in doing an interview, she opened up."

"You mean you applied pressure and she caved in." Phila sighed. "So you *are* the muscle for your families. Poor Thelma. She tries, but she isn't very good at resisting pressure. She's been a bureaucrat too long."

"You, I take it, are better at it?" Nick's brows rose skeptically.

"I'm a pro. And I'll save you a lot of time by telling you now that there's nothing you can say that will convince me to change my mind. I'm not about to sell back the shares in Castleton & Lightfoot that Crissie left to me. Not for a while, at any rate. I have some serious thinking to do about those shares. I may have some questions I want answered."

He nodded, looking neither annoyed nor startled. He just looked disturbingly patient.

"What questions do you have, Phila?"

She hesitated. The truth was, she did not really have any questions. Not yet. She hadn't been able to think clearly enough to come up with any. She was still trying to adjust to the trauma she had been through lately.

First there had been the trial, which had dragged on for weeks, and then had come the shock of Crissie's death. Phila thought she would have been able to handle the trial

11

if that had been all there was to deal with at the time. But the news about Crissie had been more than she could handle.

Beautiful, bold, flashy Crissie with her California looks and her vow to get what was coming to her. The night of the vow came back to Phila now, a clear, strong image in her mind. It had been the first time she had tried more than a sip of alcohol.

Crissie, looking a worldly twenty-one at the age of fifteen, had talked the clerk of an all-night convenience store into selling the teenage girls the cheap wine. Crissie could talk any man into anything. It was one of her survival skills.

She and Phila had gone to the small town park near the river and drunk their illicit booze out behind the women's rest rooms. Then Crissie had outlined her plans for the future.

There are people out there who owe me, Phila. I'm going to find them, and I'm going to make them give me what's mine. Don't worry. When I do, I'll cut you in for a piece of the action. You and me, we're like sisters, aren't we? We're family and family sticks together.

Crissie had learned the truth of her own words the hard way. She had found the people she felt owed her and when she had tried to make them accept her, she had discovered the real meaning of a family sticking together. They had formed a solid wall against her and her claims of kinship.

"I don't know if I'm ready to ask my questions yet," Phila told Nick. "I think I'll wait and ask them at the annual C&L stockholder's meeting in August."

"The stockholders of Castleton & Lightfoot are all family."

"Not anymore." Phila smiled, really smiled, for the first time in weeks.

Nick Lightfoot appeared amused. "Planning to make trouble?"

"I don't know yet. Possibly. Crissie deserves that much, at least. Don't you think? She loved to stir up trouble. It was her way of taking revenge on the world. Making a little trouble on her behalf would be a fitting memorial."

"Why was Crissie Masters important to you?" Nick asked. "Were you related?"

"Not by blood or marriage, and that's probably the only kind of relationship you would understand."

"I understand friendship. Was Crissie your friend?"

"She was much more than a friend. She was the closest thing to a sister I ever had."

He looked politely quizzical. "I never met the woman, but I've heard a lot about her. From what I've heard, the two of you don't appear to have had much in common."

"Which only goes to show how little you know about either Crissie or myself."

"I'm willing to learn."

Phila thought about that, and she did not like the direction her mind was taking. "You're different from the other two who called me."

"How am I different?"

"Smarter. More dangerous. You think before you choose your tactics." She spoke carefully, giving him the truth. She was accustomed to relying on her instincts when it came to judging people, and she was rarely wrong. She had developed survival skills, too, just as Crissie had. But she had not been born with Crissie's looks, so those skills had taken a different twist.

"Are you complimenting me?" Nick asked curiously.

"No. Just stating obvious facts. Tell me, who will the Castletons and Lightfoots send if you screw up your assignment to browbeat me out of the shares?"

"I will try very hard not to screw up."

"How's your track record in that department?" she taunted, although she suspected it was excellent.

"Not perfect. I've been known to screw up very badly on occasion."

"When was the last time?"

"Three years ago."

The apparently honest answer surprised her, and thereby

13

threw her off guard. "What happened?" she asked, with somewhat too obvious curiosity.

He gave her a slow, remote smile. "We both know that what happened to me three years ago doesn't matter a damn right now. Let's stick with the issue at hand."

She shrugged. "You can stick with it if you like. I've got better things to do."

He studied the brochures on the table again. "Are you sure you want to go to California?"

"I think so. I feel the need to get away, and it would be a sort of memorial trip in honor of Crissie. She loved Southern California. We were both born and raised in Washington, but she always said California was her spiritual home. She went down there to work as a model after she graduated from high school. It seems fitting somehow to spend some time there. She would have wanted me to have some fun."

"Alone?"

Phila smiled, showing her teeth. "Yes. Alone."

Nick appeared to consider that for a moment, and then he switched back to the only topic that really mattered to him. "Are you going to fight the Castletons and Lightfoots every inch of the way, or is the word *cooperation* a part of your vocabulary?"

"The word is there, but I use it only when it suits me."

"And right now it doesn't suit you to cooperate by selling those shares back to the families?"

"No, I don't think so."

"Not even for a great deal of money?"

"I'm not interested in money right now."

He nodded, as if she had verified a personal conclusion he had already reached. "Yeah, well, that settles that."

Phila was instantly wary. "What does it settle?"

"My job is done. I was asked to approach you about the shares. I've done that, and I'm convinced you aren't about to cooperate with the families. I'll report my failure, and that will be the end of it."

She did not believe what he said for a moment. "You said you were going to try very hard not to screw up."

"I gave it my best shot." He looked hurt that she would think otherwise.

Phila grew more alarmed. His best shot, she sensed, would never be this ineffectual. "You never answered my question about who they'll send next."

"I don't know what they'll do. That's their problem."

She put her glass down on the table and eyed him narrowly. "That's the end of it as far as you're concerned?"

He shrugged. "I don't see that I have much option. You've made it clear you don't even want to talk about the shares."

"You're not the type to give up this quickly," Phila stated.

His eyes widened. "How do you know what type I am?"

"Never mind. I just do and you're not acting true to form at the moment."

"Disappointed?"

"No, but I am very curious about what you're up to."

"Yeah." His smile came and went again. "I'll bet you are. And I'm equally curious about what you're planning to do. But I guess we'll both find out all the results eventually, won't we? I'll look forward to hearing about whatever trouble you manage to stir up, Phila. Should make for an interesting annual meeting. Too bad I won't be there to watch you in action."

"Why won't you be there? You're a Lightfoot. Don't you hold stock?"

"I still have the shares I was given when I was born and the shares I inherited from my mother, but they're a long way from constituting a controlling interest. I haven't paid much attention to them lately, anyway. For the past three years I've let my father vote my shares."

"Why?"

"It's a long story. Let's just say I've lost interest in Castleton & Lightfoot. I've got other things to do with my life these days."

Phila's fingernails drummed a quick staccato on the arm of her chair. Mentally she flipped through a variety of possibilities she had not yet considered.

Crissie had never mentioned this particular member of the clan. Maybe that was because he was estranged from the families for some obscure reason. He was certainly implying as much when he claimed he no longer voted his shares at the annual meeting. If that was the case, Phila told herself with a sudden rush of interest, she might find him very useful.

"If you're no longer involved with Castleton & Lightfoot, just what are you doing with your life these days?" she asked bluntly. Almost immediately she sensed she had made a tactical error. The last thing she should do was show any interest in him. She should have been more subtle. But it was too late to take back her words.

Nick seemed unaware of any blunder on her part. "I'm running my own business in Santa Barbara—Lightfoot Consulting Services. I just agreed to get in touch with you as a favor to the families. But the bottom line is that I'm not really sure I give a damn how much trouble you cause Castleton & Lightfoot. Have fun, Phila."

But he did not rise from the sofa and head back out into the heat, Phila noticed.

"What does Lightfoot Consulting Services consult about?" she asked.

He gave her an unreadable look. "We provide advice and information to firms trying to open overseas markets. A lot of companies want a cut of the world pie, but they don't have the vaguest idea of how to do business in Europe or the Pacific Rim countries."

"And you do?"

"Some."

"Would you still be working in the family firm if you hadn't shot yourself in the foot three years ago?" Phila demanded.

"I didn't exactly shoot myself in the foot three years ago."

"You said you screwed up badly."

"It was more like a family quarrel. But to answer your question, yeah, I'd probably still be with the firm if things

16

hadn't happened the way they did. In fact, I'd still be running Castleton & Lightfoot if I'd stayed."

"You were running it?" She frowned.

"I'd just gotten myself appointed CEO the year before I walked out."

"This is getting more and more weird. Why did you walk out if you'd just gotten appointed chief executive officer? What are you doing down there in California? Why did you do anybody the favor of contacting me? What is this all about?"

A slight, oddly tantalizing light appeared in his eyes. "I've told you what this is all about, Miss Fox. I am no longer with the family firm. I got a phone call from the one person connected with Castleton & Lightfoot who still speaks to me on occasion, and I agreed to talk to you as a favor to her. I've talked to you. End of favor."

"And that's the end of the matter as far as you're concerned?"

"Yeah."

"I don't believe you." Something was very wrong here.

"That's your prerogative, Phila. Have dinner with me tonight?"

It took a minute for the invitation to penetrate. She looked up at him blankly, aware that her mouth had fallen open. "I beg your pardon?"

"You heard me. It's too late to start for California this evening. I'm going to be spending the night here in town. I just thought we could have dinner. After all, I sure as hell don't know anyone else in Holloway. Unless you have other plans?"

She shook her head slowly as the light dawned. "I don't believe this."

"What don't you believe?"

"You aren't really going to try to seduce me in order to get back those shares, are you? I mean, it would be such a trite, old-fashioned, dipstick dumb sort of approach. Also a useless one."

He thought about that for a while, meditatively studying the ivy growing from a red pot on a nearby table. When his

17

eyes came back to Phila's, she did not like the cool intensity she saw in his gaze. She had the impression he had made a major decision.

"Miss Fox," Nick said with a disconcerting air of formality, "just for the record, I would like you to know that if I tried to seduce you it would be because I wanted to sleep with you, not because I wanted to get my hands on those C&L shares."

She stared at him with narrowed eyes, trying to analyze, assess and categorize him. She had thought she had known precisely what to expect from any member of the wealthy, powerful Lightfoot and Castleton clans. But Nicodemus Lightfoot was refusing to fit into the mold she had prepared for him. That just made him all the more dangerous, she reminded herself.

But she couldn't get the idea out of her head that it might also make him all the more useful.

"If I had dinner with you, would you spill any juicy family secrets?" she asked.

"Probably not."

"Then what would be the point?"

"The point would be that neither of us would be forced to eat alone."

"I don't mind eating alone. I often eat alone."

"You know something, Miss Fox? That does not surprise me. I eat alone a lot myself. Too often." He got to his feet. "I'll pick you up at six. You know the local places. I'll let you make the reservations."

He walked to the front door and let himself out into the late-afternoon sun. He did not look back once.

Phila took that as another danger signal. It was a minor point, that business about not looking back to see if she was watching him, but it was significant. Any other man could not have resisted one small glance over his shoulder to see how she was reacting to his sudden departure.

She knew that his having failed to do so was not a reflection of unconcern on his part; it was a matter of self-discipline. The man was obviously in complete control of himself and was accustomed to being in equal command of the situation around him.

The soft, husky roar of the silver-gray Porsche filled the empty street outside the house. Phila listened to the powerful car as it drove off and decided that Nicodemus Lightfoot was going to be a problem.

Maybe that was what she really needed, Phila thought suddenly. Maybe she needed a problem she could sink her teeth into. It might do a lot more for this vague sense of depression than a trip to California.

Foxes thrived on exercising their cunning, she reminded herself.

CHAPTER TWO

"I thought you'd better know, Hilary, that I phoned Nick and asked him to contact that Fox woman." Eleanor Castleton did not look up from her plants as she spoke. She moved around the heavily laden tables of the greenhouse, her gloved fingers working with assurance amidst the deceptively delicate blooms and leaves.

"You called him?"

"Oh, yes, dear. I do call him occasionally, you know. I don't want him to think he's totally out of touch with the families. He is a Lightfoot, after all."

"Did he agree to meet with Philadelphia Fox?" Hilary Lightfoot examined a small cream-colored flower. The bloom was amazingly innocent-looking, she thought, rather like Eleanor Castleton.

"Yes, dear, he agreed. Why shouldn't he?" Eleanor asked in the faintly astonished, slightly vague way that never failed to irritate Hilary.

Eleanor Castleton was in her sixties, but Hilary was certain she'd had that sweet, distracted, charmingly flighty air since the cradle. It went well with the faint traces of an aristocratic Southern accent.

"Nick hasn't been interested in family business for some time. I'm a little surprised he would get involved now,"

Hilary Lightfoot said. It was warm and humid in the greenhouse and Hilary hoped she could get out before her clothes began to stick to her. She intended to drive into the village as soon as she finished this annoying little chat with Eleanor.

She was dressed in a cream-colored silk blouse and fawn-colored pants. A row of narrow wooden bracelets clinked lightly on her wrist. Her dark red hair was drawn straight back from her face and caught at the nape of her neck in a classic knot that revealed her patrician features to fine advantage.

The only ring she wore was her wedding ring, a simple band of gold. A woman who was thirty-five years younger than her husband had to be careful about appearances. Hilary had always felt a gaudy-looking diamond would have been tacky under the circumstances. Besides, she was not the gaudy type.

"Nick is family," Eleanor said as she clipped a small, bowl-shaped leaf and discarded it. "He might have walked out three years ago, but that doesn't mean he doesn't care about something as serious as this situation with Philadelphia Fox."

"I doubt if there is anything Nick can do," Hilary said. "I tried to call her and got nowhere. Darren has also tried. She refused to even meet with him. I don't know what you think Nick can do. Frankly, if she were susceptible to masculine charm, your son would have had those shares back by now, Eleanor."

"You never know what will work with that sort of woman."

Hilary smiled. No one could convey subtle contempt for the lower classes quite the way Eleanor Castleton could. "True, I suppose. But our best bet will probably be to let her come to the annual meeting and then offer to buy her out."

Eleanor gave a small shudder. "I can't bear to think of an outsider at a C&L meeting. I'd much rather clear this up beforehand, wouldn't you? We'll see if Nick can accomplish anything."

"You really believe Nick can accomplish what Darren and I couldn't?" Hilary asked, forcing herself to keep her voice at a smooth, polite level.

"Nick has his own way of doing things," Eleanor said vaguely. "Hand me that watering can, will you, dear?"

Hilary picked up the metal vessel and handed it to the older woman. For a moment their eyes met. Hilary looked down into Eleanor's slightly vague pale blue gaze and thought she caught a glimpse of something that could have been steel. It wasn't the first time she had seen that expression, and it never failed to disturb her. But in the next instant it was gone, replaced by Eleanor's relentlessly distracted air.

"Thank you, dear." Eleanor maneuvered the spout of the watering can along a row of pots. "Mustn't let these new Nepenthes get dry. They're coming along so nicely. See how well the little pitchers are starting to form? Where's Reed today?"

"Playing golf." Hilary examined the delicately shaped leaves at the base of the plant Eleanor was watering. They were as innocent-looking as the fragile flowers.

"It seems he's always playing golf these days, or else he and Tec are busy fiddling with their guns out on the firing range. He wouldn't even talk to Darren about the Fox woman."

"My husband is enjoying retirement," Hilary said coolly. "He's earned it."

"I suppose so," Eleanor said softly. "But you know, dear, I never thought Reed would ever stop taking an interest in the firm the way he has. Castleton & Lightfoot was his whole life for so many years. He and Burke put everything they had into the company. It just doesn't seem right that Reed shows so little concern with company business these days."

"Reed trusts me to look after things for him," Hilary said coolly.

"Yes, of course he does, dear. And rightly so. You're doing an excellent job as CEO. An excellent job, indeed.

Would you hand me that little trowel? No, not that one, the other one. Going into town?"

"I've agreed to have lunch with the new chairwoman of the Port Claxton Summer Theater Guild."

"Oh, dear. I suppose the guild will be wanting more money from C&L this year."

"Undoubtedly."

"I do think we've given enough to that group over the years, don't you? I was very disappointed in that production they put on last summer."

"War Toys?"

"It painted the military in a rather uncomplimentary light, didn't you think? Not to mention the business interests that are connected to the military establishment. We don't need that sort of theater here in Port Claxton."

Nor were the good people of Port Claxton likely to be treated to another play with a strong antimilitary theme in the near future, Hilary thought wryly. The Castletons and Lightfoots had made no secret of their reaction to *War Toys*.

Last year's guild chairman must have been temporarily insane to have authorized the production of the play in the first place. Then again, perhaps it hadn't been insanity, Hilary decided. Perhaps it had been a final, defiant stab at artistic freedom by the outgoing bureaucrat.

Hilary hoped the chairman had enjoyed thumbing his nose at the guild's largest contributor, because Port Claxton's struggling summer theater program would be paying the price for a long time to come. The new chairwoman would no doubt be scrambling today to apologize for the mistakes of her predecessor. Hilary did not look forward to lunch.

"I believe I'd better ask Tec to run out to the nursery for me," Eleanor said as she frowned over a tray of greenery. "I need some more sphagnum moss for my *Dionaea* leaf cuttings."

"I'll tell him you want to see him." Hilary turned toward the greenhouse door just as it burst open.

"I've got one! I've got one! I've got one!" An excited

five-year-old boy dressed in a striped polo shirt and jeans came rushing into the greenhouse. His light brown hair was cut cute and short and his small face already showed the promise of the chiseled good looks he had inherited from his father.

Eleanor Castleton smiled down at her grandson. "What have you got, Jordan?"

"A dead fly." Jordan opened his palm to reveal a plump, moribund housefly. "Can I feed one of the plants? Can I? Can I? Can I?"

"*May* I," Eleanor corrected gently. "Yes, dear, I think we can find one hungry enough to eat your fly. Let's see, what about this little *Dionaea?* It hasn't eaten in ages."

Hilary watched in reluctant fascination as Jordan carefully dropped the now-dead insect into the open leaves of the Venus's-flytrap. The small carcass rolled across the trigger hairs and, with a speed that made all three onlookers blink, the spined leaves snapped shut. The fly was locked inside.

"Wow," said Jordan. "Wow, wow, wow. Did you see that, Hilary?"

"Yes, Jordan, I saw it." Hilary took one last glance around at the lush-looking plants that filled the greenhouse. Some were in hanging baskets, a few aquatic species floated in aquariums, others were planted in rows of boxes that covered the workbenches.

Eleanor Castleton had developed a very interesting collection of pitcher plants, flytraps, sundews, butterworts and bladderworts. They all had one thing in common: they were carnivorous.

Nick walked into the brightly lit diner behind Phila and took in the surroundings with a sense of resignation. The place was classic: red vinyl seats in the booths, wood-grained plastic-laminated tables with chrome legs and a long counter with stools that appeared to be a size too small for the people sitting on them. Loud waitresses in grease-stained uniforms that were also a size too small scurried between the tables. The open doorway to the kitchen revealed a smoky, sizzling grill filled with meat that dripped fat into the flames. The classic decor was capped by a stunning view of the parking lot.

"This is the best you could do?" Nick asked Phila politely as he followed her to a booth.

"This is it," she answered cheerfully. "Best place in town. Everyone eats here on Saturday night."

"This is Friday night."

"Which explains why we didn't have to wait for a table," she concluded smoothly. "I recommend either the chicken or the steak. Anything else is liable to entail a certain risk."

"I'll bear that in mind." Nick gazed idly around the room again before bringing his attention back to the woman sitting across from him. He smiled. Being with Phila was like sitting in a lot full of parked cars and finding himself next to the one vehicle that had its key turned on in the ignition.

Tonight Phila was dressed in a pumpkin-colored silk blouse and a pair of jeans belted with a sliver-and-turquoise-studded strip of leather. He was learning that Miss Fox favored bold colors. They went well with her air of restless energy.

A waitress came by to take their order for drinks. Nick asked for scotch and was not unduly surprised when Phila ordered a prim white wine. The drinks came immediately. He gazed around the busy restaurant for a moment, thinking.

"What's the matter, Mr. Lightfoot," Phila purred as she examined her menu. "Not accustomed to such fancy surroundings?"

"I've eaten in worse." He opened his menu. "I've also eaten in better. Tell me, Phila, what made you decide to accept my invitation for dinner this evening?"

"I figured we might as well get it over with. The suspense was killing me."

"Get what over with?"

"Whatever approach you plan to use to convince me to give back the shares." She studied the menu with a small frown, as if having a tough time choosing between a baked potato or fries.

"I told you, I've already given it my best shot."

"Hah. I don't buy that for a minute." She glanced up. "What are you having?"

"The special."

"You don't even know what it is yet. You're supposed to ask the waitress."

Nick shrugged, unconcerned. "I'll take my chances."

"I told you it would be risky."

He smiled faintly. "I'm good at taking risks."

Phila scowled and snapped her menu shut. "Suit yourself. I'll have the chicken. As usual." She put her elbows on the table, folded her hands together and rested her chin on her interlaced fingers. Her hazel eyes regarded him broodingly. "So tell me, Nicodemus Lightfoot, how long have the Lightfoots and the Castletons been in the business of building death machines for the government?"

"Since before you were born, little girl."

She blinked. "You're not even going to deny it?"

"Well, technically they're electronics and instrumentation products, not death machines. Some people think of them as a kind of technological insurance, a way to balance power in the world. In fact some people might even say C&L is a very patriotic company. But I suspect the definition of a death machine is in the mind of the beholder."

"Castleton & Lightfoot makes the kind of electronics and instrumentation used in fighter planes and command posts, from what I've been able to determine. It designs to order for the military establishment. That means you build death machines. It also means that C&L is intimately involved in some cozy financial arrangements with the Pentagon."

Nick nodded. Things were falling into place quickly. "I get it," he said gently. "You're one of those."

"One of what?"

"You're," he paused delicately, "shall we say, of the liberal persuasion."

Her answering smile was grim. "If you think I'm bad, you should have met my grandmother."

"A flaming-pink, radical left-wing anarchist, right?"

"Let's just say she didn't care for the idea of the world being run by your kind."

"My kind?"

"Aristocrats with everything but the title. Too much money and too much power. She felt very strongly that having both power and money corrupts."

"So does a lack of either. Show me ten people who don't have enough money and power to control their own lives, and I'll show you nine dangerous human beings. The tenth is probably a wimp."

The vibration in the air around Phila was almost palpable now, and there were sparks in her eyes. Her engine was definitely shifting into gear.

Having all that feminine energy focused on him was doing things to his groin region, Nick discovered—things that hadn't been done in quite a while. He could tell that Phila had no concept of how she was turning him on, and that was as amusing as it was frustrating.

"Is that how you justify having been born into a privileged class? You pretend you're more noble than those who aren't as wealthy as you are? That you wouldn't stoop to some of the things a poor person might have to do in order to survive?"

"There seems to be some misunderstanding here. The Castletons and Lightfoots are not Rockefellers or Du Ponts. When you look at me you're only looking at second-generation money and I, personally, haven't even had that for the past three years."

"Now I'm supposed to feel sorry for you?"

"Look, Phila, I don't know what Crissie told you, but the fact is my father, Reed Lightfoot, and his buddy, Burke Castleton, were a couple of shitkickers who got an education in the Army when it turned out they showed an aptitude for electronics. When they got out of the service they had some big plans and big ambitions and the advantage of an inside view of the way the military works. They built

C&L from the ground up. They were lucky. Their timing was good, and they turned out to be as shrewd about business matters as they were about electronic design."

"And they were smart enough to get into the death machine business," Phila finished with satisfaction.

Nick discovered he was enjoying the new enthusiastic gleam in Phila's eyes. He wondered if the expression was anything like the one she would have when she was lying naked under a man.

The prospect made him feel a little light-headed while the rest of him began to feel heavy and tight. He realized just how long it had been since he had genuinely anticipated going to bed with a woman. He could remember the date clearly: September twenty-fifth, four and a half years ago. It had been his wedding night. Things had gone downhill from there until the divorce eighteen months later.

There had been one woman since his marriage had ended, another shell-shocked veteran of the divorce wars who had been as terrified of the singles scene as Nick. They had consoled each other for several months in what had become a safe and comfortable, if totally uninspired, relationship.

It had been a healing time for both of them. Neither had been looking for or expecting to find a great love. Five months ago Jeannie had put an end to the affair, saying she was ready to search for something more substantial and meaningful. Nick had been vegetating in peaceful celibacy ever since.

Until tonight. Tonight everything was changing. Tonight he was relearning the simple masculine joy of sexual anticipation.

With an effort, he pushed his sensual feelings aside and concentrated on looking for the key to Philadelphia Fox.

"To be perfectly truthful," Nick said, swirling the scotch in his glass, "I used to have a few questions myself about all the military contracts Castleton & Lightfoot handled. That was back when I was involved with the firm, of course."

"Really?" Phila looked skeptical. "What happened when you asked those questions?"

"I was told I was in serious danger of becoming a left-wing liberal establishment dupe," he said dryly. "I was also called a coward and potential traitor to my country. Among other things."

Phila's shocked expression was priceless. It warmed Nick to the core because it told him he was on the right track. To catch a wary little liberal Fox, one used bait that was bleeding from the heart.

"How dare they call you that just because you stood up to them?" Phila demanded, instantly indignant on his behalf. "Is that when you left Castleton & Lightfoot?"

"Yeah. Right about then."

"You had a falling-out with the families over the business of making death machines?"

"That wasn't the only problem," he felt obliged to confess. "There were other things going on at the time."

"What other things?"

"Do you always get this personal this fast in a relationship?"

She immediately settled back against the vinyl seat and put her hands in her lap. "We're not talking about a relationship. We're talking about business."

"I don't want to talk about business tonight, Phila. Not unless you want to discuss those shares."

"I don't."

"Then we're left with a relationship discussion."

She looked him straight in the eye. "Are you going to try to seduce me after all?"

"Are you in a mood to be seduced?"

"No. Absolutely not, so don't get any ideas." She waited a beat and then, drawn inevitably back to the bait, asked, "Did you really walk away from Castleton & Lightfoot because they make military electronics?"

"As I said, there were a lot of things going on at the time besides that argument." He had her now. He was certain of it. The pleasurable sense of anticipation increased. The bright, glittering little Fox was hooked. It would take skill and subtlety to close the trap, but Nick looked forward to the challenge. "Let's talk about something else."

"I'd rather talk about what made you decide you wanted Castleton & Lightfoot to get out of the death machine business," she said.

He took a firm grip on his patience and chose his words carefully. "Let's just say that military contracts are often more trouble than they're worth from a business point of view. It's a damned nuisance having to get security clearances for so many employees, there's too much paperwork involved in tracking costs and there's too much interference from bureaucrats trying to make brownie points by playing the role of government watchdog."

Disappointment dawned immediately in her expressive eyes. "Those are the reasons you wanted your firm to stop working for the government? You didn't like the paperwork?"

His lips curved slightly. "You want me to tell you that I suffered a liberal conversion and saw the light?"

"I'd like to think that there was some vague form of ethics involved in your decision, yes."

"Well, there may have been a few other reasons besides the paperwork problems, but as I recall they didn't carry much weight with the other members of the families."

"What reasons?" Phila demanded, on the scent again.

"I don't think this is a good time to go into them," Nick said smoothly. "Let's talk about you for a while. Tell me why you quit your job. You were a social worker or welfare worker or something, I take it?"

"I was a caseworker for CPS," she said, her voice cooling.

He tried to place the initials and failed. "CPS?"

"Child Protective Services."

"Foster homes? Abused kids? That kind of thing?"

"Yes," Phila said, her voice growing even colder. "That kind of thing."

"Your ex-supervisor said something about your trying to avoid interviews. What was that all about?"

"There was a trial involving a foster parent. I had to testify. After the trial a lot of people wanted interviews."

The more reticent she became, the more curious Nick grew. "You decided to quit your job after the trial ended?"

"People in my line of work have a high rate of burnout." She smiled gratefully at the waitress who arrived to take their order. "Oh, good," she told him. "I'm starving."

Nick watched her make a major production out of ordering the chicken and sensed he wasn't going to get her back on the topic of her former job.

"I'll have the special," Nick told the waitress.

The woman looked up from her order pad. "It's macaroni and cheese," she said in a warning tone.

"Fine."

"Macaroni and cheese?" Phila murmured in deep wonder as the waitress left.

"I happen to like macaroni and cheese. I'm a man of simple tastes."

"Sure. That's why you drive a Porsche and drink scotch."

"Having simple tastes does not imply a lack of standards," Nick said blandly. "I also like beer. Now, where were we?"

"I'm not sure. I think you were trying to get the story of my life so you could figure out how to use it to convince me to turn over the shares. That's your way, isn't it? You're sneaky."

"You flatter me."

Phila tilted her chin aggressively. "Not likely. I wouldn't go out of my way to flatter a Lightfoot or a Castleton. In fact, I think it's time we put our cards on the table."

"What makes you think I'm holding any cards?"

"Because you're the type who always keeps an ace up his sleeve. Now, then, why don't you just be straightforward with me, Mr. Lightfoot? And whatever it is you're going to offer or threaten, you can rest assured I'll give you a straightforward answer in return."

"And that answer will be no, right?"

"Right." Phila's eyes were alight again with the promise

of battle. She started to say something else but stopped abruptly, her gaze going to the door behind Nick. The gleam went out of her eyes instantly, to be replaced by a wary, almost nervous expression. "Oh, damn," she said very softly.

Curious, Nick glanced over his shoulder, wondering if he was about to encounter an irate boyfriend of Phila's. What he saw was a thickly built woman in a faded, tie-dyed cotton dress. She must have been around forty but she was wearing her thin, graying hair in braids that hung to her waist. Her face was singularly lacking in character, showing no signs of maturity or past beauty. She wore no makeup to compensate for the unusual lack of color in her skin and lips. Her small eyes took in the crowd in one glance and alighted on Phila. She started down the aisle of booths.

"Friend of yours?" Nick asked, turning back to Phila.

"No."

"Trouble?"

"Probably." Her fingers were clenched around the edge of the table.

Nick wasn't sure what to expect of the coming confrontation. The last thing he wanted to get into was a cat fight between two women. Nor did he want to see Phila get hurt. "Does this by any chance involve a man?" he asked.

Phila's gaze met his. Her eyes were bitter. "In a way. Her name is Ruth Spalding. Feel free to leave."

"Not yet. I'm hungry, and here come our salads." He glanced at the waitress who was bearing down on the booth at the same rate of speed as the woman with the braids. With any luck the salads would get to the table first.

They did—or rather, Phila's did. Ruth Spalding spotted the tray and leaped for it with a muffled cry of rage. She seized one of the platefulls of iceburg lettuce, swept it off the tray and hurled it straight at Phila.

Nick managed to reach out and intercept the heavy plate before it struck Phila but the lettuce, together with its blue-cheese dressing and cherry tomatoes, cascaded down over her bright pumpkin blouse. Phila did not move. She simply sat staring at Ruth Spalding with an expression of resigned sorrow in her eyes.

"*Bitch*. Lying, scheming bitch." There was an ugly mottling of red in the Spalding woman's thick face now as she screamed at Phila. Her eyes were feverish with hatred. "You lied, damn you. You lied and they came and took the children away. Those kids were all we had. He loved those children. And now they're gone. Now my husband's gone. And it's all your fault, you rotten, lying whore!"

Phila was shaking as she slowly got to her feet. Nick saw the fine trembling in her fingers and he slid out of the booth to stand beside her. He was startled by the fierce, protective instincts that were suddenly surging through him. Nobody else in the restaurant had moved, but all eyes were on the scene taking place in front of them.

"I'm sorry, Mrs. Spalding." Phila spoke with a calm gentleness that amazed Nick. She took a step toward the heavy woman. "More sorry than I can say."

"You're not sorry, you meddling bitch," Ruth Spalding hissed through her teeth. "You did it on purpose. You ruined everything. *Everything*, damn you!" She swung a huge hand in a wide arc.

Phila did not even try to duck the blow. Ruth Spalding's palm cracked against the side of her face with enough force to make Phila stagger backward a step.

"Jesus. That's enough." Nick spoke very softly. If a man had acted this way toward Phila he knew he would have thrown a punch by now. He moved in front of the Spalding woman, looming directly in her path. She did not appear even to see him. She was staring rigidly over his shoulder, her entire attention focused on Phila.

"It's all right, Nick. Please. I'll handle this."

Phila stepped around Nick, reaching out to the other woman. Nick watched in amazement as Phila put a hand on Spalding's plump shoulder. Spalding flinched as if she had been struck.

"*Don't you dare touch me, you bitch.*"

"I'm sorry, Ruth. I know you're hurting."

Huge tears formed in Ruth Spalding's tiny eyes and

coursed down her cheeks. "Bitch," Spalding whispered again, her large body shaking with barely stifled sobs. "He was doing okay. We were gonna make it. He was doing good until you came along and messed it all up."

"I know. I know." Phila moved closer, putting both arms around the big woman. "I'm sorry, Ruth. So sorry."

For a few seconds Ruth Spalding simply stood there, her head against Phila's shoulder as she sobbed heavily. Then she jerked herself back a step, as if ashamed to find herself taking comfort from the enemy. She pushed Phila away and wiped the back of her hand across her eyes.

"You'll pay for what you did," Spalding said as she backed slowly away down the aisle. "I swear to God you'll pay for ruining everything." Then she turned and lumbered awkwardly out of the diner.

Nick took one look at Phila, who was standing very still as she watched Ruth Spalding leave the diner, and he pulled out his wallet and threw enough cash on the table to cover the tab.

"Let's go." He took Phila's arm and steered her firmly toward the door.

She did not resist. Every eye in the restaurant was on them, but she appeared oblivious as Nick urged her out into the warm night. He helped her gently into the Porsche and leaned down to study her face in the harsh neon light of the diner sign. She looked exhausted. All traces of the battle flags that had been flying earlier were gone. Without a word he closed the car door and went around to the driver's side.

Phila said nothing until he parked the Porsche in front of the little white house. Then she seemed to come slowly back from some distant place as she realized she was home.

Nick turned off the engine and shifted slightly in his seat. "You want to tell me what that was all about?"

"Not particularly. It's none of your business."

"Somehow I had a hunch you'd say that. You okay?"

"Just tired." She massaged her temples. "I've been feeling very tired lately."

"Who was that woman?" Nick persisted gently.

She hesitated, her eyes drifting to the front steps of her house which were illuminated by a pale light. "Ruth Spalding. She and her husband used to run a foster home on their farm outside of town. I . . . didn't like the way things were going for the kids. I was responsible for taking the children away and putting them in other homes. She hasn't forgiven me, as you can see."

"What I saw was you trying to comfort a woman who obviously hates your guts. You do that kind of thing a lot? If so, I can see why you got burned out. Sort of a thankless job, isn't it?"

"It gets to you." Phila shook herself like a small terrier throwing off water after falling into a cold stream. She blinked twice and opened the door. "Guess I really do need a vacation." She climbed out of the car.

Nick immediately slid out from behind the wheel and followed Phila up the path to her door. "Phila, wait."

She was fumbling in her shoulder bag for her keys. "I don't feel like talking any more tonight, Mr. Lightfoot."

"I do." He removed the keys from her hand, deliberately taking advantage of her distracted state. He was good at taking advantage. He shoved the key into the door and stood aside.

"Are you always this obnoxious?" Phila asked as she stepped into the hall and turned on a light.

"Yeah. So I've been told. Sit down and I'll fix us a tuna-fish sandwich." He headed for the kitchen without waiting for permission.

Phila trailed after him and sat down in one of the small kitchen chairs. She scowled. "You think this is amusing?"

"No. I think I'm hungry and I think I've got a few more questions. That's all." He opened a cupboard door and located a bowl. Tried another drawer and discovered a can opener. He was on a roll.

Phila's eyes followed him without much enthusiasm, but her shoulders had already relaxed a bit from the hunch of tension and depression she'd been sitting with in the car. "What questions?"

35

"Let's see. How about we start with how long did you know Crissie Masters?" he asked casually.

The vibration she'd emanated earlier abruptly returned. He was not even touching her, but he could feel her immediate reaction. She was on the alert again; the exhaustion cleared from her eyes.

"I met Crissie when I was thirteen."

"You know she raised hell when she descended on the families last year, don't you?" he said quietly, spooning mayonnaise out of a jar. He remembered the barely concealed despair in Eleanor's gracefully accented voice when she had phoned to tell him of the trauma the family was experiencing at the hands of Crissie Masters. No one had suffered as much as Eleanor Castleton during the time Crissie was on the scene.

"I know she raised hell, but I'm sure they deserved it. She only wanted what she felt was rightfully hers. After all, she was Burke Castleton's daughter."

"A daughter he never knew he had."

"Hardly Crissie's fault. Did you know she spent years looking for him? She used to fantasize about him all the time when she was a teenager. I remember lying awake in bed at night listening to her make up elaborate tales of how he must be searching for her and how he would find her someday. He lived in a mansion, she would say. And he was handsome and rich and dynamic."

"She wasn't far off," Nick admitted.

"I know." Phila smiled wistfully. "Except for the part about his actively searching for her. He never bothered to look, did he? I still remember the day she phoned to tell me that she had finally traced her father and that he had turned out to be everything she had fantasized he would be. Wealthy, attractive and dynamic. And to top it all off, he welcomed her with open arms."

"He was the only one who did, from what I hear. What did you say when she told you the good news?"

Phila's mouth tightened. "I pointed out that since he hadn't even been aware of her existence, he was probably an irresponsible bastard by nature. Any man who goes around fathering children and not being aware of it has a serious character flaw."

"I can hear the lecture now."

"Then I asked her how she could be certain he hadn't known about her or even suspected she existed. In which case he was even more of a bastard because it meant he'd deliberately ignored her all those years."

Nick took a deep breath, remembering an aesthetically lean, good-looking, charismatic man whose sensual appetites had apparently been inexhaustible. He had rarely been without a cigarette in his long-fingered hands. Burke Castleton had been larger than life, with a beguilingly wicked grin and the kind of eyes that made women catch their breath. *The Castletons got the looks and the charm.*

"The bastard, as you call him, is dead, Phila."

"I know. Crissie was stunned when she got word of Burke's heart attack a few months ago."

"And was she just as stunned when she found out he'd left her a big chunk of his shares in Castleton & Lightfoot?" Nick asked blandly.

"No. By the time he died, Crissie had gotten to know him well enough to believe he wouldn't leave her out of his will. She was right about that at least, wasn't she?"

"Yeah. But Burke Castleton rarely did anything out of the kindness of his heart. He always had a motive, and sometimes that motive was nothing more than a desire to stir up trouble."

"Sounds like that might have been a family trait," Phila murmured. "One Crissie inherited." She watched as Nick spread tuna-fish salad on slices of bread.

"Apparently so."

"Tell me something, Nick. Just how badly did the families hate Crissie?"

He hesitated, thinking of what he had learned from Eleanor. "She didn't go out of her way to make herself lovable, from what I understand. Why did she leave the shares to you?"

"I was the sole beneficiary of her will, just as she was in mine."

"The two of you made out wills? Isn't that a little unusual under the circumstances? How old were you when you did that?" Nick was amazed.

"We made them out the day we turned twenty-one. It wasn't that we had much to leave to each other, you understand. It was sort of a symbolic gesture. But the wills exist, and I am Crissie's legal heir."

"Okay, okay, I believe you. What were you implying with that question about how much the families hated Crissie?" Nick asked quietly as he served the tray of sandwiches. He sat down at the small table and helped himself to one of his own creations. "You're not crazy enough to think someone might had tried to kill her, are you?"

Phila made no move to touch the sandwiches. "The thought crossed my mind, so I hired a private detective to look into it. His report says it was clearly an accident. She was driving too fast that night, and she'd had a few drinks. She took a turn too quickly, went through a guard rail and landed in a ravine. There was no evidence of foul play. Just tragedy. Lots of evidence of tragedy."

Nick stopped chewing. "I don't believe I'm hearing this. You actually checked out the possibility of foul play?"

"Of course. I told you. Crissie was like a sister to me. Do you think I'd take a Castleton's or Lightfoot's word that her death had been an accident?"

"What about the word of the cops who investigated the scene of the accident?" Nick asked with set teeth. He was suddenly feeling angry.

"Cops can be bought. Especially by people as powerful as your precious families."

"Jesus." Nick forced himself to breathe slowly. "Who the hell do you think you are to hurl those kinds of accusations?"

"Me? I'm the only real friend the deceased had, remember? Who else has a better right to hurl accusations? Besides, I'm not hurling them. Not any more. I already checked them out. The families are technically off the hook—technically, at least."

"Technically? What the hell does that mean?" Nick was having a hard time controlling his rage now.

"I mean that as far as I'm concerned the Lightfoots and the Castletons bear some moral responsibility for what happened to Crissie."

"Moral responsibility."

"Oh, nothing that would ever hold up in court, I'll grant you that."

"Thank you very much." He wanted to pick her up and shake her. "You've got a lot of nerve, Philadelphia Fox."

"Why? Because I dare impugn the honor of the noble clans of Lightfoot and Castleton? Let me tell you something, Nicodemus Lightfoot, there are plenty of ways to ruin a person's life short of murdering her. Believe me, in my line of work I've seen a whole lot of examples of just how it can be done."

"You can't blame us for what happened to Crissie Masters."

"No? The fact that she even came into this world was Burke Castleton's fault. And he didn't stick around to help raise her, did he? Who knows how she might have turned out if she'd had a loving home and a father who cared? What's more, when she did find her roots, no one tried to make her welcome. None of you accepted her. She knew you all hated her. What do you think that does to a person? None of you even gave a damn when she died until you found out she had left the shares to someone outside the families."

Nick almost lost it then. He forced himself to put down the remainder of his sandwich very carefully. "When you're drawing up your list of people you believe hated Crissie Masters, don't include me. I never met her, remember?"

"So what? You probably wouldn't have been any kinder to her than the others were. She was an outsider."

"You know what you are? You're a bigoted, narrow-minded, totally biased little fool who is automatically against anyone who makes more money than you do."

"Is that right?"

"Yeah. And you know what else?"

"What?"

"You're making me lose my temper, and I haven't done that in a long time."

"Don't worry, it's just a right-wing, knee-jerk reaction to what you perceive as a threat to the privileged upper classes. And don't get any ideas about getting out of that chair and coming over here to manhandle me. I'll call the cops. I've been abused enough this evening." But Phila didn't look like the victim of abuse; she looked as if she was almost enjoying the blazing light of battle in her eyes.

"What's the matter, Phila?" he challenged softly. "Aren't you going to put your arms around me and offer me a bit of comfort and understanding the way you did Ruth Spalding when she attacked you?"

"I feel sorry for Ruth Spalding. I don't feel any pity at all for you. You're a Lightfoot. You don't need any of my comfort and understanding."

Nick bit back an oath and watched in amazement as Phila reached for a sandwich. The battle with him had obviously whetted her appetite. He watched her take a huge bite and wondered what the hell he was going to do next. Things were spinning out of his control and that he was unaccustomed to.

"Phila, let's take this from the top. One way or another, you're going to have to make some decisions about those C&L shares you inherited."

"One way or another," she agreed, reaching for another sandwich. "But I'll make my own decisions. I've been doing that for a long time, Lightfoot. I'm real good at it."

"You are really irritating is what you are."

She smiled, showing a lot of little white teeth. "You haven't seen anything yet. Good night, Mr. Lightfoot."

He drummed his fingers on the table, caught himself and stopped immediately. "We need to talk."

"Not tonight. I'm tired. We've talked more than enough this evening. Go."

He knew there was no point forcing the issue further now. She was too wired from the aftereffects of the confrontation with Ruth Spalding and the short battle she had just conducted with him. Nick knew when to stage a strategic retreat. He got to his feet without a word and started for the door.

"Thank you for the sandwich, Mr. Lightfoot," she called after him, her tone sarcastic.

"Anytime," he said dryly, his hand on the front doorknob.

"And thanks for trying to fend off Ruth Spalding," Phila added softly, no longer sarcastic.

He said nothing, stepping out into the night and closing the door quietly behind him. He had the feeling Phila wasn't accustomed to anyone trying to fight her battles for her.

It was then he realized there probably was no man in her life, at least not at the moment.

That thought cheered him up for some reason as he climbed into the Porsche and headed back toward the Holloway Park Motel.

41

CHAPTER THREE

Nick stalked into his motel room, then turned around and stalked back out again when he realized that he was in no mood to sleep or watch television. He headed for the flashing promise of a neon sign that signaled a tavern across the street.

Five minutes later, ensconced in a booth with a beer and a hamburger, he gave himself over to brooding.

He could not seem to get a handle on Philadelphia Fox, and that worried him. What worried him even more was the fact that he was attracted to her.

It made no sense. She was definitely not his type, although after the fiasco of his marriage he had never been quite sure what his type was.

But his father had taught him to admire courage and his mother had taught him a grudging respect for compassion, and Nick had to admit Phila had shown both tonight when she had dealt with the Spalding woman. On top of that, he automatically gave a few points to anyone who had the guts to defy the combined forces of the Castletons and the Lightfoots. There was definitely more to Phila than met the eye.

Still, he did not normally get turned on by feisty, mouthy, left-wing types who had the arrogance to lecture others on matters of moral responsibility. Nick grimaced and pushed aside his personal reaction to the Fox. He knew he had to think with his head, not his balls. Too much was riding on his next move with Phila.

Unfortunately for all concerned, Phila was not the simple, straightforward opportunist Eleanor Castleton wanted to believe she was, that much was for certain. There appeared to be a steel core of something that looked suspiciously like integrity running through Phila's spine. Integrity combined with the bleeding-heart compassion of a true liberal always made for a volatile combination: warrior and saint.

Such people tended to be quite zealous in their approach to problem solving.

Such people were never really happy until they felt justice had been done on behalf of the weak and wretched of the earth.

Such people hired independent investigators to verify the true nature of what everyone else considered an accident.

Nick concentrated, seeking the right method for dealing with his quarry. He knew there had to be a way to get to Phila. It was just a matter of pulling the right strings.

Quickly he summarized the basic facts. The woman had no job at present, she had just been through a courtroom trial, and she had lost her best friend. All in all, that added up to a lot of stress.

He remembered his initial impression of her, an idling engine that normally moved through life at full speed.

Maybe what she needed was a fresh focus, something to fill up the void in her life that had been left by the loss of her job and friend; something that would galvanize her natural sense of integrity and tap into the fire of both the warrior and the saint.

Nick sat for a long time, worrying the problem like a dog with a bone. The beer went down slowly and the hamburger disappeared bite by methodical bite.

When he had finished the hamburger he sat turning the empty beer bottle slowly between his palms. Philadelphia

Fox was his ticket home, and he was not about to lose her at this stage.

It wasn't until he reached for his wallet to pay for the meal that he acknowledged the whole truth. He needed a way to keep Phila within reach not only because of the C&L shares she possessed, but also because some part of him was never going to be satisfied until he had gotten the Fox into bed.

Phila's fingers touched cold metal the next morning while she was rooting around in her drawer for a pair of panties. She paused, pushed back a spare nightgown and stared at the 9-mm automatic pistol she had bought the week before.

She hated the sight of the handgun. Talk about a death machine. She had a lot of gall hurling accusations at Nick Lightfoot because of the products his family manufactured when she herself was carrying a thing like this around. Owning the weapon violated every principle she had ever been taught about gun control.

But she was scared, and Phila was discovering that fear changed a few things. It hurt, though, to remember her grandmother telling her that her parents had never carried guns, not even into the terrible jungle where they had died.

Phila sighed. She was angry and depressed because she had given in to the fear and bought the gun, but she knew she wasn't going to take it back. She covered up the pistol with the nightgown and several pairs of pantyhose.

Aside from her natural dislike of the thing, she was very uncomfortable with the automatic. The salesman at the sporting-goods store had shown her how to load the magazine, and she understood the necessity of removing the safety before firing. But she had never been able to bring herself actually to practice shooting the gun. It felt obscene and ugly in her hand.

Every time she looked at the automatic Phila could almost hear her grandmother's outrage. *This country is running amok with guns. Every Tom, Dick and Harry has one. It's because of all that nonsense about winning the West.*

People act as if they've got to keep on winning it! They say they're protecting themselves against crime. What a ridiculous argument. The surest way to cut back on crime in this country is to get rid of handguns.

Matilda Fox had strongly supported gun-control measures. She had waged a personal, one-woman, ongoing war with the National Rifle Association as well as every congressman who had ever dared come out against gun control.

Her grandmother wasn't the only one Phila heard scolding her in her imagination when she looked at the lethal automatic. She could also hear Crissie Masters. *If you're going to carry one, Phila, for God's sake, learn how to use it.* Crissie had had a pragmatic approach to most things.

The knock on her front door distracted Phila from her reveries. She found the underpants she had been searching for, pulled them on and reached for a pair of gauzy cotton pants. It was going to be hot again today. It would get hotter here in Holloway as the summer wore on. Another depressing thought.

The knock sounded again, more demanding this time. Phila decided that since the gauze pants were turquoise, her yellow T-shirt would go nicely. She slipped into it as she called out to whoever was making the racket.

"Who is it?" These days she thought twice about throwing open a door without first checking to see who was on the other side. The scene with Ruth Spalding last night had increased her wariness.

"It's Nick."

Phila didn't think twice about opening the door; she thought three times. Then, with a muttered groan, she went down the tiny hall into the living room and flipped the dead bolt.

Something told her that Nick Lightfoot was the kind who would either stand out there on the steps all day waiting for her to emerge or go fetch a cop and claim something was seriously wrong inside her house. Either way he would see her today. She braced herself as she opened the door, not certain how to handle him.

She stood blinking up at him in the bright morning sunlight. He was wearing a khaki shirt and a pair of jeans, and his hair was still damp from his shower. He looked good, she thought with some surprise. He was still much too large, of course, but there was something very appealing about him, nevertheless.

"Good morning." His gray gaze moved over her with a delight that made her self-conscious.

"What do you want?" Phila did not particularly care if she sounded ungracious.

Nick held up a hand, palm outward. "I come in peace bearing gifts." He waved a white paper bag in front of her.

"What's in there?" Phila asked suspiciously.

"After watching you devour my tuna sandwiches last night, I decided that food was the way to your hard little heart. I stopped at the fast-food joint next to my motel and picked up some breakfast. I figured the least you could do was make the coffee."

"Why?"

"So that we can have something bracing to drink while we eat my food and discuss your summer vacation." He flattened his palm against the door and pushed slowly, steadily inward.

With a groan of resignation, Phila fell back. "All right, you're in. What about my summer vacation?" She led the way into the kitchen and turned on the drip coffee machine.

"Sit down, Phila, I have a proposition to make, and I would very much appreciate it if you could manage to sit through my entire presentation before jumping on top of it with both feet." He dropped into one of the kitchen chairs and began unpacking the egg-and-muffin sandwiches.

"Let's hear it." Phila sat down in the other chair, unable to ignore the food any longer. She realized with some surprise that she actually was hungry this morning, just as she had been last night. That was a nice change. Her appetite had been off lately. The only meal she had been eating on a regular basis was dinner, and she usually had to down a couple of glasses of wine to work up enough enthusiasm for that.

"You are going to have to make decisions soon that will affect a number of people."

"Castletons and Lightfoots."

Nick's eyebrows rose behind his glasses. "This may come as a shock to you, Phila, but Castletons and Lightfoots are people, just like Ruth Spalding and the kids you put into foster care."

"Do me a favor, okay? Don't try to make me feel charitable toward Castletons and Lightfoots. The thought of it nauseates me." She picked up one of the breakfast sandwiches and sniffed appreciatively.

"You don't look nauseated." Nick eyed her narrowly for a moment before continuing. "I think you should get to know us before you decide what you're going to do about the shares, Phila. I think you could put your mind at ease if you spent some time with the families. You'd realize we're all human, just like everyone else."

"What are you suggesting I do? Hold a party and invite them to it?"

"I'm serious about this. Everyone's in Port Claxton now, and they'll be there for a few weeks. Sort of a summer tradition. Castletons and Lightfoots are very big on tradition. You could go over to the coast, too. You'd have a chance to get to know the families, ask questions and make an informed decision about what to do with your shares. You hold a lot of power. Don't you want to use it intelligently?"

"I already know a lot about the families. More than I really want to know, in fact."

Nick's mouth turned grim. "You've judged us all and found us wanting, haven't you? And you've never even met any of us except me."

The truth of his words made Phila feel uneasy. She concentrated on the second egg sandwich. "I just don't think I'd get any satisfactory answers by spending time in Port Claxton."

"The Castletons and Lightfoots have their problems,

Phila, and one or two family skeletons in the closet, but none of us are monsters. I think if you got to know us, you'd realize that. And you should realize it before you make any permanent decisions regarding your inheritance."

She stared at him intently. "You know something? I tend to forget sometimes that you're one of 'them.' Probably because Crissie never mentioned you. You told me yourself you walked away from the clans three years ago. But it's beginning to dawn on me that every time you mention the families you include yourself in the group. You always say 'us.'"

"What do you expect me to do? Deny I'm related to the Lightfoots? I can't do that. I've got the nose, you see." He tapped it with an air of importance.

Phila surveyed his nose gravely. "Did the women in your family also get that nose?"

"We never found out. I was the only kid my parents had. The nose is from my father's side of the family."

"And your mother?" Phila asked carefully.

"My mother was very lovely," Nick said quietly. "She died seven years ago."

"I see. I'm sorry." Phila wished she'd kept her mouth shut.

"You've mentioned a grandmother, but what happened to your parents, Phila?" he asked after a moment.

"They died when I was very young."

"Who raised you? Your grandmother?"

Phila nodded. "Until I was thirteen. Then she died."

"Who raised you after that?"

"I went into foster care."

Nick frowned. "Jesus, Phila. You went into one of those places? You didn't have any other family? No one who would take you in?"

His genuine shock was almost humorous. "Don't look so horrified, Nick. Lots of people wind up in 'those places,' as you call them. There are some very good, kind people running them. It's not so bad, given the alternative."

"But wasn't there *anyone?*" he persisted.

"I think there are a couple of distant relations out there

somewhere. But they didn't bother to come forward when they heard of my grandmother's death. My caseworker tracked down one of them, an aunt on my mother's side, but she said she couldn't possibly afford to take me in. She had her hands full with her own three kids, and her husband had just walked out on her."

"Jesus," Nick said again, making it sound halfway between a prayer and an oath.

Phila shook her head, smiling thinly. "You say that as if you can't imagine a world in which you would have been sent into foster care."

"I can't," he admitted. "As long as I can remember there's always been family around, Lightfoots and Castletons both. If something had happened to my parents when I was younger, the Castletons would have taken me in and raised me as their own. My folks would have done the same for Darren. There would have been no question about it. Hell, if anything happened to Darren and his wife tomorrow, I'd take their little boy." He shrugged. "It's just understood."

"Not everyone has an extended family clan like that, much less the financial resources to raise a relative's orphaned kid."

"You think I'm a little naive on the subject, don't you?" he asked wryly.

"Not any more than I was when I first went into foster care." Phila closed her eyes briefly. "I was so scared in the beginning. Then I met Crissie. She was the same age I was, but years older in some ways. She'd been through the wars. In and out of foster care most of her life. She preferred it to living with her mother, who tended to have the kind of boyfriends who abused helpless little girls."

"Things must have been bad at home if she actually preferred foster care," Nick said quietly.

"They were. At any rate, for some reason neither of us ever fully understood, she took me under her wing and helped me find my feet that first year; helped me to survive, in fact. I owe her, Nick."

He got up to pour coffee from the pot into two mugs.

"And that's why you feel you can't let go of her now that she's dead? You feel some sense of obligation?"

"We were a team. As close as sisters. She was all I had for a long time. And now she's gone." Phila felt the familiar burning sensation at the back of her eyes. She seemed to cry on the slightest pretext lately. She found this new tendency extremely annoying. This morning she refused to let the tears fall.

There was a long silence before Nick spoke again. "Come to Port Claxton this summer, Phila. Find out what the families are like and what really happened while Crissie was with them."

"What if no one in the families will talk to me, let alone answer questions?"

"They'll talk to you."

"How do you know?"

"Because you'll be with me. They'll have to be polite to you. Besides, you said yourself, you need a vacation. The coast will make a nice change from Holloway, I guarantee it."

Phila wondered if he was even remotely aware of the arrogance in his words. She downed the last of the egg sandwich and brushed crumbs off her turquoise pants while she tried to think.

There were several advantages to the strange, unexpected offer. Going to Port Claxton would get her out of Holloway, and after last night's meeting with Ruth Spalding that seemed more desirable than ever. And Nick was right. It would give her a chance to meet the people Crissie had thrust herself upon last year. It would give her a chance to learn what she could about the long-lost family Crissie had discovered. Phila knew she would be better equipped then to make her decision about what to do with the C&L shares.

But with her usual perception she sensed that Nicodemus Lightfoot rarely did things for altruistic reasons. He had an angle. She wondered what it was.

"Why are you doing this, Nick?"

"I told you."

"You mean that garbage about allowing me to put my mind at ease? I don't buy that for one minute. You're looking for a way to get those shares back, aren't you? Until you find one you figure it might be a good idea to keep an eye on me."

"It's your decision, Phila."

"It would be impossible to get a summer place on the coast at this late date," Phila said slowly, still thinking it through.

"You could stay at my family's cottage. Plenty of room."

"Not a chance," Phila answered instantly. She knew he was right about the room. Crissie had described the "cottages" the Lightfoots and Castletons had built side by side in Port Claxton, Washington. From all accounts they qualified as mini-mansions by most standards. Still, she had no intention of taking up residence in either of them.

Nick paid no attention to her response. He just reached for the phone on the wall. He got directory assistance, obtained the number he requested and then he dialed it.

"Harry, it's Nick Lightfoot. Yeah. A long time. Listen, Harry, I'm coming to Port Clax for a while and I've got a friend who needs a place to stay. What have you got available?"

Phila glowered as the conversation continued for a few more minutes. Nick saw her expression, and his brows rose in polite inquiry.

"The old Gilmarten place sounds fine, Harry. We'll be there on July fourth. Any problem? I didn't think so. Thanks, Harry. See you on the Fourth." Nick tossed the receiver back into the cradle. "That settles it. You've got a nice little place near the beach. Not far from the family cottages, in fact. Fully furnished. How does that sound?"

"It sounds too good to be true. What poor soul got evicted?"

Nick shrugged. "Some couple from Seattle will be given another place when they arrive next week. They'll never know the difference."

"I take it good old Harry owed the families a couple of favors?"

"I've known Harry for years. Dad and I used to go fishing with him."

"Sure. So now you can casually pick up the phone, and Harry rearranges his whole schedule of summer rentals. Just like that."

Nick smiled blandly. "Not much point in being a Lightfoot if you can't throw your weight around once in a while."

"'Evenin', sir. I just finished building the martinis. How was the golf game?" There was more than a shade of deepest, darkest Texas in Tec Sherman's accent, but after years of self-discipline it had become overlaid with standard military drawl.

"Not bad. Won fifty bucks off Fortman." Reed Lightfoot sauntered over to the small bar where Tec Sherman was using a swizzle stick with crisp authority. A row of large green olives stuffed with pimientos was arranged nearby. Reed tossed ice into a glass and helped himself from the pitcher of martinis. "The poor, benighted fool landed in the goddamn trap on the sixteenth hole, and by the time he got out he was dead meat."

"Congratulations, sir." Tec Sherman paused expectantly.

Reed took a healthy swallow of his martini and eyed the other man. William Tecumseh Sherman was built like a slab of beef. He was an ex-Marine who managed to give the impression he was still in uniform, even though he habitually dressed in garishly patterned aloha shirts and loose cotton slacks. Sherman was in his mid-forties, bald as a billiard ball, with huge, bushy brows and a chronically pinched expression around the mouth. He had worked for the Lightfoots for years and he was as loyal as the rottweilers that guarded the front gate. Reed would have trusted Tec Sherman with his life.

"Something wrong, Tec?" Reed finally inquired.

"No, sir. Just heard the good news, sir. Wanted to tell you I was damned glad. It's about time."

Reed wandered over to the window and gazed out toward the sea. Through the trees he could see the Pacific. It was steel blue today under a sun still high in the early evening sky. "You know something I don't know, Tec?"

Tec cleared his throat and clasped his hands behind his back in a parade-rest stance. "I heard about Nick, sir. That's all. Saw Harry in town today. He told me about it, sir."

Reed went still. "What the devil are you talking about, Tec?" he asked very softly.

Sherman coughed slightly. "Sorry, sir. Assumed you knew. Harry said he talked to Nick on the phone the other day. Nick told him he was comin' home on the Fourth. Bringin' a friend with him. A lady friend, sir. Needed a place for her to stay. Harry's lettin' 'er have the Gilmarten place down the road."

Reed's martini sloshed perilously close to the rim of the glass. "Nick's coming home?" He turned his head to pin Tec Sherman with a piercing gaze. "He told Harry he was coming here to Port Clax?"

"Yes, sir. Like I said, thought you knew."

"No, I did not know." He wondered if Hilary did. It would be just like her to keep the information a secret until the last minute. Hilary liked games of one-upsmanship, and she was very good at them. "Nick hasn't seen fit to notify his family yet."

Sherman turned a dull red. "I'm sure he will real soon, sir. Probably wanted to line up the Gilmarten place for his, uh, lady friend first before he made his plans."

"This lady friend. Is she by any chance named Fox?" Hilary, Darren and Eleanor had been nagging him about Philadelphia Fox for weeks. So far he'd been ignoring them.

"I believe so, sir."

"Philadelphia Fox ?"

"I believe that's what Harry said, sir."

"Goddamn it, what is Nick up to now?" Reed asked under his breath.

"Sir?"

"Never mind, Tec. I was just wondering what the devil is going on."

"Beggin' your pardon, sir, but sounds to me like Nick got word the families had gotten themselves in a bind and he decided to do somethin' about it. It's just what you'd expect of him, sir."

"You have a lot of faith in my son, Tec."

"Known him a long time, sir, under some interestin' conditions. He's a Lightfoot. When the chips are down no Lightfoot is gonna stand by and let the families get into trouble."

Nick was coming home. Something that had been frozen for a long time began to thaw inside Reed. The sensation was almost painful. He looked out toward the distant horizon, and for the first time in nearly three years he permitted himself to think seriously about the future.

Until three years ago a sense of the future had been the guiding force in Reed Lightfoot's life. The need to create something substantial that could be handed down through the generations had kept him going during the lean years when Castleton & Lightfoot had struggled to survive and gain a foothold in the competitive world of high-tech electronics. It had sustained him even in the dark time seven years ago, after his first wife's death.

But Reed's passion for the future had begun to wither and die in him the day Nick had walked out. It had vanished altogether when Hilary had lost the baby.

But now, with a few simple words, he could feel the embers rekindling within him.

Nick was coming home.

He warned himself not to put too much stock in the event. Nothing had really changed. The past could not be altered. Everything that had occurred three years ago still stood locked in time. They all had to live with it.

But no matter how hard he tried to maintain a realistic view of his son's return, Reed could not prevent an overwhelming sense of relief from surging through his veins. *Nick was coming home.*

It looked as though he owed that fact to that brassy blond troublemaker who'd landed like a bomb in the Castletons' laps last year. Reed wondered if the Fox woman was going to prove equally explosive.

No need to worry, he told himself with gathering satisfaction. It sounded as if Nick already had her under control. When Nick bothered to exert himself, he could handle anything. He was a Lightfoot.

"Hello, Reed, I suppose you've heard the news? It's all over town."

Reed turned at the sound of the cool, beautifully modulated voice. His wife was gliding through the doorway, dressed in flowing silk trousers and an artfully draped blouse that framed her elegant throat. As always, his eyes went once, briefly, to the gold band he had put on her finger.

"Tec just told me." He kept his voice perfectly neutral. He found himself doing that a lot around Hilary. It was as if he took some petty pleasure in not giving her whatever reaction she wanted or anticipated.

"Trust Nick to make his reappearance in a suitably spectacular fashion. He'll probably parachute onto the lawn in a blaze of fireworks. Pour me a drink, please, Tec."

"Yes, ma'am. The usual?" Tec's voice was more clipped than before. It was always that way when he spoke to Reed's second wife.

"Of course, Tec." Hilary did not look at him. She concentrated on her husband while Tec prepared a martini straight-up for her. "I suppose Nick's return has something to do with those shares?"

"Sounds like it," Reed said quietly.

"I wonder what he thinks he can do." Hilary picked up her martini and toyed with the spear holding the olive. "Harry referred to the Fox woman as Nick's *lady* friend. You don't suppose Nick is trying his hand at seducing those shares out of her, do you?"

"Beats me." Reed wasn't about to give her the satisfaction of speculating aloud about his son's intentions, although privately he was wondering the same thing. He sighed inwardly at his own pettiness. This was what it had come down to between himself and his beautiful, young wife. A grim, silent battlefield had been carved out between them, a battlefield where the fighting was done not with words but with a chilling display of courtesy and a total lack of outward emotion.

"Harry says Nick made it clear the Fox woman was staying alone at the Gilmarten place. How quaint. Imagine Nick worrying about the proprieties. Oh, well, I suppose that means we'd better prepare a room for him here."

"Goddamn right," Reed muttered, some of his control slipping for an instant. "Of course he'll be staying here. This is his home." He swallowed the rest of the martini in a single, numbing gulp.

The small towns of eastern Washington all had a certain similarity about them, Phila had often thought. Her job had taken her to a number of them. Hardworking and unpretentious, they were generally oriented toward the farms and ranches that surrounded them.

Holloway was no different. There were more pickup trucks than anything else on the main street. The downtown shopping district consisted of three banks, a couple of gas stations, two fast-food places—including an old-fashioned drive-in hamburger joint—and a variety of small shops.

The shops sold such things as yarn, hardware, work clothes and real estate. Most of the stores looked vaguely depressed, and with good reason. The new mall in the next town had siphoned off the majority of Holloway's downtown business.

The landscape around Holloway was also typical of this part of the state. The endless vista of arid desert, which always astonished visitors who thought of Washington as a rain forest, were broken by acres of lush farmland. At certain times of the year hot, dry winds cut a swath through the area, raising dust that hung suspended for hours in the air. When the wind blew, the effect was similar to a snowstorm. Traffic came to a halt and people stayed indoors.

But today the air was still. The sky was clear, cloudless

and free of dust, a vast blue bowl that stretched over the desert to the jagged peaks of the distant mountains.

There was nothing wrong with Holloway, Phila thought. She had been raised in towns just like it. She knew them intimately. But she realized suddenly that she would be very glad to leave this place.

She sat at a table that was sheathed in chipped, gray Formica in Emerson's Four Star Café, a cracked mug full of coffee in front of her. Outside on the hot sidewalk a few people hurried from their cars to the nearest air-conditioned business establishments.

"Going to be a hot one today," Thelma Anderson announced as she slid into the seat across from Phila.

Phila smiled faintly at her friend and former supervisor. "You've been living here too long, Thelma."

"What makes you say that?" the older woman demanded, her dark eyes snapping.

"It's a sure sign you've been in Holloway too long when the first thing you mention is the weather."

"This is farming country," Thelma pointed out casually. "Farmers always talk about the weather. I'm just trying to blend in. How's the coffee?"

"As bad as ever."

"Good. I'll have a cup." She signaled to the waitress, who nodded to her from the other side of the counter. Then Thelma turned back to Phila with an assessing eye. "So you're really going to do it, huh? You're going to quit for good? I can't talk you into coming back to your old job?"

Phila shook her head. "No. But I'm going to miss you, Thelma." And she meant it. She would miss her friend's short, no-nonsense haircut, her functional navy-blue skirts and white blouses and serviceable walking shoes. Thelma, who knew all the secret methods of shoving paperwork through an overburdened system that periodically tried to choke itself to death on forms and multiple copies and reports done in triplicate.

Thelma was dedicated and she was good at what she did, but somewhere along the line she had learned the trick of detaching herself enough emotionally from her work to ensure her own survival. Phila knew after the Spalding trial that she herself would never be able to develop that detachment. She was finished as a social worker.

"I have to get out, Thelma. I need a change."

Thelma regarded her soberly. "Yes, I think you do," she said finally. "You've been through hell. It takes awhile to recover. Feeling any better?"

"Some." Phila smiled again, realizing it was the truth. She had been feeling better, more *focused*, since she had made her decision to go to Port Claxton.

"A summer on the coast will be good for you. You always did like the ocean. Can you handle it financially?"

"Yes, thanks to Crissie's insurance policy. It wasn't much but together with my savings, it will keep me going for a while."

"How did you manage to get a place near the beach at this time of year?" Thelma demanded. "Port Claxton summer houses are always booked months in advance. I know, I've tried to get in once or twice, myself."

"Someone I know pulled a few strings for me."

Thelma grinned. "A man?"

"Uh huh."

"Well, good for you. Just what you need to take your mind off that trial and your friend's death. It's time you put it all behind you, Phila."

Phila shrugged. She did not want to explain to Thelma that Crissie's death was still very much on her mind and that she was far from letting it go. "You'll keep in touch, won't you, Thelma?"

"You know I will. We won't be forgetting you around here anytime soon, Philadelphia Fox. If it hadn't been for you we never would have nailed Elijah Spalding. You're a heroine in the office."

"You'd have gotten him sooner or later."

"Later, maybe." Thelma sounded skeptical. "After a lot more kids had been abused and psychologically scarred for life. Later would have been too late for a lot of them." She shook her head. "Cases like that are so blasted frustrating. Everyone in the office knew what was going on, and no one could prove a thing. Every time we sent the sheriff out to the Spalding farm things were in apple-pie order. The kids were too frightened to talk, and Spalding's wife was useless."

"Ruth was as frightened of him as the children were. She was also desperate to hold on to him. In her own way, she loved him."

"A sick kind of love, if you ask me."

"We see that kind of love a lot in this business, don't we, Thelma? The sick kind."

"Well, Spalding's in prison now, and he'll be there another year and a half. Thanks to you. Too bad it had to happen the way it did, though. You could have been seriously hurt or even killed. I shudder every time I think about how close it all was."

"So do I," Phila admitted. And sometimes she did more than shudder. Sometimes she dreamed about it. And woke up in a cold sweat.

"I heard you had a run-in with Mrs. Spalding last night at the diner. True?"

"It's true. She's hurting, Thelma."

"I think she could be dangerous, Phila. Watch yourself around her, okay?"

"Maybe it's just as well I'm leaving town." But Phila's instincts told her Ruth Spalding was not the real threat.

"I agree. Go off to the coast, friend, and see if you can't get that old gleam back in your eye."

"I didn't know I had an old gleam to recover." Phila smiled.

"You do, you know. In fact, I think I detect a few returning sparks already. You look a lot better than you did a couple of weeks ago."

"Thanks. I think." Phila drew a deep breath. "Thelma, I'm a little scared."

"Leaving a career is always a little scary," Thelma said gently.

"I feel I'm changing more than just a career. I think I'm changing my whole life, and I can't see what the new direction is going to be."

"You're strong, kiddo. Don't ever forget that. Want some advice, though?"

"Sure. You're one of the few people whose advice I trust and you know it."

"Choose carefully when you choose your next line of work. You were a good caseworker, one of the best, but you were a maverick. An urban guerrilla trying to work within the system. You were always twisting, bending and pushing the rules. That can be very frustrating after a while."

Phila wrinkled her nose. "I hadn't realized you noticed."

Thelma shrugged. "I let most of it go by because I wanted the results I knew you could get. But that's a hard way to work. Hard on you. I don't think you were really cut out to work in a bureaucratic system of any kind, let alone one like ours where you can see your failures in a string of little ruined lives. But you're a born crusader. A rescuer of others. it's your nature, Phila. It's one of your strengths. It's also your greatest weakness. Take that into consideration when you go job hunting again."

Later that evening Phila finished packing the last of her things and stood surveying the little house she had been renting for the past two years. It had been the closest thing to a home she'd had since the day her grandmother died. It hurt now to see her once cozy retreat looking empty and lifeless.

There would be another house, she told herself. That was one of the things you learned in foster care. There was always another house. And one of these days she would have one that really belonged to her; a real home. For keeps.

She was taking very little with her, just her personal belongings and the books she could not bear to give away. Most of the furniture and kitchenware had been put into storage. The phone would be disconnected in the morning.

Phila realized she did not even know where she would be living a month or two from now. She felt as though she were starting over from scratch, and she knew that was the way it had to be.

She had closed the door on her career as a social worker the day she had testified at the Spalding trial. She could no longer lay claim to being a professional, and she knew it. Everything for which she had trained and worked was over.

The stupid tears started to burn in her eyes again. She dashed them away with the back of her hand just as the phone rang. Grateful for the interruption, she snatched up the receiver.

"Hello?"

"Hello." Nick Lightfoot's voice was as calm and quiet over the phone as it was in person. "I called to see how the packing was going."

"It's done. I'll be leaving tomorrow." Phila sank down onto a suitcase, clutching the receiver. For some silly reason she no longer felt like crying. "Don't worry, I'll be in Port Claxton on the Fourth."

"Got a pen? I'll give you directions to the cottages."

"Yes. Yes, I've got one here somewhere." She fumbled for a pen and a pad of paper in her purse, hoping it would take him a long time to give her the directions. She wanted companionship tonight, any companionship, even that of a Lightfoot. "All right, go ahead."

Nick gave her directions in a crisp, well-organized fashion that made her realize he was, by nature, a very methodical, organized man. She would have to keep that in mind, she told herself. Methodical, organized, conservative thinkers rarely did things without specific reasons. Definitely not impulsive types.

When he was finished, she dropped the pad back into her purse and tried to think of some way to keep the conversation going. There was a long silence on the other end of the line.

"What are you doing?" she finally asked, somewhat inanely.

"Right now? Taking care of some things here at the office in Santa Barbara so I can leave town for a few weeks without worrying too much about Lightfoot Consulting Services falling apart."

"Oh."

"Yeah. Not too exciting."

"About on a par with packing."

"Yeah. What did you have for dinner?"

"Nothing. There's nothing left in the house to eat."

Nick muttered something that sounded like an oath. "Why don't you go into town and have a burger or something?"

"I'm not hungry."

"Promise me you'll have breakfast before you start the drive to Port Claxton tomorrow, okay?"

"Why should I promise you that?"

"Humor me. I get the feeling you don't eat properly."

She was not up to arguing. "All right, all right, I'll have breakfast. Satisfied?"

"For now. I'll see you soon, Phila. Good night."

"Good night." Reluctantly she put the phone back in the cradle. Her stomach rumbled. It occurred to her that she was a little hungry, after all. Maybe she would run into town and grab a burger.

Phila was still sitting on her suitcase, feeling bemused and confused and wondering how hungry she really was, when the phone rang again. She jumped and picked up the receiver, ruefully aware that she was half hoping Nick had thought of some small twist in his directions that needed to be explained in greater detail.

"Hello?"

"It's not over, you bitch, just because you're leaving. It's not over. *You lied.* You lied about my husband. He's in prison because you lied. They took away the children. All the children are gone and my man is in prison because of your lies. You've ruined everything—"

Phila cringed and gently lowered the phone back into its cradle, cutting off Ruth Spalding's sobbing accusations.

CHAPTER FOUR

It was not the first time Phila had stood at the gate and stared through the bars at a large family party that didn't include her. She and Crissie had spent most of their teen-age years knowing what it was to be on the outside looking in.

But Phila had to admit this was the first time she'd stood outside such an elegant gate or observed such a huge bash. When the Lightfoots and Castletons celebrated the Fourth of July, they went all out. It looked to Phila as if the entire town of Port Claxton had been invited.

She curled her fingers around the wrought-iron bars and stared at the festive scene. The sweeping expanse of in-credibly green lawn was filled with people in shorts, halter tops, short-sleeved shirts and jeans. Four long barbecue pits had been set up, manned by a team of professional-looking chefs. The fragrance of broiling steaks and ham-burgers wafted through the air. Ears of corn on the cob wrapped in aluminum foil were sunk deep into hot coals. Massive bowls of potato salad, pickles and relish were ar-ranged on side tables. Beer and soft drinks were being dis-pensed under a striped awning.

All very patriotic and traditional and, done on this scale, very expensive.

Two stately homes with long, graceful porticos dominated the crest of the hill above the lawn. Behind them was
a sloping, wooded hillside that fronted the wide expanse of
beach.

The Lightfoot and Castleton *beach cottages* were each
two stories high and painted a fresh, crisp, classic white.
The charming, multi-paned windows had dark green shut-
ters. Phila could see green porch swings behind the col-
umns of the porticos. She just knew there wouldn't be a
stick of furniture inside that dated from any later than
1850.

For a minute she thought she must have taken a wrong
turn and wound up in the wrong place and the wrong year.
Virginia, say. Or Maryland, sometime in the early eigh-
teen-hundreds.

The biggest American flag Phila had ever seen waved
from the top of a tall flagpole set in front of the two homes.

"May I help you, ma'am?"

It wasn't a polite inquiry; it was a direct challenge. Phila
jumped as the masculine voice cracked behind her. She
whirled around, half expecting to find herself facing a uni-
formed guard armed with a high-powered rifle and a big
dog.

What she saw was a heavily built bald man in a truly
spectacular aloha shirt. The shirt, colorful though it was,
did not reassure her. All her ingrained animosity toward
people who thought they could tell her what to do rose to
the fore.

"Help me?" she repeated sweetly. "I doubt it. You don't
look like the helpful type." She swung around to continue
staring through the bars at the Castleton-Lightfoot Fourth
of July picnic.

"This party isn't open to tourists, just local residents,
and I sure don't recognize you, ma'am. You'll have to be
on your way."

"It's all right, General, I'm here at the request of his
lordship." Phila didn't turn around again.

"What's this lordship crap? Cut the comedy, sister, and
move your little ass on out of here. This is private property.

No one goes through those gates unless they're local residents or friends of the families."

A palm the size and weight of a steer carcass closed around her shoulder.

Phila lost her temper. She tried to shrug off the heavy palm and failed. That only made her angrier. "Take your hand off me, you big ape. I told you, I've got an engraved invitation."

"Is that right? Then suppose you show it to me?"

Phila looked up into a face dominated by a nose that had obviously been broken more than once. A thin, severe little mustache crowned the man's tight lips. There was something in his painfully upright posture that clued her in.

"Ex-Marine, right?" she hazarded.

"For your information, ma'am, there ain't no such thing as an ex-Marine. A Marine's a Marine till the day he dies."

"How unfortunate for you," Phila retorted. "That will certainly be a terrible burden for you to carry the rest of your life."

A dark red flush rose beneath the man's leathery tan. The severe little mustache twitched, and the beady eyes bulged with outrage. "Why you smart-mouthed little—"

"Take your hands off me this instant or I'll get myself an ACLU lawyer and sue you from here to the shores of Tripoli!"

"Is that right? Well, I might as well give you something to sue about." Without any warning, he put his huge hands around her waist and tossed her over one massive shoulder.

Phila screeched at the top of her lungs, but apparently no one on the lush green lawn heard her above the general laughter and chatter. "Put me down or so help me I'll see you in jail." She started pounding his back furiously with her fists. It was like hitting an elephant. He was not crushing her so she did not panic, but she fiercely resented the manhandling. "You're a perfect example of the sort of imbecile produced by this country's military mentality. Where did you come from? Some secret government breeding program that's run amok? *Put me down.*"

"Hello, Tec. I see she got to you real fast. She's good at that."

"Nick!" Phila raised her head at the sound of the familiar—and infuriatingly calm—voice. "Thank heavens you're here. Do something quick. This jerk is crazy."

"*Sir*. It's you, sir." The ape sounded thrilled, Phila thought in disgust. "Welcome home, sir. We're damn glad to have you back again."

Phila twisted frantically. "Nick, do something. Tell this monster to put me down. Then call the cops. This man is extremely dangerous. I want him arrested for assault."

"Tec wouldn't hurt a fly unless he was really provoked," Nick said casually. "Of course, if you're going to go around provoking people, you've got to expect some response, Phila."

"I was not provoking him. I was standing on my constitutional rights, damn it. Make him put me down this instant or I'll sue Castleton & Lightfoot as well as this creep. I'm sure a good lawyer could prove that anybody who hired this guy was guilty of extremely bad judgment."

"Holy shit, sir, this isn't her, is it? Is this that lady friend you told Harry you were bringin' with you?"

"I'm afraid so. Philadelphia Fox, allow me to present William Tecumseh Sherman. An old friend of the family. He's worked for the Lightfoots for years. Ever since he got out of the service, in fact."

"Fire him," Phila answered.

"You'd better give her to me, Tec. She gets a bit temperamental at times."

"Sure thing, sir. Real sorry about the mistake." Tec began to shift his burden. His hands went around Phila's waist and he lifted her off his shoulder. "I asked her who she was, and she just gave me some sass."

"That sounds like her."

"I was supposed to keep an eye on everyone who tried to get through the gates this year. Last year a couple of bikers tried to crash the party. Caused a little trouble before I could get rid of 'em."

"Do I look like some kind of motorcycle mama, you

idiot?" Phila closed her eyes as the sky spun overhead. She waited impatiently for her feet to touch the ground. She kept talking while she was in midair. "This is absolutely intolerable. I can't believe this man has kept a position with your family all these years, Nick. Do you people booby-trap your front lawn, too? Put alligators in swamps around the front door maybe? Are there any more military robots like this one hanging around? Uzi machine guns in the hall . . . Ooof! *Nick!*"

A second pair of large hands caught her around the waist, and the next thing Phila knew she was hanging over Nick's broad shoulder.

"I'm going to use my shares in Castleton & Lightfoot to drive both families into bankruptcy," Phila swore.

"Take it easy, Phila. I'll handle it from here, Tec. See you a little later?"

"Yes, sir. You better believe it, sir. Sure is good to have you back."

"Thank you, Tec. I wonder if the others will feel the same way."

"I'm sure they will, sir. Not much doubt about it."

From her upside-down position Phila caught the expression on Tec Sherman's face. He was grinning widely at Nick. This was one member of the clan who was apparently happy to see the prodigal son. Of course, she reminded herself, Tec wasn't exactly family. Just hired help.

"Put me down, Nick. The joke has gone far enough." She saw the wrought-iron gates slip past her field of vision as Nick strode through them. When she looked down she saw a sea of deep, verdant green under his feet.

"This is the Fourth of July, Phila," he explained. "You're supposed to have a little fun on the Fourth."

"This is a Lightfoot's way of having fun? Manhandling innocent women?"

"I've never tried it before," Nick said thoughtfully. His palm slid higher up along her jean-clad thigh. He squeezed gently. "It's not half bad."

Before he could continue, another male voice interrupted. This voice was vaguely familiar. Rich, well modulated, very smooth. An excellent speaking voice that could make the listener believe anything. She had heard it once on the telephone. It belonged to Darren Castleton.

"Hey, Nick. What the hell have you got there? Your technique with the ladies undergone a few changes during the past three years?"

"I never did have your finesse, Darren."

"That goes without saying. You're a Lightfoot, not a Castleton. But you sure as hell never used to go in for the kind you had to bring home over your shoulder. This one must be interesting."

"She is."

"Good to see you, Nick." Darren's voice turned earnest. "Damn good. It's been too long."

"I just hope it's been long enough."

Phila felt Nick's right arm move from across the back of her thighs and she realized he was shaking hands with Darren. "If you two have finished the grand reunion, I would appreciate it if someone would let me stand on my own two feet."

"I think she's irritated, Nick."

"Not my fault. She had a small altercation with Tec down at the front gate." With an easy movement, Nick put Phila down and watched, grinning, as she pushed hair out of her eyes and straightened her fuchsia-and-green-print camp shirt. "Darren, meet Miss Philadelphia Fox."

Phila glowered at the remarkably handsome man in front of her. He looked to be about the same age as Nick, but that was where the resemblance stopped. While Nick was big and solid and blunt of feature, Darren Castleton was graceful, lean and aristocratic.

There were just enough craggy edges on his fine features to save him from being pretty, Phila decided. He had the kind of teeth that would grace any campaign poster. His light brown hair and clear, blue eyes gave him the sort of all-American look that people tended to trust on sight.

There was, she had to admit, something quite attractive about Darren Castleton, something beyond the nice features and the charm. The word *charisma* came to mind when she realized she was smiling up at him. When he held out his hand, she took it.

"Hello, Mr. Castleton."

"Darren," he corrected instantly. His handshake was solid. "Glad to meet you, Phila. Sorry about whatever happened down at the gate. Tec tends to take his duties seriously."

"It's probably the military mentality," Phila explained. "It's a severe handicap."

"You may be right." Darren exchanged a quick grin with Nick.

"I guess the Castletons and Lightfoots suffer a lot from that sort of thing," Phila murmured.

"Some of us endeavor to rise above it," Darren said, still smiling.

Crissie had had little respect for males in general and had not dwelt on them in her correspondence or phone calls. Men were just creatures to be maniuplated when it was useful to do so. But she had made one or two observations about Darren Castleton that Phila remembered. *They're talking about a political career for him,* she had remarked. *He'll probably be good at it. Endless teeth and a wife Eleanor handpicked especially for the job of being a politician's wife. Hilary says she's willing to have the families finance Darren's campaigns. Running for office takes a ton of money, she says, and lots of clout. The Lightfoots and Castletons have both.*

"Let's get you two something to eat. Reed's supervising things at the barbecue as usual. You know how he loves it." Darren looked at Nick. "Your dad's looking forward to seeing you again, Nick."

"Is he?" Nick threw a casual arm around Phila's shoulders and started walking toward the barbecue pits.

"Give him a chance, okay?" Darren suggested softly.

"Think he'll give me one?"

"I think things are going to work out just fine if everyone gives them a chance to do so," Darren said. "Are you hungry, Phila?"

She inhaled the aromas coming from the direction of the

barbecue pits and was again surprised to find herself anticipating food. "Yes, I think I am."

"Good. Plenty for everyone."

Phila glanced at him. "Do you people put on a Fourth of
July party every year?"

"Every year for as long as Nick or I can remember. It's a
C&L tradition. People around here count on it."

Phila nodded, aware of the weight of Nick's arm around
her shoulders. She wondered at it. His casual air of possessiveness disconcerted her, but it also intrigued her. This
was the first time she had seen him since he had left Holloway, and she was startled at the strange little leap of excitement that had shot through her a moment ago when he had
put her over his shoulder.

Halfway to the barbecue pits two large, muscular-look-
ing dogs came bounding through the crowd. They clustered
around Nick, who played with their ears for a few minutes
and spoke to them quietly.

"Looks like they remember you," Darren observed.

"What kind of dogs are they?" Phila asked warily as the
black-and-tan dogs turned their broad heads in her direction.

"Rottweilers," Nick said.

"I knew it," Phila muttered. "Killer dogs." She tried to
step back when the animals thrust their inquisitive noses
into her hands, but she wasn't quick enough. With a sigh
of resignation she gingerly patted their heads. They seemed
overjoyed at the attention and eagerly demanded more.

"How about that?" Darren said. "They're taking to you
right off, Phila. They don't usually do that. Normally it
takes them awhile to accept a stranger."

"They're probably just sizing me up for dinner," Phila
said. "Figuring the easiest, quickest way to tear out my
throat. What are their names? Bruno and Devil?"

"Cupcake and Fifi," Nick told her.

"Oh, sure."

"It's true. My father bought them just before I left. He
named them." Nick pushed his glasses higher on his nose
and smiled faintly as he watched the dogs' antics. "Dar-

ren's right. You've got them eating out of the palm of your hand. Very unusual."

"I can't tell you how thrilled I am," Phila said. The rottweilers laughed up at her, tongues lolling, as if she had said something very funny. "They remind me of you."

"Crissie Masters hated the dogs," Darren said quietly.

"Crissie was terrified of dogs," Phila explained coldly. She gave the rottweilers a last pat and tried to step back.

"Come on, let's get that food we were talking about," Darren said, leading the way. "How about a beer, Nick?"

"Sounds good."

The dogs danced around Phila's heels all the way to the barbecue pits. She finally gave up trying to discourage their attention. It was not the first time she'd found herself in this position. Animals and kids frequently reacted this way around her.

People were standing three-deep near the barbecue pits, but the crowd parted almost magically as Nick, Phila and Darren approached. When the last hungry guest stepped aside, a big, broad-shouldered man in his mid-sixties was revealed. He held a spatula in his right hand as he supervised the half dozen other men dressed in chef's aprons.

Phila recognized the nose immediately as the silver-haired man turned to glance in her direction. She also recognized the cool gray eyes and the high, blunt cheekbones. Reed Castleton. She felt Nick's arm tighten around her shoulders, but his voice was as calm as ever when he spoke.

"Hello, Dad."

Reed nodded once casually but there was an intensity in his hooded gaze as he examined his son. "Heard you were coming back. Glad you could make it to the picnic this year." The words sounded stilted but genuine. "This is Miss Fox, I take it?"

"Phila, this is Reed Lightfoot. My father."

"How do you do?" Phila said, carefully polite. She wasn't sure what to expect. Crissie had said very little about Reed Lightfoot. *He's always out on the golf course. Stays out of Hilary's way.*

"Nice to meet you, Phila," Reed said, flipping a meat patty with a deft movement. There was an awkward silence before he added, "You two want a burger?"

The question seemed to be directed at Nick, but when he failed to respond to it Phila automatically stepped in to answer. "That sounds great," she said.

Reed nodded, obviously glad to have something constructive to do. "We'll get you fixed up here. Eleanor, where are you? We need more buns over here."

"I'll have one of the caterer's people bring out some more, Reed."

Phila glanced around to see a polished-looking woman in her early sixties approaching them through the crowd. She had a clever little nautical cap perched atop her discreetly tinted beige-blond hair, and she was wearing a red-white-and-blue silk top over a pleated white silk skirt. Her smile was vague, but polite. Her pale blue eyes went immediately to Nick.

"Nick, dear! You're here. It's so good to see you, darling. We heard you were due to arrive today, and we're all so delighted."

Nick released Phila to accept Eleanor Castleton's hug. "Hi, Eleanor. Good to see you again. Meet Philadelphia Fox."

Eleanor turned to Phila, her smile still gracious but her eyes cold. "Of course. Miss Fox. You were a friend of Crissie Masters, I believe?"

"That's right. She was my best friend. Like a sister, in fact." Might as well get the cards on the table at the start of the game, Phila decided. She already knew how Eleanor Castleton felt about Crissie. *She hates my guts. But that's okay. I'm not real fond of her, either,* Crissie had said once.

"Such a dreadful accident," Eleanor said dismissively. She turned toward an attractive, slim, black-haired woman whose striking dark eyes were on Phila. "Vicky, dear, meet Phila Fox. Crissie's friend."

"How do you do, Miss Fox? I'm Victoria Castleton, Darren's wife."

"How do you do?" Phila said quietly as she held out her hand and silently remembered Crissie's description of this clan member: *Handpicked by dear Eleanor to be an asset to her son's political career.*

Victoria Castleton looked at Nick and smiled warily. "Hello, Nick. Good to see you again."

"Hello, Vicky." Nick nodded toward her. "Where's Jordan?"

"I'm here," announced a small boy as he stepped out from behind the shelter of his mother's legs. "Who're you?"

Nick went down on his haunches. "I'm Nick. You don't remember me, but I remember you. The last time I saw you, though, you were only about two years old and only about that high." He held his palm out about a foot above the grass.

"I'm big now." Jordan grinned proudly, standing beside Nick's hand to demonstrate the difference in height. He looked up at Phila. "Hi."

"Hi, yourself. My name is Phila." The boy's self-confidence spoke for itself, she thought. This was a child who had always received a great deal of love and attention; a boy who was sure of his place in his family and therefore sure of his welcome from others. The children she usually worked with rarely demonstrated this kind of comfortable confidence. She caught herself on that last thought. She would not be working with such children in the future. Her career was finished.

"D'you like seaweed?" Jordan asked.

"Yes, as a matter of fact, I do," Phila answered readily. "I like seaweed a lot."

"I got some in my room. Wanna see it?"

"Some other time, Jordan." Victoria took her son's hand and tugged him back a step from Phila. "Phila and Nick want to eat now."

"I believe the hamburgers are ready," Eleanor Castleton said smoothly. She picked up two plates and handed them to Nick and Phila. "Do help yourselves to salad and all the trimmings."

73

"Thanks, Eleanor." Nick took his plate and steered Phila toward the potato salad table.

"Lots of real genuine regret over Crissie's death there," Phila muttered. "Such a *dreadful* accident." She added, mimicking Eleanor Castleton's dismissive tone.

Nick scooped potato salad onto Phila's plate. "You'd better get realistic about this business, Phila. You can't expect her to feel a lot of sorrow over Crissie's death. Your friend made Eleanor's life hell while she was here."

"It's wasn't Crissie's fault Burke Castleton cheated on his wife twenty-six years ago."

"You're absolutely right, of course," said a new voice from behind Phila. The newcomer spoke with a hint of a New England accent. "It was not her fault at all. But don't expect Eleanor Castleton to ever admit it. She's put a lot of effort into polishing the Castleton image."

Phila knew who the speaker was without being told. When she turned around she was not surprised to see a sleek thoroughbred of a woman with chestnut-red hair and emerald-green eyes. She was dressed in beautifully cut camel-colored trousers that emphasized her long legs and an off-white silk blouse, an elegant outfit that perfectly complemented her features. She wore a gold wedding ring on her left hand.

"Hello," Phila said.

"Hello, Phila. I'm Hilary Lightfoot." Hilary put out a perfectly manicured hand. "I want to tell you how sorry I am about Crissie. She was a fascinating creature, bright and full of life. I miss her."

Phila accepted the long-fingered, long-nailed hand. "Thank you, Mrs. Lightfoot. It's a pleasure to meet you. Crissie liked you." This was the only member of the clan Crissie had liked, Phila recalled, and because Crissie had liked her, Phila was prepared to like Hilary Lightfoot, also.

"Call me Hilary." She withdrew her hand from Phila's and turned to Nick, who was munching potato salad. Her expression was serene but oddly unreadable. "Hello, Nick."

Nick nodded once. He did not offer his hand. "Hilary."

"I was surprised to hear you had decided to return."

"Were you?" Nick bit into a pickle and glanced out over the throng. "Quite a crowd this year."

"It gets bigger every year. One of these days we may have to start limiting the invitations to just friends of the families." Hilary followed his gaze. "This business of inviting the whole town is getting awkward, not to mention expensive."

"Castleton & Lightfoot can afford it." Nick's voice was neutral, but Phila thought she detected an undertone of annoyance.

"True, but it's hardly worthwhile."

"The Fourth of July picnic is a Castleton & Lightfoot tradition. I don't see Dad ever giving it up." Nick took a sizable bite out of his hamburger, his eyes still on the crowd.

"Reed is leaving more and more of the important decisions in my hands these days," Hilary told him quietly. "In fact, you might be interested to know that at last year's annual meeting he turned both his shares and yours over to me to vote. He trusts me to do what's best for the firm."

"He's always trusted you, hasn't he, Hilary?"

"Why shouldn't he trust me? I've always had the best interests of C&L at heart, unlike you."

Phila edged closer to the relish tray and concentrated on slathering her hamburger bun with mustard and pickles. She could feel the eerie crackle of emotional tension around these two and it sent shivers down her spine. It also raised a few interesting questions. She wondered just what Nick's relationship with Hilary had been. It was obvious he hadn't wasted any money on Mother's Day cards for his father's wife during the past few years.

Darren wandered over, a couple of cans of beer in his hands. He handed one to Nick as Hilary nodded at Phila and moved off into the crowd.

"Here," Darren said. "Figured you could use one of these."

"You figured right." Nick took the can and popped the tab.

"Since you're here," Darren said easily, "you can give us a hand with the fireworks later."

"Sure. Why not?"

"I knew there would be fireworks," Phila said under her breath.

Nick looked at her. "I've got a feeling the ones tonight are only the beginning."

The first crackling display of pyrotecnics lit up the evening sky at precisely ten o'clock that night. Phila sat cross-legged on the lawn in front of one of the colonnaded porticos to watch. She was surrounded by the women of the Lightfoot and Castleton clans. The only male in the group was young Jordan, who was so excited he could not sit still.

The townspeople sprawled across the wide lawn. Some were drinking a final can of beer, and others were trying to put away one more slice of apple pie. The dogs had stuffed themselves and were laying supine nearby. Somehow one of them, the one called Fifi, Phila thought, had managed to get her head lodged on Phila's lap.

Nick had vanished along with his father, Tec Sherman and Darren.

"Do all the Castleton and Lightfoot males get involved with the fireworks?" Phila asked Vicky, who was sitting next to her.

"It's a tradition," Vicky explained, her tone brusque. She looked at her bouncing son. "In a few years Jordan will get to help stage the fireworks display."

"Next year, next year, next year," Jordan chanted and then shrieked as another flash of color filled the night sky.

"Fireworks are dangerous," Phila said with a frown. "Basically, they're explosive devices. Small bombs. They're supposed to be handled by experts."

"Reed and Darren and Nick are experts. So was Burke."

"Is that right? Where did they all get this expertise?" Phila glanced up again as a starburst of red exploded overhead.

"Oh, every Castleton and Lightfoot male does his military service," Vicky said. "I suppose when Jordan is out of college he'll go into the Marines or the Air Force for a while."

"Another tradition?" Phila asked dryly.

"You wouldn't believe how many traditions these families have established in just two generations. My people have lived in Virginia since the seventeen-hundreds and we don't have as many rites and rituals as the Castletons and the Lightfoots."

"Nick and Darren went into the service?"

"Their fathers would have kicked them out of the business if they hadn't done their military duty. Don't worry. They all know what they're doing around explosives and firearms."

"How reassuring."

Hilary spoke softly out of the darkness to the right of Phila. "I'm going to get something to drink. Anyone want anything?"

Phila shook her head. "No, thanks."

"Nothing for me, Hilary," Victoria murmured.

"I'll come with you, Hilary, dear." Eleanor Castleton got out of the porch swing and followed Hilary into the house.

Victoria and Phila sat in silence for a few minutes as fireworks shrieked overhead. Phila absently played with Fifi's ears. The dog shuddered with pleasure.

"Are you going to pick up where Crissie left off?" Victoria finally asked quietly.

Phila had been wondering about the woman's tense tone, and she was glad the reason for her unfriendliness was finally out in the open.

"What do you mean?"

"Are you going to cause trouble for us?"

"Do you think I can?"

"Crissie certainly did."

"I'm not Crissie."

"No, you're different. Very different. I knew that the minute I saw you. But you're in a position to cause all kinds of trouble. You've got the shares now. Why did Nick bring you to Port Claxton?"

"To let me find out for myself what happened while Crissie was here. I want to know what you people did to her, Vicky."

"It's more a case of what she did to us," Victoria snapped. "I'm sorry for your sake that she's dead, but she did a lot of damage during the short time she was around, Phila. I hope you won't do more of the same. The families have been through enough."

"What, exactly, have the families been through?"

"Never mind. It doesn't concern you. I just thought you ought to know that what happened between the families and Crissie wasn't all one-sided."

"Perhaps."

They were silent again for several minutes before Victoria Castleton spoke. "Nick came back today because of you, didn't he? You have no idea what a shock that was to everyone, except maybe Eleanor. She always believed he'd return sooner or later. I wonder what he's planning?"

"He's planning to get his hands on my shares, just like everyone else." And if she were smart, Phila thought, she would not forget that simple fact for one minute.

Another brilliant display crackled overhead, and in the faint glow of the explosion Victoria eyed Phila with cool interest. "I saw that little scene down by the gate this afternoon. We all did. Quite an entrance."

Phila winced. "It certainly wasn't my idea of a grand entrance."

"I'd have said it wasn't Nick's idea, either. At least, not the Nick I knew three years ago. I'd have bet my last dollar Nicodemus Lightfoot was not the kind of man who would ever throw a woman over his shoulder and carry her through a crowd of people."

"Maybe he's been living in California too long."

"Whatever the reason, it certainly revealed a new side of him. And it's a side Hilary never saw, that's for sure. I can't imagine Nick throwing her over his shoulder. Never in a million years."

"Hilary?" Phila went still. "Why would he want to toss her over his shoulder?"

Victoria studied her for a moment in the flare of another explosion. "Don't you know?"

"Know what?"

"I'm sorry. I shouldn't have said anything. I just assumed Nick would have told you by now."

"Told me what, for heaven's sake?"

"Hilary is Nick's ex-wife. They were divorced three years ago. She married Reed the day after the divorce was final."

CHAPTER FIVE

The silence in the library was oppressive. Nick lounged in one of the mahogany cabriole chairs, his legs stretched out in front of him, and watched his father pour brandy at the early-nineteenth-century butler's tray. Old crystal clinked melodically. Nick wondered what Phila was doing at that moment.

He decided she was probably sound asleep. He had walked her back to the Gilmarten place half an hour before. She had been suspiciously silent. He had thought about attempting a kiss and decided not to risk it. Her mood had been a dangerous cross between thoughtful and volatile.

As Reed fixed the brandies Nick shifted his gaze to the familiar book-lined walls of the high-ceilinged room. He knew the library was a fine example of the Federal period. Eleanor Castleton had designed it and overseen the selection of furnishings here as in every other room in the beach cottages and the main homes on Bainbridge Island. He had it on the best authority that if Eleanor said this room was decorated in the Federal style, then it undoubtedly was.

I'm sure it's perfect, Nick, his mother had once said with a wry smile. *Eleanor knows how to do everything perfectly. She was raised to be a lady.*

The books lining the shelves ranged from *Moby Dick* to a recent exposé of the inner workings of a beleagured CIA. They resided in glass-paned Duncan Phyfe—style bookcases made of mahogany and poplar and pine. In one obscure corner of a particular bookcase, stuffed behind a three-part series on nineteenth-century American history, was an aging copy of *Playboy* magazine. Nick assumed it was still there. He had shoved it there himself, a long time ago when he thought he'd heard his mother's step in the hall. He'd never gotten around to retrieving it.

To the best of his recollection the women featured in it were top-heavy in the extreme. Not at all like Phila, who had delicate, pert little breasts and a neat, lush rear he was pretty sure he could cup in both palms.

His gaze moved on around the room to the girandole mirror with its American eagle decoration. The antique crewelwork fire screen was still in front of the fireplace. The circular library table covered in green baize was positioned as usual near his chair.

There were echoes of Nick's childhood as well as his more recent past in every corner of this room. He had not been here in a long time. He did not feel comfortable now.

"Goddamn fireworks get trickier every year, don't they?" Reed remarked in a determinedly conversational tone as he handed Nick a glass. He sat down in a blue wing-backed armchair across from his son.

A truce had apparently been declared. Nick sought to hold up his end of it. "It was a good show tonight. The kids got a kick out of it."

"They always do." Reed sipped his brandy. "So how's business? Much demand for this consulting work of yours?"

"Enough." That seemed a little brusque. Nick tried to expand his answer. "California's full of fast-food geniuses who think the time has come to open a chicken-fried grapefruit outlet in downtown Tokyo or Milan. They're all willing to pay for advice."

"What do you know about chicken-fried grapefruit?"

"Nothing," Nick said, forcing himself to ignore Reed's

skeptical tone. "But I know a lot about doing business in places like Tokyo or Milan."

"Thanks to having been raised a Lightfoot."

"Yeah. Thanks to that. No substitute for a good, well-rounded background, is there, Dad?"

"Didn't think you bothered to remember your background these days."

"I get reminded of it every once in a while." Nick heard the belligerence in Reed's voice, but he had questions of his own. "Speaking of the old family background, how are things going with Castleton & Lightfoot?"

Reed regarded him with hooded eyes. "Fine."

"That tells me a lot."

"If you cared about getting more details, you'd come to the annual meetings."

"I think that would be a little uncomfortable for everyone, don't you?"

Reed got to his feet and walked to the end of the room without speaking. He stood looking out the window into the darkness for a long moment. "If you weren't so goddamned stubborn, none of it would have happened."

"Be reasonable, Dad. You can't blame me for the stubbornness. It runs in the family."

"We could have worked things out."

"The business about getting C&L out of government contract work? Maybe. But we both now we couldn't have worked out the other glitch."

"Damn it, Nick . . ."

"You didn't have to marry her, Dad. I'm a big boy now. I can clean up my own messes."

"Well, you sure as hell didn't bother to clean this one up, did you? You just left it for someone else to fix."

Nick felt his temper flare. "I knew what I was doing. You could have shown a little faith in me."

"Goddamn it, I had to do something. I couldn't just turn my back on her. It wasn't right. If you hadn't . . ." Reed made an obviously heroic effort to swallow the remainder of the sentence. "Let's change the subject."

"Yeah. Let's."

Reed swung around abruptly. "All right, what the hell's going on between you and that Fox woman?"

"Not much. Yet." The brandy glass dangled from Nick's fingers.

"You can at least tell me what you're planning."

"I'm not sure."

"Why did you bring her here?"

"She's got some questions she wants answered."

"Questions about what? Castleton & Lightfoot?"

"No, she already knows the firm makes death machines." Nick smiled slightly.

"*Death machines*. Oh, hell, she's not one of those, is she?"

"I'm afraid so."

"I was hoping she'd be more like her friend, the Masters woman. Out for what she can get."

"Sorry. It's not going to be that simple."

"You said she had some questions she wants answered."

"About us and about what happened to her friend, Crissie Masters."

Reed looked exasperated. "What about her?"

"She wants to know how the families treated her and whether they bear some moral responsibility for what happened to Miss Masters. What she decides about us will determine what she does with the C&L shares, I think."

"*Moral responsibility*. For Crissie Masters's death? Is she crazy? Masters got drunk and got into a car. End of story. No one else is involved, and we sure as hell don't bear any *moral responsibility* for what happened. It's just like some muddle-brained liberal type to try to put responsibility on everyone else except the one person who really was responsible."

"What can I say?" Nick shrugged. "Phila's an ex−social worker or something. That's the way that type thinks."

"For Crissake." Reed's brows beetled threateningly. "You don't believe any of that moral responsibility nonsense, do you?"

"No. I haven't been living down in California long enough to start thinking like that."

"Well, that's something at least."

"Thanks."

Reed paid no attention to his son's dry tone. "What's the point of bringing her here?"

"I thought if she had a chance to meet the families and ask her questions, it would put her mind at ease. Phila's been through a lot lately, from what I can tell. She needs something to focus on, something to help her get her feet back on the ground. Crissie Masters was more than her best friend; she was like family to Phila. I thought if she had a chance to satisfy herself that the Castletons and Lightfoots aren't a couple of demon clans, she might be inclined to be reasonable about the shares."

Reed nodded slowly. "I see your point. Might work. Unless she's too much like Crissie."

"What do you know about Crissie Masters?" Nick asked.

"Not much. Hilary got to know her better than I did. All I know is that she landed on Burke's doorstep a year ago and proceeded to set everyone's back teeth on edge, except Burke's. Christ, I felt sorry for Eleanor. Whole thing was such a goddamn shock to her. It can't have been easy having to accept Burke's bastard daughter."

"Especially after having spent nearly forty years turning a blind eye to Burke's running around," Nick agreed.

"Eleanor's no fool. She knew what was going on. But she was too much of a lady to acknowledge it."

"Unlike mother?" Nick asked with a small smile.

"Nora would have had my scalp on a silver platter if I'd tried chasing outside tail." Reed smiled reminiscently. Then he shook his head. "But Eleanor was different. Nora always said you could put Eleanor to work shoveling shit and she'd find a way to make it look as if she were planting tea roses. As long as Burke didn't parade his conquests in front of her, Eleanor could pretend everything was all right."

"But when Crissie appeared with proof she was Burke's daughter, there was no way to pretend any longer, was there?"

Reed shook his head. "No, although I'll give Eleanor credit for trying goddamn hard to ignore her. Treated Crissie as though the gal was just some shade tree relative instead of Darren's half sister.

"But there was never any doubt Crissie was Burke's daughter and Eleanor knew it. Even if the girl hadn't spent a fortune on private detectives to trace her father, you'd have known who she was the minute you saw her. Crissie had the Castleton looks."

"What about Burke?"

"Burke took to Crissie right from the start. Made it clear he was pleased as all get-out with her. Called her a chip off the old block. Kept saying she was the one who had inherited his guts and nerve."

"Must have made Darren feel like a real second-class citizen."

"You know Burke. He made a big production out of Crissie. It gave him a chance to hold center stage. He always liked to be the center of attention."

"Yeah," Nick agreed. "He did. And he was good at it."

Reed scowled. "No getting around the fact that Crissie Masters caused a lot of trouble while she was here and, besides Burke—really because of Burke's behavior—no one went out of their way to make her feel like one of the family, that's for sure. But the shit flew both ways."

"I know that."

"Think you can convince the Fox woman we're not 'morally' responsible for Masters's death?"

"It's not up to me to convince her, is it? It's up to the rest of you."

"Bullshit. You've obviously got a handle on her. Use it."

"A handle?"

Reed went back to his chair and sat down. "Come on, Nick. I'm your father, remember? I know you better than anyone now that Nora's gone. I saw that scene down at the gate when Phila arrived and I saw the way you watched the woman all afternoon. If you're not sleeping with her already, you soon will be. Is that your scheme? Are you going to get those shares back by talking her out of them in bed?"

"An interesting thought. Think I could?"

Reed studied the ceiling for a moment. "Don't know. She strikes me as a sharp little cookie. Gutsy, too, or she wouldn't be here waving those shares in our faces."

"You could be right."

Reed's eyebrows rose, revealing a gleam of humor in his eyes. "Better be careful, son. She may be too goddamned smart to let you climb into bed with her."

"Yeah. After all, as far as she's concerned, I'm one of the enemy."

"She's goddamn right. You are the enemy. Don't let yourself forget it for one minute. You're a Lightfoot. If you do wind up in bed with her, you'd better watch your ass."

"I'll do that."

Reed's grin came and went. "She sure set Tec off today."

"Yeah."

"Got to say I've never seen you throw a woman over your shoulder before, either."

"Not my style," Nick agreed.

"What did you say this Phila did for a living?"

"She was a social worker."

"Sounds like a real bleeding-heart type."

"The kind of bleeding hearts who practice what they preach are always the most difficult ones to deal with, aren't they?" Nick offered his father a wry smile.

Reed's gaze sharpened perceptively. "You're finding this really funny, aren't you?"

"Let's just say I think it will prove interesting."

Reed stared at him. "Interesting," he repeated thoughtfully. "You may be right."

"Why did you let Hilary vote my shares and yours at the last annual meeting?" Nick regretted the question as soon as the words left his mouth, but he also knew he could not avoid asking it. It had been gnawing at him all afternoon.

Reed's face went taut. "If you give a damn about who votes your shares, come home and vote 'em yourself."

"You've made a mistake turning things over to her, Dad."

"Have I? She's devoted to Castleton & Lightfoot. It's all she cares about."

"Unlike me? You're only partially right. Hilary is devoted to herself, not C&L and if you ever forget that, you're in real trouble."

Reed's expression turned cold. "You've said enough, Nick. Goddamn it, Hilary is my wife now. You'll show her the proper respect or you'll get your ass out of this house."

"She's a piranha. Haven't you realized that yet?"

"Shut up, Nick. *Now.* Before I have to do something about it."

"How did it happen?"

"How did what happen?"

"How did it get to the point where you turned over complete control of the Lightfoot half of the company to her?" Nick insisted coldly.

"You want to know how it happened?" Reed leaned forward, his face taut and angry. "I'll tell you how it happened, goddamn it. She was devastated after she lost the baby. She was on the edge of a nervous breakdown. I thought it might help if she had something to do, something else to think about besides the miscarriage. I let her start getting involved with the company. She took to it like a duck to water."

"Yeah. I'll bet she did."

"It's true. The woman's got a real talent for management. And she cares about what happens to Castleton & Lightfoot."

"And you don't anymore?"

"I'm discovering the joys of retirement." Reed sat back in his chair and gulped his brandy. "Golf game's better than it's been in years."

"Don't give me that crap. Running Castleton & Lightfoot was the only game you ever really liked."

"The whole point of building up a firm like Castleton & Lightfoot is to create something worth leaving behind. I don't have anyone to leave my half of the firm to, now do

I? When you walked out you made it goddamnn clear you weren't coming back."

Nick exhaled slowly and closed his eyes for a moment. "You could try for another baby."

"That would be a little tricky, given the fact that Hilary and I have separate bedrooms," Reed shot back bitterly.

Nick opened his eyes and stared at his father. "Don't tell me you found out the truth."

"What truth?"

"That going to bed with her is like bedding an ice sculpture."

Reed slammed his fist against the arm of the chair. "Goddamn it, Nick, I told you to keep your mouth shut and I meant it. She's my wife, and I won't let anyone talk about her, not even you. Especially not you. Not after what you did to her."

"Shit. I knew this was going to happen."

"If you hadn't walked out on your responsibilities three years ago none of us would be in this situation. You've got real balls to sit there and talk about Hilary and me having babies." Reed set the brandy glass down on the table with a violent snap. The fragile crystal shattered.

Nick watched the shards sparkle in the light from the table lamp for a long moment. Then he got to his feet. "So much for the big reunion scene. Thanks for the brandy. I think it's time I went to bed."

Reed looked up instantly. "Your room's the one across from mine. Hilary had it made up for you."

Nick nodded and walked to the door.

"Nick."

"What?"

"About those shares the Fox woman owns."

Nick glanced back over his shoulder. "What about them?"

"They belong in the family," Reed said bluntly. "Stop playing your goddamnn games with me. Give it to me straight. Are you going to get those shares back for us?"

"Yeah," Nick said as he turned the doorknob. "I'll get them back for you."

He stepped out into the hall and closed the door behind him. There was no noise at the top of the stairs, but something made him glance up. Hilary stood on the landing, her hair a gleaming mass of dark fire around her shoulders. Her emerald eyes blazed at him, and he could see the outline of her slim body through the fabric of her flowing robe. He remembered that body all too well. A beautifully molded alabaster statue he had never been able to bring to life.

"I won't have you upsetting Reed."

"I've got news for you, Hilary. My father can take care of himself. Be careful or one of these days he might show you just how well he can do it."

Hilary glided one step down from the landing. The silky peignoir flowed around her ankles. "What game are you playing, Nick? Why are you here? Why did you bring that woman here?"

"You don't really expect me to tell you, do you?" He started toward the front door.

"Where are you going?"

"To find a warm place to sleep." He let himself out into the cool night air.

It was a ten-minute walk to Phila's cottage.

The loud knock on the cottage door brought Phila up out of a surprisingly sound sleep. Fear lanced through her. She sat bolt upright in bed, orienting herself to the cheerfully shabby surroundings of her new bedroom.

The knock came again, harsh and demanding. Automatically Phila swung her legs over the edge of the bed and reached for her purple velour robe. She was almost to the bedroom door when she remembered the gun.

The gun. This was what it was for, she thought wildly. She rushed back to the nightstand and yanked open the drawer. She fumbled for the weapon in the darkness, her fingers closing around the awkward, square grip.

The knock sounded once more, and this time it was accompanied by a familiar masculine voice.

"Phila. It's Nick. Open the door."

Relief poured through Phila. She dropped the gun back into the drawer and whipped around. She took a few deep breaths on the way to the front door. Her pulse was almost back to normal by the time she opened it.

"What are you doing here?" she demanded, opening the door and peering up at Nick. He looked larger than ever standing there in the shadows.

"Mind if I come in?" he asked impatiently. It wasn't a request. He was already halfway through the door.

"You can come in, but what do you want?" She stepped back and flipped on the light switch. "For heaven's sake, Nick, it's nearly one o'clock in the morning."

"I know what time it is. I've got a two-thousand-dollar watch that tells the time with absolute accuracy." He strode past her, crossing the comfortably shabby living room with its sagging furniture and bare board floors. He went straight into the kitchen and began opening and closing cupboard doors in a methodical fashion.

"Is that right? Who gave you the watch?"

"My father. He gave it to me the day I took over the reins for Castleton & Lightfoot. I thought for sure he'd ask for it back along with my sword and brass buttons the day I walked out, but he didn't. Probably forgot about it."

Phila hurried after him. "Nick, what is going on here?"

"Questions. All I get are questions. Haven't you got anything to drink?"

"You mean something strong like scotch or bourbon? No. I just got into town this morning, remember? I picked up enough groceries for breakfast, and that's all. Nick, what are you doing here at this time of night?"

He turned around and leaned back against the chipped tile counter top, his arms folded across his chest. "I'm looking for a place to spend the night."

That stopped her for a few short seconds. "I thought you were going to spend the night up at Tara West."

"I changed my mind."

"Why?"

"Let's just say that I had an unpleasant father-son chat

with Reed Lightfoot, and by the time it was over I felt I'd worn out my welcome."

"Already?"

"I can do it really fast when I put my mind to it. Are you sure you don't have anything to drink?"

Phila sighed. "Warm milk."

"What?" He looked startled.

"You heard me. I can heat some milk for you."

"That sounds disgusting."

"Well, there's tea."

"I don't drink tea."

Phila started to lose her temper. "I'm sorry, *sir*, but that's all I've got in the place. If I'd known you were going to be dropping by in the middle of the night I'd have picked up some brandy to sedate you, sir."

"I've already had enough brandy. That's what I was drinking with Dad when I decided I was going to have to spend the night somewhere else."

"What brought you to that conclusion?"

"We got into an argument. It was a totally predictable scene, and I'll give us both credit for trying to avoid it. We both started out with good intentions. To be perfectly honest, I broke first."

"What did you argue about?" Phila asked cautiously.

"A number of things."

"Hilary, for instance?"

Nick's eyes narrowed behind the lenses of his glasses. "Now, what makes you say that?"

Phila folded her arms under her breasts, tucking her hands into the sleeves of her robe. She noticed her feet were getting cold. "I know she's your ex-wife, Nick."

"You pick up information fast, don't you?"

"That's what I'm here for, remember? To find out things."

"Who told you about Hilary and me?"

"Vicky."

"Yeah, that figures." Nick nodded as if confirming something to himself. "I didn't think it was Eleanor.

Eleanor's committed to keeping family secrets locked in the closet where they belong."

"You must feel the same way, or you would have told me about Hilary being your ex-wife."

That seemed to surprise him. "Why would I have told you about her? She's not important one way or the other."

"Women look at these things a little differently."

"Only a woman who was seriously thinking of getting involved with me would look at it differently. Are you thinking about getting involved with me, Phila?"

She flushed but refused to be drawn. "It must be a little awkward for you," she offered hesitantly. "I mean Hilary being your ex-wife and all."

"Yeah, sure. Awkward. Just to set the record straight, Dad and I did touch briefly on the subject of Hilary this evening, but our chief argument concerning her had nothing to do with any father-son rivalry. Dad's welcome to her, although from what I can gather his bed's as cold as mine used to be when she was married to me."

"She's a beautiful woman."

"That's something you tend to notice right off, isn't it? Coldest bitch this side of the Arctic Circle, though. But what the hell. Maybe that was as much my fault as hers. God knows I'm no Casanova."

"Nick . . ."

"Maybe you've got something to drink in the refrigerator." He opened the door and stood scanning the empty shelves. His face looked harsh in the glare of the appliance light. After a moment he swore softly in resignation and gave up the search. He reluctantly slammed the door.

"I told you there was nothing to drink except milk. How did you meet her?"

"Who? Hilary?" Nick went back to leaning against the counter. "Eleanor introduced us. Hilary's the daughter of some old friends of Eleanor's family. They all go way back together."

"The original boat people, hmmm? An awful lot of upper-class East Coast folks seem to think they came over on the *Mayflower*. Must have been a crowded ship." So that's what it was, Phila thought. Hilary had been another of Eleanor's handpicked brides.

"Skip the lecture on inbreeding among the upper classes, will you? I'm not in the mood for it tonight."

"The bit about Hilary marrying your father after being married to you does sound a bit incestuous."

"Well it's not, so don't try to make it sound that way."

"I've heard that in some old, established East Coast families it's almost traditional to pass girlfriends around from brother to brother or father to son," Phila asked.

"Jesus, Phila."

"It's true. I've read about it."

"If the girlfriend happens to be a movie star and the family is tilted to the extreme left, I suppose it's a possibility," Nick growled. "Trust me, Phila, no one in my family holds liberal views."

"Was Hilary the only thing you and Reed argued about?"

"We talked about a few other things," Nick answered casually.

"Such as?"

"Your shares in Castleton & Lightfoot."

"Hah! I knew it. I just knew it."

"What did you expect us to talk about? Your shares are the reason I've returned to the bosom of my family, remember?"

"It's not a joke, Nick."

"Who's laughing?"

Phila studied him intently. "Your father wanted to know if you would be able to get your hands on my shares, I suppose?"

"Yeah. That's what he wanted to know, all right."

She lifted her chin. "Well? What did you tell him?"

Nick shrugged. His eyes met hers in a level look. "I told him I'd get the shares back."

Phila's feet felt colder than ever. "Yes, of course you did," she whispered, almost to herself. She went back out into the living room, heading for the bedroom. Nick followed.

"Phila?"

"Yes?"

"About the little matter of where I'm going to spend the night." His voice was rough around the edges, but otherwise as calm as ever.

"Use your Lightfoot pull to get yourself a motel room in town."

"I'd rather stay here."

She spun around to confront him and discovered he was practically on top of her. Instinctively she backed up. She wondered how he'd gotten so close without her realizing it. "Why do you want to stay here?"

He reached out and gently caught hold of the lapels of her robe, drawing her close. "You know the answer to that."

Phila tried to tamp down the energy that was beginning to sizzle through her. "Going to bed with you would be a very stupid thing for me to do."

"You think I'm one of the enemy."

"Aren't you?"

"No, Phila. I'm not."

"You want my shares."

"That's a side issue. The shares belong in the family, and sooner or later I'll get them back. But the fact has got nothing to do with you and me. It doesn't make me your enemy."

"How can you say that?" She searched his face. "Damn it, Nick, how can you *say* that?"

"It's easy because it's the truth. I can say it loud or soft or anywhere in between." His thumb moved along the angle of her jaw. "Take your pick."

"I could never really trust you," she pointed out, feeling desperate. A heady sense of awareness, a feeling of being gloriously, recklessly alive was kicking in for the first time in months.

"Yes you can. You can trust me, Phila." His thumb moved across her lower lip, tugging it gently away from her teeth.

Phila shivered. "If push comes to shove, you'll side with your family."

"Will I?"

"You've already admitted as much."

"I've said I'll get back the shares. That's the only thing I've admitted. Don't read any more into it than that. What goes on between you and me has nothing to do with the families or those damn shares."

She thought he was going to kiss her, but he did not. He just stood there, holding her lightly by the lapels, and waited.

She fought herself for a long moment, holding herself stiff and proud, trying to step back from the brink.

"Will you kiss me?" Nick asked softly. "I've been going out of my head wondering what it would be like."

So had she. Phila finally admitted it to herself, moaned softly and surrendered to the unfamiliar driving force of passion.

She gripped his shoulders fiercely as the excitement raced through her. No man had ever sent her senses reeling this way, and she was frankly fascinated with her own responses.

Crissie had laughed at her in the past, telling Phila that her disappointment in sex was directly attributable to the fact that she'd never met the right mate. Crissie had encouraged greater experimentation, but Phila had shied away from that approach. It wasn't just her inbuilt sense of discretion that kept her from it. There was an old fear to contend with, a fear that made sex seem less that attractive. Because of what had happened to her, the thought of a man climbing on top of her was enough to awaken a primitive panic.

But tonight her sense of caution was a dim and distant voice. She ignored it in favor of the heat that was waiting for her in Nick's arms. Impulsively she brushed her mouth quickly, awkwardly against his, tasting brandy and desire.

"Yeah, that's it. That's what I want—" Nick's voice was growing thick. His hands framed her face. "Come on. Eat me up. A hundred miles an hour."

A firestorm was building inside Phila. She was shaking with need, longing to know more about the tantalizing feelings flowing through her. She grabbed Nick's head in both hands and held him still so that she could plunge her tongue between his teeth.

Her fingers twisted in his hair, and her nose bumped against his glasses. When her teeth grated against his, Nick chuckled softly.

"It's okay, honey. I'm not going anywhere tonight. I'm all yours." Nick caught her around the waist and lifted her high against him. "Why don't you try wrapping your legs around me," he suggested softly.

"Nick, wait. I . . . we shouldn't . . ."

"It's okay," he soothed gently. "Nothing to worry about. I'm healthy as a horse. Want to see my blood donor card?"

She shook her head frantically. "I'm healthy, too. That's not what I meant." But she could no longer think clearly.

"Put your legs around me," he urged again, his eyes brilliant with desire. "Do it, Phila."

She did so instantly, hugging his hips with her thighs as if he were a stallion she intended to ride. Her arms locked around his neck, and her mouth fastened onto his again. Teeth clinked once more. His glasses were in the way, she thought.

Nick carried her down the short hall to the darkened bedroom and fell with her onto the bed. He rolled onto his back, one leg drawn up. His eyes gleamed in the shadows.

"Nick?"

"I'm here."

Dazed and hungry, filled with emotions that left her shaking, Phila needed no further encouragement. She knelt beside him, fumbling with the buttons of his shirt. She was in such a hurry now that when one button got stuck she yanked at it. There was a soft plink as it flew across the room and bounced off the window. She looked up. There was just enough light to see the grin on Nick's face.

"So help me, if you're laughing at me, you son of a . . ."

He stopped the words with two fingers across her lips. "I'm not laughing. I want this more than you do."

Phila decided to take him at his word because in that moment she wanted desperately to believe him. She went back to work on his clothing, stripping the shirt from him with impatient, wrenching movements. Then she groped for the buckle of his belt.

Nick sucked in his breath as she unzipped his jeans. His manhood sprang free. He groaned heavily when she captured him in her hands.

For a short while Phila contented herself with exploring him intimately. She was enthralled with the fullness of him, captivated by the hard tension in his thighs. She laced her fingertips in the crisp curling hair of his groin and stroked the unbelievably hard length of his shaft.

"You're magnificent," she whispered, awed.

"Oh, Jesus," Nick's finger twisted in her hair.

The fire in her was very close to the surface now. She wanted to know what it would be like to quench it. Eagerly she pulled the last of Nick's clothing from his body. When he was lying naked on the bed, Phila knelt between his legs, drinking in the sight of him. He was a beautiful beast in the shadows.

"What about you?" he urged softly, toying with the hem of her robe.

"Oh, yes. Right." Phila stripped off her robe and nightgown, almost unaware of what she was doing. She was too excited to think clearly. Nick was a treasure she had discovered and unearthed all by herself. He was hers to do with as she pleased, and she was so excited by the prospect that she could not decide what to do first. Her hands slid over him in soft wonder.

"You look like a kid in a candy factory," Nick observed, his smile wicked and warm.

She heard the laughter in his voice but she no longer cared if he was amused. She could concentrate only on her own chaotic emotions. There was a liquid warmth between her thighs, an aching need that she knew Nick could satisfy.

"What are you waiting for?" Nick asked with a soft chuckle.

What was she waiting for? He was just lying there. He was not trying to climb all over her. He was not going to crush her beneath his heavy body. Phila hesitated briefly as the old memories and the primal fear they always brought with them surfaced. But an instant later the secret dread dissolved. He was offering himself for her pleasure, not forcing himself on her.

She moved upward, straddling him. With eager fingers, she guided him toward the center of her pulsating desire. Quickly she lowered herself, trying to impale herself on him.

"You're tight. Small and tight." His fingers slid up along her thighs to where she was fumbling with his manhood. He parted her softness gently. "You're hot but not quite ready for me. Give it awhile. There's no rush."

But she *was* in a rush. Phila had never felt like this, and she was very much afraid that if she did not take advantage of the sensations immediately she would never experience them again. It was imperative to hurry. Frantically she pushed herself downward.

"Not so fast. Take it easy," Nick murmured.

She paid no attention, forcing him into her snug sheath. It felt good, but it was not very comfortable. In fact it was almost painful. Phila gasped as her softness suddenly felt stretched beyond its limits. She eased herself carefully back up the length of him.

"I told you to slow down." Nick's voice sounded half-strangled.

But Phila wasn't listening. She began to glide up and down more quickly as her body adjusted rapidly to his. He was big, but she wanted him and she was determined to have all of him.

He still felt huge inside her, but the sensation was quickly becoming pleasurable again. She splayed her fingers across his chest, clinging to him, lost in the wonder of it all. She increased the tempo of her rising and falling movements, her knees pressing tightly against his hips.

"*Nick.*"

"Yes. Oh, God, yes," Nick muttered as she moved faster and faster on him. "I shouldn't let you run wild like this. Not yet. You're going too fast. A hundred miles an hour. But it feels so good. *So good.*"

And then he went taut beneath Phila, shouting hoarsely, shuddering heavily as he exploded deep within her.

CHAPTER SIX

"Nick is sleeping with her." Victoria stabbed her grapefruit with her spoon.

Darren glanced up from the head of the table, frowning. "How do you know that? Nick was supposed to spend the night over at the Lightfoot cottage. Hilary told me she'd had her housekeeper prepare his old room."

"Well, I guess Hilary lied," Victoria said, taking some small pleasure from making the comment sound terribly casual.

"Vicky, really, dear. That's no way to talk." Eleanor, seated at the other end of the gleaming fruitwood dining table, glanced first at her daughter-in-law and then at her son. "Hilary certainly did not lie. Why on earth would she do a thing like that? I know Nick was expected to sleep at the Lightfoot cottage last night."

"Well, he didn't." It wasn't often she got the satisfaction of surprising both her husband and Eleanor. Castletons were notoriously difficult to startle. It took something on the order of an unknown illegitimate daughter's sudden appearance out of the blue to do that. "Jordan and I stopped by the Gilmarten place a while ago when we came back from our walk along the beach. I wanted to talk to her, so I thought I'd see if she was up. She wasn't. Nick was. He opened the door when I knocked."

"I see," Eleanor said blandly. "Darren, dear, would you please pass the cream? Thank you. Maybe Nick went for a walk this morning, too, and just decided to say good morning to Miss Fox."

"He was barefoot and he wasn't wearing a shirt. All he had on were the jeans he was wearing yesterday at the party. I asked if Phila was awake, and he said she wasn't but that when she woke up he would tell her I'd stopped by to say hello. Take my word for it, he spent the night there."

"It's hardly any of our business," Eleanor proclaimed primly.

"You don't think so?" Victoria looked at her.

"No, I do not. Really, dear, this is hardly a subject for the breakfast table."

"Don't fret, Eleanor. I think we're all adult enough to handle it," Victoria said. Jordan was safely out of earshot, having eaten breakfast earlier in the kitchen.

Darren ate a wedge of grapefruit. "I don't know why you're acting like it's a big deal, Vicky. It was pretty obvious yesterday Nick had something going with her."

"Maybe he's trying to seduce the shares out of her," Victoria suggested, thinking about it. "Or, maybe she's just a little tramp like Crissie was."

"Quite possible," Eleanor agreed with a sigh of resignation. "Probable, in fact. They both come from the same sort of background, I understand."

"You think she's a tramp?" Darren shook his head. "I doubt it. Not the type."

Victoria was irritated. "For heaven's sake, Darren. You're a man. That doesn't make you a good judge of women."

"No?" Darren regarded his wife with a level look.

Victoria flushed angrily and went back to work on her grapefruit. "Whatever the reason, Nick's sleeping with her and I'll bet Hilary is furious."

"Why should Hilary be upset?" Eleanor inquired politely.

"Because she probably figured she could manage Nick if he ever returned to the fold. It would be just like her to assume she could manipulate him the way she does everyone else around here. She's never really understood Nick. She doesn't know him."

"She was married to him for eighteen months," Eleanor pointed out. "I'd say that gives her some insight into the man. We all know what she went through because of him."

"Well, she was wrong about one thing. She thinks Nick left three years ago because he was weak. That was a stupid assumption. He left because he was sick of the whole mess. Who can blame him?"

"Vicky, I think you've said enough," Darren began warningly.

"But," Victoria continued, "the first night Nick's home, he goes off with another woman. Poor Hilary didn't even get a chance to sink her claws back into him."

"I said that's enough, Vicky." Darren did not raise his voice, but his tone was harsh.

Victoria slanted him a scornful glance. "I'm merely mentioning a few facts. Hilary is accustomed to having men make fools of themselves over her."

"Now, dear," Eleanor murmured, dabbing at her lips with a white linen napkin. "I really do think you've said enough."

"Damn it, Vicky, close your mouth. You don't know what you're talking about." Darren poured himself another cup of coffee from the silver pot.

Victoria smiled grimly. "You're wrong, Darren. I do know what I'm talking about. I'm not blind. Hilary's an expert. She knows how to make men jump through hoops."

"How can you say that after what she went through?" Darren demanded.

"It's easy to say because it's the truth."

"Would anyone like some more fruit?" Eleanor asked, picking up a heavily scrolled silver-plate tray that contained a selection of fresh strawberries and grapefruit.

Darren ignored his mother. "Let's close the subject."

"I don't feel like closing it," Victoria retorted. "Nick got free of her three years ago and from the look of him this morning, my guess is that he's in no danger of falling into Hilary's clutches a second time. But we all know the situation with Reed. During the past three years he's gradually turned over the entire Lightfoot half of the company to Hilary. He's given up. Now she's working on you, Darren."

"What the hell is that supposed to mean?" Darren snapped.

"She wants to run the Castleton side of things as well. And she's going to do that by offering you what you want most."

Darren pushed aside his grapefruit dish and folded his arms on the table. "What can she offer me that would make me give up running our half of the business?"

"Freedom. The freedom to devote all your time to your political career. And C&L money to wage your campaigns." Victoria glanced from one startled face to to the other. "Don't you see? She's already starting to do it. This past year she's graciously taken over more and more of the daily decision making so that Darren can be free to set up the foundations of his gubernatorial campaign. Little by little, Hilary's assuming full responsibility, and you two don't even see what's happening."

"Hilary is the current CEO. She's not *taking over*, she already has the day-to-day responsibility of running C&L," Eleanor said soothingly. "I, for one, feel the firm is doing very well under her management. We can rely upon her."

"You don't understand, Eleanor. She's acting as if she really owns the business, not as if she's just been elected by the rest of us to run it."

"Hilary is family. She has the firm's best interests at heart, and that's all that really matters." Eleanor paused. "Actually, now that you mention it, I've been giving the whole matter some serious consideration. It could be an excellent arrangement, you know."

"What would be an excellent arrangement?" Victoria demanded. "Letting her handle C&L while Darren runs for office? Believe me, there would be a price to pay. One of these days we're all going to wake up and find out we're just puppets, totally dependent on her."

"Damn it, Vicky, you're acting like a spoiled brat," Darren said. "You know what's wrong with you? You're jealous. Hilary's worked hard to get involved with the business, and you're envious of her ability. That's what this is all about. She pulled herself together after Nick walked out and she lost the baby. She's made a career for herself, and you resent her for it."

"Maybe you're right." Victoria felt the angry, resentful tears welling up in her eyes. "After all, the only thing I've done during the past few years is bear your son and play the part of an up-and-coming politician's wife. Putting on dinners for a hundred potential backers and serving tea to fifty campaign workers is hardly a worthwhile career, is it?"

"Take it easy, Vicky. I didn't mean that the way it sounded," Darren said lightly.

"How did you mean it?"

Eleanor picked up the silver bell on the table and tinkled it loudly. When the door to the kitchen opened, she turned to smile at the housekeeper. "Oh, there you are, Mrs. Atkins. I believe we need more coffee."

"I'll bring it right out, Mrs. Castleton."

"Thank you." Eleanor looked from her son to her daughter-in-law as the housekeeper disappeared. For a moment the sweet, vague look disappeared from her eyes. "I really do feel it would be best for all of us if Hilary stays in charge of C&L. The most important consideration now is that Darren have the freedom and the financial backing to run for governor. We can only be assured of his having both if Hilary remains at the helm."

The queen had spoken. Victoria knew she had been given her orders. As always, she would follow them. She folded her napkin and placed it beside her coffee cup. Then she got to her feet and rose from the table. She was aware of Darren watching her in angry silence as she left the room.

* * *

Phila shifted drowsily under the covers. Something was missing, something she had grown accustomed to having next to her during the night. Something warm and comforting and male.

She came awake slowly. Memories trickled back; memories of strong, gentle hands guiding her; memories of a masculine voice laced with husky amusement, wicked and urgent and exciting as it commanded and cajoled and pleaded; memories of coming very close to a thrilling promise of release, a promise that had slipped out of her fingers at the last moment but one that she was sure she could capture the next time around. She just needed another shot at it, that's all.

At least she now knew for certain that there was, indeed, something to go after the next time. Crissie had been right, after all.

Phila opened her eyes and saw Nick sitting, legs spread wide, on a reversed ladder-back chair. He had his arms folded across the back of the chair and he was leaning forward, watching her intently. He had on his jeans and a shirt, although he hadn't bothered to fasten the buttons of the shirt. She could see the heavy mat of his chest hair through the opening.

The expression on his face was the one she remembered from the occasion of their first meeting: hard, remote, unreadable. A faint trickle of dread lanced through her. Then she saw the gun.

It lay on top of the nightstand, gleaming dully in the early light. The ammunition clip lay beside it. Too late she recalled she had carelessly left the drawer open last night in her rush to answer the door. Nick must have seen the gun the minute he opened his eyes.

Phila sat up slowly, her eyes going from Nick's cold, set face to the gun and back again. As the blankets fell away she remembered she was nude. Automatically, she pulled the sheet up to her chin.

"Nick? What's wrong?"

"You tell me."

"I don't understand."

"The hell you don't."

"You're wondering about the gun?" she hazarded.

"Yeah. Good guess. I'm wondering about the gun. You said you had some questions about what happened to Crissie Masters. You said you thought the Castletons and Ligthfoots might bear some 'moral responsibility' in the matter. But you forgot to mention you intended to play lady vigilante if you didn't like the answers you got."

She stilled, shocked by his interpretation of events. "Nick, you've got it all wrong."

"You really had me fooled, lady. I've got to hand it to you. What do you think you are? A hit woman? You put on a hell of an act. I went for it every step of the way, didn't I? Brought you right through the gate myself. Introduced you to all the Castletons and Lightfoots. Gave you free run of the place. And just to top it all off, I even let you seduce me."

"You can't possibly think I've come here to kill someone."

"What else am I supposed to think?" He nodded toward the gun. "That's an expensive 9-mm automatic pistol, not a squirt gun." He studied her with chilling detachment. "What the hell do you think you're doing? And what made you think I'd let you get away with it?"

Phila edged backward, taking the sheet with her. The look in his eyes frightened her as nothing else had since the Spalding trial. "You don't know what you're talking about. Please. Give me a chance to explain."

He reached out and snagged the sheet, tearing it from her grasp. "That's exactly what I'm going to do. You're going to explain the gun, your plans and what you think gives you the right to hunt my people."

"Your people," she repeated scathingly as she battled another jolt of fear. She felt horribly vulnerable. She was crouched naked in front of him, the wall at her back. She felt dizzy. Once before she had been in a position like this, and the old memories were starting to get tangled up with the present reality. "I suppose we're talking about your precious Lightfoots and Castletons?"

"Yeah, we're talking about Lightfoots and Castletons."

"I told you last night that when the crunch came, you'd side with them."

"Against a nut with an automatic? You'd better believe it."

She could not tolerate this position any longer. Fear was gnawing at her stomach now. It was as though a mask had been thrown aside and she was finally seeing the real Nicodemus Lightfoot. This was not the man she had felt so gloriously free with last night, the man whose body she had learned to enjoy with such wholehearted abandon. This was a very dangerous stranger.

Phila began to inch carefully toward the foot of the bed. She was trapped and defenseless as long as she was caught between Nick and the wall. The first thing she had to do was put some distance between herself and this large, threatening male.

Nick tracked her with his eyes. Phila lost her nerve. She gave up inching and launched herself full tilt toward the end of the bed, wildly seeking escape.

"Oh, no you don't—" He shot out an arm that caught her around the midsection.

It was like running into an iron railing. Phila fell back, gasping for breath. She twisted to one side, pulling herself into a ball and kicking out frantically.

Her foot struck Nick's thigh. He grunted in pain but he did not stop. He moved so fast Phila never stood a chance. He came down on top of her, pinning her wrists above her head and using the weight of his body to still her thrashing legs.

"Let me go, damn you!" Phila's head snapped around as she tried to find some vulnerable spot into which she could sink her teeth. Panic swamped her. She could not tolerate being held down like this. Old terror and fresh fear rampaged through her. She fought like a wild thing.

"Phila. Stop it."

Her hair lashed the pillow. He weighed a ton, she realized vaguely as she struggled to wriggle free. She had been on top of him last night. Last night she had been the one in control. She hadn't fully comprehended just how large and powerful Nick really was. Now she was crushed beneath him. She could hardly breathe. Her mouth opened on a scream.

"Stop it," Nick ordered again as he clamped a hand over her lips. "Just calm down, will you? Jesus, you're going crazy." He waited a moment and then slowly removed his hand from her mouth.

"Calm down? You're assaulting me! Let go of me and I'll calm down."

"Not a chance. Not until I get some answers. What did you plan to do with that pistol?"

"I have a right to own a gun."

"That depends. Don't tell me you really believe the Castletons and Lightfoots deserve a bullet just because they didn't welcome Crissie Masters with open arms?"

"I don't have to explain anything to you, damn it." The defiance was dangerous, Phila knew that. But in her anger and fear and outrage, it was also instinctive. It was the way she had always responded to that which threatened to control her. In that, she and Crissie had been very much alike.

"Don't be stupid, Phila. Tell me why you had that gun stashed in the bedside drawer."

Phila stopped struggling, exhausted. She inhaled deeply, trying to recover her strength. Frantically she tried to contain her fear so that she could keep talking. Words were all she had left at the moment. She knew how to use words.

"I don't owe you an explanation, but I'll give you one if you'll promise to get off of me," she said stiffly.

"I'm listening. Talk fast."

"Elijah Spalding."

Nick stared down into her face. His eyes glittered behind the lenses of his glasses. "Who?"

"Elijah Spalding. Ruth Spalding's husband. Remember her? I told you I testified at a trial a few weeks ago, remember?"

"I remember. You said the guy went to prison."

"The man was Spalding. And they sent him to one of

those minimum-security places. When he gets out, he'll come after me."

"Why?"

"Because he said he would," Phila said fiercely. "He hates me. It was my testimony that sent him away. He'll never forget that. He's a dangerous man. He likes to hurt little kids and women."

Nick studied her for a moment longer, his eyes implacable as he searched her expression. "When did you buy the gun?"

"Right after the trial. Believe me, at the time I wasn't even thinking about Castletons and Lightfoots. Crissie was still alive."

"That would be easy enough to check out."

"Check it out. I don't give a damn."

Nick contemplated her for a long moment, seemingly unaware of the way her bare breasts were crushed beneath his chest. "I think," he said at last, "that you had better tell me a little more about this trial."

Phila held her breath, sensing that he was about to release her. She gathered herself. "Please," she whispered, hating herself for resorting to pleading.

"Please what?" Nick scowled.

"Please. Get. Off. Of. Me. I can't stand it."

He levered himself slowly away from her, watching her warily. "Phila? Are you all right? What the hell are you looking at me like that for? I didn't hurt you."

The instant she could move out from underneath him, Phila flung herself to the side of the bed and shot to her feet. She grabbed her brilliant purple robe, holding it in front of her like a shield as she backed as far away as she could get. She was brought up short by the closed door of the bathroom. She swallowed quickly a few times, trying to still her nervous stomach. Her fingers were white as they clutched the velour robe.

"Get out of here," she ordered tightly.

Nick sat on the edge of the bed, watching her. "I'm not going anywhere," he said quietly. "I think you're smart enough to realize that. Go take a shower, comb your hair, get dressed and calm down. I'll fix us some coffee and we'll talk."

"I don't want to talk to you."

"You don't have much choice." He stood up.

Phila flinched, her eyes widening. She fumbled with the bathroom doorknob. "Don't touch me."

"I'm not touching you. You're irrational."

"I'm not the irrational one around here. You're the one who was waiting for me with a gun this morning."

"I wasn't holding the gun on you." He raked his fingers through his hair in exasperation. "I just wanted some answers. I had a right to a few after I found that automatic." He took a step forward.

"No. Don't come any closer." Phila got the bathroom door open. She backed quickly into the small room.

"Take it easy, damn it. I'm not going to hurt you."

"You already have. I'm not going to give you a second chance."

He glanced over his shoulder at the bed where he had recently pinned her. "I didn't hurt you. I just held you down so you couldn't get away or do me any damage."

Technically, he was right, but Phila's emotions and memories weren't dealing in technicalities. Her chin lifted. "Will you get out of my bedroom?"

"Yeah. I'll get out of your bedroom." He paced to the door. "The coffee will be ready when you get out of the bathroom. Then we'll talk."

Phila slammed the bathroom door and locked it. The lock was a weak little device that probably would not last long against a determined assault, but it was all that was available.

Leaning back against the closed door, she listened carefully until she was satisfied that Nick had actually gone down the hall to the kitchen. Only then did the adrenaline begin to slow its wild rush through her bloodstream.

She stayed where she was for several minutes before she finally decided she could risk taking a shower. For the first time since she had awakened she began to pay attention to her body.

She wrinkled her nose at the hint of a faint, alien, musky scent. A man's scent. Something that had been damp and sticky a few hours ago had dried on the inside of her thighs. A new terror ripped through her. It was superseded almost instantly by raw fury. How could she have forgotten! How could he have— She vaguely remembered a short discussion on matters of health, but not one on the subject of birth control. Fury at her own appalling stupidity only served to fuel her anger at Nick.

Phila wrenched open the bathroom door, still clutching the robe in front of her. She flew down the hall, through the living room and came to a halt in the kitchen doorway.

"You didn't use anything last night, you bastard," she yelled.

Nick glanced up from where he was calmly measuring coffee into a drip machine. "No, I didn't. I didn't even think about it until it was too late. You mean you're not taking pills?"

"No, I'm not taking pills," she bit out furiously. "I haven't had any reason to take them. Do you go around doing this sort of thing a lot?"

"No." He finished spooning coffee and put down the container. He picked up the pot and started to run water into it. "You're a first. Normally, I'm the cautious type. Very cautious. But I went a little crazy last night when you swept me off my feet and carried me into the bedroom. Are you always that impulsive?"

"No. *Never.*" Phila was beside herself with fury. "Oh, my God, I might be pregnant, you big jerk."

"I'm sorry, but the truth is, you have a strange effect on me, honey. No one's ever dragged me off to bed before and made wild love to me until I couldn't think straight."

"This is not funny." Phila drew herself up ramrod straight. "Listen to me you son of a bitch and listen good. You wanted to know what I planned to do with that gun in the bedroom drawer? I'll tell you what I'll do with it. If I'm pregnant, I'll come after you with it. *Do you hear me?*"

"I hear you." Nick poured the water into the machine and flipped the switch.

Phila choked on a sob of helpless rage, whirled and ran back to the bathroom. Too late she recalled that she was holding her robe in front of her, not behind her. The image of Nick watching her bare derriere as she made her exit was almost too much to handle on top of everything else that had happened. She was on the edge of bursting into tears.

She dashed into the bathroom, slammed the door shut and turned on the shower full blast. She would not cry, she vowed. She would not cry this morning.

Twenty minutes later she felt calmer and more in control of herself. The long shower had helped. She had scrubbed herself thoroughly in an effort to get rid of any outward traces of Nick's lovemaking. She could only cross her fingers about inner traces. Every five minutes she asked herself how she could have been so stupid. Her whole life seemed to have become unbelievably muddled lately.

Stress. It had to be the result of too much stress. She was just not thinking clearly these days. It seemed to her that she hadn't been able to think clearly since the news of Crissie's death.

She pulled on a pair of green jeans and an orange-and-green striped T-shirt, stuffed her feet into a pair of soft leather moccasins and headed back toward the kitchen. The aroma of brewing coffee was an irresistible lure.

Nick was sitting at the table near the window scanning an old fishing magazine that had been left behind by a previous tenant. Two bowls of cold cereal, a carton of milk and and a couple of spoons were sitting on the table beside him. He looked up when Phila appeared in the doorway.

"I thought you might be planning to spend the day in the shower," he remarked.

"It was a tempting idea, but there wasn't enough hot water."

Phila went over to the coffee machine and poured herself a cup of the dark brew. She gazed out the window over the sink, trying to collect her thoughts. An early morning fog squatted above the ocean. Peering through the trees, she found it impossible to tell where water ended and the thick mist began. It was all just one solid wall of gray. The world looked as if it ended right there on the other side of the woods.

"Sit down and eat, Phila. You'll feel better."

"How do you know?"

"Call it a wild hunch. Eat some cereal and then we'll talk."

"I'm not hungry, and there isn't anything left to talk about. I told you the whole story."

"Not quite. Who is this Elijah Spalding?"

Phila swore under her breath, knowing she was going to have to explain everything to Nick before she could get rid of him. He was that kind of man. "Spalding and his wife, Ruth, have a large farm outside of Holloway. Two years ago they started taking in foster children. It looked like a great setup. To the authorities, the Spaldings seemed like a stable couple. Ruth was into organic gardening and health foods. Elijah came from a farming family and knew how to run that kind of business. He had served in the military for several years, including some time in Southeast Asia and Latin America."

"The Army?"

Phila's mouth twisted in disgust. "Not exactly. During the trial it came out that he hadn't been on active duty with U.S. forces during his time out of the country. But he had been waging war. Independently, you might say."

"A mercenary?"

"Yes. Nothing more than a hired killer. But no one knew about that part of his background when they started sending the kids to him. All they knew was that he and Ruth couldn't have kids of their own and they seemed to want to care for children. The farm they were running appeared to be prosperous, and it looked like a healthy environment for kids. Lots of fresh air, exercise, chores, wholesome routines. By the end of the first year there were five children living with the Spaldings."

"But there were problems?"

Phila wandered over to the table and sat down. She kept her eyes on the gray mist beyond the trees as she talked. "Thelma Anderson started to get suspicious because when she made her visits to the farm the kids were too well behaved. Too quiet. Too polite. They gave all the right answers to her questions. Every one of the children seemed to have adjusted perfectly to life on the Spalding farm."

"I don't know much about foster-home situations, but I do know that anything that looks too good to be true usually is."

"It was. Spalding is a huge, powerfully built man. He has a big, bushy beard and he wears overalls and plaid shirts. The picture-perfect image of a farmer." Phila sipped coffee. "He's got weird eyes, though."

"Weird eyes?"

"Like blue ice. Mesmerizing. Piercing. Maybe a little bit mad. Nobody seemed to notice his eyes except me. I didn't like the man the minute I met him."

"When was that?"

"About a year ago. I went to work in the region that included Holloway, and Thelma assigned me the job of keeping tabs on the Spalding farm kids. I knew she had her suspicions. After my first trip to the farm, I agreed with her. Something was very wrong. The difference between me and Thelma was that she only had an instinctive feeling things were bad. I'd had enough personal experience in foster homes to be certain things were bad. The hard part was proving it." Phila sighed. "That's always the hard part."

"The kids were still saying everything was fine?"

Phila nodded. "Oh, yes. They all claimed they liked living on the farm. But I could see the fear in their eyes, and I knew I had to act. Unfortunately, I had nothing concrete to go on. No obvious indications of abuse. No complaints. Nothing. I needed real evidence. But before I could figure out how to get it, one of the youngest kids was brought into the emergency room of the local hospital. Little Andy. He was unconscious. The Spaldings said he'd gone climbing against their orders and suffered a bad fall."

"What did the boy say?"

"He never regained consciousness. He died."

"Oh, Christ."

"Thelma was more suspicious than ever, and I was sure the boy had been beaten. I talked to the doctors who said the injuries could have been caused by a severe beating, although they were not inconsistent with a bad fall. Thelma and I sent the sheriff out to the ranch to see if he could turn up anything. Nothing."

"What happened next?"

"I went out to see Spalding myself, several times. I wanted him to know he was under close observation. I hoped he would watch his step while I bought myself some time to work with the kids. But the kids were better behaved than ever. So I went to work on Spalding's wife, Ruth. I thought she might be a weak link. But she was more terrified of Spalding than she was of me or the authorities."

Nick considered that. "What did you do?"

"I finally phoned Spalding and told him I wanted to talk to him away from the farm. Neutral territory, so to speak. He agreed to meet me at a diner in town."

"What did you think you were going to accomplish by getting him away from his farm?"

Phila fiddled with her coffee cup. "I just thought it would be easier to talk to him away from that environment. But I was wrong. He was angry and belligerent when he arrived in the parking lot. I was still in my car, waiting for him. I got out when I saw his truck pull in. He came over to me and starting yelling. Called me a lot of names and accused me of interfering with the sanctity of the American home."

"How did you respond?"

"I told him I was doing my job and I was very worried about the children in his care. He lost his temper."

"He threatened you?"

"He did more than that. He told me those children were his and he could do with them as he pleased. He told me he was going to teach me to keep my nose out of his business. Then he hit me."

Nick's fingers clenched around his coffee cup. "He hurt you?"

"Oh, yes, he hurt me." Phila smiled grimly. "He was used to hurting people and he was very good at. it." She touched the side of her jaw, remembering the bruise she had worn for days after the assault. Her lawyer had taken photographs. "But then he made his big mistake. He tried to drag me to his truck."

"Did anyone see what was happening?"

"Not at that point. It was about ten-fifteen and the parking lot of the diner was empty. I started to scream, naturally, and he put his hand over my mouth. He was . . . very big." The memory of that huge palm smothering her made her stomach turn over. "He got me to the truck and opened the door. I was struggling, and I guess he thought he had better do something to make me keep quiet. He reached into the glove compartment and pulled out a gun."

"Jesus, Phila."

"That's when I got very lucky. That particular diner happens to be the spot where the local cops take their morning coffee break. A police car pulled into the parking lot just as Spalding tried to force me into the pickup. The cops saw what was happening and came to the rescue. They caught him with the gun, but that wasn't all. When they searched him, they found some heroin on him."

"He was carrying drugs?" Nick looked startled.

Phila nodded grimly. "The narcotics, together with the weapon and the obvious evidence of physical assault on me, were enough to get him put away for a while. More than enough to make certain he never qualified as a foster parent again."

"Which was the important thing as far as you were concerned," Nick concluded softly.

Phila glanced at him directly for the first time. His eyes were colder than she had ever seen them. It seemed to her she could feel the chill even sitting two feet away. Phila drew a deep breath.

"That's the whole story," she said. "They arrested Spalding for assault on me, not the kids. We never could prove he had done anything to the children. I'm the one who testified against him at the trial. I'm the one he intends to punish when he gets out."

CHAPTER SEVEN

Nick walked back to the Lightfoot beach cottage twenty minutes after he'd heard Phila's tale. He was still burning with a cold rage against the unknown Elijah Spalding, but he was well aware he had more immediate problems. Spalding, at least, was safely tucked away for a while.

One of the things that was hammering at him now was the memory of the panic in Phila's eyes when she'd fought him this morning. There had been more to her fear than a simple desire to escape. She had struggled as if she had thought he might rape her or beat her.

Something had happened to her at some point in the past, Nick concluded. Something that made her fear a man's weight on top of her.

Nick allowed himself a brief, self-satisfied smile. Through a combination of sheer luck and brilliant male intuition he had stumbled onto the key to seducing Phila. She was as full of feminine fire as any man could want. The trick was to let her light her own fuse.

But he was definitely going to have to work on the problem of teaching her how to burn a little more slowly. When she finally got turned on, she approached sex the same way she did everything else—at Mach speed.

He thought fleetingly of all the long, cold months he had

labored to find the right approach to use with Hilary. His failure with her had not totally crushed his masculine pride; he had been intelligent enough to understand that it was not all his fault. But it had left him with some serious qualms about his appeal to the opposite six.

More specifically, it had made him wonder frequently how much of whatever attraction women did feel for him was induced by the name of Lightfoot. There was no denying he did not come equipped with the Castleton looks and charms. Business savvy only took a man so far in this world.

But right from the start he had not had to worry about Phila being interested in him because of the Lightfoot name. If anything, the name was a distinct turnoff for her.

Yet last night, even though she had tried to resist, she had gone crazy for him. He must have the magic touch with her, Nick told himself. His smile turned into a wide, laughing grin.

Contemplation of how he would proceed with Phila started doing invigorating things to his system. To get his mind off sex he switched his thoughts to the automatic he had found in the bedside drawer earlier. That sobered him immediately.

He was halfway up the long, curving drive when the white Mercedes convertible appeared from the back of the cottage and roared toward the gate. Reed Lightfoot was at the wheel. He was wearing his golfing clothes. The sleek car glided to a halt near Nick, and Reed scanned his son's rumpled shirt and unshaven face.

"You look like you just spent the night in some god-damned cathouse. Don't let Eleanor see you," Reed said.

"Eleanor's not that easily shocked. I wasn't planning on visiting her at this hour, anyway. It's only seven-thirty. You off to the golf course?"

"Got a game at eight." Reed's eyes narrowed. "I take it the status quo has changed? You're sleeping with her as of last night?"

"I'll make a deal with you, Dad. You don't pry into my

love life and I won't make any more comments about yours, okay?"

"Suit yourself. As far as I'm concerned you can do anything you goddamn well please with Phila Fox as long as you get those shares back." Reed put his foot down on the accelerator, and the Mercedes roared through the open gate.

Nick watched for a moment until the car was out of sight and then resumed his walk toward the cottage. Phila was right. The Castleton and Lightfoot summer homes did look a little like some film-set version of a couple of plantation mansions.

Cupcake and Fifi spotted him as he drew close, and both bounded forth to greet him. He scratched their ears, and they fell into step beside him as he headed toward the colonnaded porch.

"'Morning, sir," Tec Sherman said from the doorway. He was wearing a bilious-green aloha shirt. His bald head gleamed in the morning sunlight. "Breakfast is just about to hit the table. You interested?"

"No, thanks, Tec. All I want right now is a shower and a shave."

"No problem, sir. Your things are in your bedroom."

"I know." Nick took another look at the aloha shirt. "I think Phila has a shirt that color. The two of you would probably have fun shopping together."

"She may have good taste in clothes," Tec allowed magnanimously, "but she's sure got a mouth on her."

"You get used to it."

Tec cleared his throat. "Uh, we sort of wondered where you'd gone last night."

"Yeah?"

"Your dad figured you went to visit Miss Fox."

"Is that right?"

Nick went up the steps and into the house. Phila was not going to be thrilled when she found out their relationship was common knowledge. He probably should have warned her that it was inevitable everyone would figure out what had happened last night.

But, then, Phila was not going to be thrilled when she found out they still had a relationship, period. As far as she was concerned, the previous evening was going down as a deeply regretted one-night stand.

She had certainly done her best to kick him out of the Gilmarten place this morning. Nick had finally left when he came to the conclusion they both needed time to cool down.

He wondered if she would have been more relaxed about things if it had not hit her that, on top of everything else, she might be pregnant.

He made a mental note to pick up a package of condoms in town that afternoon. He also made a note to maintain more control the next time he took Phila to bed. Next time, he promised himself, he was going to make damn sure she had a climax. He desperately wanted her to associate physical satisfaction with being in his arms. Nick shook his head, still unable to believe the effect she'd had on him last night. No other woman had ever broken through his iron-clad self-control the way Phila had. She had made him go wild, a totally unique experience for him.

Half an hour later, shaved, showered and dressed in jeans and a black pullover, Nick went back downstairs.

"If you manage to get those shares back by sleeping with her, I'll be very surprised." Hilary spoke almost idly from the breakfast-room doorway. "After all she was a friend of Crissie's and I can't see any friend of Crissie's being that stupid."

Nick swore to himself and halted in the middle of the hall. He turned halfway around to confront Hilary. She looked as stunning as ever this morning. Her dark red hair was tied at the nape of her neck, her wide-sleeved blouse flowed gracefully from the high-waisted, pleated trousers she wore.

"Good morning, Hilary. Beautiful day, isn't it?" Nick kept his voice perfectly bland.

"I think I've got this all figured out, Nick. You're going to try and buy your way back into Reed's good graces by prying those shares away from Phila, aren't you? Why bother? Or have you decided you want to be a part of Castleton & Lightfoot again, after all?"

"And if I have?" he asked softly.

Her green eyes glinted savagely. "If you think you can just walk back in here after three years and take over, you're out of your mind."

"It's my inheritance, Hilary. If you're smart, you won't forget that. One of these days I might just decide to take it back and if I do, your ass will be out the door."

She smiled coldly. "You really believe you could do that? After what you did to me? The families are on my side, Nick."

"If I decide I want to run the families and the company, I'll do it, Hilary." It was a statement of fact as far as Nick was concerned. But he knew from the confident expression in her eyes that Hilary did not believe him.

"Stop bluffing. I'm Reed's wife now. You can't touch me or the company. You shouldn't have come back, Nick. No one wants you here."

"Maybe no one wants me, but they all sure as hell want those shares, don't they? And right now I've got the best chance of getting them back into the family. So it looks as though everyone will just have to tolerate my presence."

"Do you really think anything's going to change if you do manage to get back the shares?"

Nick did some fast mental calculations and made an executive decision. It was time to rattle Hilary's cage. "Yeah, Hilary. I do think things are going to change. You see, I could do just about anything I want if I decide to have Phila give those shares to me instead of to Darren." He watched the anger form in her eyes as the full impact of what he was saying dawned on her.

"But those were Castleton shares. They belong to Darren now that Burke is dead, not you."

"They belong to whoever can get them out of Philadelphia Fox's hands."

"You bastard."

"Right, first time, Hilary. I think you're getting the point."

"Damn you, Nick."

"I told Dad I'd get the shares back into family hands, but I didn't say which family and I didn't specify whose hands. If I started voting my own shares again plus Phila's, I could begin to make some interesting waves in the moat around your little castle. Think about that when you sit in front of your mirror and tell yourself you're safe."

"I am safe," Hilary answered swiftly. "I'm family and I'm here to stay. No one is going to accept you back into the fold after what you did three years ago. You think about *that* while you screw your new girlfriend. You might also spend some time thinking about why she's willing to sleep with you in the first place. You aren't exactly hell on wheels in bed, as we both know. Better find out who's using whom." Hilary turned on one well-shod heel and walked back into the breakfast room.

Nick let himself out the front door. "Hey, Tec."

"Over here, sir." Tec came toward him, a garden hose looped around one burly shoulder. "What can I do for you, sir?"

"Let's hunt up Darron and see if he wants to get in a little target practice down at the range."

Tec's face lit up like a Christmas tree. "Great idea, sir. Your dad picked up a beautiful Ruger .44 a month ago that needs a workout. Let's hit the deck."

There was a storm coming in from the west. Phila stood barefoot in the gritty sand at the water's edge and watched the clouds boil toward shore. The wind was picking up, carrying a hint of rain. The sea was choppy with whitecaps cresting every small wave. Several hundred yards out an aging fishing boat was laboring toward port.

Phila had walked down to the beach with the hope of getting the morning's scene with Nick out of her mind. She was not having much luck. She was supposed to be gathering information on Castletons and Lightfoots in preparation for making an intelligent decision about what to do with Crissie's shares. She was supposed to be analyzing, judging, perhaps seeking some revenge for the way the families had ostracized poor Crissie.

Instead she had gotten herself tangled up in an affair with a Lightfoot.

Phila winced as she recalled the expression on Nick's face when she had awakened to find him watching her, the gun on the table beside him. But as hard as she tried to keep that memory firmly in mind, the one that kept pushing it aside was the one of last night.

Nick had been exactly what she had been looking for in a lover. Phila realized that now. He was perfect in every way except one: he was a Lightfoot. Crissie probably would have found the entire situation vastly entertaining.

Phila had known she had some problems when it came to sex. She was realistic enough to have guessed that some, if not all, of those problems stemmed from what had happened to her when she was thirteen. But she had not known how to overcome the problem. The few halting attempts she had made to get involved physically with a man had usually ended in disaster. At best she had just managed to endure groping hands and a heavy, male body.

But last night with Nick, Phila had felt gloriously safe, secure and in control for the first time. That was obviously the way she needed to feel if she was to enjoy sex.

Nick was a big man, the kind she normally felt most uneasy with. But last night he had not used his strength against her. He had not tried to overwhelm her. He had let her set the pace. For the first time she had sensed she did have her share of normal resonses. For the first time she had discovered she was capable of satisfying a man.

And she had loved the feeling.

It was too bad Nick had ruined everything this morning, she thought bitterly.

If she was pregnant, she was going to make good on her threat to use that gun on him, she vowed angrily. The thought of having possibly conceived threw her into a whole different realm of panic.

She was trying not to remember that she had been as irresponsible as Nick last night, when she realized she was not alone on the beach. She could hear nothing above the wind and the waves, but when she turned her head she saw Hilary approaching. Phila froze and waited.

"Crissie liked to walk on the beach in the mornings, too." Hilary said as she came to a halt next to Phila and gazed at the fishing boat in the distance.

Phila was silent for a moment before she said, "Crissie and I were both raised in eastern Washington. The sea always symbolized freedom to us. We used to talk about the day we would move to the coast."

"Crissie went to Southern California."

Phila smiled. "Marina Del Rey. She had an apartment overlooking the water. All chrome and white leather. Very flashy. Very beautiful."

"Like Crissie."

"Yes. Just like Crissie. California was her kind of place. She was a golden girl in a sunny, golden land."

Hilary put her long-nailed hands into the pockets of her pleated trousers. "She talked about you frequently."

"Did she?"

Hilary nodded. "She loved you, but she thought you were hopelessly naive about some things."

Phila laughed and realized it was the first time she had been amused by anything connected with Crissie since the day she'd learned of her death. "We were opposites. I'm sure if we hadn't been thrown together in a foster-home situation we would never have become friends. We had absolutely nothing in common."

"Maybe it was the fact that you were so different that drew you together. Maybe you needed each other in some ways."

"Maybe. Whatever it was, Crissie and I didn't question it too much. We were too young for that kind of introspection. We were friends, and that was all that mattered. We knew we could depend on each other."

"That's why you're here, isn't it? Because you were Crissie's friend and you need to know what happened during those last months with us." Hilary's voice was soft with understanding. "I'd feel the same way. Perhaps even more so. Because, unlike you, I did have a great deal in common with Crissie."

"You're as beautiful as she was," Phila observed.

"I wasn't talking about looks. I meant we had more important things in common. Crissie was a lot like me in some ways." When Phila gave her a sharp glance of surprise, Hilary smiled indulgently. "It's true, you know. We understood each other. Oh, I had private schooling and holidays abroad while I was growing up, but I didn't have any more love than Crissie did. My parents turned me over to nannies, tutors and boarding schools whenever possible. After they were divorced, I spent most of my time being shuttled from one place to another. I might as well have been raised in an institution."

"A nicely furnished institution," Phila said dryly.

"I won't argue that. But the result was the same, I think. Crissie realized that when she got to know me. We used to talk about what we wanted out of life, and it turned out that we both had very similar goals."

Phila chuckled. "Crissie always said her goal was to use her looks to get so rich she'd never have to worry about anything again as long as she lived. She wanted to be able to live in a big mansion and have lots of people at her beck and call. She wanted to be so powerful no one would ever dare try to hurt her or abuse her again."

"Umhmmm."

"Is that your goal?" Phila asked.

"Something very similar, I'm afraid."

"Would you do anything to achieve that goal?"

Hilary's mouth tightened. "Just about. I refuse to be prized only for my beauty and my background. I was forced to trade on those commodities for too much of my life. First while I was growing up and then in my marriage. From now on people will have to deal with me as a financially independent woman."

"Maybe you and Crissie did have a lot in common. She was certain money could buy her freedom."

"She could never understand why you chose to go into social work, you know. She said it was stupid and that you'd never last. You'd burn out, she said. You weren't hard enough for that kind of thing."

"She was right," Phila admitted. "I resigned my job a few weeks ago. I don't plan to ever go back into that field again."

"Crissie was shrewd when it came to knowing what made people tick. She could manipulate them."

"She had to learn how or she would never have survived her childhood," Phila explained.

"She certainly enjoyed herself pushing the families' buttons while she was around us. She used to think of it as a game. I was the only one she never played games with."

Phila wondered about that. "You do seem to be the only one who has anything kind to say about her."

"I told you, I liked her. Reed said something this morning at breakfast about your feeling the families bear some responsibility for Crissie's death. Is that true?"

"I don't know, Hilary," Phila said quietly. "I honestly don't know. I need to think about it, though, before I decide what to do with the shares."

Hilary nodded, as if in understanding. "I would just like to caution you about one thing. Don't get the idea that because Nick was not physically present during those last months when Crissie was here that he's somehow more trustworthy or innocent than any of the rest of us. Nick wouldn't be here now if he weren't working some angle."

"But he was estranged from the families during the time Crissie was involved with them."

"I've known Nick Lightfoot a long time, Phila. He's a very dangerous man. Be careful."

"Sure."

"Keep something else in mind about Nick. His reasoning processes don't always follow a normal, predictable pattern. He's hard to read, and his motives can be very obscure. Think about that if he tries to talk you into giving her shares to him instead of back to Darren."

Phila became lightheaded for an instant. She took a deep breath, and the world righted itself. "He's said nothing about having me turn the shares over to him."

"But he does plan to get the shares back into family hands. He told Reed that much last night."

"He told me the same thing. He was very up-front about it."

"Nick is at his most dangerous when he looks you right in the eye and tells you what he's going to do." Hilary paused for a moment, then asked, "What are you going to do, Phila?"

"I don't know," Phila answered honestly.

Hilary drew a deep breath. "I'd like to make you an offer for those shares."

Phila turned her head to look at Hilary's beautiful profile. "You want to buy them from me?"

"I'll give you an excellent price for them. More than enough cash to keep you from having to go back into social work. I'll give you what I would have given Crissie."

"Crissie was going to sell the shares to you?"

"Crissie wanted me to have those shares. But she was practical. She needed financial security," Hilary said. "I understood that. I was going to make sure she got it in exchange for the shares."

"I see."

"By the way," Hilary said easily, "I have an invitation to extend to you from Eleanor. She would like to have you join us for dinner tomorrow evening."

"A family affair?" Phila asked wryly.

Hilary smiled, showing perfect teeth. "Precisely. A family affair." She turned to walk back along the beach, pausing to say over her shoulder, "Think about my offer, Phila."

Port Claxton was a picturesque mixture of old Victorian homes, white picket fences and weathered seaside cottages. The small marina with its collection of sailing boats, fishing vessels and cruisers was the heart of the community.

Port Clax, as the locals called it, was typical of Washington's seaside towns in that it hibernated during the winter months and got rudely jolted wide awake during the summer when the tourists and vacationers descended on it.

But even at the peak of the season, it was still possible to park right in front of the entrance of either of the two small grocery stores. Phila chose the one at the north end of town.

Inside she went quickly down the short aisles, selecting salad makings, bread, cheese and other essentials. When she came to the wine shelves she remembered Nick going through her cupboards the previous night looking for something to drink. She picked up a bottle of northwest Cabernet Sauvignon, telling herself it was for her, not uninvited midnight visitors. When she got to the checkout counter a young man with curly blond hair and a shy smile greeted her.

"Hey, didn't I see you at the big Fourth of July party yesterday? You were with Nick Lightfoot, weren't you? You a new member of the family?"

"No. I am definitely not a new member of the family." Phila softened the curt response with a smile.

"Just wondered. Lotta folks did. Haven't seen Nick around for a long time. Thought when he showed up with you he might be bringing home a new wife or something."

"I take it the folks here in Port Claxton keep close tabs on the Castletons and Lightfoots?"

The young man grinned. "Sure do. Guess it's kind of a local pastime. They're big wheels around here. We've had Castletons and Lightfoots in this town since before I was born. My mom remembers when Reed and Burke built those fancy places out there near the beach. She always liked Reed's first wife, she said. A real down-to-earth person. Kind of looked after things here in town, Mom says."

"Looked after things?"

"You know what I mean. While Nora Lightfoot was alive, the Castletons and Lightfoots did lots of things for the town. Got a nice park built out by the marina. Got a theater group going. Gave a lot of money to local charities. Helped folks out when they needed it. Real nice lady, my mom says."

Phila was intrigued. "Don't the Castletons and Light-foots still help out locally?"

"Well, when Nick Lightfoot was around we did get some new equipment for the hospital, I think, and there used to be a scholarship fund for local kids who went on to college. He kept that up for a while after the first Mrs. Lightfoot died. But it's different now."

"How are things different?"

"Don't get me wrong. The Castletons and the Lightfoots still make some local contributions occasionally, but it's not like in the old days. My dad says Eleanor Castleton and the others think people should stand on their own feet and not get used to handouts. Says it makes folks dependent."

"I can see how that philosophy would suit them."

"The Castletons and Lightfoots still put on one heck of a Fourth of July picnic, though, I'll say that for 'em. Everybody around here really looks forward to it. Sort of a local tradition."

"I take it people in town enjoy gossiping about them, too?"

The young man flushed. "I guess so." He brightened. "Way things are going, according to my dad, we may be voting for a Castleton for governor one of these days. Everyone says Darren's getting set to go into politics in a big way. Wouldn't that be somethin'?"

"Would everyone in town vote for him if he ran?"

"Are you kiddin'? Like a shot. He's one of us." The young man beamed with pride.

"Amazing," Phila muttered, picking up her bag of groceries. "You do realize that the Castleton and Lightfoot fortunes are founded on machines used for military purposes? That if Darren Caslteton got into public office he would probably hold extremely right-wing, militaristic views due to his background and family business? If he ever went into national office he would undoubtedly vote to increase the defense budget every chance he got."

The clerk gave her a puzzled look. "Castletons and Lightfoots are real patriotic. Proud to be Americans. They got a way of making everyone else proud of it, too."

"I give up." Phila headed for the door with her groceries.

The storm finally hit the coast later that evening. Phila closed the windows of her little house when the rain began pouring down. It was all very cozy, she told herself as she cleaned up after a simple dinner of soup and salad. She wondered what everyone was doing up at the family mansions. She had seen no sign of a Castleton or a Lightfoot all afternoon.

When she had washed the last of the small stack of dirty dishes she wandered into the living room and stood at the front window. For a while she toyed with the notion of going down to the beach in the storm. It would be a good place to think.

Lord knew, she needed to do some thinking.

She was going to have to make a decision about what to do with the shares by the date of the annual meeting of Castleton & Lightfoot. If she opted to keep them and vote them, she was going to be fighting an open war with the families, a war she could not win.

She did not own enough shares to outvote them on critical issues. All she could accomplish was to be a gadfly, a troublemaker in their midst. She would always be an outsider, just as Crissie had been.

But it seemed wrong just to return those shares to the families. They constituted Crissie's inheritance; the inheritance she had always fantasized would one day be hers. Any kind of inheritance meant a lot when you had grown up in foster homes. It symoblized something important, a sense of belonging, a sense of being part of a family, of having a place in the world.

But Crissie was dead and the inheritance was now hers, Phila reminded herself.

And soon she would have to make a decision.

Thunder partially masked the first knock on the front door, but Phila heard the second quite clearly. She recognized the blunt summons at once and gave serious thought to not answering. But she knew that would be a waste of time.

She went to the door and found Nick on the step. His dark hair was wet, and the black windbreaker he wore was soaked. His gray eyes gleamed as they moved over her.

"Do me a favor and don't go for the gun yet, okay? I've had a hard evening."

"Am I supposed to feel sorry for you?" Phila stepped back reluctantly, unable to think of a way to keep him out and not really certain she wanted to achieve that goal, anyway. "It's your family."

"You don't have to remind me." He moved over the threshold, shaking raindrops onto the scarred boards of the floor. He slipped off the windbreaker and hung it over the back of a chair. "I heard you went into town this afternoon. Can I assume you picked up something for me to drink?"

"We went through this routine last night. How did you know I went into town?"

He shrugged, heading for the kitchen. "Better get used to the reality of being associated with Lightfoots and Castletons. Everyone knows what you're doing, when you do it and who you do it with. I even know about the conversation with the Wilson kid in the grocery store."

He found the cabernet inside the first cupboard he opened. He started opening drawers, apparently looking for something he could use to pull the cork. "So you think Darren would be a hawk if he ever got into public office, huh?"

"Second drawer on the left," Phila volunteered when she realized he was going to go through each drawer systematically until he found what he wanted.

"Thanks." He went to work on the cork, removing it with a few swift, deft twists. "I don't suppose you have anything to eat with this? Some cheese, maybe?"

"Don't look so innocent. Your sources probably told you exactly what I bought in town today." She went to the refrigerator and withdrew the package of cheese. "Must be nice owning a whole town and everyone in it."

"We don't own it. We're just real neighborly and folks around here appreciate that."

"I'll bet they'd appreciate it even more if you went back to contributing heavily to scholarships and civic-improvement projects."

"The Wilson kid got real chatty, I take it?" Nick poured the wine into a water glass. "Don't worry, the families still give lots of money away."

"To whom?"

Nick gave her his slow, faint smile. "Mostly to the political campaigns of right-thinking politicians and a number of good, solid, all-American organizations."

"Such as the National Rifle Association?"

"You're hardly in a position to complain if it's on the list. The NRA is one of the reasons you can legally pack that automatic you've got stashed in the nightstand."

"The Constitution gives me that right, not the NRA."

"Odds are you would have lost the right years ago if the left-wing antigun lobbyists had had their way. I'll bet you held some pretty narrow views on the subject of gun control yourself until a few weeks ago."

Phila knew she was turning pink under his shrewd gaze. It was true. Until she had come to fear Elijah Spalding, she had been a staunch supporter of strict handgun legislation. "My views on gun control can hardly be of major interest to you," she said, her tone aloof.

"I've got news for you. Everything you do is of great interest to me. How much have you worked with that pistol, by the way?"

"Worked with it?"

"Fired it. Practiced with it."

"Oh. I've never had occasion to use it, thank God."

"You've never even fired the damn thing?"

"Well, no."

"You bought a fancy 9-mm automatic pistol and you don't know the first thing about it? How the hell do you expect to be able to use it in an emergency?"

"I read the manual."

"Jesus. You read the manual. That's just terrific, Phila.

I'm really impressed. Did you figure out which end to point away from yourself?"

"I do not have to tolerate your sarcasm."

He sighed. "Yeah, you do, I'm afraid. I'm spending the night."

Phila stared at him. "Are you crazy? After the way you behaved last night and this morning? I'm not about to let you spend the night."

He took a sizable swallow of the cabernet and bit into a slice of cheese. "You were the one who dragged me into your bedroom last night. And as for what happened this morning, you know as well as I do that my reactions were understandable under the circumstances. When I came out of the bathroom and spotted that pistol in the drawer, I assumed I had just spent the night with a professional hit lady."

"You thought no such thing. Even you couldn't have been that stupid."

"Thank you, I think. In any event, I feel I am not entirely to blame for either the sex or the scene in the bedroom this morning and if you are half the logical, intelligent, fair-minded human being you claim to be, you'll agree with me."

She felt cornered. "If you stay here tonight, you'll sleep on the sofa."

"I'll take what I can get."

She couldn't believe it. "You want to spend the night on that lumpy monstrosity?"

"No, I'd rather spend the night in your bed, but as I said, I'll take what I can get. How much did Hilary offer you today?"

Phila blinked. "I beg your pardon?"

"I just wondered how much Hilary offered you for those shares of yours." Nick poured himself another glass of wine. "She did make an offer, didn't she?"

"She said something about paying me for the shares, yes," Phila admitted warily. "But how did you know? Did she tell you?"

"No. I just had a hunch she'd try something like that."

"What gave you the hunch?" Phila was now very suspicious.

Nick leaned back against the counter. "I set her up for it."

"You encouraged her to try to buy back the shares? But why?"

"Because I knew it would annoy you. I don't want you dealing with Hilary, and I figured the fastest way of cutting her off at the pass was to have her push you too far, too fast. Trying to buy you off is a surefire way to make you dig in your heels."

"My God." Phila felt winded.

"Money might work eventually, but this was the wrong time to make an offer to you. You're still feeling loyal to Crissie's memory. Those shares are a tie to that memory. You need awhile to think through what you want to do, and you're bound to resent anyone trying to force your hand."

Phila stared at him. "So you pushed Hilary into doing just that. You must think you're a very clever man."

"Honey, when it comes to business, I'm as clever as they get."

CHAPTER EIGHT

It was irrational and annoying, but Phila woke up the next morning with the realization that she had slept better the past two nights than she had at any time since Elijah Spalding had been arrested.

There was no denying that having Nicodemus Lightfoot sleeping nearby, whether in her bed or out in the living room, was a comfort.

She was so accustomed to having only herself to rely on that it had taken her awhile to understand just what was happening. The fact was that in spite of all the evidence to the contrary, in spite of all the obvious warnings, and against her better judgment, she was starting to trust Nick. The man was too big, too mysterious and a little too clever for her taste, but there was a steel core she found irresistibly comforting under all those troublesome traits.

A woman might not always have the comfort of knowing just what Nick Lightfoot was thinking, but she could be certain he would not bend once he had made up his mind. He could be relied on.

He had certainly been honest about his intentions regarding the shares, she reminded herself as she stepped into the shower. If she got burned in that department, she would have only herself to blame.

She was still lecturing herself about Nick Lightfoot when she emerged from the bedroom half an hour later to find him standing at the door talking to his father. A white Mercedes convertible was visible through the open doorway. Reed was dressed for golfing in a monogrammed polo shirt and plaid slacks.

Nick, on the other hand, was hardly dressed at all. He'd taken time to put on his jeans, but that was it. The couch, Phila noted, had already been made up and the blankets stowed. Nick had clearly taken time to do that before answering the door.

Apparently Nick did not want early-morning callers to know he'd been consigned to the living room. Simple male pride or something more devious? Phila wondered.

"Phila," Nick called over his shoulder, "Dad stopped by to ask you to play a round of golf with him this morning."

Phila raised her brows. "Sorry, I don't play."

"It's a great morning," Reed himself insisted. "A little nippy, but the sun's out. Why don't you walk the course with me while I hit a few balls?"

"Oh, I get it," Phila said yawning. "You want to get me off by myself so you can make your pitch for the shares. Hilary already offered me mucho bucks, and that didn't work. What have you got to offer?"

Reed shot a quick, questioning glance at his son. Nick just shrugged. Reed smiled broadly again at Phila. "I thought we'd spend some time talking. Get to know each other. Nick tells me you have some questions concerning what went on while Crissie Masters was here with us. Maybe I can answer a few of them."

"You don't look like the sort who volunteers answers."

Reed's smile vanished. "Well, I'm volunteering now, am I not? So go get a goddamned jacket and let's go."

"You don't have to go with him, Phila." Nick absently polished his glasses with a soft white handkerchief.

"I know. But I think I will," Phila decided. "If he'll guarantee to provide breakfast. I'm hungry."

"I'll buy you breakfast at the clubhouse," Reed promised.

The eighteen-hole course followed the cliffs along the ocean for half its length and then curved inland. The thick, carefully cropped grass stretched before Phila like a lush green carpet. It glistened with traces of the previous night's rain. Reed had been right. It was chilly this morning, but the sun was shining and it felt good to be outdoors.

"You don't use a cart?" Phila inquired as they approached the second green. Her yellow running shoes were already wet, and the cuffs of her pink-and-green pants were getting damp.

"Not unless the course is crowded. I like the exercise. Now keep quiet for a few minutes while I get this sucker on the green."

"Sorry."

"Umm." Reed selected an iron from his bag, stationed himself over the small white ball and took a slow, powerful swing.

The ball hit the green, bounced and rolled to within three feet of the cup.

"You missed," Phila observed.

Reed scowled at her, reminding her momentarily of his son. "That was a damn fine shot, young lady, if I do say so myself."

"Are all golfers this snappish?"

"Yes, ma'am, they are. Especially when they're getting a lot of unnecessary backchat from the gallery."

"You brought me out here to talk, remember?"

"About Crissie Masters and related family matters. Not about my golf game. What's all this crap about the Castletons and Lightfoots bearing some kind of responsibility for Masters's death, anyway?"

"I don't think she was treated very well while she was with the families, Mr. Lightfoot. I think that rejection could have been devastating for her after she'd spent so many years dreaming of finding her father. Indirectly it could have been a contributing factor in her death."

"No one drove her to her death. She drove herself. Literally," Reed's voice was rough.

"I've seen the cops' report of the accident, and I hired a private investigator to check it out. I know it really was an accident, but I'd like to hear what happened the night she died. Why did she have so much alcohol in her bloodstream? Crissie wasn't normally a heavy drinker."

Reed glared at her. "You hired a private investigator to double-check the accident report?"

"Of course." Phila shoved her hands into her pockets. "I never completely trust official reports. I've written too many myself. And I certainly had no reason to accept any assurances from the Castletons and Lightfoots, did I? Naturally I double-checked. It was the least I could do for Crissie."

"Christ almighty. No wonder Nick didn't know what to do with you. Who the hell do you think you are to question us, girl?"

Phila smiled grimly. "Your son asked me the same thing. I question everything all the time, Mr. Lightfoot. It's in the blood. Now why don't you tell me what happened the night Crissie died?"

"The hell with it. There's nothing much to tell. It was the night of Eleanor's birthday party," Reed said. "We'd all had a few drinks, including Crissie. There was a large crowd at the Castletons' cottage that night. No one saw her leave, but the accident report was clear. She had alcohol in her blood and the weather was bad. She had been driving a dangerous stretch of road. Put all that together and you have more than enough explanation for what happened to her."

"Did you dislike her, Reed?"

He considered that. "Didn't actively dislike her, but I can't say I took to her the way Burke did. But, then, Burke had his reasons for making a fuss over his long-lost daughter."

"What reasons?"

Reed pulled a putter out of the bag and walked over to where his ball lay on the green. "Burke Castleton was a man who admired nerve and gumption. Crissie had plenty of both. Take the pin out of the hole, will you?"

"What do you want me to do with it?"

"Just hold it, for crissake."

Phila obeyed and stood back while Reed lined up his putt. "Don't you think you should aim a little more to the right?" she asked just as he tapped the ball with the putter.

Reed swore as the ball rolled to within half an inch of the cup. "Are you this goddamned chatty with Nick at all the wrong moments?"

"Sorry."

"Huh. Put the pin back."

"The ball isn't in the cup yet. Isn't it supposed to go in?"

Reed glared at her and pushed the ball into the cup with the tip of his putter. "Satisfied?"

Phila smiled blandly. "This is certainly an interesting game. Do you play a lot?"

"Every day unless the weather is bad."

"Does Hilary play with you?"

Reed shook his head. "My wife prefers tennis."

"What about Nick?"

"Nick and I used to play together occasionally. But that was a long time ago. Haven't played with him for over three years." Reed picked up his bag of clubs and started for the next hole.

"You haven't played with him since Hilary and Nick got divorced and she married you?"

Reed spun around abruptly, his expression forbidding. "The circumstances surrounding my marriage are not something we discuss much in this family. I'm sure you've figured that out by now. Haven't you ever heard of tact, Philadelphia?"

"Tact doesn't always get the job done. My grandmother taught me that. She used to say that when your kind of people start getting extra polite you could pretty well figure they were up to something."

"My kind of people?"

"Yup."

Reed was grimly amused. "You might be interested to learn that I didn't know diddlysquat about genteel politeness until Eleanor married Burke thirty-six years ago."

"Eleanor taught you everything you know?"

"Goddamn right. Burke said we needed a real lady to get us all shaped up so we could mingle with the money crowd. We were raking in the dough, you see, but we didn't have the manners to go with it. Burke and me, we were just a couple of shitkickers with too much cash for our own good at that point."

"The money didn't buy you into the right crowd?"

"Money only takes you so far, even out here on the West Coast. Burke went looking for a genuine lady and when he found Eleanor, he married her."

"And Eleanor took you all in hand?"

"She did her best. Sometimes we don't all live up to her standards, but she keeps workin' on us. She's devoted to the project. Making Castletons and Lightfoots socially acceptable is her mission in life. I reckon if Darren gets to be governor, maybe she'll figure she's finally succeeded."

"Why did Eleanor marry Burke if he wasn't up to her standards to begin with?"

"You want to get real down and dirty, don't you?"

"I'm curious."

"Then you ask her why she married him. I'm not going to satisfy your goddamn curiosity, Philadelphia. I don't see that the answer is any of your business."

"You're probably right."

"I know I'm right. I'm always right. Now keep quiet while I tee off."

"No wonder you and Nick have a hard time communicating," Phila mused as Reed readied his swing. She waited until Reed's club started its descent before concluding, "You both seem to have developed the same nasty habit."

"*Goddamn* it, woman, can't you keep your mouth shut while I'm hitting the goddamn ball? Look what you made me do. I'm clear out in the rough. Jesus H. Christ." Reed slammed the wood into his bag. "What nasty habit?"

"Each of you thinks he's always right. You're both as stubborn as a couple of bricks." Unperturbed by Reed's furious glare, she started off in the direction in which his ball had disappeared. "I think it landed over there behind that bush."

"What kind of a fairy tale did Nick tell you about his divorce?" Reed demanded, overtaking Phila in four strides.

"We haven't discussed it in great detail but I'm sure we'll get around to it eventually."

"You're sleeping with my son and you haven't even bothered to find out why his marriage went on the rocks? If you don't know that, then there's sure as hell a lot more you probably don't know, either. It'd think a smart cookie like you would find out the details before she got too involved with a man like Nick. Which bush?"

"Over there." Phila pointed.

Reed shielded his eyes under his palm. "Goddamn. I'm going to lose two strokes on this hole thanks to your mouthiness."

"Do you always look for someone else to blame when things go wrong?"

"Take some advice. If you want to make it back to the clubhouse in one piece, you will keep your mouth shut while I get this goddamn ball back onto the fairway."

"Why don't you just pick it up and throw it back on the grass?"

Reed did not dignify that with an answer. In fact, he didn't speak again until he had shot the ball onto the green.

Phila decided to keep quiet for a while, at least until Reed lined up his tee shot on the next fairway. Then she said, "Are you hoping Nick will marry again?"

"Why should I care one way or the other if my son marries again?" Reed concentrated on the ball.

"I thought maybe you'd like some grandchildren, your kind being so family oriented and all. I mean, what's the good of founding an empire if you haven't got a dynasty to leave it to, right?"

"For Crissake, you're not thinking of trying that old trick, are you?"

"What old trick?"

"Trying to get a permanent piece of the action by marrying into the families. If that's your game, you're barking up the wrong tree. Don't think for one moment that if you get pregnant, Nick will feel obliged to marry you." Reed took a powerful swing at the ball and sent it sailing a good two hundred yards down the fairway.

"If I get pregnant," Phila said, her tone very even, "Nick will damn sure meet his responsibilities."

Reed's head came around abruptly, his eyes unreadable under the brim of his hat. "What makes you think so?"

"He feels as strongly about family as you do," Phila explained patiently. "He'd want his child. In fact, he'd demand it."

"You sound pretty goddamn sure of that."

"I am sure of it."

"Is that right?"

"The real question," Phila continued thoughtfully, "is whether I'd lower myself to marrying into this nest of ultraconservative right-wing pit vipers. Would you mind if I tried hitting the ball a couple of times?"

Reed looked momentarily baffled by the switch in topics. When he saw her enthusiastic expression, he finally nodded brusquely and handed her a club.

"No, no, you don't clutch it like a stick," he said as he stood over her. "Your thumb goes along the grip like this. That's it. Okay, take it back like this. Real easy. The backswing is slow and controlled. Don't rush it. All right, bring it down nice and easy. I said, *easy,* damn it."

Phila ignored the last bit of advice and swung the club with all her might, eager to drive the ball as far as Reed had. There was a nice sensation of power, a satisfying whoosh and a loud, despairing groan from Reed.

She paid no attention to the groan, certain that she had hit the ball halfway down the fairway. When she couldn't spot it, she glanced down and saw that the little white ball had gone about three feet.

"Slow and easy, I said. Do you always rush into things that way?" Reed asked as he repositioned the ball.

"What way?" Phila planted her feet for another swing.

"Full speed ahead, no holds barred?"

"I guess so, why?"

"You're going to drive Nick crazy."

"Might be good for him. He needs to loosen up a bit. Now stand back. I'm going to try this again." She swung this time with even greater enthusiasm. The ball dribbled about four feet from the tee. "Well, damn."

"I told you, Phila. Slow and easy does it. You really believe my son would stand by you if you got pregnant?"

"Of course. After all, he is your son, isn't he? Would you walk out on a woman you'd gotten pregnant?"

"There's a word for people like you."

"Liberal? Left wing? Commie sympathizer?"

"No. *Naive.* I hate to shatter your illusions, Philadelphia, especially if Nick is playing on them in order to get the shares back from you. Hell, I want those shares back in the families, too. But the fact is, I think you would be very foolish to put too much stock in Nick's sense of obligation."

"Mr. Lightfoot, I may not play golf very well, but I've had a lot of experience dealing with different kinds of families. Many of them not very nice. Believe me, since the age of thirteen, I've been able to tell the good guys from the bad guys at a glance. It's one of the reasons I used to be very good at my job."

"Who taught you a neat trick like that when you were thirteen?" Reed asked, brows arching derisively.

"Crissie Masters." Phila smiled. "She always said I had a lot of natural ability, though. She claimed that all she did was fine-tune it a little for me."

Nick went to lounge in the Gilmarten doorway when he heard the Mercedes pull into the drive. Sending Phila off with his father had been a calculated risk. He was curious to find out the results.

As the convertible came to a halt, Phila waved and smiled at him. She looked good, he thought, cheerful and exhilarated. He had an overpowering urge to take her to bed right then and there and sample some of that sweet, sexy enthusiasm.

"How was the game?" he forced himself to ask politely as he opened the door for her.

"I nearly strangled her on the third, sixth and fifteenth greens," Reed said. "She's a mouthy little thing, isn't she?"

"Yeah. But you get used to it after a while."

"I resent that," Phila announced.

"I let her try a few shots," Reed said. "But she has a bad habit of rushing her swing. She'll have to learn to slow down a bit if she ever wants to be able to play."

"I'm working with her on the problem," Nick said calmly. *A hundred miles per hour.*

Reed's eyes were cool and curious. "She seems to think you're one of the good guys. Did you know that?"

"A good guy?"

"The kind of man who'd marry her if she got pregnant, for instance."

Nick glanced at Phila and saw the color staining her cheeks. "Did she tell you that?"

"Yup. Real sure of herself. Seems to think she can tell the sonsobitches a mile off."

"She's just bragging. Did she mention that she threatened to come after me with a gun if she gets pregnant?"

"No." Reed gave Nick a thin smile. "But she did say the real question wasn't whether you'd marry her, it was whether she'd lower her standards far enough to marry into our family."

Phila drew herself up to her full height, her eyes gleaming with irritation. "If either one of you continues to discuss me as if I were not present, I will hand over my shares in Castleton & Lightfoot to the Revolutionary Workers Brigade of America. I'm sure they'll make quite an impression at the annual meeting in August."

Reed glared at Nick. "Goddamn it. Do something about her. Fast."

"Yes, sir." Nick quickly removed his hand from the car door as the Mercedes shot forward.

"It's very tacky to discuss someone as if she weren't present," Phila announced as she turned to march into the cottage. "I'd have thought Eleanor would have taught you all better manners than that. By the way, your father certainly swears a lot, doesn't he? Eleanor should have cleaned up his language by now, too."

Nick followed her over the threshold. "You and Reed discussed the possibility that you might be pregnant?"

Phila was already in the kitchen, rummaging through the refrigerator. "He brought it up, not me. I think he felt he had a gentlemanly obligation to warn me not to use pregnancy as a means of getting a piece of the precious Lightfoot family pie. I wonder where he got the idea that the Great American Dream is to become a Lightfoot or a Castleton." She removed some carrots from the crisper. "Arrogant redneck."

"Dad?"

"Sure. He may drive that fancy Mercedes and dress in designer polo shirts, but deep down he's just a redneck cowboy. I'm surprised he doesn't wear a six-gun on the golf course." She went to the sink and began peeling the carrots.

"The holster would probably interfere with his golf swing. You told him you didn't think I'd walk out on you if you got pregnant?" Nick was fascinated with the way she wielded the peeler. Little strips of carrot flew into the chipped enamel sink.

"You're not the type to walk out."

"You know the type?"

"I'm an ex–social worker, remember? One who specialized in children? I've hunted down more deserters than the U.S. Army. If there's one thing I know, it's the type. Want a carrot?" She held one out to him. "Your cheap father only bought me a cup of coffee and a Danish at the clubhouse before we went out on the course. Said he had a scheduled tee-off time and we couldn't stand around eating."

Nick took the carrot and crunched down on one end, his eyes never leaving Phila's face. "If I'm not the type to walk out, what was that business about threatening me with the gun yesterday morning?"

"I said if you'd gotten me pregnant, I'd come after you with a gun. I didn't say I expected you to run."

Nick finished his carrot. It occurred to him that when a man took a calculated risk, he expected either success or failure. Having the whole business go off on some crazy, unforeseen tangent was a novelty. Nick was dumbfounded. "Sounds like you and my father had a very interesting morning."

"Uh huh. Why did you send me off with him, anyway?"

"I didn't send you off with him. It was your decision to go to the course."

"Come on, Nick, this is me, Phila, remember? Sell that bridge to someone else."

He smiled faintly. "All right, when he showed up at the door I figured it was a good opportunity for the two of you to get to know each other. You wanted to get to know Castletons and Lightfoots, remember?"

"There's more to it than that," Phila said. "Did you hope he'd bully me? Did you think he'd make me mad the way Hilary did when she offered to buy the shares?"

"It was a possibility," Nick admitted.

"I'll just bet it was. Why did you want him to try to push me around?"

"So you'd get really stubborn. I don't want you turning the shares over to him."

"Why not?"

"Because he's letting Hilary vote his shares these days, and I don't want her getting her hands on any more shares than she already controls."

"Got it."

"Speaking of not getting pregnant—" Nick continued and broke off as Phila began choking on the carrot. He slapped her helpfully on the back until she could swallow properly. "I picked up a package of condoms in town yesterday afternoon."

"Oh, fine. Why don't you just broadcast the fact on the local radio station? Buying condoms in a town the size of Port Claxton at a drugstore where the clerk has probably known you since you were born is real subtle, Lightfoot. What are you trying to do? Sink my reputation completely?"

"Everyone already assumes we're sleeping together," Nick pointed out gently.

"Well, everyone's wrong. You're sleeping on the couch, remember? A one-night stand does not constitute an affair or even a short-term shack-up."

"Does this mean you don't have any immediate plans to seduce me again in the near future?"

"My immediate plans are to take a book down to that little cove at the bottom of the hill. I've had it with Lightfoots this morning."

"That little cove is full of rocks, not nice, soft sand."

"Life is full of rocks. With a little practice you get used to sitting on them."

The book was good, a thriller in which the hero, an aging ex-hippie from the sixties, halted a fanatical, power-hungry, right-wing businessman who was secretly financing a band of guerrillas with the intention of taking over Texas.

Phila was halfway through the story when she realized she was concentrating on it in the old, familiar way. Reading had always been a secret pleasure for her, a treasured escape. But ever since the Spalding trial and Crissie's death, she'd had trouble keeping her attention on any book, even a very good one. It was a relief to sense she was getting back to normal in some areas of her life.

She squirmed a bit on the small patch of rough sand she had managed to find in the cove and resettled herself against a large, sun-warmed boulder. Gulls wheeled overhead and several long-legged wading birds darted back and forth in the foam of the retreating surf.

A high-pitched, childish screech of delight mingled with the cries of the birds, and Phila glanced up to see Jordan Castleton running across the wide beach toward the water at full speed. He was wearing a tiny pair of shorts and a shirt that flapped around his waist. His mother was right behind him.

"That's close enough, Jordan," Vicky called as her son showed every sign of charging straight into the waves. "We have to stay on the beach. That water is cold."

Jordan protested vociferously until his attention was caught by the sight of Phila sitting near the tumble of rocks in the cove. He stopped complaining to his mother and stared at Phila. Then he waved both arms excitedly and dashed toward her.

"Hi, Phila. Hi, Phila. Hi, Phila." He got sidetracked by a pile of wet seaweed. Seeing it, he halted immediately and squatted down to investigate.

Victoria turned to see what had first captured her son's attention. She hesitated when she saw Phila, then she started toward her.

"Good afternoon," Victoria said with restrained politeness as she came close to Phila. "I didn't realize you were down here on the beach."

"I had a hard morning playing golf with Reed. I decided to rest this afternoon."

Jordan now came running to join them, a long length of seaweed in his hands. "Look, Phila."

"Hi, Jordan. How's the world treating you today? Why, thank you. Just what I've always wanted," she added as he triumphantly placed the seaweed in her hand. She put it on display on the rock behind her. "There. How's that?"

Jordan cackled in delight. "Pretty."

"It's beautiful. Does wonders for that rock."

He nodded in ready agreement and started looking for more seaweed to add to the collection. Victoria hesitated and then put a towel down on a nearby rock. She sat on top of the towel.

"You went golfing with Reed?" Victoria finally asked.

"In a manner of speaking. I've never played before, and I'm afraid Reed was a tad impatient with my backswing."

"Hilary never plays with him."

"I'm sure he'd rather play with men."

"Eleanor says Nora, his first wife, learned. She used to go around with him sometimes in the evenings when the course was quiet."

"Reed was happy with his first wife?"

"According to everything I've ever heard. She died shortly before I was introduced to Darren. Eleanor says when she first met Nora, the poor woman didn't know where to shop for her clothes or which glass to set where at a formal dinner. But Reed was madly in love with her. It's too bad he got stuck with Hilary for a second wife, but I imagine he felt he didn't have a choice."

Phila decided to bite. "Why didn't he feel he had a choice?"

"He felt duty bound to marry her after she found out she was pregnant. Nick made it clear he wasn't going to take responsibility."

Phila's mind went totally blank for a split second. She accepted another bit of seaweed from Jordan and placed it carefully on the rock next to the first piece. "Hilary was pregnant when she married Reed?"

"Another family secret the Lightfoots haven't bothered to divulge, I gather? She was pregnant, all right. She made a major production out of it."

"But Nick denied the baby was his?"

Victoria nodded, her attention on the small stick Jordan was uncovering amid the rocks. "I heard he refused even to discuss it when his father called him and confronted him with the news. Reed was already feuding with Nick at the time, and he was angry about the divorce. The pregnancy pushed him over the edge. He rushed into marriage with Hilary. Felt sorry for her, I guess. Or maybe he felt duty bound to protect her. I don't know."

"Why was Reed feuding with Nick?"

"I'm not sure exactly. Something to do with the direction

in which Nick wanted to take the firm. Darren explained it, but I don't remember all the details. I just recall that Nick and his father were battling tooth and nail over it while the divorce was in progress. Then came the announcement about Hilary being pregnant. Nick had already walked out by the time she realized she was carrying the baby."

"So Hilary became Mrs. Reed Lightfoot."

"She managed to lose the baby two months after Reed married her. Hilary's timing is usually very good."

"Why are you telling me this, Vicky?" Phila asked quietly.

Victoria flicked a quick glance at her and then looked away again. "I just thought you ought to know what you're up against. Hilary is a manipulator. And Nick is just as clever in his own way, if not more so."

"What are you afraid of? That I'll fall for Lightfoot lies or Lightfoot seduction techniques and decide to turn the shares over to a Lightfoot instead of a Castleton?"

"That's exactly what I'm afraid will happen." Victoria stood up and hugged her arms around herself as she looked down at Phila. Her fine dark eyes burned with resentment. "Those shares belong to the Castletons. By rights they should have gone to Darren when Burke died, not to that cheap little trollop who wandered into our lives and ruined everything!"

Phila was on her feet in an instant, rage heating her blood. "Don't you dare call Crissie names. I don't care what you think she did, she was my friend and I won't let anyone call her names. Apologize, damn it. Right now."

Victoria's eyes filled with hurt and anger. "Why should I bother? Crissie Masters came very close to wrecking my marriage. She enjoyed driving a wedge between me and Darren, and I hated her for that."

"How could she drive a wedge between the two of you unless there was one sitting around waiting to be driven?" Phila snapped.

"There are things you don't know. Private matters that concern only Darren and myself. I hoped they'd been buried three years ago, but your precious Crissie found out about them and brought them to the surface again. She took great delight in throwing them in our faces."

"You can't blame Crissie for everything, damn you."

"Believe what you want, but I'll tell you one thing, Philadelphia Fox. Those shares you got from her are my son's inheritance. I want them back in the Castleton family."

"Crissie had as much right to them as anyone in that family. They constituted *her* inheritance, not Jordan's. Burke was her father, remember?"

"She's dead."

"Right," Phila said tightly. "So now they're my inheritance, aren't they? Crissie was family to me, Vicky, the only family I had left in this world. No one insults her and gets away with it. Apologize for calling her a cheap trollop."

"All right, I apologize," Victoria said wretchedly. She dashed away the tears that had formed in her eyes. "But it changes nothing. She was a troublemaker while she was alive, and she's still making trouble even though she's dead. I'll never forgive her for turning Burke against Darren. And I'll never forgive her for leaving those shares to you. She gave away a portion of my son's future, and I want it back. If you don't give the shares to us, you're no better than she was."

Victoria whirled around, grabbed Jordan up into her arms and stood staring for an instant at a point just beyond Phila's left shoulder. Then she burst into more tears and hurried toward the cliff path with her small son.

"Well, well, well," Nick observed quietly from just behind Phila. "Aren't you a little ray of sunshine in everyone's life today?"

She swung around to see him leaning against a large boulder. He had one hand braced against the rock's surface, and his face was set in familiar, unreadable lines.

"How long have you been standing there?" Phila demanded, struggling to regain her self-control.

"A few minutes. You and Vicky were both so wrapped up in your girlish conversation you didn't hear me arrive."

Phila sank wearily back down onto her towel and picked

up her book. Her fingers were trembling. She was fighting her own tears. "I didn't mean to upset her," she said. "But I won't let her or anyone else call Crissie names."

"Even if Crissie deserves them?"

Phila nodded resolutely. "Even if Crissie deserves them."

"I can understand that. Family is family." Nick sat down beside her and leaned back against the warm boulder. He drew up his jeaned legs and closed his eyes against the sun. "Ever made love on a beach?"

CHAPTER NINE

"No, I certainly have not made love on a beach and I don't intend to try it now, so don't get any ideas." Phila picked up her book and buried her nose in it.

Nick waited. While he waited he picked up a handful of small pebbles and tossed them idly into the waves. Two or three minutes passed.

"I suppose you have?" Phila eventually asked, sounding petulant. She did not remove her nose from the book.

Nick smiled to himself and picked up another handful of smooth, sea-washed pebbles. "No, can't say that I have. But I've always secretly wanted to do it."

That caught her attention. "Do you have a lot of weird unfulfilled desires?"

"As you get to know me better you'll find out, won't you?"

"I can't imagine why you would want to make love on a beach." She turned the page in her book. "It seems to me it would be extremely uncomfortable."

"Not for you."

"What do you mean, not for me?"

"The way I fantasize it, you'd be on your feet most of the time."

"On my feet!"

"Yeah. Kind of leaning over me. You'd have your legs wide apart and I'd . . ."

"Stop it. You're getting kinky." She flipped another page in her book.

"Thank you, Phila," he said gravely. "No one's ever said that to me before. It must be something you bring out in me." Nick was not concerned by her apparent interest in the book. It was obvious she had not read the last two pages. She was as aware of him physically as he was of her. The sense of primitive masculine power gave him a real rush. He was getting hard already.

"Don't blame me for your sexual fantasies," Phila muttered.

"How can I help but blame you? You're the subject of them. All of them."

"Will you please stop talking like that? I told you earlier, we are not having an affair. You're using my sofa, remember?"

"I'd like to have an affair with you," Nick said very humbly.

"Why? Because you think you could control me better if you were sleeping with me?" she retorted.

Nick heard the wariness in her voice and knew he had to move very carefully through this particular mine field. "I'm the one who should be worrying about being controlled by sex," he said softly. "I told you that you have a potent effect on me, Phila. No other woman does to me what you do to me."

"Hah."

"It's true." He paused a few seconds. "I'm thirty-five years old and I've never felt as good with anyone as I felt with you the other night when you made love to me . . ."

"That sounds like a line, Nick. An old, dumb, sappy line."

"It's not. That is, it may be a line, but it's certainly the first time I've ever used it. I like to think that I wouldn't use anything that sappy for a routine seduction. Would you at least kiss me here on the beach? My fantasies can take over from there if necessary."

Phila finally lifted her head and studied him cautiously. There was an urgent curiosity in her eyes as she searched his face. She was visibly torn by her own conflicting needs. She wanted him, he could tell. Even when she was doing her best to conceal the fact, it showed.

The knowledge made him feel great.

Nick dropped his handful of pebbles and touched the corner of her mouth.

"Kiss me, Phila. Please."

She hesitated, a dainty wild creature consumed by her own curiosity and a desire she did not yet know quite how to handle. Nick got even harder knowing he was the cause of her confusion. He vowed to himself he would satisfy both the curiosity and the sweet, hot desire.

"Are you laughing at me?" Phila demanded accusingly.

"No. You make me happy, Phila. Is that so terrible?" He traced the shape of her soft mouth. He felt the gathering excitement in her and knew she was practically his.

"Do I really make you happy?" she asked.

"Yeah." He smiled again, realizing how true that was. "Why does that surprise you?"

Her shoulder lifted in a small gesture of uncertainty. "I don't know." She looked down at the book in her lap. "I don't think of myself as a very sexy person, and I guess I just figured I'm not the type to turn a man on. The few times I've tried it things always went wrong."

Nick was fascinated by the tension in her. "What went wrong, Phila? You didn't find any satisfaction in it? Is that what you're trying to say? Don't worry about it. Some things just take practice."

She shook her head violently, not looking at him. "No, it's not that. I mean, what you just said is true, I don't . . . haven't ever experienced a . . . well, you know. But that's not the problem."

"What is the problem?"

"I get turned off as soon as some man starts pawing me," she said in a tight little voice. "It's hard to explain. I just get scared and I freeze. I can't stand to have some man on top of me, crushing me. That seems to be the way most men go at it."

"Probably because they're usually made to feel they're responsible for taking the initiative."

"Yes. I suppose so. And I didn't think to suggest reversing things. I just assumed I wasn't a very sensual person. But with you everything was different. You let me do what I wanted. I felt safe. I guess being in command like that, being on top is going to be the one way sex will work for me." She paused. "It was reassuring to know there's hope for me, if you want to know the truth."

"I'm glad," he said simply. "Why do you think you have the hang-up about the traditional missionary position?"

"It's probably because of something that happened to me when I was a teenager." She leaned her elbows on her knees and studied the sea.

"Tell me about it, Phila." His insides tightened. "Did some jerk force you?"

"He tried to rape me. He was the brother of a man who ran the foster home I was living in at the time. He used to visit a lot and help out around the place. He watched the girls all the time. I think he picked me because I was the most naive. I didn't like him; none of the girls did, but I didn't know how to handle him. He probably sensed that I was afraid of him and that's why he zeroed in on me."

"He attacked you?"

"He hung around the house until he found me alone one afternoon after school. He came into my room and started telling me how he was going to show me what women were made for. He said a lot of horrible things, mostly about how he knew that all the girls in the home were tramps and whores and how we'd all grow up to be prostitutes so I might as well get started learning my future profession." Phila shuddered. "I was so scared I was paralyzed with fear."

Nick touched her arm and she flinched. He started to withdraw his hand but changed his mind at the last minute. He let his fingers rest lightly on her skin and breathed a sigh of relief when she did not pull away. "You should have kicked the bastard in the balls."

"I know but at the time I was too frightened to try it. I was afraid I'd only make him more aggressive. I tried to get out of the room, instead. He let me get almost to the door and just when I thought I was safe, he grabbed me. He had just been playing with me, you see. He wanted me to try to escape. It made the game more fun for him."

"Oh, Phila."

"He caught me and threw me down on the bed. I kicked and scratched and struggled and he just kept crushing me into the bed. I thought I would go mad. I felt so helpless. He was so big and heavy. Like a mountain of meat. Whenever I think about it, that's the image that comes back to me; being crushed beneath a man. I can't stand the feeling."

Nick closed his eyes briefly. "What happened?"

"He had an arm across my throat and he was starting to tear off my clothes when Crissie came in."

Nick took a breath. "I should have known. Crissie Masters to the rescue again, hmmm? No wonder you're so devoted to her memory."

"She picked up a lamp that was on the bedside table and brought it down over his head," Phila said. "Crissie could always think fast in situations like that. I was safe, but then came the real problem."

Nick frowned. "What was that?"

"Explaining it to the foster parents and our caseworker. The man who ran the home claimed I must have led his brother on. The brother said that he hadn't done anything. He claimed he'd been fixing a light socket in the bedroom. He said Crissie and I set him up to make it look like attempted rape."

"Hell."

"There was no proof either way. But our caseworker was an old pro in the business, and she knew what had happened. She believed me. She pulled strings and called in a few favors and got me and Crissie and the other three kids out of the home within forty-eight hours. I think that was when I first considered social work as a career. I wanted to be able to rescue people the way she had rescued me and Crissie and the others."

That figured, Nick thought. Thus was a sweet little liberal do-gooder born. "I wish I knew where that jerk is now."

"The guy who attacked me? Why?" She gave him a puzzled look.

"Because I would like to tear him into small pieces."

Phila just stared at him. "You would? You don't even know him."

"Phila, I would want to tear anyone who hurt you into small pieces," Nick explained carefully. "Don't you understand?"

"No. I can see where you might feel that protective toward someone in your family, but I don't see why you should feel that way about me. You hardly know me."

"You know that's not a fair statement. You and I are getting to know each other very well."

"Is that right?" she challenged. "What do you really know about me?"

"For openers, I now understand why you like to be on top when we make love."

She flushed. "You make it sound as if we do it all the time."

"I'd like to."

"Forget it."

"Will you at least fulfill part of my beach fantasy?"

"What part?" she asked suspiciously.

He couldn't help himself. His mouth twitched in a smile he struggled manfully to conceal. "Just kiss me."

"If I do, will you stop pestering me about having an affair?"

"Just kiss me," he repeated softly, his fingers sliding up and down the length of her arm. "Please. You make me feel so damn good, honey."

For an instant he thought she was going to draw back. But just when he thought he'd miscalculated badly, she started leaning toward him, her arms going lightly around his neck. Nick exhaled in relief as her soft mouth brushed his.

"So sweet. You're so sweet." A shudder went through Nick.

Phila began to pull away but she made the mistake of dropping a small, warm kiss on his chin and after that she could not seem to resist running the tip of her tongue over his bottom lip.

Nick felt her tremble and knew everything was going to be all right. "Again, honey. You taste so good."

She crowded closer and her fingers began to clutch at him. "Nick," she whispered. "How do you do this to me?"

"I don't do anything to you, sweetheart. You do it all by yourself. I'm just lucky enough to get invited along for the ride."

"No, it's you. Something you do. I haven't figured it out yet, but I'm sure it's dangerous."

"No, Phila, it's not dangerous. Not as long as you're with me. You're safe with me. Remember that." He moved his hand soothingly down her back, tracking the sensual length of her spine. Her fragrance filled his head, triggering a flood of dazzling need throughout his body. He wasn't the only one who had to learn to slow down, he thought. Phila had the knack of catapulting him into a full state of arousal almost instantaneously.

She knelt in the coarse sand and began to nuzzle him hungrily, nipping at his earlobe, kissing his eyelashes. Nick groaned, leaned back against the warm rock and let her have her way with him.

Within a matter of minutes she had worked herself and him into a feverish state. He felt her fingers fumbling with the buttons of his shirt. He swore in frustration when she got everything tangled up, but he did not offer to help. He endured the sweet torture nobly until her palms at last flattened on his bare chest.

She found his lips again and drove her tongue boldly into his mouth, pressing herself against him. Nick gave himself up to the pure sensual joy of being a sex object until he realized that Phila, true to form, was once again charging full speed ahead. It wasn't going to happen that way this time. This time she would get it right.

"Slow down," he muttered into her ear.

She paid no attention. Her hands went to his belt buckle. She got it undone after several attempts and then she reached for his zipper.

"No," Nick said, although it nearly broke him. He gently caught her hand. "This time we're going to find out what you like."

"Please, Nick. I want to feel you again the way I did the other night. It was so good. I was so close."

"I know. The problem is you're rushing things."

She went still. "You don't like the way I do it? I thought you did."

He was exasperated by the uncertainty in her voice. "I go crazy and you know it. But as much as I like it, I think you need to give yourself more time." He guided her fingers to the snap of her jeans.

"More time?" She sounded confused. "But we must be doing it right. I've never felt like this with anyone else."

"Good." He kissed her forehead and then the tip of her nose and his hand rested on her thigh. "Now, if you'll just take it a little more slowly, you'll feel even better. Don't worry," he added, seeing the expression of concern on her face. "It's not going anywhere."

"You're laughing at me," she said with a resigned groan.

"Never." He urged her fingers to undo the snap of her jeans.

Slowly and then with increasing speed, she stripped off her jeans. Nick had to close his eyes and think of flag and country for a moment when he saw the dark triangle of hair showing through the sheer fabric of her panties. When he had control of himself again he opened his eyes and saw Phila watching him closely.

"Are you all right?" she asked. She paused in the act of unbuttoning her shirt.

Nick realized she was not wearing a bra. "If I were any better I'd go out of my mind."

She looked relieved and quickly finished undoing the

last buttons of her shirt. She let the ends of the garment hang free. The soft curves of her breasts were barely visible, half-hidden in tantalizing shadow. "Then can we do it now? Please? Before this feeling goes away?"

"The feeling isn't going away. I told you that. Just give yourself a chance to experience it."

"That's what I'm trying to do," she replied impatiently. She grabbed his zipper again.

"No, not yet. Here." He held out his hand.

She stared down at his palm, mystified. "What am I supposed to do with it?"

"Use it any way you want," he instructed softly. "Show me what you need and how you like it. Teach me how to touch you."

Her head came up so swiftly she nearly cracked his chin. "You want me to show you how to touch me? Don't you want to get inside me?"

"Eventually," he promised through his teeth. "We'll definitely get to that part eventually. But let's try a little foreplay first."

"Oh. Foreplay." She leaned against him, nibbling his throat. "Okay. Do it."

"No, sweetheart, you're going to do it. You're the teacher, remember?"

She was quiet for a moment, and Nick began to worry. Then she gripped his hand and pulled his fingers toward her breasts. She shivered as she moved his palm over her nipples, and Nick experienced a few shudders of his own as he felt her harden beneath his touch.

"Look at you," he whispered, awed by her response. "Hard as little pebbles. Just the right size for my hand."

Phila made a small sound of pleasure and pushed her breast more tightly into his cupped palm. Nick carefully caught the nipple between thumb and forefinger and tugged gently.

"*Nick.*"

"Feel good?"

"It feels strange." Eagerly she adjusted herself so that she was sitting on his lap. "Do the other one."

He obeyed, kissing the nape of her neck as he gently prodded her other nipple erect. She felt tight and full.

"I'm ready," she informed him, clutching at him. "Let's do it now."

"Not yet."

"Damn it, Nick . . ."

"You haven't taught me all I want to learn."

"Now what?" she demanded.

"I don't know. Show me."

She moved on his legs. He felt the lush curve of her bare thigh pushing against his trapped manhood and thought he'd lose it all inside his jeans. He counted stars and stripes for a minute until he'd regained a portion of his control.

"Nick, please, I feel so hot. I want to do it."

He let his fingers curl invitingly in her palm. When he made no further move Phila grabbed his hand and plunged it down between her legs.

"There. Do something," she ordered.

"Yes, ma'am."

Nick allowed his fingertips to trace light designs over the silky material of her underwear. The soft stuff quickly grew damp under his touch. He could feel her growing plump and soft.

"You get wet so fast for me, baby. Know what that does to me?"

"Do that again," Phila said, moving against his hand with sudden urgency.

"Do what again?"

"Touch me like that." She grabbed his hand, held him steady and then slid along the length of his finger. "Yes, like that. Harder. No, here." She edged aside the elastic leg band of her panties and maneuvered his hand inside.

Nick sucked in his breath almost painfully as the full impact of her moist, welcoming warmth nearly overwhelmed him. "Show me exactly how you want it."

Phila was beyond protesting the torment. She fumbled with his hand, getting him thoroughly wet in the process. Nick felt so tight and hot he had to grit his teeth to maintain any kind of control.

He started to search out the little bud of feminine sensation but held off until she finally managed to find it for him. She cried out when he stroked her, cried out and clung to him with all her might, her face buried against his chest.

Then she moved against his finger with a woman's instinct.

"Oh, Nick, that feels so good."

"I told you it wasn't going anywhere. Just relax and enjoy."

Some of the frantic quality seemed to evaporate from her. A sexy, dreamy expression crossed her vivid features. She began to guide him with more certainty. Her tiny little sounds of increasing pleasure were muffled against his chest.

Nick was rigid with his own desire but he refused to ruin everything at this point by losing control. Nothing was more important in that moment than having Phila learn her first taste of satisfaction at his hands.

She shifted position after a few minutes, kneeling astride him and leaning over him. Then she started to move more and more aggressively against his finger. Her head tipped back as the excitement flowed through her.

Nick allowed one finger to slip slowly inside her slick, tight channel. Phila's reaction was immediate. She went over the edge. She called out his name in a muffled shout. Her body went taut with sexual tension. Then she was convulsing gently around his fingers, clutching him fiercely.

For a long, wondrous moment she clung to him as her climax rippled through her. Nick knew he was more thrilled than she could ever be. He had never seen anything so glorious as Philadelphia Fox in the full flower of her womanly passion.

Slowly, slowly, she crumpled against him until she was sitting once more on his thighs. Her head rested against his chest and her whole body was filled with a gentle languor that was as sensual in its own way as her climax had been. Nick stroked her slowly, seeking the little aftershocks.

When his fingers drifted over the small button that was

the chief focus of her recent pleasure, she flinched and mumbled a soft protest.

"Sensitive?" he asked.

"Um hmmm." She didn't open her eyes.

He grinned but he did not relax. He was still iron hard with his own need. He wanted to bury himself in her but he was reluctant to break the magic spell.

"Nick?" Her voice was drowsy.

"Yeah?"

"That was incredible. I've never felt anything like it. Fantastic. Thank you."

"You're fantastic. And don't thank me. You did it all by yourself."

She moved her head in a small negative gesture against his shoulder. "No, it was you."

"Let's not argue about it." He opened his eyes and watched a gull soaring out over the sea. "The last thing I want to do right now is argue about anything."

"Okay." She shifted into a more comfortable position.

Chagrined, Nick realized she was about to go to sleep. "Phila?"

"Hmm?"

"You know that package I told you about? The one I bought at the pharmacy in town?"

Her eyes flew open. She looked up at him from under her lashes. "What about it?"

"Check my back pocket."

Shock filled her eyes. "Oh, Nick, I forgot about you. I'm so sorry. I didn't mean . . ."

"It's all right." He smiled heroically. "I understand. But now that you've remembered me do you suppose we might try it your way again?"

She giggled, reaching around behind him to withdraw the small package from his jeans pocket. She handed it to him. "Here you go."

He made no move to take the package from her hand. Instead, he looked at her. "You do it."

She blinked, a new gleam of interest in her eyes. "You want me to put it on you?"

"Apparently I'm a sucker for an aggressive, take-charge female."

A long while later Phila finally roused herself sufficiently to pay attention to her surroundings again. She was sitting across Nick's thighs and he had his eyes closed. He was still wearing his jeans but they were unfastened and unzipped. He looked wicked and sexy.

"Nick? We'd better get dressed. Anyone could come down here."

"Not likely. I checked before I came looking for you. Dad's gone into town with Tec, Eleanor's in her greenhouse and Hilary's working. Darren's having lunch with some of his local campaign staff. Vicky and Jordan have already been here and left. Trust me, we're safe."

"You're so thorough," she said, half in mockery and half in genuine respect for the care he'd taken. Leave it to Nick to orchestrate things behind the scenes so that nothing went wrong with a supposedly spontaneous sexual encounter. "You think you're so clever, don't you?"

Nick's eyes narrowed, but still glittered with amusement. "No, I just like things to work out the way I want them to work out. Which reminds me."

"About what?" She reached for her shirt which had somehow been abandoned, and slipped it on.

"We've done this twice now. That definitely takes our association out of the one-night-stand category."

She glanced at him out of the corner of her eye, wondering what he had up his sleeve now. "So?"

"So, I think it's time we agreed we're having an affair, don't you? Otherwise, what are we going to call this relationship of ours?"

Phila was feeling too pleasantly relaxed to argue. "Call it whatever you want," she said with an air of grand indifference.

"Fine. I'm calling it an affair. A full-time, monogamous, one-on-one affair."

Phila frowned in warning. "Just don't get the idea you can control me with sex."

"I wouldn't think of it."

"One of these days, Nick, I'm going to wipe that smug grin off your face."

"Why? You're the one who put it there in the first place."

Reed was at the wheel of the Mercedes with Tec Sherman sitting beside him as they drove back from town, when he spotted Nick and Phila. He saw the two figures in the distance as they came up the path from the cove and started toward the Gilmarten place. He knew from the casually possessive way his son's arm rested on Phila's shoulders that the pair had probably just made love down on the beach.

"That little gal's damn sure caught Nick's attention, hasn't she, sir?" Tec observed.

"That she has."

"Think it's serious?"

"I don't know. What do you think?" Reed knew Nick never did anything without a reason. That reason was not always fathomable to others, but it always existed. Had he truly fallen for little Miss Philadelphia Fox, or was he engineering some scheme to get back the shares?

"I don't know either, sir. Nick can be tough to figure out at times. But I'll tell you one thing. I've never seen him act like this around a female. It's like he's not real sure what to make of her, but he damn sure knows he can't let her out of his sight."

What game are you playing, Nick? Reed asked himself silently. "I know what you mean, Tec."

"Good havin' him back, ain't it, sir?"

Goddamn right. "About time he remembered he's got family."

The Mercedes came abreast of Nick and Phila a few moments later. Reed saw the faint flush in Phila's cheeks and the lazy, satiated look in his son's eyes. For a second he knew a flash of pure male envy. In the old days he and Nora had sneaked off to that cove a time or two and gone at it like a couple of mink.

"You two been for a walk on the beach?" Reed asked, slowing the car to a halt.

"Yeah." Nick put one hand on the frame of the windshield and leaned down. "Tec, I want to do some shooting with Phila this week."

"Sure thing, sir. Got a preference?"

"A .38, I think. Some nitwit sold her a spiffy little 9-mm automatic even though she's never used a handgun in her life. She's never even fired the damn thing."

"An automatic? Bad choice. Too complicated for a beginner," Tec said. "Unless she wants to put in a lot of work gettin' used to it."

"I think we can safely assume she's not going to become a handgun enthusiast. But I want her to be able to use something, so I think we'll educate her with a revolver."

"No problem."

"Wait a second," Phila interrupted. "I don't recall saying I wanted to practice shooting a gun."

Reed frowned at her. "Nick's right. An automatic is a poor choice for a novice. Too fancy. Takes practice to master. A revolver is simpler and easier to use in an emergency. Just point it and pull the trigger."

"But I . . ."

Reed turned to his son. "Make it the morning after tomorrow, and I'll join you. I've got a game tomorrow or I'd say make it then."

Nick stepped back from the car. "All right," he said. "We'll make it the day after tomorrow."

"Don't forget Eleanor's dinner party tomorrow night," Reed added as he put his foot down on the accelerator.

Ten minutes later Reed walked into the house and went in search of Hilary. He found her in the study that had once been his personal domain. As he walked into the room he realized that through the wide windows a person could see a portion of the cliff road. He wondered if Hilary had been watching Nick and Phila return from the beach.

"Hello, Reed." Hilary looked up from the file she was examining. She leaned back in her chair and smiled politely. "Did you want something?"

"Just wanted to let you know I've got a game at three o'clock."

"All right. I'll tell the housekeeper to plan dinner accordingly. Will Nick be eating with us tonight?"

"No, I don't think so." Reed looked at the beautiful, perfectly groomed woman who was his wife. Every hair was in place. Her makeup was flawless. She was the picture of elegant femininity.

Then he thought about Phila looking tousled and flushed, slightly embarrassed and happy. He could not imagine Hilary ever looking that way. He was pretty sure Nick wouldn't be able to imagine her looking that way, either.

His son had definitely missed out on something important during his disastrous marriage, something he appeared to be finding with Phila Fox.

169

CHAPTER TEN

Eleanor presided over dinner the following evening with the elegant ease of one who has spent a lifetime cultivating the fine art of formal entertaining.

Phila eyed the array of cutlery and glassware in front of her and felt like a guerrilla heading into combat. She would not screw up, she vowed silently. She was a well-educated human being who, although she had not been raised amid upper-class surroundings, had learned somewhere along the line how to tell a seafood fork from a salad fork. *She would not screw up*.

She was not about to let Eleanor intimidate her, especially since she had a sneaking suspicion that that had been the purpose of the dinner party. Eleanor sat at the far end of the impossibly long table smiling vaguely out over a sea of Wedgwood creamware, Sheffield silver plate and Waterford crystal, and Phila just knew what she was thinking. Eleanor was taking the opportunity to demonstrate how out of place Crissie had been here and, by extension, how out of place Phila herself was.

Phila was very glad that Crissie had told her about the Wedgwood and the Sheffield and the Waterford. It made it easier to act casually when the stuff was plunked down in front of her. *I just pretend it's all plastic*, Crissie had said.

"I understand you're a social worker, dear," Eleanor said as she delicately separated a slice of fish from the halibut steak on her plate. "How did you meet Crissie?"

"I met her when I was sent to a foster home after my grandmother died."

"Your grandmother? Then you weren't an abandoned child?"

"You mean like Crissie?" Phila smiled brilliantly as she saw Eleanor's eyes flicker. "No, I was far more fortunate. My parents cared about me, but they were both killed when I was very young. My father's mother took me in and raised me until I was thirteen."

Reed looked up from his fish, his expression curious. "How did your folks die?"

"In a helicopter crash in South America. The 'copter was shot down."

"Shot down! What in blue blazes were they doing in South America?" Reed demanded, ignoring Eleanor's frown over the harsh language.

"They were involved in helping Indians who were being systematically hunted and shot by their own government. The local government always claimed it was Communist rebels who shot down the 'copter, but everyone knew it was the government's own forces that did it. It was an open secret."

Nick's eyes narrowed. "Did your parents do that kind of thing routinely?"

"You mean helping people like those Indians?" Phila picked up her water glass, aware of the diamond shapes of the cut crystal beneath her fingertips. "Oh, yes. They were devoted to doing what they could to help those less fortunate than themselves. They traveled all over the world on behalf of an organization called Freedom for the Future Foundation. Have you heard of it?"

Reed groaned aloud, and Nick's brows rose in amusement. Darren shook his head, and Victoria sighed. Hilary winced, and Eleanor made a tut-tutting sound and quickly passed a plate of asparagus.

Phila was pleased with the reaction. "Ah hah. You *have* heard of it."

"A troublemaking, anarchistic, radical left-wing fringe group that's always sticking its nose in where it doesn't belong," Reed declared, stabbing at his asparagus. "Financed by a bunch of hypocritical do-gooders who don't have the sense to know they're nothing but Communist dupes."

"Are you calling my parents hypocritical Communist dupes?" Phila asked very softly, more than ready for battle on this front.

Reed finally noticed the look in her eyes and muttered something under his breath. "I'm sorry about what happened to your folks, but you can't expect me to condone an outfit like that goddamned Freedom for the Future Foundation. They're all a bunch of wild-eyed crazies, and everyone with an ounce of common sense knows it."

"I don't expect you to condone the foundation. That would be asking too much, given your ridiculously narrow-minded views, but I do expect you to show some respect for my parents. They died working for something they believed in, and I would think even a Lightfoot could appreciate that."

"I'm sure Reed didn't mean to be unkind," Hilary said in a soothing tone.

"Of course he didn't," Eleanor confirmed. "Have some more asparagus, dear. Washington grown. It's excellent this time of year."

Darren regarded Phila thoughtfully. "Did you travel with your parents when you were a child?"

"No, I stayed behind with Grandmother. The places my parents had to go on behalf of the foundation were usually dangerous."

"I'm sure your parents meant well," Nick said seriously. "But as far as I'm concerned, they had no business risking their necks all over the world when they had a daughter to raise. You should have been their first priority."

Phila, who had often harbored similar disloyal thoughts in moments of great loneliness, began to get really angry.

"They had a right to follow their consciences. If no one did, this world would be a much worse place to live in than it already is."

"I agree with Nick," Darren said unexpectedly. "Once you were born, your parents had an obligation to think of your future. Their first duty was to protect you, not a bunch of strangers."

Victoria nodded, her dark eyes shadowed. "I think it's very sad that you were left alone in the world because your parents were out trying to save other people."

"You're all speaking so piously on the subject because you don't happen to approve of the work my parents were doing. I'm sure if I'd said my father was in the armed forces and had got sent into dangerous trouble spots all over the world on behalf of the good old U.S. of A., you'd say it was his duty to go."

Reed scowled. "That's a different matter entirely."

"Talk about hypocritical reasoning." Phila smiled triumphantly and pointed her fork straight down the table at Reed. The asparagus stalk on the end of the fork wavered in the air. "Your logic is totally messed up. My parents were doing what they saw as their duty. Just as if they were in the military."

"There is one important difference," Nick pointed out. "If your father had been in the military, chances are your mother would have been at home with you. You wouldn't have lost both parents."

"Now you're saying that women shouldn't be allowed to serve in the military? I suppose you're one of those chauvinists who doesn't think women should serve in combat positions?" Phila made this point so emphatically that the piece of asparagus fell off the tines of her fork.

Phila glanced down at the green spear lying on the priceless antique lace and did the only thing she could think of to do. She snatched the stalk up off the tablecloth and popped it into her mouth. When she caught Nick's eye, she saw he was laughing silently at her. It was the same kind of laughter she saw in his eyes when she made love with him.

"I see no reason to put women into combat." Nick sank

his strong white teeth into a large chunk of crusty sour-dough bread. "They're not cut out for it."

"If you feel that way, I'm surprised you're so gung-ho about teaching me how to use a gun."

"I have nothing against a woman being able to take care of herself," Nick retorted.

Darren nodded soberly. "I taught Vicky to use a revolver a few years back. It's just common sense."

"Nick is an excellent teacher," Hilary murmured from the far end of the table. "He taught me how to use a gun the year we got married."

A lot of the wind went out of Phila's sails at that point. The thought of Nick teaching Hilary anything was depressing. Hilary's simple remark had the effect of forcibly reminding Phila that the other woman had once shared the most intimate of relationships with Nick. When she glanced across the table she saw that Nick's expression had reverted to a hard, shuttered look. That irritated her.

She considered launching into a lecture on the evils of handguns but then remembered she was hardly in a position to make a fuss on the subject. But she couldn't resist one small comment, if only for the sake of form.

"If we had better gun-control legislation in this country, none of us would have to worry about learning how to use a gun for protection. There wouldn't be so many weapons floating around in the hands of criminals."

"The world is a dangerous place," Eleanor said serenely. "One must do what is necessary." When everyone turned to glance at her she quickly summoned up her distracted smile. She looked down the length of the table at Reed. "By the way, I wanted to remind everyone about Darren's fund-raiser in Seattle at the end of the month. Not long now, hmmm? I'm sure we'll get a substantial turnout. Just the sort of thing we need to kick off the gubernatorial campaign." She turned to look at Nick. "I do hope everyone will be there? So important to show a united family front, don't you think?"

There was a soft stillness around the table before Hilary said briskly, "I'm sure that whoever needs to be there will be there, Eleanor. We all want to see Darren's campaign get off to a strong start. Isn't that right, Reed?"

"Sure." Reed did not look terribly interested, one way or the other.

Victoria looked anxiously at Nick. "What do you think about Darren's chances of being governor, Nick?"

"I think," said Nick, picking up his wineglass, "that the Castletons and Lightfoots are businessmen, not politicians."

There was a stark silence following that remark. Darren broke it with an easy smile. "I think you're definitely a businessman, Nick. And, to be truthful, a much better one than I am. But I think I can make a contribution in the realm of politics. I do have some ideas and some skills that can be useful in governing this state. Washington is one of the last frontiers and at the rate it's being discovered, we need to start managing our resources well. If we don't, we'll lose them the way California did."

"It takes money to run for office," Nick pointed out. "A lot of it."

Darren nodded, meeting Nick's eyes squarely. "No one makes it into public office these days without the backing of family money. Everyone knows that."

"That's certainly true," Phila interjected spiritedly. "Certainly makes politics a game for the wealthy upper classes, doesn't it? Not much chance for another Abe Lincoln these days."

Reed glowered at her. "If a man can't prove he can make a success of his own life, I don't want him running the country. How's he going to keep the economy strong if he doesn't even have any talent for managing his own finances?"

"Oh, for heaven's sake . . ." Phila began. But before she could continue, she realized that Nick and Darren were still contemplating each other very thoughtfully.

"In your case, Darren," Nick murmured, ignoring Phila, "it wouldn't just be Castleton family money involved, would it? It would be C&L money."

"Yes," Darren agreed. "It would, wouldn't it? I prefer to

think of it as an investment in our future as well as the state's future. Castletons and Lightfoots have a major stake in Washington and the Northwest. Our destinies are linked."

"C&L will survive, regardless of what happens politically in this state," Nick stated.

Before Darren could argue, Victoria made a frantic stab at redirecting the conversation. "Well, I understand we're giving the townspeople a lot to talk about this summer," she observed with false brightness.

"People will always talk," Darren said with a shrug.

"You can't blame them for being curious under the circumstances," Victoria persisted, sliding a sidelong glance at Phila.

Phila smiled back benignly. "The least you can do is give the good people of Port Claxton something to talk about, since you've apparently cut off the scholarship money and most of the contributions to local charities and civic-improvement projects."

Everyone at the table turned to stare at her in astonishment.

"I believe we're ready for dessert," Eleanor announced quickly. "I'll ring for Mrs. Atkins." She picked up the silver bell beside her fork.

Bowls of fresh raspberries and cream arrived within minutes. In the subdued flurry of clearing dishes and serving dessert, Phila thought her last conversational gambit had been quashed. But she was wrong.

"What did you mean about cutting off scholarship and charity money?" Darren asked with a frown as Mrs. Atkins disappeared into the kitchen.

Phila swallowed a raspberry. "I recently had a very interesting chat with a nice young man who works in one of the grocery stores in town."

"The Wilson kid," Nick put in dryly, his eyes on Phila.

"He was complaining about a lack of charity handouts from us?" Hilary demanded.

Eleanor shook her head sadly. "People expect so much

these days. There was a time when everyone had enough pride and gumption to stand on his own two feet."

"You misunderstand," Phila said smoothly. "He wasn't complaining. In fact, he admires you all tremendously. He even intends to vote for Darren, if he gets the chance. He merely commented on the fact that the Castletons and Lightfoots didn't seem to be taking as much of an interest in the town as they once did. I'm the one who's complaining about it."

"What the hell have you got to complain about?" Reed demanded.

"Reed, please," Eleanor said reprovingly.

"I think it's disgusting that people with as much money as you folks have don't pour a little of it back into the community," Phila declared.

"We pour a shitload of it into a whole bunch of causes and organizations," Reed retorted furiously. "Don't let anyone tell you otherwise."

"Really, Reed. Your language." Eleanor frowned at him.

"If you're talking about contributions to a lot of stupid ultraconservative lobbies and the campaigns of right-wing politicians, I've got news for you," Phila said. "They don't count. Helping people is what counts." She aimed her fork at Reed again. This time there was a raspberry on the end of it. "Scholarships for local kids who couldn't go on to college otherwise count. Books for libraries count. Educational-assistance programs for disadvantaged youngsters count. Food and housing programs for the homeless count."

"Jesus H. Christ," Reed exclaimed in exasperation. "She sounds like Nora. Nora was always having us give money to every fast-talking sharpie who showed up at the front gate with a sob story."

"That's an exaggeration, Dad, and you know it." Nick interrupted calmly. "Mom investigated each cause carefully. She only had us give to the ones she'd personally checked out."

"You know what they say about money," Phila murmured. "It's like manure. It doesn't do any good unless you spread it around."

Nick studied the fork she was waving in the air. "Phila, are you going to eat that raspberry or throw it at one of us?"

Phila blinked. "I don't know. It's a toss-up." But she redirected the fork toward her mouth and bit into the fruit. She glared across the table at Darren. "I suppose you're going to be one of those wrongheaded, right-wing, ultraconservative Republican candidates?"

Darren grinned slowly, displaying the kind of charm that would undoubtedly carry him a long way on the campaign trail. "If I am, you can bet I'm not going to admit it here and now. I may be a Republican, but I'm not totally stupid."

Phila blinked again and then burst out laughing. Darren joined her. After a second's hesitation, Reed started to chuckle. The chuckle turned into a roar of laughter that filled the room.

When Phila glanced at Nick, she saw that he was smiling to himself, looking quietly pleased.

Eleanor rang for the cheese tray.

Much later that night Phila lay sprawled on Nick's chest, her chin resting on her folded arms. She was feeling delicious and powerful and happy, having just finished duplicating the marvelous sensation she had experienced earlier that day on the beach. Nick threaded his fingers through her hair, his eyes gleaming in the shadows. His skin still glistened with the sweat of their recent lovemaking.

"Did you have fun showing off tonight at the dinner table, foxy lady?" he asked.

"Was I showing off?" She toyed with a lock of his crisp, curling chest hair. "I thought I was just participating in the conversation as required by proper etiquette."

"You had Dad and Darren eating out of the palm of your hand by the end of the evening."

"I think they just like to argue. They get off on it."

"They certainly enjoyed arguing with you."

"Hilary and Vicky and Eleanor weren't so excited about it." Phila squirmed slightly, seeking a more comfortable position.

"They're not sure what to make of you yet. You're a threat. I think they understand that better than Dad and Darren."

Phila frowned. "I'm not a threat."

"Depends on your point of view. Stop wriggling like that. You're going to get me hard again and I'm too old to recuperate that fast. Right now I want to talk."

Phila grinned, thoroughly delighted that she could make him react to her so quickly. "What do you want to talk about?"

"I have to go down to California for a couple of days."

"California." Phila stopped grinning. "Why?"

"I've got a business to run in Santa Barbara, remember? I've left a good man in charge, but there are some things only the boss can handle. I won't be gone long."

"Oh." It was funny how fast you could get used to having someone around, Phila thought bleakly. The little beach house was going to seem quite lonely without Nick.

"You sound disappointed," Nick said.

"Don't look so thrilled with yourself."

"Going to miss me?"

"Yes," Phila admitted starkly.

"Good. Now you can start wriggling again."

"She's a lot different from Crissie Masters, isn't she?" Darren observed as he came out of the bathroom. He was wearing only the bottom half of a pair of black silk pajamas. "Remember how Crissie used to raise everyone's hackles?"

"I remember." Victoria lay back against the pillows and studied her husband. "But I think Phila's a lot more dangerous than Crissie was."

"Why the hell do you say that?" Darren turned off the light and climbed into bed beside Victoria. He did not reach for her. Instead he folded his arms behind his head and stared up at the ceiling.

"It was easy to tell what Crissie was after. She wanted to cause trouble, to punish this family for abandoning her all those years ago. She wanted to make certain we all paid for what she had been through. Remember how she taunted all of us every chance she got? But I can't tell what Phila wants."

"I don't know what Phila wants, either, but I'll tell you one thing: Nick wants her. Bad."

"You mean he wants those shares. Nick's up to something," Victoria said quietly. "Eleanor thinks he'll get those shares back for us, but I wonder. Do you think he'd have the gall to seduce Phila into giving those shares to him instead of convincing her to give them back to you?"

"Nick's never been short of nerve."

Victoria was horrified. "For God's sake, Darren, we can't let him do that. Those are *Castleton* shares. They belong to us, and Nick knows that. Eleanor only called on him for help because she trusted him to do the right thing. She trusted him to get the shares back for *us*."

"Even if he were planning to have Phila turn the shares over to him instead of us, you're assuming he can get her to do it. You can't be sure he can manage that. Phila strikes me as a woman who has a mind of her own."

"Why else would he be sleeping with her unless he was seducing her into handing over the shares?" Victoria was impatient with Darren's lack of common sense. "Phila is not his type at all."

"You think Hilary is more his type?" Darren inquired.

"In a way, yes. Oh, maybe temperamentally they're not perfectly suited and God knows I'll never be fond of the woman, but you have to admit she's got breeding and background and poise and all the things Nick should have in a wife. You wouldn't catch Hilary dropping a stalk of asparagus on the dining table in the middle of an argument."

Darren grinned in the darkness. "No, probably not."

"Darren," Victoria said after a moment's thought, "if Nick did get those shares from Phila and if he used them together with the ones he inherited from his mother and his own block, would he have enough to take control of the company away from Hilary?"

Darren hesitated. "He'd need another large block."

"Reed's?"

"That would do it. Or mine together with yours."

"Nick will never get his hands on Reed's block," Victoria said with certainty. "Reed would never back him in a move to unseat Hilary. Not after what he thinks Nick did to her three years ago."

"What he thinks Nick did? You mean you don't believe the baby was Nick's?"

Victoria bit her lip, wishing she had not spoken. "Never mind. It doesn't matter now what happened. No point dredging up old news. It's the future we've got to think about. I'm worried, Darren. Your political chances depend on having the families back you both financially and by freeing you to run for office. Hilary's willing to do that on the Lightfoot side. Eleanor says we need her support."

"I know."

"You heard Nick tonight. He has the same attitude toward your going into politics that he had three years ago."

"I realize that."

"If you're going to make a successful run for governor, you've got to have the backing of C&L's chief executive officer. No, as much as I hate to admit it, Eleanor's right when she says we need Hilary in charge of the Lightfoot side of Castleton & Lightfoot. We have to support her."

"You're always so clear sighted and rational when we discuss my political future, Vicky. Sometimes I get the feeling my future is more important to you than it is to me."

Victoria caught her breath. "That's a terrible thing to say."

"Tell me something. I've always wondered how much my father offered you to stay with me three years ago when you were getting ready to file for divorce."

Victoria closed her eyes in silent anguish. They had been through this before. Twice. Once in the beginning and later when Crissie Masters had dredged it all back up again. "He didn't pay me a dime. I told you that three years ago and I told you that last year when Crissie found out about it from Burke and taunted you about it."

"Oh, come off it. You had an appointment with a lawyer three years ago. Something changed your mind. Dad always claimed he bought your loyalty. I figured he must have promised you a lot to compensate you for the trouble of being a politician's wife and your role as mother of his grandson. He had no intention of letting you walk off with Jordan. Dad must have made it worth your while."

"Stop it, Darren. I stayed because I wanted to be with you. I've told you that. Didn't I grovel enough the day I told you I wasn't going to get a divorce?"

"I just want to know what Dad promised you. A fortune in his will?"

"If he did, then the joke's on me," Victoria said bitterly. "Because he didn't leave anything extra to me, did he?"

"Maybe Crissie got what he had planned to leave to you. Crissie threw everyone's plans into the wringer."

"And Burke loved it. He loved watching her effect on all of us."

Darren exhaled heavily. "Nothing's been the same since she arrived last year."

"It wasn't Crissie who started changing things for all of us," Victoria muttered. "The real changes began three years ago when Nick left."

"Let's drop it. I'm sorry I brought up the subject."

"Not nearly as sorry as I am."

Darren sighed. "You know," he said softly, "when Reed laughed at Phila tonight, I realized it was the first time he's really laughed during the past three years."

"I know. God, I wish we knew what Nick was up to. Maybe Eleanor was wrong to bring him into this situation."

"She should have thought about the possible consequences before she called him."

"One's thing's for certain. We can't let Nick take control from Hilary," Victoria declared.

"It could complicate things. On the other hand . . ."

"No." Victoria stared at the ceiling. "It will ruin everything. Eleanor says we need Hilary at the helm while your career is getting started. Maybe sometime in the future Nick can come back, but not yet."

"The trouble with Nick is that he tends to make his own decisions in his own time and he doesn't always bother to inform everyone else until it's too late to stop him."

Eleanor sipped her late-night glass of sherry and stared out into the darkness. Too late she was beginning to wonder if she had made a serious mistake in bringing Nick back into the picture. She had realized as she watched him at dinner tonight that she was no longer certain she could depend on him to do exactly what she had wanted him to do.

She had pleaded with him to get the shares back from the little nobody to whom Crissie had left them, and Eleanor did not doubt that Nick would do exactly that. He would get them back. After all, he was family and he could work magic when it came to business. He had more of a talent for it than either his father or Reed or Darren.

But she was old enough now to know that magic never came cheap. What would this magician take as a fee for getting the shares out of Philadelphia Fox's hands? Perhaps, Eleanor, thought, the Castletons would lose them altogether. Perhaps Nick would get those shares for himself and use them.

She tried to imagine what he would do with them, and every option led back to one crucial point: Nick would have to get rid of Hilary if he came back to stay. The two of them could not coexist for long. The tensions between them were too violent.

But Nick would need more than the shares Phila now held if he wanted to wrest back control of the firm.

Eleanor knew she had to face the fact that if Nick succeeded in regaining control of C&L from Hilary, Darren's chances for a successful start in politics were going to be dimmed severely. Nick showed no indications of being enthusiastic about a gubernatorial campaign for Darren, and it would take combined family money to win an election. Money and the freedom to campaign actively.

Nothing must get in Darren's way.

"He's more of a man than you ever were, Burke, even though you could never admit it. But that's probably one of the reasons you were always so hard on him, always baiting him. You saw him as competition, didn't you? One of these days he'll have more power than you ever dreamed of having. He's going to be the next governor of this state."

Eleanor turned away from the window and gazed around the Federal-style bedroom with its fine old dressing table, high-post bedstead, and dimity hangings. She was so much happier here in this room these days. She had moved all Burke's things out, claiming it saddened her to be reminded of him. Everyone had accepted that explanation without questioning it.

But the truth was, she had experienced an enormous sense of relief the day Burke died. She had felt freed at last.

She was far from free, however. She knew that now. None of them was free.

"Did you plan it this way, Burke? You'd be happy if you knew that we're all still paying for your cruel games. I should have known you'd find a way to reach beyond the grave to hurt us."

She could envision him laughing as he watched those he had left behind struggle with the results of the disasters he had set in motion. Some people were destined to go through life wrecking the happiness of others. Burke Castleton had been an expert at doing exactly that, and his bastard daughter had inherited his talent.

But Darren was different. Darren was her son. He had inherited his father's looks and charm but not his callousness.

Eleanor's fingers tightened around the sherry glass. She

refused to contemplate failure. She would not let her dead husband ruin her son's future.

"Did you enjoy the evening, Reed?" Hilary asked casually as she climbed the stairs ahead of her husband.

"Sure. Eleanor always puts on a good feed. If she weren't so hung up on proper wineglasses and forks we'd probably all enjoy ourselves more, but what the hell. The halibut was good." He tugged at his tie, amazed at how automatically he concealed his true feelings from Hilary these days. It was almost instinctive.

"Phila is an amusing character at times, isn't she?"

"She'll give Nick a run for his money, that's for sure."

"Did she really remind you of Nora?"

Reed wondered where all this was leading. He grew even more cautious. "Just once with that little lecture on charitable contributions. Nora was always after the rest of us to spread the money around a little. She used to quote the same bit about it being like manure, as I recall."

"You know most charities are scams," Hilary said as she rounded the corner at the top of the stairs. "One has to be so careful. Much more effective to donate money to the conservative organizations and politicians who are working to keep the country on the right path. In the long run, everyone benefits that way, rich and poor alike."

"Goddamn right."

"Nick certainly seems taken with Phila."

"You can never tell with Nick," Reed heard himself say carefully.

"I know." Hilary walked into her room. "We all learned that the hard way three years ago, didn't we? Good night, Reed." She smiled wistfully before she closed the door.

Reed stood staring at the closed door for a long moment before moving slowly off down the hall to his bedroom. He walked inside and shut his own door. His gaze caught on the carved maple bed. He tried to visualize Hilary in that bed, her beautiful red hair cascading around her breasts, her fine body stretched out languorously beneath the sheets.

It was impossible. No matter how hard he worked at it, he could not summon up an image of Hilary in his bed. Nora was the only woman who had looked at home there.

In spite of everything, Reed realized he was glad that Nick was finding some happiness and satisfaction with Philadelphia Fox. Nora would have wanted her son to be happy.

CHAPTER ELEVEN

The revolver roared, the noise penetrating even the thick headgear Phila wore over her ears. The heavy gun jumped in her hand, and she struggled to bring it back in line with the target.

"Take it easy, Phila."

"What?" Phila shouted in return, squinting at the paper target in the distance to try and see if she had come remotely close.

"You're doing everything too fast. Slow down. This isn't a quick-draw contest."

"What?"

"I said," Nick repeated, lifting the muff-shaped headgear away from her ears, "this isn't a quick-draw contest. You want the whole operation to be smooth and easy. Try doing it in slow motion."

"I don't think I like this gun."

"You don't like guns, in general, so you're hardly a good judge."

"Why can't I practice with my own gun?"

"Because for someone who doesn't really like guns, someone like you who won't ever want to practice, a revolver is a much better option than an automatic. I've already explained that. You'd have to fire hundreds of rounds with your 9-mm to break it in and to get yourself familiar with it. Somehow I don't see you being willing to do that."

"This thing's hard to load."

"Stop bitching. You'll get used to it. Even if it is a little more awkward to load, a revolver is a lot less complicated to use. For your purposes you want something simple and direct, not fancy. Trust me, Phila, you're better off with a .38 than your 9-mm."

"This sucker's heavy. My arm's getting tired, and my hand is sore from pulling the trigger so many times."

Nick gave her an exasperated look. "You've been complaining since we got here this morning. Close your mouth and reload your gun, lady."

"You're getting impatient with me, Nick." She fumbled with the ammunition, feeling like some desperado in an old-time western movie. "You'll make me nervous if you start yelling."

"It was your idea to carry a gun. I'll be damned if I'll have you running around with something you can't handle. If you're going to keep a gun beside your bed, you're sure as hell going to know how to use it. That's final."

"You're starting to raise your voice, Nick."

"That's not all I'm going to do if you don't start paying attention. All right, step up to the firing line and for God's sake, try to remember what I just told you. Easy does it."

"Must be something about guns that brings out the macho in men, huh? Is that why you're talking so tough this morning?"

"Another five minutes and I won't be talking tough. I will be acting tough. Be interesting to see if that approach works any better." Nick shoved the muffs back down over her ears.

Phila groaned, took her stance and brought the revolver up with what she thought was a smooth, sweeping motion. She snapped off two shots in the general direction of the target and lowered the gun.

"Not bad," Tec said loudly behind her. "She's got a tendency to pull to the right and she's still trying to get the shot off too fast, but she's starting to hit the paper."

Phila removed the muffs and smiled loftily. "Why thank you, General Sherman. So kind of you to pass along some encouraging words to the troops. If I paid too much attention to Nick, I'd get very depressed. He hasn't said one nice thing to me all morning."

"Nick," said Nick, "is taking this seriously and you'd better do the same, Phila. Try it again."

Phila ignored him for a moment, eyeing Tec's orange-and-pink aloha shirt with some envy. "Nice shirt, General."

Tec beamed. "Thought you might like it."

"Get your little ass over to the firing line, Phila," ordered Nick, "or I will drag it over there, myself."

"Sheesh. What a way to spend a perfectly good morning." Phila grumbled and went through the motions once more. She didn't hear the Mercedes arrive but when she finished firing several more rounds and glanced around for approval, she saw that Reed had driven down from the house to join them at the outdoor firing range.

"She's rushing it," Reed announced as he strolled over to the small group near the firing line. "Just like she rushes her backswing."

"I know." Nick handed Phila more ammunition. "I'm working on the problem."

"I don't need any more of an audience," Phila said, annoyed. "It's hard enough doing this with Nick and Tec glaring at me."

"Why *are* you doing it, Phila?" Reed asked in a conversational tone as he picked up a .357 Magnum Tec had brought along. "It's fairly obvious you don't think much of handguns and you don't seem to approve of individuals owning them. Why are you so goddamned bent on carrying one?"

"I have my reasons," Phila muttered, not wanting to go into the whole story for the benefit of Reed and Tec.

"She had some trouble a while back with one of the operators of a foster home," Nick explained as he unpacked more ammunition. "The guy jumped her with a gun, roughed her up a bit and landed in jail. He made some threats about what he was going to do when he got out."

"Holy shit," said Tec, looking both reverent and awed. "Were you hurt?"

"No, just shaken up. The police arrived in the nick of time." Phila concentrated on the targets in the distance.

Reed frowned at Phila. "But the creep threatened to come after you when he got out of prison?"

"I know it sounds melodramatic," Phila said, examining the heavy weapon in her hand, "but the fact is, I'm scared of Elijah Spalding."

Reed looked at Nick over Phila's head. "Have you checked into this?"

"Not yet," Nick said. "But I intend to. All right, Phila, try it again and this time make it very slow and very smooth, understand?"

She stared at him, alarmed. "What do you mean, you're going to check into it? What's to check into?"

"Never mind. Stop arguing and for once in your life try following orders."

"I never follow orders if I can help it," Phila announced with fine hauteur.

"You'll learn," Nick replied, unconcerned.

"Who knows?" Tec added. "You might even get used to it."

"Not a chance," Phila retorted. "Antiauthoritarian, ultra-liberal, anarchistic tendencies are bred in my bones. Just ask Reed here."

"With all three of us yelling at her," Reed said equably, "she'll learn to follow a few orders."

"Make that four," Darren drawled as he strolled up to join the crowd.

Phila surveyed the small circle of determined male faces and knew she was outnumbered. Feeling mutinous but temporarily subdued, she turned back toward the target.

It was an odd sensation to have all these people hovering over her, concerned with making certain she got this gun business right, she reflected as she lifted the .38.

It had been a very long time since anyone had worried

about her personal safety and even longer since anyone had felt obliged to ensure it by teaching her how to take care of herself.

It made no sense, but for the first time since Crissie's death Phila didn't feel quite so alone in the world.

Nick arrived in Seattle at four o'clock that afternoon. The trip was another calculated risk, he acknowledged as he parked his Porsche in one of the company lots. But this whole project was dependent on a series of such risks. He had to keep things teetering on the brink until he was ready to send a few of them over the edge.

He turned off the engine and sat for a moment behind the wheel, examining the jumble of plain two- and three-story buildings that comprised the headquarters of Castleton & Lightfoot, Inc.

The company had grown in rapid spurts during the early years. Reed and Burke had paid scant attention to such niceties as coordinated office and manufacturing plant design. Business was booming and they'd had no time for frills.

They had acquired building space in the south end of Seattle and as needed erected the cheapest, most efficient structures they could find. The parking lots were scattered willy-nilly around the buildings. At some point in the distant past someone had planted a few scraggly bushes near the doorways in a futile attempt to soften the no-nonsense surroundings.

There was nothing about the Castleton & Lightfoot headquarters that would win any industrial-design awards, but that wasn't nearly as important to the work force as the fact that there had never been any layoffs in the entire history of the company. Jobs had been steady, even during the worst periods of the notoriously cyclical aerospace boom-and-bust industry.

The company had managed to tread water during the bad times and bounce back as strong as ever when the economy picked up again. Avoiding mass layoffs was just another Castleton & Lightfoot tradition.

There was no denying that C&L had done phenomenally well during the initial growth period when Reed and Burke had been at the helm. But for the past several years things had become comfortably staid as far as Nick was concerned. The company was set in its ways; it no longer responded quickly to the promise of new markets. Competitors nipped at its heels. When Nick had been given the CEO mandate, he'd immediately started making some changes.

He had contracted several relationships with new suppliers whose operations were more modern than some of the older companies C&L had always used. He had begun to expand the overseas markets, with a special emphasis on Pacific Rim countries. And he had started to expand product development so that it would be less necessary for C&L to depend on government contracts.

That was the area where he had found himself going toe-to-toe with both his father and Burke Castleton. They liked doing business the old-fashioned way, which meant the government way.

Nick felt strongly that sophisticated electronics and instrumentation had as many uses in industry·and the home as they did in military hardware. To Reed and Burke the nongovernment market niches were afterthoughts, nothing more than casual sidelines in which Castleton & Lightfoot occasionally dabbled.

But Nick had seen the future of the company in those niches and had focused an increasing amount of Castleton & Lightfoot resources toward developing them. Darren had been receptive to the new ideas, but Nick had been forced to fight his father and Burke Castleton all the way.

It occurred to Nick as he parked the Porsche that if he'd had Phila on his side in those days when he'd been battling his father and Burke, he would probably have won the war.

He smiled briefly as he got out of the Porsche. It was obvious that once Phila gave her friendship or her love, she was fiercely loyal. She would have backed her husband to the hilt, unlike Hilary who had undermined Nick's position every chance she got. Nick had made few mistakes in his life, but he readily admitted that marrying Hilary had been a costly one.

He walked across the wide parking lot, cutting between rows of cars until he was on the sidewalk that led to the building that housed the corporate offices. He pushed open the glass doors and looked around with a sensation of possessiveness he could never quite suppress. It had been three years since he had walked into this lobby, but the feeling that he had a right to be here, that this was where he belonged, had never wavered during that time.

Over the years he had done everything in this business from emptying the wastebaskets to negotiating multimillion-dollar contracts. He knew C&L from the ground up, and half of it was his.

The Lightfoot portion of Castleton & Lightfoot constituted his rightful inheritance. Three years ago he had told himself to forget that inheritance, but he knew now as he walked through the front door again that one of these days he was going to reclaim it.

The receptionist at the front desk was new, thin and terrifyingly young. She looked as if she had done her apprenticeship behind a cosmetics counter—nothing but perfect skin, perfect hair, perfect makeup.

The nameplate read Rita Duckett. Nick wondered what had happened to Miss Oxberry, who had been thirty years older, gray haired and capable of fending off an entire battalion of nosy government bureaucrats.

"May I help you, sir?" Miss Duckett inquired with a smile that suggested Nick was probably in the wrong building.

"I'm Nick Lightfoot, and I'm going upstairs to the CEO's office."

Miss Duckett frowned over the name. "I'm sorry, sir, but Mrs. Lightfoot is not here. She's on vacation for a few weeks. I'm afraid her assistant, Mr. Vellacott, has already left for the day. You said your name was Lightfoot?"

"That's right. And you don't have to worry about my going upstairs. The office is mine. I just haven't been using it for a while." He headed for the elevators.

Miss Duckett leapt to her feet. "Mr. Lightfoot, wait a minute. I can't let you just barge upstairs."

Nick spotted the guard who was ambling forward to see what the fuss was about. "Hello, Boyd. How are the wife and kids?"

The guard's leathery face creased first in surprise and then in a wide grin. "Mr. Lightfoot. Good to see you again, sir. Been a long time."

"I know." Nick stepped into the waiting elevator. "Please tell Miss Duckett I belong here. She's a little nervous."

"Oh, sure. I'll let her know. She's new. You coming back to work here again, Mr. Lightfoot?"

"Soon," Nick promised as the elevator doors closed. "Very soon."

He stepped out of the elevator on the second floor and found himself facing another woman seated behind a desk. But this face was familiar.

"Mr. Lightfoot! So good to see you again, sir."

"Hello, Mrs. Gilford. How are you doing these days?"

"Just fine, just fine. But we've missed you around here, sir. Are you here to see your, uh, wife . . . I mean Mr. Lightfoot's wife?" Mrs Gilford's competent, middle-aged face flushed with embarrassment. "I mean, are you here to see Mrs. Lightfoot?" she finally got out.

"It's confusing, isn't it?" Nick said. "The answer is no."

"Oh, good. Because she, I mean they, I mean everyone's at the place on the coast. Port Claxton, you know." She flushed a darker red. "Good grief, listen to me, as if you don't know where Port Claxton is."

"Don't worry about it, Mrs. Gilford," Nick said gently. "I'm here to do a little work while the families are off enjoying a hard-earned vacation."

"Work?" She stared at him in confusion. "You're coming back to work here at Castleton & Lightfoot?"

"That's right, Mrs. Gilford."

She smiled broadly. "That's wonderful, sir. But what about Mrs. Lightfoot? Excuse me, I didn't mean to pry. I was just wondering if there had been an official change in duties?"

"The change will occur officially in August at the annual meeting. But I thought I'd come in today and look things over. Sort of get the feel of the place again, if you know what I mean."

"Certainly, sir. Go right on in. If you have any questions, I might be able to contact Mr. Vellacott and have him return to the office. He left a little early but I'm sure I can reach him."

"Don't bother, Mrs. Gilford. I won't be needing Vellacott."

"Fine, sir. Uh, Mrs. Lightfoot has made a few changes in the office," Mrs. Gilford added on a note of warning.

"I'm not surprised."

Nor was he, but Nick winced anyway when he opened the door of the inner office. This had been his private kingdom when he had been the chief executive officer of Castleton & Lightfoot. The style he had maintained it in had been in keeping with the rest of the firm's physical plant: functional, unfussy and austere.

Now it was filled with exotic plants, lustrously polished Queen Anne–style furniture and an Oriental carpet on the floor. Hilary had moved right in and made herself at home. Probably with Eleanor's expert help.

Nick walked slowly around the office, opening desk drawers and examining the paintings on the wall. As far as he could tell, there was not a single Northwest artist represented in the collection of muted abstract works. Hilary had never really liked the Northwest, much less its art.

Nick paused beside the walnut desk, frowning at its delicate lines and curved, mincing little legs. Then he leaned forward and punched the button on the intercom. Time for another calculated risk.

"Mrs. Gilford, would you please bring me the Traynor file?"

"Certainly, sir. Just a minute."

Nick sat down at the desk and waited. Time passed.

Five minutes later, Mrs. Gilford's voice came over the

intercom. She sounded worried. "I'm sorry, Mr. Lightfoot. Did you say Traynor?"

"That's right." He spelled it out for her, but he was already accepting the fact that this particular shot in the dark was not going to pan out. Hardly surprising. That would have been a little too easy.

"I can't seem to locate a file with that name on it. I'll take another look. Perhaps it's been misplaced."

"Don't worry about it, Mrs. Gilford. I think I know where it is."

"Very well, sir. Let me know if you want me to initiate a search."

"Thanks." He sat back and surveyed the room. Hilary had hung a subtly colored painting done in shades of mauve over the old wall safe. His father had always kept a portrait of a springer spaniel there. When Nick had moved in, he had left the spaniel in place. Something about the patient, mournful gaze had amused him.

He got up, went over to the painting and lifted it down from the wall. If Hilary had changed the combination on the safe, he would have to call in a professional locksmith. That would take time, but he didn't have much choice. He tried the old combination on the off chance that she had left it alone. Funny how he could still remember the numbers after three years.

The safe did not yield. Nick was about to get out the phone book to find a locksmith, when it occurred to him that Hilary had no talent for memorizing numbers. You couldn't help learning a few things about someone when you lived with her for eighteen months. Hilary could not even remember a telephone number. She always wrote down addresses, phone numbers and bank-card codes. She was very meticulous about that kind of thing.

Nick started going through the small drawers of the old desk, looking for a string of digits that might have been jotted down in a convenient location. Eventually he gave up on the desk and tried other places in the room. He finally got around to turning over the abstract painting that had covered the wall safe. He found the combination neatly lettered in Hilary's precise handwriting on the back. Very convenient.

Three minutes later he reached inside the safe and removed two thin files. Neither of them carried labels, but it did not take long to figure out which one was the Traynor file.

There was probably little new to be learned from the file, but the fact that it even existed confirmed what Nick had already concluded. The rumors he'd picked up in California had been true. Hilary was working a deal with Traynor. C&L was about to be slowly and quietly drawn and quartered. By the time the families realized what was happening, it would be too late.

Half an hour later Nick put the files back in the wall safe and rehung the painting. He had been right, there wasn't much in the folder that was new but it had made fascinating reading, nevertheless.

He shook his head as he stepped back to be certain the painting was hung straight. He knew, because Eleanor had assured him of the fact, that Hilary had great taste. But there was no way he was ever going to learn to like mauve. He thought of Philadelphia in her bright plumage and smiled. Then he turned and walked out the door.

"Mrs. Gilford, I have one other project for you this afternoon."

"Of course."

"Would you contact whatever newspaper is published in Holloway and see if they've got anything in their files on the conviction or sentencing of an Elijah Spalding?"

Mrs. Gilford frowned as she jotted down the name. "Spalding?"

"That's right."

"I believe there's a Holloway in eastern Washington; is that the town you mean?"

"Yeah. If you turn up anything, see if they'll fax us a copy of the article. Thank you, Mrs. Gilford."

"Not at all." She smiled expectantly. "Will you be back on a permanent basis soon, Mr. Lightfoot?" Mrs. Gilford asked.

"Soon," Nick promised.

Out in the parking lot, he eased the Porsche from its slot and headed downtown. The cluster of high-rise buildings that dominated Seattle's central business area stretched upward into a cloudless July sky.

Elliott Bay looked like a blue mirror on which someone had artfully arranged a variety of long cargo ships and bright white ferryboats. There were very few pleasure craft on this part of the bay, however. This was a working port, and there was little room for frivolous vessels. The yachts and sailing boats stuck to Lake Union or Lake Washington or ventured out into Puget Sound to go island-hopping.

Nick took 99 into town, traveling the elevated viaduct along the waterfront. He glanced down once and saw the ferry from Bainbridge Island docking. The sight gave him an odd feeling. Bainbridge was where the Castletons and Lightfoots had built their main residences.

Nick turned off the viaduct on Seneca Street. He went left on First Avenue and drove past Pike Place Market to a concrete-and-glass condominium building that overlooked the bay.

He hadn't been in the condo for three years. On occasion he'd toyed with the idea of renting it out or even selling it, but he had always changed his mind at the last minute. Instead, he'd kept paying a cleaning and maintenance service to keep it in good condition even though he had not been certain until recently that he would ever come back to it.

Set near the year-round street fair that was the Market and equipped with a wall-to-wall view of Elliott Bay and the Olympics, the condo had been the one place he could be sure of being alone when he wished. Hilary hadn't liked the place. She preferred the Bainbridge Island home.

Even though she had not cared for downtown living, Hilary had managed to leave her mark on the condo. He had brought her here in the early days of their marriage, hoping that being away from the family home might help solve their problems.

No problems had been solved, but Hilary had immediately dedicated herself to redecorating the condo, and Nick walked in the door now to find things exactly as she had left them. The rooms were filled with dark mahogany, pine and walnut furnishings that could have come straight out of a New England colonial home.

Lightfoots, Nick reflected, appeared to be doomed to live in the past even though their business was strictly high-tech.

As he poured himself a glass of scotch from the bottle he'd left behind three years ago, Nick speculated idly on what Phila would do with the condo if she were given free rein. He'd probably wind up with fuschia walls and a lime-green carpet. He grinned at the thought.

The phone rang just as he was wondering where in the Market he would go for dinner.

"Mr. Lightfoot, I'm glad I caught you. We just got the article from the *Holloway Reporter*," Mrs. Gilford announced. "Will there be anything else?"

"No, thanks, Mrs. Gilford. You've been a great help. I'll pick up the fax sheet in the morning before I leave town."

His father had been right. It was time he checked into the story surrounding the trial that had put Elijah Spalding in jail. Nick realized he was beginning to feel a strong sense of responsibility toward one Philadelphia Fox.

On the morning after Nick had left to fly down to Santa Barbara, Phila found a pay phone at a gas station on the outskirts of Port Claxton. Her conversation was brief, and after she replaced the receiver she stood for a moment watching the gas-station attendant wash the windows of her car.

The words of Nick's secretary at Lightfoot Consulting Services in Santa Barbara rang in her ears.

"I'm sorry, but Mr. Lightfoot is not in the office and is not expected for some time. He's on vacation. Mr. Plummer is in charge. He'll be glad to talk to you. Whom shall I say is calling?"

Phila's response had been short and to the point. "Nobody."

She studied the gas-station attendant more closely as she stood mulling over what she had just learned. The grizzled, middle-aged man was on the scrawny side. He was wearing grease-stained coveralls and a cap that looked as if it had been run over by a car. He appeared to have made a career out of this line of work. Phila eased away from the pay phone and started toward her car.

So Nick had not flown down to California, or if he had, he hadn't bothered to check in with his office. That was nothing short of upsetting—even alarming—given the fact that he had said he was going down there on business.

No matter how you looked at it, Nick had lied to her.

She did not know precisely what had made her call. She had told herself she certainly was not checking up on him, but when you got right down to it that was just what she had done. She'd checked up, and Nick had not checked out. She wished she knew what to do with the unsettling information.

"Thanks for doing the windows," Phila said to the attendant as she climbed into the car. There was a twinge in her shoulder as she got behind the wheel. That heavy, ugly revolver she had been forced to practice with for two solid hours under the watchful eyes of Nick, his father, Darren and Tec Sherman yesterday had made itself felt. Her arms and shoulders were aching as if she'd been doing a lot of push-ups. She wrinkled her nose as she recalled that she was scheduled for another workout with Tec later in the afternoon.

"You're that lady who's stayin' out at the old Gilmarten place, ain't ya? The one who's shacked up—I mean, the one's who's here with Nick Lightfoot?" The attendant peered at Phila as he took the cash from her hand.

"Yes, I am staying at the Gilmarten place," Phila confirmed with a well-chilled smile. Small towns were all the same. Everyone felt a proprietorial interest in everyone else's business. "No, I am not with Nick Lightfoot. I am on my own."

The attendant did not seem to understand that he was displaying bad manners. He just looked puzzled. "But he's stayin' there with you, ain't he? I heard you and him were there together. Everyone wondered when he'd come back. Can't blame him for staying away so long, though. Not after his wife up and married his father. Kinda weird, you know? Maybe Nick thought it'd be easier to come back if he had another woman in tow. A man's got his pride."

Phila refused to respond to that. She turned on the compact's ignition and whipped the steering wheel to the right. Without more than a cursory glance to the left, she swung the little red car out onto the main street and headed back toward the Gilmarten place. The two-lane highway that followed the beach was clogged with campers, trailers and motor homes.

Nick had his pride, all right. Phila did not doubt that for a moment. But somehow she did not think he would need to have a "woman in tow" before he felt he could face the families again.

He might, however, find a certain woman—one Philadelphia Fox, for example—extremely useful as a means of regaining a toehold in Castleton & Lightfoot.

Damn it, why had he lied to her about going to Santa Barbara? That hurt. But more importantly, it made no sense. Nick Lightfoot sometimes moved in mysterious ways. Dangerous ways.

She was pulling into the Gilmarten drive when she saw Tec Sherman coming toward her in the open jeep he used for running around. He peered out at her from under the brim of a fatigue cap. Today's aloha shirt was lavender, yellow and black. She had to admit that, obnoxious as he could be at times, the man did have excellent taste in clothes.

"Been lookin' for you, Phila," Tec called from the jeep. "Mrs. Castleton wants to see you. Can you come up to the house for a few minutes?"

"I suppose so. What does she want?"

"Damned if I know. Don't forget we have another session at the range scheduled today."

"You know, it had just about slipped my mind, Tec."

Tec grinned evilly. "I won't let you forget. Nick'd nail

my hide to the nearest barn door if I let you get away without more practice."

"That's just an excuse. The truth is, you like the idea of having me under your thumb, don't you? You like giving me orders. Were you ever a drill sergeant, by any chance?"

"Spent a coupla years at Pendleton," Tec admitted, looking cheerful at the recollection.

"I'll bet you had fun beating up on new recruits."

"No fun in it. Just a job. But teachin' you to shoot straight is gonna be kind of fun, I think. Hop in the jeep. I'll drive you up to the house."

With a groan of resignation, Phila got into the vehicle. "Are you sure you don't know why Eleanor wants to see me?"

"No. But I reckon she'll tell you."

Five minutes later he brought the jeep to a halt in the Castleton drive. "She's around back in her greenhouse."

"Okay. Thanks for the lift. I guess. One never knows around here." A welcoming yip made her turn around, and she groaned in dismay. "Oh, no. The killer dogs."

Cupcake and Fifi came dashing around the side of the house, charging happily toward Phila. They were all over her in an instant, thrusting their noses into her palm and fidgeting with delight over her presence.

"Look at it this way," Tec said, "they make better friends than enemies. Same goes for Castletons and Lightfoots. I'll pick you up at three o'clock for target practice."

"I'll see if I can fit another practice session into my schedule."

But she could tell from the way Tec was grinning that she didn't have any choice. She followed the dogs around to the front portico of the Castleton beach cottage, wondering if her coming meeting with Eleanor Castleton would offer her any more leeway than Tec did.

CHAPTER TWELVE

"There you are, dear. Do come in. I was just puttering." Eleanor looked up with her slightly distracted air as Phila appeared in the greenhouse doorway.

"This is quite a setup." Phila gazed around in wonder. The greenhouse was warm and humid and redolent of tropical smells. The curiously appealing scent of rich soil underlay the entire medley of odors. Water gurgled in a large aquarium. Phila's nose twitched appreciatively. "I've never been inside a private greenhouse. I think I'd like one of these myself."

Eleanor peered at her from under the brim of her denim gardening cap. She was busy snipping leaves from a plant that had a number of cup-shaped appendages. "You're interested in plants?"

"I like plants and flowers. I'd love to have a place where I could grow them year round." Phila leaned over to examine an oddly shaped red leaf that had a row of spines around its edge. "What is this? Some sort of cactus?"

"No, dear. That's a *Dionaea muscipula*. A Venus's-flytrap."

Phila, who had been about to touch the unusual leaf, jerked her finger back out of reach. "A carnivorous plant?"

"Yes, dear."

"How interesting. I'm sort of into ivy and philodendron, myself." Phila looked around, frowning as she realized she did not recognize any of the abundant, healthy plant life that filled the greenhouse. "That plant you're pruning, the one with the little cups. What is it?"

"A variety of sarracenia. I'm working on developing a hybrid. Notice the nicely shaped pitchers?"

"Is that a pitcher plant? The kind unsuspecting bugs fall into and can't get back out of?"

Eleanor smiled fondly at the plant under her hands. "Yes, indeed, dear. The pitchers are modified leaves, of course. Quite fascinating to watch the insect discover the nectar and begin feeding on the lip of the leaf."

"I can imagine."

"The silly creature just keeps moving farther and farther into the pitcher until all of a sudden its little feet start sliding on the tiny little hairs inside the leaf. The insect slips and slides, trying to get its feet back under itself and then it reaches the waxy area where there's no footing at all. Before it knows what's happened, the little thing just falls straight down into the bottom of the pitcher."

Phila eyed the innocent-looking plant. "Then what?"

"Why then it gets eaten, dear." Eleanor smiled. "Once inside, it can't escape from the bowl of the pitcher, you see. It's trapped."

"How does the plant digest it?"

"The bottom of the pitcher has a set of special glands that secrete digestive enzymes," Eleanor explained. "A bacterial reaction is produced, too, which aids in the digestion of prey." She glanced around vaguely. "Jordan was playing with that row of sarracenia over there the other day. If you look inside some of the pitchers you might see some bits and pieces of ant chitin at the bottom."

"That's okay, I'm going to have lunch soon." The aquarium caught Phila's attention. "Are those plants in that tank carnivorous, too?"

"Oh, yes. A species of *Utricularia*. The common name is bladderworts."

"Everything in this greenhouse is carnivorous, isn't it?"

Phila looked straight at Eleanor, wondering if she would be insulted by her double meaning.

"Yes, dear. Carnivorous plants are my specialty." Eleanor snipped off another leaf.

Apparently the double entendre had been a bit too subtle. Either that or Eleanor was too much of a lady to rise to the bait. "How long have you been interested in these plants?" Phila asked.

"Let me see, how long has it been now? Over thirty years, I believe. I used to raise orchids before I became fascinated with carnivorous plants."

"Is that right?" Phila decided she'd had enough of the horticultural discussion. "Thank you for dinner last night, Eleanor. I had a very interesting time."

"You're quite welcome. I thought it might be nice for you to have an opportunity to spend an evening with all of us together."

"So I'd understand that I don't fit in with the Lightfoots and Castletons any more than Crissie did? What are you worried about, Eleanor? That I might be entertaining the notion of becoming part of this happy-go-lucky family group?"

Eleanor flinched at the blunt attack, but she rallied quickly. "I'm sure your background is considerably different from ours, just as Miss Masters's was."

"The amusing thing is that if Crissie's father had accepted his responsibilities, Crissie's background would have been exactly the same as Darren's. Makes one stop and think, doesn't it? Raises all sorts of interesting questions on the old subject of heredity versus environment."

Eleanor's pleasantly vague expression hardened as she took visible hold of herself. "I asked you to come here today because I wish to talk quite frankly to you about the shares in your possession."

"That doesn't surprise me. What's your pitch, Eleanor? Hilary tried to buy them back. Vicky cried and tried to put a guilt trip on me by telling me I was stealing her son's inheritance. I'll be interested to hear your approach."

"You're not so different from Crissie Masters, after all,

are you? The others are beginning to think you might be, but I can see the truth. I've had a little more experience in detecting it, you see." Eleanor worked the garden shears with a small, violent movement. A handful of leaves cascaded to the table. "Oh, yes, I've seen the way the men in the families are starting to change toward you. Men are so blind, aren't they?"

"Are they, Eleanor?"

"You think you'll soon have them eating out of the palm of your hand, don't you? Reed was laughing at the table last night. Actually laughing. He hasn't done that in a long time. And Nick looks at you in a way he never looked at Hilary. Even Darren found you entertaining last night. Vicky told me this morning that he's not nearly as worried as he should be about you."

"You think your son should be worried?"

"Of course he should be worried. His whole future is in the hands of a hustling little opportunist who's obviously out for the best deal she can get. You're just like Crissie. Just as cruel and vicious as she was."

"If you're going to attack someone, attack me, not Crissie. She's dead, remember?"

The distracted expression vanished from Eleanor's eyes as her head came up sharply. Her gracious accent was taut with controlled fury. "Hilary tried to make an honest bargain with you, Miss Fox, but you turned her down. Vicky tried to reason with you. If you had been a decent person, you would have accepted the money and given back the shares. You did no such thing. You're out to cause pain and destruction, just as Crissie did."

Phila dug her nails into her palms. "This family caused Crissie a lot of pain. Eventually it destroyed her."

"That's not true."

"She's dead, Eleanor, and you're all still alive," Phila pointed out softly. "So don't talk to me about who caused the pain and destruction. The results speak for themselves."

Eleanor stopped clipping leaves. Her eyes were very bright with a mixture of anger and what looked like anguish. "Crissie Masters was cheap and spiteful. She caused trouble from the moment she appeared in our lives, always trying to set one of us against the other. Don't you dare try to make me feel sorry for her. I will never forgive her for what she did while she was here. She had no right to descend on us the way she did. No right at all."

"Crissie was not the one who originally caused the pain," Phila said. "She was another victim of the one who was responsible, just like you. Your husband caused your pain years ago when he had a tacky little one-night stand and got some poor young woman pregnant. Crissie is the result of your husband's indiscriminate womanizing."

"You have no right to talk about my husband that way. Burke Castleton was a fine man. A successful, influential businessman. A credit to his community. His son is going to be the next governor of this state, so you will do well to keep a civil tongue in your head, young woman."

"I'll admit it wasn't particularly charitable of Crissie to come crashing into your lives, but Crissie didn't know much about real charity. You learn things like that by example, Eleanor, and no one ever showed her any warmth or kindness while she was growing up."

"I don't have to listen to this."

"You started it. If you're going to insist on blaming Crissie for all the trauma your husband caused, I'm damn sure going to insist on setting the record straight. Put the blame where it belongs, on the man you married." Phila thought her nails were breaking the skin of her palms, but she was determined to keep a level tone to her voice.

"Stop it. Stop it. Stop it right now, do you hear me? The blame belongs on that cheap little tramp." Eleanor's voice was becoming shrill.

"No, Eleanor," Phila whispered through set teeth. "It belongs on a man who cheated on his wife all those years ago. And I'll tell you something else. If he did it once, chances are he did it several times. Let's hope for your sake you don't have to deal with any more surprises from the past on your doorstep."

"Shut your foul mouth, you little slut."

"Ah, now I get it. That's the real source of your anguish, isn't it? You know deep down what kind of man your husband really was. I'll bet you knew it back then. You're a smart woman, Eleanor. Too smart not to know what Burke Castleton was like. Was that why you gave up growing orchids and started cultivating carnivorous plants? Is this how you started working out your frustration with a marriage you knew would never become what you wanted it to be?"

"You are a monstrous woman," Eleanor gasped. *"Monstrous."*

"I'm just spelling out a few facts." Phila could feel herself shaking.

"I will not let you talk to me like this." Eleanor gripped the workbench very tightly. "You're nothing but a no-account little whore, and I'm certain Nick realizes it. You've got no looks, no money and no background. Use your head, you fool. If you had any sense you'd see that Nick is only using you for his own ends. How could he possibly be interested in you except for some cheap sex? After all, he was once married to Hilary."

"You think Hilary is more his type?" Phila asked scathingly.

"Hilary is beautiful, well mannered and well bred. Her family goes back to the *Mayflower*. She's everything you're not, and Nick must know that. How can you possibly hope to compete with her?"

"I didn't notice there was a competition going on," Phila got out tightly. "Hilary's married to another man, or have you forgotten? I'm sure she's too much of a *lady* to go after one man when she's wearing another's ring. Besides, Nick doesn't show any signs of being interested in her. Don't get your hopes up about a grand reconciliation between those two, Eleanor. I know you handpicked her for Nick, but that doesn't mean you picked the right woman."

"You don't know anything, do you?" Eleanor's voice was as brittle as glass. "You silly little fool. You have no idea of what you're dealing with here. You're just standing on the outside looking in, trying to stir up trouble. But for your information, you're quite right. Hilary would not go out of her way to get Nick back. Why should she want him back after what he did to her?"

"Just what did he do to her, Eleanor?"

"Vicky said she told you about the baby."

"So what? You think the baby was Nick's?"

"I know the baby was Nick's." Eleanor's eyes had never appeared less vague. *"He raped her.* The next time you go to bed with him think about that, you little whore. You've got a lot of nerve calling my Burke a womanizer when you're sleeping with a man who raped his own wife."

"You don't know what you're talking about."

Eleanor smiled thinly. "Don't I? It's the truth. Nick forced himself on Hilary because he was furious with her for asking for a divorce. She got pregnant and nearly had a nervous breakdown."

"I don't believe you."

"Then you are a very stupid woman, Philadelphia Fox."

"Did Hilary tell you she was raped?"

"Yes, after she realized she had gotten pregnant. She took some tranquilizers and came to see me the next morning. Nick had already left a couple of weeks earlier. Hilary was rambling, almost incoherent. But she told me everything, including how she had been assaulted by Nick before he left. She didn't know what to do. I'm the one who called Reed."

"And Reed did the noble thing, of course?"

Eleanor drew herself up stiffly. "Reed is a good man. A bit rough in his ways still, even after all these years, but he's a good, decent man."

Phila forced herself to think through the swirl of emotions that threatened to blind her. "All right, I'll go along with you on that. I think he is a decent man. But so is Nick. And you know it."

"I don't wish to discuss Nick any further."

"Umm hmmm. Tell me, Eleanor, if you really believed he had treated Hilary so badly, why would you have bothered to keep in touch with him during the past three years?"

Eleanor tossed aside the clippers and picked up a small watering can. "Nick is family. I couldn't just let him be cut off completely," she whispered.

"Especially when you knew in your soul he'd gotten a bum rap?"

"You don't know what you're talking about."

"Maybe. Perhaps I'm being too charitable. I'm assuming that you kept in touch with Nick because you suspected he was innocent, but maybe the real reason was a lot more practical—a lot more mercenary. Did you keep in touch with him because you knew that someday the families would need him back to run Castleton & Lightfoot? Did you want to leave the door open in case you decided to recall him for active duty?"

The spout of the can trembled as Eleanor tried to water a plant. "I do not have to explain my actions to someone of your type."

"Fair enough. I don't have to stand around and explain myself to someone of your type." She turned toward the door.

"Miss Fox."

"Yes, Mrs. Castleton?"

"I demand that you tell me what you are going to do with those shares."

"When I decide, I'll be sure to let you know."

"Those shares belong to my son, damn you."

"Crissie had as much right to them as Darren did. She was Burke's daughter, remember?"

"No. No, damn you, no. *She was an outsider.*" Eleanor's eyes filled with tears, and her proud face began to crumple.

Phila went through the door and closed it behind her with shaking hands. Her legs felt weak. When the dogs danced over to greet her, she nearly collapsed beneath their assault.

But there was something very comforting about their cheerful, overflowing affection. Phila sank to the ground and hugged the animals close.

* * *

That afternoon on the firing range, Phila concentrated fiercely on Tec's instructions. He seemed to sense that her attitude toward the handgun lessons had undergone a major change. He gave his orders in a crisp, no-nonsense voice, and Phila did exactly as she was told. When she finally succeeded in putting a whole group of shots into the target, he nodded with satisfaction.

"Nick'll be pleased," Tec said. "Let's do it again."

She went through the routine over and over again. Time after time she gripped the revolver as she had been taught, found the trigger with her index finger, brought the weapon up in a sweeping motion and fired. Round after round went into the paper targets. The muffled roar of the .38 and Tec's harsh voice became the only sounds in the world.

"Don't worry about speed. It doesn't do any good to get off the first shot if it's a bad one. Just take it slow and easy for now."

When Tec finally signaled a halt, Phila had to yank herself back to reality. She pulled the hearing muffs off her head and rubbed her temples with thumb and forefinger.

"You're lookin' good," Tec said. "Damn good. Nick'll be real happy with the way you're comin' along."

"We must please Nick at all costs, mustn't we?" Phila said wearily.

Tec looked up from where he was packing away the .38. "Somethin' wrong? You sound kinda funny this afternoon."

"I'm fine, Tec. I think I'll walk back to my place."

"It's a long walk."

"I don't mind."

"I'll drop the .38 off at the Gilmarten place on my way back to the house. I've got a key."

"Thanks. You can leave it in a drawer in the kitchen."

"Right. But move it into you bedroom tonight, huh?"

"Yes, Tec."

Tec straightened and started for the jeep. Then he stopped. "This guy who jumped you. What's he look like?"

"Very big. Huge through the shoulders. Strange blue eyes. The last time I saw him, he had a beard and long hair, but that may be gone now."

"You're sure he didn't hurt you?"

"No, he didn't get the chance. The cops arrived just as he was trying to drag me into his pickup."

"Damn lucky for you."

Phila smiled fleetingly. "Yes. Very lucky. I'll see you later, Tec."

"Hey, you don't have to worry about that bastard, you know," Tec said gruffly. "Nick'll look after you."

"I've been looking after myself for a long time, Tec. I'm pretty good at it."

Hilary poured coffee from the early-nineteenth-century pot and handed a cup to Eleanor. The beautiful coffee service had been a wedding gift to Eleanor and Burke nearly forty years before, she knew. It had descended through Eleanor's family and had been used by generations of her female ancestors.

Hilary wondered if a loveless marriage was also a family tradition. How many of Eleanor's forebears had poured coffee from this lovely Georgian silver pot and secretly wondered if it and all the other things they had were worth the price they had paid?

"She upset you, didn't she?" Hilary asked quietly as she sat back on the sofa, her own cup and saucer in hand.

Eleanor took a fortifying sip of coffee. "She's a very difficult young woman."

"We knew that from the beginning. What did she say to you that disturbed you so much?"

"So many things. She made more of her vile accusations and refused to tell me what she's going to do with the shares."

Hilary sensed there was more to the story than that, but she also sensed this was not the time to find out what it was. "I think we can assume she's going to hand the shares over to Nick or at least vote them the way he tells her to vote them."

Eleanor sighed. "I was so certain Nick would do the right thing. I thought he could convince her to return the shares to us. Nick was always good at business matters. So good at making deals. I never dreamed it was going to get this messy."

"What made you think Nick would do the right thing in this matter when he didn't bother to do the right thing three years ago?"

Eleanor shook her head vaguely and looked away. "This is business. Family business. I thought surely . . ." She let the sentence trail off. "I was wrong."

"You thought that in a pinch he would come through for you? For the sake of the families?" Hilary smiled regretfully. "I know you did what you thought was best, Eleanor. But the net result is to make things infinitely more complicated than they were before you involved Nick."

"I know. I just wish I knew what that Fox woman wants from us."

Hilary looked at her pityingly. "Don't you know yet what Philadelphia Fox wants from us? It's rapidly becoming perfectly clear. She wants exactly what Crissie wanted. To be a part of the families."

Eleanor shuddered. "My God. Do you think she honestly believes she can get Nick to marry her?"

"Why not? Nick is obviously encouraging her to think precisely that." Hilary set her cup and saucer down on the table. "After all, he is sleeping with her."

"That means nothing. I warned her not to put too much stock in that kind of sordid maneuvering. She must realize she's far beneath him and that he's just using her."

"Perhaps. But she may be shrewd enough to put a price tag on those shares before she hands them over to him."

"Marriage being the price tag?" Eleanor shuddered. "Do you think he would pay that price, Hilary? She's such a little nobody."

"He wants those shares very badly," Hilary reasoned. "I think it's possible that, if he can't seduce them out of her, he might marry her for them. After all, he can always divorce her later."

"She'd make him pay heavily for a divorce."

Hilary lifted one shoulder negligently. "Her notion of a large settlement would probably be small change to Nick. He can afford it. Or perhaps I should say Castleton & Lightfoot can afford it."

"What are we going to do, Hilary?" Eleanor asked wearily. "Whatever are we going to do?"

Hilary ran her finger lightly along the delicate carving of the scroll-back sofa. "Nick can't do anything drastic at the annual meeting with just his shares and Phila's. He needs another large block to be able to control things."

"I know. But if he can talk Darren or Reed into going along with him, he could take control of the firm."

"Or you. He could do it if he had your block of shares, Eleanor."

"Don't say such things. I'm hardly likely to back him."

"It would certainly put Darren's future at risk, wouldn't it? If Nick regains control of C&L he's not going to make it easy for your son to go after the governor's mansion. You heard Nick the other night at dinner. He doesn't have any interest in financing a political campaign for Darren."

"No," Eleanor said uneasily. "It's obvious Nick's attitude toward a member of the families going into politics is as negative as it ever was."

"We must make certain no one in either family wavers."

Eleanor shot Hilary a searching look. "Do you think Reed might? He's starting to change toward Nick. I can feel it."

"Reed will do what he knows is right, regardless of how he feels about Nick. He might soften toward his son, but he would never back him to take control of Castleton & Lightfoot. He would never really trust Nick again." Hilary hoped she was right on that count. "But in any event, I think I will make another personal stab at getting the shares back from Phila."

"If she turned down your offer, what makes you think you have any chance of talking her out of them?"

"Crissie used to talk a great deal about Phila. I know more about her than she realizes."

"What's to know about that cheap little hustler?" Eleanor's cup rattled in the saucer. She set it down quickly. "She's just like Crissie."

"No," Hilary said thoughtfully, "she's not just like Crissie. And that's why I may be able to use another tactic."

Phila had intended to go straight back to the cottage from the firing range, but when she passed the path down to the beach, she changed her mind. The beach was empty. The promise of windswept solitude lured her. She started down the path.

She was halfway along the trail through the trees when a familiar yelp alerted her. She glanced back just as Cupcake and Fifi started to bound down the path. Darren Castleton followed more leisurely in their wake.

The dogs crowded around Phila for a moment. She patted them absently, her eyes on Darren. He was watching her with a thoughtful gaze.

"Hello, Phila. Tec said you were walking home from the range. Thought I'd meet you. I wanted to talk to you."

"What about? Or is that a dumb question under the circumstances."

"Not so dumb." He followed her down to the beach, his hands in the pockets of his windbreaker. "I'm not sure myself what I want to say."

Cupcake and Fifi raced to the water's edge and began chasing sea gulls.

"The dogs really love it down here, don't they?" Phila shoved her hands in her jeans pockets. "Look at them. Do they ever catch the gulls?"

"No. But, then, I'm not sure how hard they really try. It's just a game to them. They're not serious about the hunt right now."

"What happens when they get serious?"

"Then they're dangerous. Just like some people I could mention."

"Is this a veiled warning about Nick's intentions?"

"I take it you've had a lot of such warnings?" Darren smiled and kicked idly at a small shell.

"From just about everyone, including his own father."

"Reed's got his reasons for warning you about Nick."

"Silly reasons."

Darren glanced at her. "What makes you say that?"

"We're talking about Hilary's famous baby, right?"

"So you know about that. You think Nick was right to let his father pick up the pieces after that disaster? Because that's exactly what Nick did. Reed felt obliged to step in and protect Hilary."

"Then he was a fool. Nick is perfectly capable of handling his own disasters. Reed should have known that."

"Wait a second. You do know the baby was Nick's don't you?"

"I know that's what everyone thinks, including Reed, apparently,"

Darren frowned. "But you don't believe it?"

"Not for a minute."

"Well, I guess your viewpoint is bound to be a little biased. After all, you're having an affair with Nick. You want to believe the best of him."

"He's no angel," Phila muttered, thinking about the phone call to Santa Barbara that morning. "I know that. He's secretive, and I know for a fact he's deliberately misled me in some things. He's also quite mysterious, and I'm not sure how far to trust him when it comes to certain matters. But I do know he wouldn't have let his father step in and take responsibility for the baby if the baby had been his."

"You sound very sure of yourself. Why would Hilary have lied?"

"Good question. Perhaps because the marriage was falling apart and she didn't want to lose everything she'd gained by marrying into Castleton & Lightfoot?"

Darren was silent for a moment. "I thought of that possibility myself, once or twice three years ago," he finally admitted. "But my mother seemed so sure of her. She was convinced Hilary had been abused by Nick and that Reed as well as Castleton & Lightfoot owed her protection. She feels very protective toward her. How much do you know about Hilary?"

"Just the little Crissie told me."

"You can probably discard most of that," Darren said. "I know she was your friend, but Crissie Masters couldn't be trusted an inch."

"I could trust her."

Darren shrugged that aside. "Back to Hilary. Eleanor introduced her to Nick about five years ago. If it wasn't a case of love at first sight, it was definitely a case of satisfaction at first sight. They both seemed to want what the other was offering. Nick was ready to marry, and Hilary was a stunning woman who looked as though she would be a perfect wife for him."

"I know." Phila wrinkled her nose. "Good family background, good looks and lots of old money. The perfect combination. Too bad she didn't love him."

"He thought she did. Or at least he thought the potential for love was there. I don't believe he would have married her otherwise. He had been raised in a loving marriage, and I think he fully expected the same sort of relationship for himself when he married. But you're wrong about one thing. Hilary didn't have a lot of old money."

"No?"

Darren shook his head. "She had the family background, all right, and the looks, but that was about all that was left. She came from an old family that had been living on its expectations for the past couple of generations. Unfortunately, they hadn't produced anyone strong enough to keep the income flowing into the family coffers during the last forty years. They made the classic mistake of dipping into capital. They were on the verge of bankruptcy when Hilary married Nick."

Phila stumbled over a small piece of driftwood. "Did Nick know that?"

"Sure. He's not exactly stupid. At least not when it comes to money."

"Do you think he worried he was being married for his money?"

"Nick's a natural risk-taker. I think he just decided to take the risk in this case. After all, everything else looked good and Hilary certainly appeared to be in love with him."

"And your mother was pushing for the match?"

"Yes. She felt that after Nora died she had a duty to find a proper wife for Nick. She liked Hilary, and her family had known Hilary's family for generations."

Phila frowned. "Did she know Hilary's family was just about broke?"

"She probably did. But she understood that kind of situation. She didn't see it as a negative. Why do you think she married my father?"

"*What?*"

Darren smiled again, briefly. "I'm afraid so. A marriage of convenience, as they used to say. Her family was Southern aristocracy. Bloodlines all the way back to the Colonial era."

"But they were out of money?"

Darren nodded. "They had enough to put up a good front, but basically they were in deep trouble when Burke Castleton went east looking for a proper lady to marry."

"Poor Eleanor!"

"She knew what she was doing. It was expected of her. She may not have had money, but she had a strong sense of family honor and obligation. Who knows? Maybe in the beginning she actually cared for my father. God knows he had a way with women."

"She tolerated nearly forty years of marriage to a man she probably considered beneath her?"

"She did her best to elevate him and the rest of us. She's spent years polishing the image. I think she sees it as her life's work."

"In other words, she fulfilled her part of the bargain. She brought a little class to the Castletons and the Lightfoots." Phila grimaced. "And so it goes. Life among the rich and famous."

"Not that rich and certainly not that famous," Darren said. "Don't act so damn condescending."

"You don't have to lecture me. I'm already feeling bad enough for the way I talked to your mother this morning."

Darren's expression hardened. "What did you say to her?"

"She was accusing Crissie of having caused a lot of pain and anguish. I pointed out that the blame belonged on Burke. He was the one who played around all those years ago. I also pointed out that if he'd played around once, he'd undoubtedly done so many times."

"You said that to my mother?" Darren's voice was grim.

"I'm afraid so."

"You are a real little bitch, aren't you?"

CHAPTER THIRTEEN

———⟡———

A real little bitch.
   Just like Crissie.

The words reverberated through Phila's mind as she fixed herself a salad that evening. They made her feel worn-out and depressed.

Phila took her plate over to the kitchen table and sat down. She'd lost her appetite again, she realized. She really didn't want to eat the salad. She didn't want to eat anything.

There was another storm moving inland. Rain was already striking the windows in big fat drops that sounded like small-weapons fire. She was becoming an expert on that particular sound.

The only thing she was accomplishing here on the coast was causing more trouble, Phila told herself, trying to face the situation clearly.

Crissie was dead. There was nothing to be done about it. There were no questions to ask. She had known that from the beginning. It was time to turn the shares back to their rightful owner and be done with it.

Strange how things had become so painfully clear this afternoon after that conversation with Eleanor. There was no point trying to punish the Castletons and Lightfoots.

They had done a fine job of punishing themselves over the years.

On top of everything else, she was a fool to stick around and play dangerous games with Nick Lightfoot. There was no sense kidding herself. Everyone was right. Nick never did anything without a reason. He was using her. She knew it; they all knew it. Phila didn't blame him particularly. After all, she had been using him. But she was suddenly very tired of dealing with the situation.

She knew she had allowed Nick to persuade her to come to Port Claxton because she had not known what else to do with herself. She had needed a focus for her burned-out emotions. She had needed something to revitalize herself. Creating trouble with the C&L shares had seemed a way to do that for a while. She could pretend she was somehow avenging Crissie. But the more Phila got mired in the quicksand of the emotional politics between the families, the less vengeful she felt.

It was time to call it quits and get out. Phila made her decision as she sat watching the storm come in. She would give the shares back to Darren in the morning, and then she would pack and head for Seattle.

Seattle seemed like a good place to start job hunting, and she had a life to put back together. It was time to get busy on that task.

Nick's Porsche pulled into the cottage drive just as Phila started on her salad. The sound of the powerful engine took her by surprise. She had not expected him back tonight. Slowly she got to her feet as Nick came through the front door. She went to meet him.

"I didn't think you'd get here until tomorrow," Phila said quietly as he set down his luggage.

He looked at her. "I finished my business and decided to come back early." He paused, eying her quizzically. "I think there's something wrong with this scene."

"Is there?"

"Shouldn't you be rushing into my arms? Climbing all over me? Ripping off my clothes?"

"Should I?"

"Oh, Christ. What happened?" He shrugged out of his jacket and tossed it across the nearest chair.

"Not much. I've decided to leave tomorrow, Nick."

He didn't move, but his eyes turned bleak and hard. "Is that right? What are you going to do with the shares?"

Phila turned back toward the kitchen with a humorless smile. "The first and foremost question, of course. What will I do with the shares. Well, you can all stop wondering. I'm going to give them back to Darren. They belong to him."

"For the past few days you've been claiming those shares were Crissie's inheritance." Nick followed her into the kitchen.

"Crissie's dead."

"That's not news. She's been dead for nearly three months."

"I guess I'm finally accepting that fact." Phila sat down at the table again and picked up her fork. "It was hard, you know. I think I was afraid to let go of her. There were times when she was all I had and it was hard to envision a world without her in it."

Nick opened a cupboard and found his bottle of scotch. "You want to tell me what happened while I was gone?"

"Not much, really. I had a talk with Eleanor today, and I felt like a piece of garbage afterward. It jolted me. It also put things into perspective."

"What did you say to her? Or was it something she said to you?" Nick watched her coolly as he poured his scotch.

"I said some nasty things to her. Afterward I felt as though I'd kicked a dog when it was down. She's obviously worked for years on shoring up an image of family unity. It was cruel of me to casually rip it apart."

"What exactly did you say?"

"I reminded her it was her husband who had caused the problem of Crissie."

"A logical deduction."

"But one Eleanor has chosen not to make. She doesn't want to admit that someone in the family, her own husband to be precise, had created the problem. She wanted to

blame it all on an outsideer. The family must remain inviolate at all costs."

"But you pointed out the truth?"

"A totally useless exercise in reality therapy. She won't
ever acknowledge it, and why should she? She's built her
life around the families. The image of the Castletons and
Lightfoots is more important to her than anything else.
What right do I have to mess with her little world?"

"I thought you wanted to avenge Crissie Masters. Repre-
sent her interests in the families. What about all that business about Castletons and Lightfoots bearing a moral
responsibility for what happened?"

"I realized today that I'm tired of playing Lady Avenger.
Crissie's dead and no one's responsible, not even Crissie.
She was the victim of cosmic bad luck. The universe is full
of it."

"I don't know if I can handle a Philadelphia Fox turned
existentialist. I liked you better when you were paranoid
about conspiracies."

She looked at him. "I'm glad you're still finding something amusing in all this. You really do enjoy playing your
little games, don't you, Nick? You should. You're very
good at them."

He scowled at her, swirling the scotch in his glass. "You
really are in a hell of a mood, aren't you?"

"You want to talk conspiracies? All right, I'll talk conspiracies. Let's start with you telling me how your trip to
Santa Barbara went?"

He winced around a swallow of scotch. "You were the
one who called my office down there? Martha said the lady
hadn't left her name. I thought it might have been Hilary."

"Maybe we both called," Phila suggested, annoyed.

"No. Martha said only one woman called asking for me
by name. Had to be you or Hilary."

"Why did you check in with your Santa Barbara office in
the first place? Worried someone might suspect you had
lied about your little business jaunt?"

"It was one of the risks involved. Just out of curiosity,
what made you suspicious?"

"I don't trust Castletons or Lightfoots any more than they trust me," she said.

"Ah, that's my old Philadelphia."

"I'm glad you find it all so damned funny."

"I went to Seattle, not Santa Barbara."

"Did you?"

"Do you care?" he retorted.

"Not particularly. Not any more. It's your business."

"Damn right." Nick set his glass down on the tiled countertop. "And I intend to get it back in August."

Phila nodded slowly, toying with the salad greens. "Everyone knows you're up to something. People keep warning me you're using me."

Nick leaned back against the counter, his eyes gleaming behind the lenses of his glasses. "What do you think?"

"That they're right, of course. You're using me."

"Any more than you're using me, Phila? You seemed to be having a great time in bed."

"Oh, I was. But the party's over. I'm tired and it's time to go home."

"Where's home? Holloway?"

She shook her head quickly. "No. Not there. Someplace new. Seattle, maybe."

He nodded. "I've got a place you can stay in while you hunt for an apartment and a job. A condo near the Market. You'd love it."

She was floored. "Why would you want to do me any favors? I've told you I'm going to give the shares back to Darren. You don't have to pay me off for returning them."

"I'm not trying to pay you off for them. I'm offering you a bribe so you'll hang on to them until the August meeting."

"Why should I do that?"

"I need them," Nick said softly. "More importantly, I need you."

She experienced a small rush of pleasure that she tried to suppress immediately. "How?"

"I want the others to know you're going to back me at

the annual meeting. I want them to think you believe in me."

"I see." She clamped a lid on the surge of disappointment, just as she had damped down the initial hope. "But I think I'm losing this somewhere. Why do you want the families to think I'm going to back you?"

"Because if you continue to do so, there's a fair-to-even chance that the owner of one of the other large share blocks will throw his or her lot in with us."

"And if one of the others does decide to back you?"

Nick smiled slowly. "Then I get my old job back."

"You'll get control of Castleton & Lightfoot again?"

"Yeah. That's the scenario." He poured himself another glass of scotch.

Phila felt chilled. The rain was falling in heavy sheets against the old windows. "What makes you think that my backing you with Crissie's shares will encourage any of the others to do so?"

"You, my sweet, are shaping up as the Good Witch. You're annoying the hell out of the families, but some of the members are starting to think you may have a few good points."

"Such as?"

"Such as the primitive, rather naive qualities of honesty and integrity."

"Even if they do suspect me of having left-wing, antiestablishment tendencies?"

"Yeah. You're putting doubts in their minds about me, Phila. This wasn't quite the way I planned it, but I think things are going to work out. They're all starting to wonder if I really was the bad guy three years ago. I'm hoping that if you spread enough doubt around, it'll act like the manure you lectured us about at Eleanor's dinner. It'll do some good."

"You mean it will benefit you."

"Right."

"Who's the Wicked Witch in this story?"

"One guess."

"Hilary?"

225

"Yeah."

Phila shook her head. "I don't think I like it. Any of it. I'm tired of being used."

"You don't have much choice," Nick said. The steel core was showing again. "You haven't had any choice since the day you inherited the shares."

"I told you, I'm out of the vengeance business. If you're trying to get back at Hilary because she let everyone think you walked out on her and the baby three years ago, then you can do it on your own. You're a big boy. I want to get on with my own life." Phila looked down at the salad. She was never going to be able to eat it. She stood up and carried her dishes over to the sink.

Nick put out his hand and caught hold of her wrist. His eyes were the color of the rain outside. "I think we need to discuss this a little further."

"No. I've made up my mind. I'm leaving tomorrow."

"I want you to support me or at least pretend to support me until the August meeting."

"Why should I? What's in it for me?" Phila asked, suddenly feeling truly angry.

Nick stared at her for a long, considering moment. "What do you want out of it?"

She exhaled heavily. "Nothing. I can't think of anything I want from a Lightfoot, so I guess that means no deal."

"Phila, I need your help."

"I doubt it."

"Believe me, everything hinges on you. Things are at a very delicate stage. If you walk out on me now it could tip the balance of power back in Hilary's direction."

"I'm not interested in helping you get even with your ex-wife, damn it!"

"Jesus. You think I'm going through all of this just to get even?"

"Why else would you be doing it?"

"I'm doing it to save Castleton & Lightfoot, you little idiot. Which means I'm doing it for the families, whether they like it or not. My own personal problems with Hilary are the least of it."

Phila wriggled her captive wrist. "Let go of me."

Nick hesitated and then released her. He folded his arms across his chest. "Please help me, Phila."

She went over to the window. "What did you mean about trying to save Castleton & Lightfoot?"

"Before I tell you the story, you've got to give me your word you won't say anything to any of the others."

"If something is threatening the company, why shouldn't they be told?"

"Because at this stage Hilary could still cover her tracks and get away with what she has planned."

Phila hesitated, knowing he was shamelessly pushing her buttons and she was responding. She could already feel herself weakening. "All right, tell me about it."

"Your word of honor you'll keep quiet until the August meeting?"

"Yes."

"All right, here it is in a nutshell. About six months ago I started picking up rumors of secret negotiations that involved Castleton & Lightfoot. It was hard to tell what was going on at first. All I got were bits and pieces here and there. I had to be careful about checking out the gossip. I didn't want word to get back to Hilary that I was on to something."

"What did you learn?"

"With the help of a couple of friends who were in a position to check the rumors, I found out that Hilary was preparing to sell off a chunk of Castleton & Lightfoot to an outsider, a guy named Alex Traynor."

"Who's Traynor?"

"A fast-moving, very smooth Silicon Valley character. He's been walking a fine line down there in California for the past couple of years. Buys into high-tech firms, bleeds them dry and then sells out, leaving a carcass behind."

"Why would Hilary want to sell off part of the company she controls? It doesn't make sense."

Nick shoved his hand through his hair. "I don't know. I've asked myself that question a hundred times. Maybe Traynor has convinced her he can make Castleton & Lightfoot bigger and stronger than it already is. Or maybe she's got something else in mind. All I do know is that she's going to do it after she gets the backing she needs at the August meeting."

"The others won't back her in a move to sell off shares to outsiders. Good grief, Nick, that's the last thing they'd do. Look at how hard they're working to get Crissie's shares back."

"The others aren't going to know what's happened until it's all over. Hilary's not stupid. She's not going to put a simple motion before them to sell off some shares. She's just going to get them to vote her a greater range of powers."

"Why would they agree to give her more power?"

"Everyone on the board has his or her own reason. My father simply doesn't care enough to get involved anymore, apparently. He'd rather play golf. Darren wants more freedom to jump into politics in a big way. He'd rather turn the entire company over to someone else to run so long as that someone else promises to back his campaign. Vicky always votes the way Darren tells her to vote and she wants a political future for Darren, too."

"And Eleanor is also determined to give Darren his chance to run for office," Phila finished slowly. "Besides, she trusts Hilary. Feels she must support her. She'll give her whatever she asks for at the meeting."

"Yeah."

"But none of them would back her if they thought it meant hurting Castleton & Lightfoot. Why not just explain to them what's going on?"

"I told you, Hilary's still got time to cover her tracks. I've got no real proof, just rumors off the California network and a file on Traynor that's stored in the office safe in Seattle."

"What's in the file?"

"Nothing incriminating enough to prove my point, unfortunately. I went through it yesterday afternoon. Given the information I have from my contacts, I know it means Hilary is dealing with Traynor, but I can't prove she's going to sell off a chunk of C&L to him. I need to get control of Castleton & Lightfoot away from her long enough to smash the deal with Traynor. I can do that if I get my old job back in August."

"You intend to get yourself appointed CEO again. To do that you need a majority of the shareholders on your side."

"You've got the picture."

Phila stared out into the storm. "Do you really believe that with my backing you will convince one or more of the others to support you?"

"It's my only real chance. What it comes down to, Phila, is that I think you can convince at least one of them to trust me again."

"Which one? Your father?"

"Maybe," Nick swirled the last of the scotch in his glass. "Possibly Darren."

"What about Eleanor?"

"I think she's too convinced Hilary's the Benevolent Queen who can give Darren his shot at a political career. Also, Eleanor has the most to protect in terms of the past, as you found out today. She won't be able to trust you because you were involved with Crissie. She can't admit anything good could have come out of that mess with Crissie Masters."

"What if I can't get any of the others to go along with you?"

"Then I lose, and Castleton & Lightfoot goes under."

"You're taking a huge risk."

"A calculated risk," he corrected with a wry smile. "I'm good at those."

Of course he was. Phila swung around to confront him with a rush of tight fury. "Tell me something, Nick. When you came looking for me was it because Eleanor had asked you to get the shares back from me or had you already figured out a way to use me to retake control of the company?"

He shrugged. "When I learned about you, I realized I had been dealt a wild card. I wasn't sure at the time what I was going to do with it. I wasn't even sure what to make of you at first. You weren't what I expected so I just decided to play it by ear."

"What did you expect?"

"Someone who would have accepted a quick payoff for the shares. I realized almost as soon as I met you that would be the wrong approach, though."

"So you offered me a chance to wallow in my anger and frustration over Crissie's death, instead. And I jumped at the opportunity." Phila shook her head. "Damn, but I hate being manipulated, Nick."

"I know. So do I. But don't you think that in this instance, we're both guilty of using each other? You were quick enough to take advantage of what I was offering."

"Don't try to make me feel guilty. I already feel stupid. That's bad enough."

"Why should you feel stupid?" he asked, his mouth hardening. "You got what you wanted out of the deal."

"A chance to torment Castletons and Lightfoots for the way they treated Crissie? That's a joke. They're already tormenting each other very nicely. They don't need me to add any more fuel to the fire."

"You weren't sure of that a few days ago. If your mind is more at ease about the whole thing now, if you've really been able to accept Crissie's death, then you've accomplished your goal. All I ask is that you let me accomplish mine."

Phila just looked at him, too weary even to cry. Then she turned and started to leave the kitchen. She got as far as the doorway before she lost her self-control. Rage boiled up within her, washing away the exhaustion. Her fist slammed against the door frame.

"Why did you have to take it as far as sleeping with me?" she got out in a choked voice, whirling around to confront him. "Why couldn't you have kept it on the level of a simple business deal?"

Nick didn't move, but there was tension in every line of his body. When he spoke his voice was soft. "I've told you from the beginning that our going to bed together has nothing to do with all this."

"That's pure bullshit, and you know it. You used the fact that I was attracted to you, just as you want to use my shares. Just as you want to use me as a Judas goat to lead one of the others over to your side in August."

"What about me?"

"What about you?" she said through her teeth.

"You've been happy enough to use me in bed. Just as you were happy enough to use me to gain entrée into the inner circle of the families."

Phila shut her eyes against the fury that was threatening to overwhelm her. "No. It wasn't like that."

"Wasn't it?"

Her eyes flew open. "I didn't sleep with you to get that entrée."

"I didn't sleep with you to get those shares."

Phila felt dazed and cornered. "I guess," she said slowly, "when you get right down to it, neither one of us can afford to trust the other. Not in bed, at any rate."

"Can't we?"

"No." She turned away again and went purposefully out into the living room. She came to a halt in the middle of the floor, realizing she had no particular destination in mind. She had just needed to escape the kitchen.

"Phila," Nick said quietly behind her, "don't run out on me. Help me. Please."

"Why should I, damn you?"

"I told you. I need you."

"To save Castleton & Lightfoot." She thought of Vicky and little Jordan and Reed and Darren and Eleanor. "It seems to me you should all be able to save yourselves."

"We can't do it without your help."

Thelma Anderson's words echoed in Phila's ears. *You're a born crusader. A rescuer of others. It's your nature, Phila.* Thelma was not the only one who understood her greatest weakness, Phila realized. Nick had caught on really fast.

"Tell me something, Nick. Why do you care what happens to Castleton & Lightfoot now after what the others did to you?"

Nick hesitated. "It's hard to explain. All I can say is that it's a family thing."

"The chips are down, and even though no one except Eleanor has spoken to you in three years you're going to try to save the family firm for everybody."

"That's a little heavy on the dramatics, isn't it?" he asked with a fleeting smile.

It may have sounded dramatic, but it also rang true. Phila realized she believed him. He was not asking this of her because he wanted revenge on Hilary, or if he did, that revenge was just a byproduct. His main goal was to save C&L for the families. She understood that need now. Family was family.

"All right," Phila said. "I'll do what I can. Just don't expect miracles."

"Thank you, Phila."

"Don't get maudlin about it, okay? Let's just keep this on a clean, businesslike basis." She started for the bedroom.

"Phila?"

"No," she said very firmly. "If you stay here again, you sleep on the couch. We're not going to get this situation any more confused than it already is."

Three hours later Nick decided he'd had enough of the lumpy sofa. He kicked aside the blankets and got to his feet. Padding barefoot to the bedroom door, he opened it carefully and looked at the bed. He could just barely make out Phila's form curled up under the covers.

He eased the door open farther and stepped inside the room. She did not stir. He went to the bed and slowly pulled back the sheet. Then he slid in beside her.

Nick touched her lightly and, without waking, she immediately turned into his arms, snuggling close. One of her legs slipped between his. He heard her sigh softly against his chest, and a great tension seemed to evaporate from his body.

Phila was wrong when she said they could not trust each

other in bed. It was in bed that she was at her most honest with him and he with her.

"Bastard," she muttered drowsily. But she did not pull away. The tip of her tongue touched his nipple.

"Do that again," he said, rolling onto his back and taking her with him.

She did, and a very pleasant tremor went through him. Then her tongue touched his other nipple, and he groaned softly. He stroked her sleek back down to her thigh, found the hem of her nightgown and pulled it up to her waist. His fingers moved lightly into the warm cleft between her buttocks. Nick felt the small shiver that rippled through her and he smiled in the darkness.

"Damn you, Nick. How do you do this to me?" But she wasn't waiting around for an answer.

She was starting to wriggle down under the sheet. Nick felt her bare teeth on the skin of his stomach. When he shifted his leg she moved lower. Her fingers blazed a trail ahead of her mouth, finding the base of his manhood and cupping him eagerly. He was already rock hard. He had been since he'd entered the room.

"Baby," he muttered. "Kiss me. Please. I want to feel your mouth on me."

She instantly started to crawl back up along the length of him, aiming for his lips. He halted her gently, his hands twining in her hair.

"Kiss me down there," he muttered thickly. "Where your hand is."

She trembled again and then she began to work her way back down his belly to the hard length of him. He felt her breath stirring the mat of hair above his thighs, and then he sucked in his breath as he felt her lips on his throbbing shaft.

"So good," Nick said. "So damn good." He lifted himself into her warm, soft mouth and she took him willingly. Her fingertips traced erratic little designs on the insides of his thighs. His whole body began to grow rigid.

"Now," he told her, reaching for a package in the bedside drawer. His fingers touched the revolver. He pushed it out of the way, scrabbling for the condom.

Phila released him as he quickly sheathed himself. Then she was flowing up and over him until she was lying on top of him. He reached down to guide himself into her, felt her tight, hot opening give way slowly as she pushed herself eagerly against him.

Then he was inside where he needed to be. Deep inside. He exhaled heavily, savoring the sweet heat that engulfed him. He slid his hands up Phila's soft, curving thighs and she cried out and clutched at his shoulders. He could feel her fingernails sinking into his skin, and he laughed silently in the shadows.

Within a few minutes she was rigid with shuddering pleasure, and he gave in to his own shattering climax. Phila collapsed on top of him.

A long time later he stirred sleepily and adjusted Phila more closely against him. He thought she was asleep, but her voice came softly out of the darkness.

"Whose baby was it?"

"Huh?" It took Nick a few seconds to orient himself to reality. He had been drifting in the pleasant aftermath and had been intending to glide straight into sleep.

She rested her chin on her folded arms and peered down at him with her big, questioning, wary eyes. "Hilary's baby. Whose was it?"

"That's a hell of a thing to bring up now."

"There was a baby. Everyone agrees on that. It wasn't yours, so whose was it?"

Nick rubbed the bridge of his nose, feeling weary. "My father's I guess. She probably started to work seducing him as soon as she realized I meant to end the marriage."

"Nah." Phila dismissed that impatiently. "Not Reed's."

Nick stopped rubbing his nose. "He was quick enough to marry her."

Phila eyed him thoughtfully. "You've been thinking all along that Reed slept with Hilary?"

"There's not much point speculating about it one way or the other. It's history."

"Wait a second. It's bad enough that Reed suspects you of walking out on your own kid, but I never realized you might have believed he was the one who got Hilary pregnant."

Nick was suddenly very tense. "You don't think that's the most logical explanation under the circumstances?"

"Good heavens, no. Reed would never have slept with your wife. Not while she was still technically married to you, at any rate. Besides, Eleanor says Hilary claims she was raped."

"Yes, I know."

"Reed would never use force on a woman any more than you would."

"No, but Hilary is quite capable of lying to Eleanor."

"Possible, but I still don't see Reed as the guilty party, either way. He only stepped into the situation because he was convinced he had to make up for what you had done. Honestly, Nick, how could you have been so dumb as to think your father had slept with your wife?"

Nick got angry. "He married her, for God's sake. The day after the divorce was final. What was I supposed to think?"

"What a pair of idiots. So smart in some ways but brick-dumb in others." Phila sat up, drew her legs up to her breasts and wrapped her arms around her knees. The puzzle was pulling at her again. "Let's think about this."

"Why bother?"

"Because I believe it may be important."

"It's old news, Phila."

She shook her head thoughtfully. "I'm not so sure about that."

"Damn it. It happened three years ago."

"It's still affecting the families."

"I'm not asking you to hang around until August so that you can play social worker. This is not a dysfunctional family situation that requires your professional counseling services. Just follow my lead, okay? Stick to the business side of things. I'll handle the details."

Phila was silent, but Nick could almost hear the wheels spinning in her head. Her engine was revving up again, and he had to admit it was a relief. She had given him a real scare earlier in the evening when he'd walked in and found her looking as though she had given up on all of them, including him.

Nick gave her a few more minutes of silent contemplation, but when she failed to stretch out beside him he grew impatient. "All right, maybe it was some outsider who got Hilary pregnant. Some man with whom she was having an affair."

"Not likely."

"Why not? She sure as hell wasn't in love with me. She could easily have had an affair, gotten pregnant at an opportune time and decided to use the pregnancy to her own advantage."

"I don't think that's the way it happened. Eleanor says she saw Hilary the morning after she found out she was pregnant. Hilary was very distraught. That's not the attitude of a mature, sophisticated woman who's simply having an affair and accidently gotten pregnant. A woman in that position would have taken care of the problem quietly."

"For crying out loud, Phila. I've told you Hilary is more than capable of lying."

"I believe you. But I don't think Eleanor was lying to me this morning. She genuinely believes Hilary was abused. She feels very protective toward her. I wonder why?"

"I've told you, Eleanor wants to keep Hilary in charge of things so that Darren's career can get launched. Naturally she feels protective toward her. Now stop looking for answers to old questions and go to sleep."

"Stop telling me what to do. You know I'm not good at taking orders."

"True. There are, fortunately, others things that you do very well, however, so I think I'll keep you around."

She looked at him, her eyes very large in the shadows. The eyes of a clever little fox, Nick thought. Even in the darkness he could tell Phila's gaze was full of energy once more.

"Just so long as you understand that this time around our relationship is strictly business," Phila declared.

He ran his thumb down the length of her graceful spine. "Lady, who are you trying to kid?"

THE GOLDEN CHANCE

CHAPTER FOURTEEN

❧

The knocking on the front door of the cottage awoke Phila the next morning. She opened her eyes slowly, aware that something heavy was weighing her down. Instinctively she shoved at the offending bulk, trying to push it aside. It didn't budge. Her fingers touched bare skin, skin with rough hair on it—masculine skin. She was suddenly, frantically, wide awake and struggling wildly.

"*Phila*. Phila, wait a second. Hold on. It's just me. Take it easy, honey."

"Get off of me," she hissed in muffled tones, shoving at Nick's broad shoulders.

"I am getting off of you. I'm sorry. I must have moved in my sleep." Nick rolled quickly to one side, disentangling his legs from hers. He had been lying half-sprawled over her, his heavy thigh anchoring her lower body, his arm across her breasts.

Phila sat up, breathing quickly, and pushed hair out of her eyes.

"Are you all right?" Nick said gently.

"There's someone at the door."

"I'll get it." Nick pushed aside the covers and stood up. He gazed down at her in concern. "Are you okay?"

She nodded rapidly, not meeting his eyes. "Yes. Yes,

I'm fine. I just panicked for a minute, that's all. You know I can't stand having a man on top of me."

"It was an accident, honey."

"I know, I know. Go see who's at the door." She waved him out of the room.

Nick stepped into a pair of jeans and went reluctantly out of the bedroom. Phila took several deep breaths and pulled herself together. It wasn't too bad this time, all things considered. The panic had been short-lived, and it was already fading.

Nick would never hurt her. He had just accidentally triggered some old reflexive fears.

She heard Reed Lightfoot's voice in the outer room. Phila got out of bed and pulled on her robe. When she opened the bedroom door she felt almost calm again.

"Well now, don't you look all bright eyed and bushy tailed this morning, Phila," Reed said cheerfully as he spotted her in the hall. "I was just telling Nick, here, that I thought you might like to take another stab at a golf ball today. What do you say?"

Phila blinked, her gaze going to Nick, who was standing barefoot near the front door. He had a watchful expression on his face, and she knew he was plotting again.

Phila yawned. "I don't think I'm up to it today, Reed. Why don't you go with him, Nick?"

There was a moment of awkward silence as both men assimilated her words. Reed cleared his throat. "It's short notice. You've probably got a lot of things to do, Nick."

"Yeah. And I don't have a set of clubs with me. Haven't played for quite a while," Nick said.

Phila's eyes narrowed. "Don't be ridiculous. The notice isn't any shorter for you, Nick, than it would have been for me. You don't have anything in particular to do this morning, and you can always rent a set of clubs at the course. Gee whiz, being Lightfoots, you could probably get the pro to loan you his personal set, if necessary."

"Course is probably crowded, anyway, this morning," Reed offered weakly. "Might be better to try it another time."

"Yeah."

Phila frowned at the two men. "Go on, both of you. I'm not used to having so many males standing around in my living room at this hour of the morning. Makes me nervous."

Reed inclined his head in an abrupt motion. "Suit yourself, Nick. Feel like a game?"

"You'd probably cream me."

Reed began to smile evilly. "Goddamn right. Especially if you're out of practice."

"I'm not that out of practice. Care to put a little money where your mouth is?"

Reed sighed. "Too much like taking candy from a baby."

"We'll see. Let me get some shoes on. I'll be right with you." Nick went down the hall to the bedroom with a long stride.

Reed looked at Phila. His brows rose. "Sure you don't want to come with us?"

"I'm sure. I want a real breakfast. Coffee and a Danish doesn't do it for me."

"We could have a real meal at the clubhouse restaurant before we go out on the course."

"Hah. I know you. You'd lure me out there with a promise of ham and eggs and then tell me we didn't have time to eat. Too many people waiting to tee off. You'd rush me out onto the course, and I'd have to walk eighteen holes with my stomach growling."

Reed glanced idly around the room. "Why did you push Nick into going with me?"

"I think it's time the two of you got to know each other again. I think somewhere along the line you've both forgotten a few important things about yourselves."

"Like what?"

"Figure it out. You're both reasonably smart. Not brilliant, mind you, but definitely above average for the male of the species. No telling what you might come up with if you try." Phila adjusted the sash of her purple robe.

Nick came out of the bedroom, his windbreaker slung

over his shoulder. He walked over to Phila and kissed her squarely on the mouth. "You remember our deal, okay?"

Phila slitted her eyes. "Go on, get out of here."

"She always this grouchy in the morning?" Reed asked as he followed his son out the door.

"No. Sometimes she's worse. Don't worry, I'm working on the problem." The door closed behind him.

Phila rolled her eyes and went toward the kitchen to start the coffee. When she had it going she trooped back into the bedroom with the intention of taking her morning shower.

She was halfway down the hall when she noticed the closet door standing ajar. She opened it and saw that Nick had gathered up the bedding she had given him for the sofa last night and shoved it inside. He must have done it in a hurry on his way to answer the door.

This was the second time he'd scrambled to disguise the fact that he'd been relegated to the sofa. Had to be pure masculine ego. She found it oddly touching to realize that his male pride wouldn't allow him to let anyone think he might have had to spend the night in the living room. He was so cool and confident; so sure of himself in so many other ways.

It occurred to Phila that being married to Hilary might have been a difficult cross for a man like Nick to bear.

She opened the closet and began refolding the blankets he had tossed inside along with his clothing.

Something crackled in the pocket of the shirt he had been wearing when he arrived the previous evening. Phila glanced inside the pocket and saw the piece of paper that had been folded into fourths.

She almost talked herself out of looking at it, but some instinct made her go ahead and remove the sheet of paper from the pocket. She unfolded it carefully and saw that it was a fax copy of a newspaper article dated two and a half months earlier.

HOLLOWAY. A Holloway area man was convicted today on a variety of drug and assault charges stemming from an attack on a social worker earlier this year.

Elijah Joshua Spalding was given a total of eighteen months in prison.

The assault took place in the parking lot of the Holloway Grill. According to testimony at the trial, Spalding had agreed to meet Philadelphia Fox, a social worker, at the restaurant to discuss matters concerning the foster home run by himself and his wife, Ruth.

Spalding and Fox arrived in the parking lot at approximately the same time. There was an argument during which Spalding attacked the social worker and tried to drag her into his pickup truck. Fox fought back and Spalding got a gun out of the pickup. He was threatening her with it when police arrived on the scene.

When Spalding was searched at the time of the arrest, a quantity of heroin was found on him. Spalding pleaded guilty to the assault charges.

His wife maintained throughout the trial that her husband had never used drugs. The children who had been in the Spaldings' care have been sent to other homes.

Phila's fingers were shaking as she refolded the piece of paper. Nick had been digging into her past. She wondered frantically what he had been looking for or, worse, what he suspected.

He could not know anything more than what the newspaper story had covered, she told herself. There was no reason for him to think there was anything more to the tale.

She sank down onto the plump arm of the sofa, trying to think logically. There was absolutely nothing to worry about. He had merely been curious about Elijah Spalding. It made sense. After all, he knew she had a definite fear of the man, and he had taken care to see that she learned how to protect herself in the event Spalding showed up in her life.

That's all it was, she decided. Nick had just been indulging his curiosity. He had told his father he intended to check into the matter, so he'd gotten a copy of a clipping that covered the story.

Phila told herself she had enough things to worry about without getting paranoid over this.

"Looks like you owe me a beer, Nick, not to mention ten bucks." Reed Lightfoot was grinning broadly as he led the way off the eighteenth green toward the clubhouse. "Easiest goddamn money I've made in a long time. When was the last time you played?"

"Six months ago. I had a game with a client."

"You beat him?"

"Yeah. But he wasn't as good as you are. Of course, you've been practicing a lot lately."

Reed stopped smiling. "That's a fact."

"Come on, I'll buy you the beer."

"Don't forget the ten bucks."

They found a couple of chairs out on the clubhouse terrace. Nick leaned back, one foot cocked across his knee, a cold bottle of beer in his hand.

Reed took a big swallow of his Rainier straight from the can. "Good thing Eleanor isn't here. Look at us. We look like a couple of blue-collar working stiffs after a long day behind the wheel of a heavy rig. She thinks beer-drinking is low class."

"Eleanor always had a problem with class."

"Nora used to say it was because Eleanor secretly thought she'd married down." Reed was silent for a minute. "Nora used to be right a lot of the time."

"Yeah."

"That little gal of yours thinks she's right most of the time."

"She thinks she's right all of the time." Nick watched a foursome getting ready to go out on the course.

"Is she?"

"I don't know yet," Nick said slowly. "But I'm beginning to think her instincts are pretty good about most things."

"She's got goddamn screwy politics, but I guess that's only to be expected, given her upbringing," Reed noted charitably.

"Yeah. Only to be expected."

"She given up that wacko idea about us having some responsibility for Crissie Masters's death?"

"She's come to the conclusion it was a case of cosmic bad luck. I think that's how she described it."

Reed considered that. "There may be a grain of truth in that. Things were chaotic during the time Crissie was around. A lot of tension. A lot of anger. Burke was the only one enjoying himself. He was like a kid with a fire-cracker."

"Makes for an unstable situation."

"That it does." Reed swallowed some beer. "What are you going to do with Miss Philadelphia Fox?"

"I think I'll keep her around."

"Until you get the shares back from her?"

Nick smiled slowly. "Even after I get the shares back from her."

"Yeah, I was beginning to get that impression. When are you going to get those shares, Nick?"

"Soon."

Reed turned his head to look at his son with a level gaze. "What are you going to do with them when you get hold of them?"

Nick settled deeper into the chair, his eyes on the four-some that was now making its way up the first fairway. "Do you think it's possible one or both of us may have made a mistake three years ago, Dad?"

Reed exhaled slowly. "No need to ask where that notion came from, is there? The little Mouth put that idea in your head."

"Did she put it into yours?"

"Got to admit it, that little gal has a way of making you stop and think about a few things," Reed finally said care-fully. "Nora used to be able to do that, too."

"Make you stop and think?"

"Uh huh." Reed swallowed more beer. "Had a way of seeing things a lot more clearly than I did sometimes. She was better with people than I ever was."

Nick decided that was as close as either of them was going to get for now. Maybe it was time to take another risk. "If you really want to know what I'm going to do with those shares of Phila's, I'll tell you."

Reed studied him expressionlessly for a long moment. "I'm listening."

"I'm going to have her back me at the August meeting."

"Why?" Reed's voice turned harsh. "The shares belong to Darren, and you goddamn well know it."

"I know it. But I can't be sure I can get Darren to back me. I need one of you besides Phila on my side, though."

"One of us?"

"You, Darren and Vicky or Eleanor."

"What the hell are you going for, Nick?"

"I'm going to try and pull Castleton & Lightfoot out of the water before it goes under."

Reed's hand flexed around his beer can. "Maybe you'd better tell me the whole story."

Nick took another swallow of beer and did exactly that.

Phila was wondering how the golf game was going and contemplating a walk on the beach, when Hilary arrived at the front door. The instant Phila saw who her visitor was, she wished she'd left for the beach five minutes earlier.

"Come on in," Phila said politely because it was the only thing she could say under the circumstances. "Would you like some coffee?"

"That would be nice, thank you." Hilary stood for a moment, looking elegantly out of place in the comfortably shabby room.

She was wearing a pair of slim black pants and an austerely cut russet shirt with wide cuffs. A handful of simple gold chains swung gracefully down the center of the shirt.

"Have a seat," Phila offered as she went into the kitchen.

245

When she returned she saw that Hilary had chosen the sofa. She was perched regally on the edge so as not to let herself get sucked back into the sagging depths of the old cushions. She examined Phila as she took her coffee.

"It's hard to believe you and Crissie were so close."

"Do you doubt it?"

"No. Crissie talked enough about you to make me realize you and she had a special relationship." Hilary paused. "Sometimes I was almost envious of that relationship."

"There was no need for you to be," Phila said gently as she took the chair across from her. "Hilary, if I ask you an honest question, will you answer it?"

"I don't know."

"Were you raped as Eleanor says?"

Hilary's head snapped around sharply. She fixed Phila with fierce eyes. "Yes."

Phila drew a deep breath as pity welled up in her. "I'm so sorry."

Almost immediately Hilary had control of herself. "I didn't realize Eleanor had told you so much. She's never told anyone else about that part of it."

"She was upset."

"You upset her," Hilary accused.

"Yes. I . . . ." Phila swallowed. "I'm afraid I hurt her."

"You're hurting a lot of people just by being here. Don't you think it's time you handed over the shares and left?"

"Probably."

There was a long silence, and then Hilary said quietly, "He called me cold, you know. Told me I was only a beautiful shell of a woman. He could not tolerate the fact that I did not respond to him."

Phila put down her mug and clasped her hands together. "You don't have to tell me about it, Hilary."

"Why shouldn't I? You're thinking of becoming part of the family, aren't you? Maybe you'd better know a little more about the kind of family you're hoping to marry into. Maybe the truth will make you open your eyes."

"I don't think you want to tell me this."

Hilary eyed her sharply. "Perhaps you're right. It isn't a very pleasant tale."

"Tell me about Crissie instead."

Hilary hesitated, her expression softening. "Crissie was special. To others she seemed very self-centered. But I understood her. She understood me."

"I know."

"I've never been as close to anyone as I was to Crissie." Phila nodded.

"You know it all, don't you?" Hilary asked tightly.

"That you and she were lovers? Yes. I did some careful thinking last night, and finally put together what I'd learned about the families with some things Crissie had said about you all. Crissie was discreet and she never would have told me outright about her affair with you. But as I got to know all of you, it wasn't too hard to figure it out."

Hilary watched her. "You're not jealous, are you?"

"Crissie and I were best friends, but we were never lovers. She knew, even before I did, that we never would be." Phila took a sip of coffee. "She disliked men intensely. She thought they were all fools, although she occasionally found them useful. She used to say I was hopelessly trapped in my heterosexuality and that it was a damn shame." *A shame because I wasn't even enjoying it.* Crissie would be genuinely glad to know that Nick had definitely changed that much, at least.

Hilary's mouth curved grimly. "I did not realize why I could not respond to Nick or any other man until I met Crissie. I put Nick off until our wedding night because I was afraid he'd realize he wouldn't ever get the kind of response he wanted. I sensed he would be a physically demanding man, a passionate man. But when I met Crissie, I finally understood. I stopped fighting myself."

"But you married Reed."

"Only because of the baby. Reed has never touched me."

"You're both living rather lonely lives, aren't you?"

"I have my goals. I'm satisfied with them." Hilary's eyes were intent but no longer fierce. "If you know Crissie and I were lovers then you must know she intended to give me those shares or at least back me at the annual meeting. She knew how important they were to me."

"But she didn't give them to you, Hilary. Nor did she will them to you. She left them to me, and they didn't come with instructions."

"Crissie was full of life. She had no way of knowing she would die before the August meeting. It never occurred to her to change her will. She was too young to think about things like that. Neither of us even considered the possibility of her death."

"I don't believe she would have altered her will, even if she had thought about it. I've told you, Crissie and I were best friends."

"But I was her lover."

"She'd had other lovers, Hilary. She did not mention them in her will."

"Damn you, I know she intended for me to have those shares. She told me she did. You have no right to them. Are you so blinded by your infatuation with Nick that you're going to let him tell you what to do with those shares?"

Phila thought about that. "I'm not backing him because I'm infatuated with him."

"You think you're in love with him?" Hilary softened. "You think he'll marry you?"

Phila shook her head. "It's got nothing to do with any of that. It's a business decision."

"A *business* decision. You mean he's offering you so much money you can't resist? Did he finally find your price?"

"No." Phila said. "He was too smart to try. He knew I'd just get spitting mad if he tried to buy me off."

"What's his secret?" Hilary demanded.

"I trust him to do what's best for the families."

"You trust him? You're crazy. After what I just told you about what he did to me?"

"You didn't say it was Nick who raped you."

"Well, it was, you little fool."

"Was it?" Phila realized her coffee was getting cold.

"Yes, yes, *yes!*" Hilary leaped to her feet, the cup and saucer clattering as she half-dropped them on the small table. "He hurt me very badly. So very badly."

Phila looked down at her coffee. "I don't believe you, Hilary. In fact, I don't believe you were raped by anyone."

"Then you're a bigger fool than I thought." Hilary rushed for the door and then halted abruptly, not looking back. "Just tell me one thing, if you can. I have to know."

"What do you have to know, Hilary?"

"Why you? Why did Crissie love you so much? You weren't even her lover."

Phila felt the tears well up in her eyes and begin to course down her cheeks. "Don't you see?" she whispered. "Don't you understand? I was the one person with whom she could lower her guard and take the risk of being kind. I was the one person who wanted nothing from her except friendship, the one person who didn't try to use her."

"I never tried to use her."

"Sure you did. Everyone did. Except me. With me she felt safe. But she was wrong, wasn't she? In the end I couldn't protect her, could I?"

There was silence for a long moment before Hilary said very distantly, "We both loved her, but I don't think either of us could have protected her. She was her own worst enemy. How do you save someone from herself?"

Phila blinked back more tears. "I don't know. Oh, God. I just don't know."

The door squeaked on its hinges as Hilary opened it. "One more thing, Phila. Don't go near Eleanor again, do you hear me? I don't want you upsetting her. She's got enough to deal with."

The door slammed behind her.

Phila waited until her legs felt strong enough to support her, and then she got to her feet and went into the kitchen. Her tears mixed with the cold coffee as she poured it down the drain.

* * *

There was nothing like the laughter of a child to jerk you out of morbid thoughts, Phila decided later that afternoon as she walked along the path in front of the Lightfoot and Castleton front gate.

Jordan's screeches of excitement echoed across the lawn. She looked through the wrought-iron bars and saw that he was having a great time rolling down a small hill. As soon as he reached the bottom, he picked himself up and ran back to the top to start the process all over again. Cupcake and Fifi were charging up and down the grassy slope beside him, thoroughly enjoying themselves.

Phila stood for a minute, her fingers locked around the bars of the gate. She was aware of a strangely wistful feeling. Before she could properly identify the odd sensation, Jordan spotted her and waved enthusiastically. Then he came racing toward her. The rottweilers trotted after him.

"Hi, Phila. Hi, Phila. Hi, Phila." Jordan sang his litany of greeting as he barreled toward her.

"Hi, yourself. What are you doing?" She patted the dogs in an effort to fend them off.

"Gettin' dizzy." Jordan grinned proudly.

"Is that a lot of fun?"

He nodded vigorously. "Wanna try?"

"Not today, thanks. I'm already dizzy. Where's your mother?" Phila glanced automatically toward the Castleton beach cottage as Jordan pointed. She saw Victoria rise from the porch swing and start down toward the gate. "Oh, there she is." Phila straightened, trying to give the dogs a farewell pat. She was not in a good mood to deal with any adult Castletons or Lightfoots at the moment. "Tell her hello for me."

"Where you going?"

"I'm just taking a walk."

"Phila." Victoria was almost at the gate.

Phila groaned. "Hello, Vicky. Jordan and I were having a chat. I'm out for a walk."

"Jordan and I will go with you."

"Yes, yes, yes," Jordan said, clapping his hands.

Phila wished she had never turned left when she walked

away from the cottage. She should have headed straight for the solitude of the beach. "Sure. Why not?"

"Where's Nick?" Victoria let herself and her son through the gate and fell into step beside Phila. Jordan scampered on ahead with the dogs.

"Playing golf with Reed."

Victoria looked startled. "He is?"

"Yes."

"They haven't played together in years."

"It's about time they did, then, don't you think?"

Victoria's eyes narrowed. "Hilary went down to the Gilmarten place to see you this morning. I saw her leave."

"Uh huh."

"What did she want?"

"The usual."

"She tried to get you to give her the shares?"

Phila watched the dogs investigating interesting odors at the side of the road. "That's about the only reason a Castleton or a Lightfoot would bother to seek me out, isn't it?"

"Can you blame us?"

"Nope. Vicky, I want to tell you something. I know your biggest concern is about Jordan's future inheritance. Rest assured that I won't do anything to jeopardize it."

"If you back Nick instead of Hilary at the annual meeting, you'll jeopardize my husband's future and, therefore, my son's."

"I think Nick has the best interests of Castleton & Lightfoot at heart."

"So does Hilary. She might not give a damn about anything or anyone else, but Eleanor's right. There's no doubt she's devoted to the firm."

"You don't like Hilary very much, do you?"

Victoria bit her lip and called out to her son. "Jordan, come back here. Stop running with that stick."

"Why don't you like her?" Phila persisted quietly.

"That's not really any of your business, is it?"

Phila thought for a moment. "I'll bet you think the baby was Darren's, don't you?"

Victoria came to a halt and whirled to face her. "You little bitch."

Phila closed her eyes and then opened them narrowly. "A lot of people seem to think of me in those terms lately. Your husband called me the same thing."

"He was right."

"Well, you're wrong. About him, at any rate. Hilary claims she was raped. Darren wouldn't have done such a thing."

"Any man might resort to rape if he's pushed far enough, just as any man might resort to murder," Victoria said tightly.

"Hilary didn't push him. Why should she?"

"Who knows how she thinks? She likes to control everyone and everything. She might have thought she could control Darren with sex. She certainly had Nick blinded for a while when they were engaged."

"Vicky, be reasonable. There's no traumatic secret past shared by your husband and Hilary."

"How do you know?" Victoria's gaze was locked on Phila's face.

"I'd sense it if there were. I'm good at that kind of thing. Darren is a little wary of her and probably with good reason. She's shrewd, and he knows it. He even admires her abilities to some extent. He's willing to deal with her because she's in a position to give him what he wants and she is, after all, family. But that's the extent of his interest in her. Believe me."

"You weren't here three years ago. You don't know what went on. Darren and I were having problems. We were on the brink of divorce. I suppose it would have been only natural for him to turn to Hilary."

"If that's what you've been telling yourself for three years, don't bother. That's not what happened. I'd know if something had gone on between those two. It would show when they're together. Hilary hates the man who got her pregnant, whoever he is. She would never be able to deal with him as serenely as she deals with Darren. I can't imagine why you thought the baby might have been your husband's."

Victoria's hands clenched at her sides. "I was never certain. But I sometimes wondered. Darren's father was, well, I'm sure you've heard."

"A man who made a career of chasing women. Yes, I've figured that much out."

"I used to lie awake at night and wonder if that kind of thing was hereditary." Victoria smiled grimly. "But mostly I managed to put the whole matter out of my mind. Then Crissie arrived on the scene a year ago. She picked up on the situation immediately. She used to go around saying 'like father, like son.'"

"And manage to revive a lot of your secret fears?"

"Yes." Victoria's face was stark. "I guess she did."

"Burke must have been a real bastard."

"Please don't ever say that in front of Eleanor."

"It's too late. I said it yesterday."

Victoria's mouth twisted. "So that was what upset her so much. That was cruel of you, Phila."

"I know. I'm sorry. I was trying to defend Crissie, as usual."

"What a mess."

"Yes," agreed Phila, "it is. I intend to get out of it as soon as the August meeting is over. Unlike Crissie and contrary to popular opinion, I don't see any real advantage to being a Castleton or a Lightfoot. I don't intend to hang around."

Victoria glanced at her assessingly. "What's going to happen at the annual meeting?"

"I'm scheduled to back Nick in whatever he plans to do. Then I'll give the shares back to Darren."

"But that will be too late," Victoria said. "We need Hilary reelected CEO at that meeting."

"Sorry," Phila said. "But I trust Nick more than I trust Hilary. Speaking of trust . . ."

"What about it?"

"You might try telling your husband you trust him."

"Why should I bother? He doesn't really trust me."

Phila's eyes widened. "He thinks you're fooling around?"

Victoria waved that aside impatiently. "No. He thinks I accepted a bribe from Burke three years ago to drop divorce proceedings."

"Did you?"

"No. I stayed because I wanted to try to make the marriage work. I love him."

"Heck of a situation, isn't it? Each of you suspects the other of having done something unforgivable, and neither of you can ever prove your innocence to the other. An interesting problem."

"With no solution?" Victoria asked, her eyes shadowed.

"I didn't say that."

"What are you going to do, Miss Fox? Wave a magic wand and make it all better?"

"No, you and Darren have to do that. But the next time the two of you discuss the matter, consider the sources of your information. You might also consider the fact that in spite of your suspicions, neither of you has gone ahead and broken up the marriage, even though you're both proud people. There must be some love and trust left to work with in your relationship."

"Darren thinks I've stuck with him because I want to be a politician's wife. He's stuck with me because he wants his son."

"Maybe."

"It's the truth, damn you."

"Only if you want it to be."

CHAPTER FIFTEEN

"No," Phila said, absolutely adamant. "Definitely not. I will not be dragged to that fund-raiser in Seattle."

Nick was patient. "It won't be that bad. You might even enjoy yourself."

"No."

"I have to go, and I want you to come with me. You wouldn't make me go alone, would you?"

"You won't be alone. You'll have all your friends and relatives with you. Everyone wants to get Darren off to a flying start in politics."

"Except you."

"I don't care what Darren does with his career. I wish him the best of luck, even if he does have the misfortune to be a Republican. But he certainly doesn't need me at the fancy fund-raiser, and his mother would just as soon I wasn't there, believe me. My presence would probably lower the tone of the whole event."

"Bigot."

"You bet."

Phila shoved her key into the lock of the Gilmarten door. It had been a hard day, what with dealing with Hilary and then Vicky.

Phila and Nick had just walked back from an after-dinner coffee-and-brandy hour arranged by Victoria. The invitation had come as a surprise late that afternoon, and Phila still was not quite certain why it had been issued.

The event had been reasonably civil, although Phila strongly suspected Eleanor of trying to use the opportunity to once more demonstrate the inappropriateness of Phila's presence in the household. Phila had ignored her for the most part, and so had everyone else.

Reed had not been able to avoid baiting Phila, of course, and Nick had appeared to enjoy the fun. But she felt she had held her own and at times had even enjoyed the arguments.

Even Victoria had gotten into the fracas over increasing financial aid and job-training assistance to single women on welfare. She had surprised everyone else by agreeing with Phila that more tax dollars should be spent in that area.

"I'm a mother," Victoria had said calmly when they'd all looked at her in blank astonishment. "This is basically a children's issue. What side do you expect me to take?"

But the argument over Phila's attendance at the fundraiser had begun after the small gathering had concluded. It had developed on the way back to the Gilmarten place and had been conducted only between Nick and Phila. Nick had blithely assumed she would go with him to Darren's first major political bash. Nick assumed a lot lately, Phila told herself resentfully.

"Phila, why are you making such a big deal out of this? You're not nervous about meeting that crowd, are you?"

"There's no point in my going." She tugged off her lightweight jacket and hung it in the closet. "I'm not a member of either family."

Nick scowled as he sat down to unlace his shoes. "You're a part of the company."

"Not for long. Not after that August meeting."

Nick sat up and leaned back into the corner of the sofa, watching her broodingly. "What if I asked you to come with me for my sake?"

"Why should you care if I'm there or not?"

"I want you there."

"Forget it."

"You're supposed to be showing support for me, remember? That was our deal. A united front and all that."

"My going to the fund-raiser won't influence our so-called united front one way or the other. I don't want to go, Nick, and that's final."

He held up a palm in surrender. "All right. If you feel that strongly about it."

"I do." Why was he pushing her on this? she wondered. The fund-raiser did not affect his goal of saving Castleton & Lightfoot, as far as she could tell.

"I accept your decision."

"You're too damn gracious." She didn't believe him for a minute. "How did your golf game go with Reed today?" she asked as she sat down in the chair.

"You heard him bragging this evening about how he beat me."

"Did you let him?"

"Hell, no. He's always been a strong player, and he's had a lot of practice lately since he abdicated the job of running Castleton & Lightfoot. He won fair and square. Cost me ten bucks and a beer."

"Did you talk to him?"

"Yeah, I talked to him. Hard to play eighteen holes of golf with someone without talking to him at some point."

"That's not what I meant, and you know it."

Nick's smile was wry. "I know what you meant. Let's just say I tiptoed around the subject of the baby and let it go at that, okay?"

"Oh." Phila was disappointed.

"It's a little hard to talk about, Phila."

"Yes, I guess it would be. After all, if I'm right the two of you are going to have to admit to some massive errors in judgment, aren't you?"

"And if you're wrong, bringing up the subject will just lead to more trouble and hostility and I don't need that right now. I've got bigger problems."

"Saving Castleton & Lightfoot?"

He gave her an odd look. "That's one of them. I did take a major risk today with Dad. I told him what I had found out about Hilary's plans to sell off a chunk of C&L."

"You did?" Phila was surprised. "That *was* a risk. What made you take it now?"

"You."

Phila sat forward in the chair eagerly. "Well? How did your father respond?"

"Said he'd think about it."

"Is that all? He'll think about it?"

"Yeah."

"But what if he talks to Hilary?"

"She'll deny everything, and I won't be able to prove a damn thing. But he didn't say he was going to talk to Hilary. He just said he was going to think about what I'd told him."

Phila examined the problem closely. "One thing in your favor is that he doesn't talk to Hilary very much at all. As far as I can tell, they're living like strangers in that big house."

"Yeah," Nick said again. "That was sort of the way it looked to me, too."

"So you decided to take the risk of telling Reed everything. Interesting."

"I'm glad you find it so fascinating since you're the one who nagged me into laying my cards on the table with Dad."

"I did not nag. I never nag."

"That's a matter of opinion. You ready to sweep me off to bed?"

"Honestly, Nick, sometimes you have a one-track mind."

"I know. It's really disgusting, isn't it? But, then," he added, brightening, "you don't love me for my mind, do you?"

She caught her breath and glowered to hide the emotions she was afraid might appear in her eyes. "Don't be crude."

"You love it; you're the earthy type at heart."

Phila wished he would stop using the word *love*. It definitely was not a subject she could joke about these days. It made her nervous. She got to her feet. "I'm tired. I don't know about you, but I've had a very wearing day."

Nick got up off the sofa in a smooth motion, smiling in sensual anticipation. "I'm pretty exhausted myself. Can't wait to get to bed."

"You're in an awfully good mood for someone who may have just made a major tactical error today."

"All because of you." He caught her hand and started swinging it as he walked into the bedroom with her.

"Sure."

He stopped and pulled her close. "Kiss me, baby," he growled. "I'm hot, and you're the only one who knows how to put out the flames."

She leaned against him, her arms stealing around his neck. "You're impossible."

"No, just hot, as I said." He kissed the side of her throat. "Make love to me until I go crazy, okay?"

"I thought you said you were exhausted."

Nick moved away from her, sat down on the bed and flopped back against the pillows, his arms open wide. "I am, but I know my duty. I'm all yours."

"Stop acting so noble. You're just horny."

"That, too."

Phila tried to restrain herself, but, as usual, she could not resist him. She stepped out of her clothes, aware of his attention on her every inch of the way. The look in his eyes was more than enough to get her excited.

"Baby, you are one beautiful, sexy lady," Nick muttered, his voice roughening as the last of her clothing dropped to the floor.

With a small, enthusiastic exclamation of delight and anticipation, Phila dove on top of him.

Nick was ready and waiting for her, silent laughter in his eyes.

A long time later, when she was feeling pleasantly drowsy, her head resting on Nick's shoulder, her leg sprawled across his heavy thigh, he spoke.

"Tell me," he said, circling her nipple with one finger, "the real reason why you don't want to go to Darren's fund-raiser?"

"You'll laugh."

"No, I won't."

"Promise?"

"I swear I won't even chuckle."

Phila took a deep breath. "I haven't got anything to wear."

Nick roared with laughter. Phila punched him in the ribs, but that didn't stop him.

"Shut up," she ordered. "I'm serious."

"I know. That's what makes it so damn funny. Philadelphia Fox, President of the Left-Wing-Left-Out-Cause-of-the-Month Club is too proud to go to a political party where she might actually meet a few of the people who finance the Right-Wing Causes of the Month because she hasn't got a fancy dress. I can't believe it. I should think you'd want to go in jeans just to make a statement."

"I'm not into statements. I'm too practical for that. And I will not humiliate myself deliberately by showing up underdressed for a black-tie affair, and that's that."

"I understand completely," Nick said, soothing her with a movement of his big hand. "We'll go back to Seattle a couple of days early and find you a dress."

"Nick, I cannot afford that sort of dress. In case it has escaped your notice, I am currently unemployed." *The man is dense*, she thought angrily.

"You happen to own a fortune in C&L stock. I'll float you a loan."

"The hell you will."

"Ah, my fine, proud lady. All right, then, I'll buy the dress for you, how's that?"

"Absolutely not."

"I owe you, Phila," he said, turning serious without any warning. "I'll buy the dress."

She looked at him for a moment, wondering how to interpret that statement. The last thing she wanted was to have him feel a sense of obligation toward her. "Never mind the dress," she finally said. "I don't want to talk about it."

"You can be a very stubborn, hard-headed little fox at times." Nick's hand slipped down over her gently curved stomach. His fingers slid between her thighs. "Lucky for you I'm so patient and understanding."

"I never knew you felt that strongly about child-welfare legislation," Darren said as he came out of the bathroom.

"You never asked." Victoria continued to leaf through her magazine, staring unseeingly at an advertisement for fine crystal sculpture.

Darren sat down on the edge of the bed. His bare back gleamed in the lamplight. "You and Phila would make a fine pair if you ever combined forces." He sounded amused. "You'd have Reed, Nick, Mother and me running for cover."

"Phila's not a member of either family, so she's not likely to be around once the issue of the shares is settled."

"I'm not so sure about that. I don't see Nick turning her loose really quickly even after he's got the shares."

"She may turn him loose." Victoria closed the magazine slowly. "Darren, Phila told me today she won't do anything to hurt Jordan's inheritance. She says she'll give the shares back after the August meeting. Said she had to back Nick until then."

"Did she?" Darren looked thoughtful. "So he is planning something, and he needs a little help."

"You know what he's planning. He hasn't spelled it out, but it's obvious he wants to take control of the company away from Hilary."

"Why now? Why wait three years and then come storming back like this?"

"Maybe when Eleanor called him about Phila he simply saw his chance and took it."

"Or maybe Nick knows something the rest of us don't know."

"What could he possibly know that we don't? He's been out of touch for three years."

Darren shook his head. "I'm not so sure about that." He looked over his shoulder at Victoria, his eyes searching her face.

"Whatever it is, I suppose we don't have any real choice. We'll have to back Hilary for the sake of your career."

Darren studied her a moment. "Tell me something, Vicky. Why do you hate her so much?"

Victoria flushed. She had known deep down where this conversation might lead. She had practically set herself up. She had been both nervous and determined, and now that the moment was upon her she was frightened. She hedged.

"We don't have a lot in common," Victoria mumbled.

"Bullshit. You've got a great deal in common. Same kind of family background, same kind of schools and you both married into the same kind of families."

Victoria tensed. "At least I didn't have to marry you for your money."

Darren went still. "No, that's true. Why did you marry me, Vicky?"

"You know the answer to that."

Darren examined his long, shapely fingers. "Tell me again. It's been a long time."

Victoria blinked back the tears. "I married you because I loved you." Her voice was so thick she could hardly understand her own words.

"What changed your mind?"

Something in Victoria snapped. "*Nothing changed my mind.* I still love you, damn it. I wouldn't have stayed with you after what happened three years ago if I didn't love you more than I love my own pride. Are you so stupid you don't even realize that?" She burst into tears, no longer caring if she humiliated herself. She felt as if she had been in a pressure cooker during all the hours since she had spoken to Phila.

Darren stared at her, his expression totally confused. "After what happened three years ago? You mean after Dad offered you cash to stay with me?"

"Oh, shut up." Victoria wiped her eyes with a quick,

angry movement. "I knew there was no point trying to ask you. I knew it would just end up like this. I wish I'd had the sense to keep my mouth shut. Damn Phila."

"Phila? What's Phila got to do with any of this?" Darren was getting angry. "What the hell did you want to ask me? I don't remember any question."

"Because I've been afraid to ask it for three years," Victoria blazed. "I didn't know if I could trust you to tell me the truth, and I would have to leave if the answer was yes. Don't you see? I would have no choice. As long as I didn't ask, I could pretend most of the time that everything was all right, that the answer was no."

"Damn it, Vicky. What did you want to ask me?"

Victoria looked at him through her tears. "Was the baby yours?"

"Baby? *What* baby?" Then he caught on. Darren's eyes widened in amazement. "Oh, for God's sake. You don't mean Hilary's, do you? You can't believe the baby was mine?"

"Why not?" Victoria retorted. "For three years you've believed the only reason I stayed with you was because your father offered to make it worth my while."

"My father told me about that damned bribe," Darren said, his face taut and furious. "I know he offered to pay you off."

"But I didn't accept," Victoria raged. "I never said I'd take his money. But I could never prove it to you. You chose to believe him. Now he's dead, and I'll never have a chance to prove I'm innocent."

"What about me? How am I suppose to prove I'm innocent?"

"Are you?" Victoria held her breath.

"Hell, yes. I wouldn't go near Hilary Lightfoot in a bed even if I happened to be wearing a full suit of armor. I'm not blind. I saw what she did to Nick during the first year of their marriage. What's more, Hilary has absolutely no interest in me or any other man as far as I can tell. She's all wrapped up in herself and the company. What in God's name made you think the baby was mine?"

Victoria could hardly breathe. "I wasn't certain. I didn't want to believe it. For three years I've tried not to believe it. But you know how it was back then, Darren. We were having so many problems. And Nick and Hilary had just split up, and I was so afraid Hilary was turning to you for . . . for consolation."

"Consolation."

"I knew she was terrified of no longer being married to a Lightfoot and I was afraid she'd decided to marry a Castleton, instead. Darren, you know as well as I do that the two of you spent a lot of time together during that period."

Darren's handsome face suffused with a dark tint. "She was upset," he agreed. "She did talk to me a few times."

"She's very beautiful."

"I know." He sighed heavily. "And she was scared. For a while I felt sorry for her."

"That's what I was afraid of." Victoria looked at the foot of the bed.

"You and I were always arguing back then. Sometimes I got damn sick and tired of it. Dad was always telling me you were probably going to walk out and take his grandson with you. He kept telling me you thought you'd married beneath yourself. He said he knew the signs. He'd seen them in Mom when she married him. He said I'd better learn how to control you. Then he told me I probably wasn't man enough to do it."

"Oh, Darren."

"So, yes, I guess there were times when it was comforting to listen to Hilary's problems. At least I knew I wasn't alone. But I never slept with her, Vicky. Christ, even if I'd wanted to, I wouldn't have done it. Hell, the divorce wasn't even final at that point, remember? She was still married to Nick, as far as I was concerned."

"And you wouldn't have gone to bed with Nick's wife any more than he would have gone to bed with yours," Victoria concluded slowly. A vast sense of relief washed over her.

Darren nodded. "That's about the size of it. Nick and I were raised together. We're practically brothers. We wouldn't mess around with each other's wives any more than Dad and Reed would have swapped Mom and Nora. But there's no way I could ever prove it to you."

"I can never prove I didn't stay with you because of your father's promise to give me an extra helping in the will. Where does that leave us, Darren?"

He sat silently for a moment and then he touched her hand fleetingly. "We're still together, aren't we? We managed to stay together for the past three years, even though we both had a lot of doubts."

Victoria tried a small, misty smile. "Yes, we did, didn't we? Phila said there must be something solid underneath or we wouldn't have made it this far together."

Darren got into bed beside her. "Tell me again why you married me."

"If you bring up the subject of the dress one more time, I will strangle you," Phila announced the next morning as she hopped out of the way of the foaming surf. She was barefoot, her jeans rolled up to mid-calf. The sea was in a frisky mood.

"I can't believe you're going to be so stubborn about this." Nick had taken off his shoes, too. He also had his jeans rolled up a couple of inches above his ankles.

"I can be stubborn about anything I want." Phila was about to continue on that theme when Jordan's voice shrilled across the expanse of beach.

"Hi, Phila. Hi, Nick. Hi, Phila. Hi, Nick. Hi, Phila."

"Kid's got a problem with his soundtrack," Nick observed as he waved at Darren, Victoria and their son, who were walking toward them.

"For Pete's sake. They brought the dogs." Phila braced herself as Cupcake and Fifi came charging toward her, their tongues lolling. At the last instant she realized they had already been swimming in the surf. They were soaking wet. "No, wait a minute, you brutes. Don't you dare shake. Stop it."

But it was too late. Nick prudently stepped aside while the rottweilers sprayed Phila. "Hi, Jordan," he said, hoisting the boy up into the air for a quick greeting. "What are you doing today?"

"Gonna find some good seaweed."

"Sounds like a great plan." Nick set Jordan on his feet. The boy immediately headed toward Phila, who was still trying to escape from Cupcake and Fifi.

Darren grinned at Nick. "His seaweed collection has a problem. The stuff self-destructs after it's been in his room for a while, and Mrs. Atkins throws it out."

"Maybe he should collect shells," Nick suggested.

Phila chuckled. "They're not slimy enough. Jordan's a connoisseur, aren't you, Jordan? He wants nice, slimy seaweed."

"Yes." Jordan nodded happily and went off to investigate a possible addition to his collection.

"Ah, now I get the picture," Nick said. "'Morning, Vicky. You're just the person I wanted to see. I'm trying to convince Phila to go to Darren's fund-raiser with me. She says she doesn't have anything to wear. Maybe you can reassure her."

"Then you will be attending, Nick? I wasn't certain." Victoria studied him with faint anxiety in her eyes.

Nick smiled coolly. "It's a family event, isn't it? I was under the impression Eleanor thinks we should present a united front. I'll be there."

Darren looked at him and nodded brusquely. "Thanks. I appreciate that. The more arm-twisters there, the better. Vicky and I are still a little new at this, but my staff tells me we'd better get used to it."

Victoria watched her son playing near the edge of the water. "It takes money to run for office. Everyone knows that. Money and time. Campaigning is a full-time job, you know."

"I can see where it would be," Nick commented calmly.

Victoria seemed to come to some inner decision. She glanced at Phila. "Don't worry about having an expensive dress. Something simple in black will be just fine. Black goes anywhere."

Phila cleared her throat. "I don't have a single black item in my entire wardrobe."

Victoria surveyed the coral-striped top Phila was wearing with her green jeans. She smiled slowly. "Somehow, I'm not surprised."

"We'll find something for her to wear," Nick said. He caught Phila's hand. "Come on, let's finish this walk you insisted we take. I want to get in another session at the range before lunch."

"I'm getting tired of practicing with that gun, Nick. I don't think I was cut out to be Annie Oakley."

"I'll settle for Matt Dillon. Let's go." He nodded to Darren and Victoria as he tugged on Phila's wrist. "See you two later."

"Right." Darren took his wife's hand and they headed off in pursuit of their son.

Phila glanced back as the little boy yelled in happy excitement and raced toward another strand of seaweed. "Mrs. Atkins is going to have another specimen to deal with this afternoon."

"She won't mind," Nick said. "She loves Jordan."

"Everybody does. Jordan is a very lucky little boy. There are a lot of kids in this world who aren't that lucky."

Nick's hand tightened around hers. "Speaking of kids, how are we doing?"

Phila yanked her gaze back from Jordan. "What are you talking about?"

"I just wondered if you were getting set to come after me with a gun."

Phila's throat felt suddenly tight, her stomach turned queasy. "I won't know for a while yet. A few more days."

"You will let me know as soon as you find out, one way or the other, won't you?"

"Worried?"

"Not particularly. Are you?"

Phila set her teeth together and did not answer.

"Phila?" Nick pulled on her hand. "I asked if you were worried."

"Of course I'm worried. Any woman in my situation

would be worried. The odds are that I'm not pregnant, though."

"It only takes one time."

"Thanks for the reassurance. You don't have to remind me," she retorted. "I've seen it happen often enough in my line of work. Ex-line of work."

"Do you ever think of having a family?" Nick asked after a moment.

"The subject has crossed my mind a few times lately," she muttered. "Hard not to think about it when you're worried you might be pregnant."

"I mean, in general, have you given the matter much thought?"

"No."

"Why not?"

Phila let out a long breath. "I'm afraid, I suppose. Families are so fragile. So much can go wrong, even when everyone's intentions are good. People get divorced so easily these days. They put themselves and their precious freedom ahead of their children and then lie to themselves and tell everyone the kids are better off because at least the adults aren't arguing over the dinner table every night."

"Statistically, you've got a point, I guess. The divorce rate is sky-high. The kind of work you used to do and your personal background probably haven't added to your faith in the stability of the American family, either."

"No."

"You've been exposed to the worst-possible-case situations, haven't you? First you lived it, and then you went into the business of dealing with children of families that were having major problems. Stands to reason you'd be a bit skittish on the topic."

"That's me. Skittish on the topic."

"It's kind of ironic, isn't it? You've made a career out of trying to salvage families and children, and yet you're afraid to have a family yourself."

"We've all got our personal hang-ups," she said.

"True." Nick was quiet for a moment, apparently lost in

his own thoughts. "Did Vicky and Darren seem a little different to you this morning?"

"Maybe they finally got around to talking to each other."

"About what?"

"This and that," said Phila.

Hilary went cold when she walked into the study and saw Reed sitting at the desk. He hadn't sat in that chair for over two years. The niggling sense that she was losing control of everything made her stomach tighten.

"Hello, Reed. Was there something you wanted?"

Reed looked up from the thick document he was studying and smiled absently at her. He took off his horn-rimmed reading glasses and put them down on the stack of papers he had been going through. "I just wandered in here and happened to see the Hewett papers sitting on the desk. I remember you mentioned something about it last month. How is the deal going? Did you get old Hewett to stop bellyaching about the delivery dates?"

"I think we finally reached a compromise. I talked to Leighton in Purchasing and Contracts and he said Hewett was calming down." Hilary moved over to the desk and glanced at the papers under Reed's glasses. They were just the Hewett papers, she saw with relief.

Reed nodded. "Old Henry Hewett has been with us from the beginning. He took a chance on us back when C&L couldn't even guarantee to pay its light bill. I'd hate to see us stop doing business with him now."

"We won't." Hilary smiled reassuringly. "I didn't realize you were interested in the outcome of the contract negotiations. The last time I mentioned it you didn't want to be bothered with those kinds of details."

"I know." Reed got to his feet and shoved his hands into his pockets. He wandered toward the window and stood looking out over the sweep of lawn. "But things change sometimes. I've been letting you carry most of the load around here for a long time. I'm sorry, Hilary. I shouldn't have pushed it all off on you. For a while I thought Burke was taking care of things."

"He was."

"But after he died, I should have stepped back in and taken the responsibility."

Hilary propped one hip on the edge of the desk, her lizard-skin-shod foot swinging gently. "I wanted the responsibility. I needed it. We both know it saved my sanity. I would have been a basket case three years ago if I hadn't had the Lightfoot portion of the company to manage. C&L means everything to me, Reed."

He nodded, not looking around. "You've worked goddamned hard."

"I've given it everything I've got." Her voice was tight with feeling. She tried to relax.

Reed nodded again, and this time he did turn around. "You're an amazing woman, Hilary. I have nothing but respect for you."

"Thank you."

"You're welcome." Reed walked out of the room.

Hilary closed her eyes and took several deep breaths. Then she got up and went around to her chair. When she reached for the telephone, her fingers were trembling. She dialed the familiar number with great care. She should have thought of this sooner. Much sooner.

"Hello, Mrs. Gilford. Please put me through to Mr. Vellacott."

"I'm sorry, Mrs. Lightfoot. Mr. Vellacott is out of the office."

The fool was probably playing tennis. He always ducked out to play tennis in the afternoons when he thought she wouldn't notice. She should have replaced Vellacott a year ago. But he had been useful precisely because he paid so little attention to details. Hilary stifled her impatience. "Tell him I want him to call me as soon as he gets in, will you?"

"Of course, Mrs. Lightfoot. How is your vacation going?"

"Fine, thank you."

"We were all so pleased to see Mr. Lightfoot in the office the other day. It's been such a long time."

The cold feeling in Hilary's stomach got worse. "Yes, it has, hasn't it? How long was he there, Mrs. Gilford?"

"Not long. Half an hour or less. Seemed anxious to get back to Port Claxton."

"Thank you, Mrs. Gilford. Don't forget I want to speak to Mr. Vellacott as soon as he gets into the office."

"Of course."

Hilary hung up the phone and forced herself to think clearly. Half an hour was not long enough for Nick to have gotten a locksmith in to open the safe. Even if he had, he could not have known what to look for in the first place. If he had gotten the safe open and found the Traynor file it would be meaningless to him. Just another file on another potential supplier. She was not stupid enough to leave anything incriminating lying around.

Hilary started to drum her long, peach-tinted fingernails on the polished surface of the desk and then caught herself. She stilled her hand.

It could not fall apart now, not when she was so close, she thought fearfully. All she had to do was keep it together until the August meeting.

But she was losing total control of the situation, and she sensed it. She probably did not have to worry too much about Darren and Vicky. Eleanor could keep them from wavering. But Reed was a different matter. She had been so sure he was not going to be a problem, but now she was no longer certain.

Reed hadn't shown any real interest in the company for so long she had convinced herself he would never again get involved. But, then, she had been certain Nick would never come back, either. She had been wrong on both counts.

It was not right. She deserved justice. She deserved vengeance. She would not allow herself to be defeated at this stage.

"Crissie," she whispered softly, "if only you were still here. I need you. I need someone to talk to. Why couldn't Phila have been more like you?"

Something was happening to the whole plan; Hilary could feel it. Her instincts warned her that she had to control Reed. He was the biggest risk at the moment.

Hilary decided she had better have a talk with Eleanor.

CHAPTER SIXTEEN

"I always felt this room turned out the finest of all the rooms in both beach cottages." Eleanor gazed around Reed's library, remembering the hours of planning and work she had put into this particular room. It had been very important to her that Reed's library be right.

"You did a goddamn good . . . I mean, you did a terrific job with it, Eleanor. Nora always said you had great taste." Reed moved over to the butler's tray. "Can I get you something?"

Eleanor glanced at the clock. "Why not? It is after five, isn't it?"

"It's definitely after five. In fact, I think it's getting a little late all the way around." Reed poured two brandies and carried one back to her.

"What makes you say that?"

"Nothing. Just an idle comment."

She took the glass from him and watched him seat himself in the wing-back easy chair. She had chosen that chair with great care, wanting it to be comfortable for him. He was a big man; he needed a strong, solid chair.

"Why did you want to talk to me today, Eleanor?" Reed asked after a moment.

"I think you know the answer to that."

"No, I don't. But I am curious."

Eleanor gripped her glass. Reed was notorious about coming directly to a point. "The August meeting."

"Ah."

She looked at him. "Tell me the truth, Reed. Is Nick going to try to take over control of Castleton & Lightfoot at that meeting?"

"I think it's safe to assume he's going to attempt it."

"The only way he can do it is with your help. Are you going to help him?" She could be as blunt as any Lightfoot, Eleanor told herself.

"What makes you think I'm the only hope he's got? Darren could back him or you could. With either of you on his side plus his own shares and Phila's, Nick could do just about anything he damn well pleased."

"The Castletons, all of us, will back Hilary."

Reed nodded. "You'll have to vote as you see fit."

Eleanor leaned toward him. "We need her running things, Reed. The only other person we could even consider is you."

Reed shook his head. "No. I'm not going to step back into that job. Not for all the tea in China. It was good while it lasted, but it's time to turn it over to someone younger. Life is so goddamned short, Eleanor. I don't want to spend the rest of mine behind a desk."

"You want to spend it playing golf? Is that all you can think of these days?"

"No. Sometimes I think about grandkids." Reed sipped his brandy. "I envy you, Eleanor. You have your son and you have little Jordan. That's more than I've had for quite a while now."

"For better or worse, your son appears to have returned. The question is why and for how long?"

"I know. Interesting questions. I ask myself the same ones every day."

"Reed, if he regains control of the company, you know what he'll do with it. He'll start moving away from the government contracts. He'll start pushing again for a broader consumer market. There's no telling how far he'll go with his changes this time. You and Burke won't be there to stop him. He'll have C&L designing home-entertainment centers, for heaven's sake. That's not the kind of business this company was founded upon. Ten years ago you and Burke would have refused even to consider going in that direction."

"That was ten years ago and Burke is dead. I may be dead myself, one of these days." Reed smiled.

"Don't talk like that." The brandy glass trembled in her hand.

He frowned at her obvious alarm. "Hey, just kidding. I'm only trying to point out that what Burke and I wanted for the company ten, twenty or thirty years ago may not be what the next generation wants. And it's their company, Eleanor. The important thing is that C&L survive and that it stay in the families. Beyond that, Nick and Darren are welcome to do any damn thing they want with it as far as I'm concerned."

"What about Hilary?" Eleanor asked, feeling desperate. "Where does she fit into all this? She has some rights, too."

"Yes." Reed took another swallow of brandy. "She has some rights. I'm not denying that."

"She's given everything she has to C&L over the past three years."

"I realize that."

"Yet you're seriously thinking of backing Nick at the August meeting, aren't you?"

"I'm thinking about it, yes. That's all I'm doing at this point, Eleanor. Thinking about it."

Eleanor forced herself to remain calm. "You'd do that, Reed? You'd back Nick? Knowing what he did to all of us three years ago?"

"Lately I've begun to wonder if we all might have misinterpreted what happened three years ago. In fact, I'm beginning to think we may have been fools three years ago."

"It's all that woman's fault." Eleanor whispered. "She started all of this."

"Crissie Masters?"

Eleanor could barely bring herself to nod once in confirmation. She hoped she would not break down in front of Reed. It would be so terribly embarrassing. "Now we have Philadelphia Fox dropping into our lives, interfering with things that should never have concerned her in the first place."

"I think that when all is said and done, I'm going to owe Philadelphia Fox," Reed mused.

Eleanor looked up sharply. "Why do you say that?"

"No matter how you slice it, she's the one responsible for giving me back my son."

"Don't give her too much credit. You don't have Nick back. Not really. Keep in mind, too, that a woman with her sort of background is only looking out for her own self-interest. What else could you expect from her type?"

"Nora used to say that you had a thing about people's backgrounds," Reed commented. "I know yours is pretty fancy, but you've got to remember that mine isn't. Neither is my son's, when you get right down to it. We're just plain folks, Eleanor, even though you've done your best over the years. Plain folks can't look back too much. Nothing there to see. People like us tend to look to the future, not the past."

Eleanor did not think she could take any more. She put down the brandy glass and got to her feet. "Please think very carefully about what you'll be doing to all of us if you back Nick."

"Darren will do all right, even if Nick does take charge," Reed said gently. "Don't you worry about that son of yours."

That comment stopped her abruptly halfway to the door. "How do you know that?" Eleanor whispered.

"I've known him for as long as I've known my own son, remember? Darren's a lot tougher than Burke ever realized. Or maybe Burke did realize it and was afraid to admit his son would go farther than he had. I don't know the answer to that one, but I do know that if Darren really wants to be governor, he'll get the job, one way or the other. He's got all of Burke's strengths but none of his worst weaknesses, thank God. He's also got a lot of you in him. The part that toughs it out to the end, no matter what the price."

Eleanor felt a curious warmth steal through her. "Burke never thought Darren would make it in politics or anything else," she pointed out, knowing that what she was really asking for was more reassurance.

"Don't mean to speak ill of the dead. God knows Burke was my best friend and partner for over forty years. But I gotta be truthful with you, Eleanor. In some ways he was a horse's ass."

Eleanor flinched. "Yes, he was, wasn't he?" she heard herself say just before her hand touched the doorknob. "Thank you, Reed. Thank you for believing in my son."

"Eleanor?"

"I'm glad you like this room, Reed," she said quickly, before he could continue. "I worked very hard on it for you."

"I know." Reed got to his feet and stood looking at her across the width of the beautiful room. "I've always been comfortable in here."

"Good."

"Why did you spend so much time on my library, Eleanor?"

"Isn't it obvious? I designed these rooms, let's see, when was it? Thirty years ago?"

"Thirty-one years ago."

"Yes. Well, no matter. I knew by then I'd married the wrong man, you see. I knew I was trapped and that I'd never have the man I loved. He was already very happy with someone else. But I wanted to do something for him. I wanted him to be comfortable in some small way and to know that I had been responsible for that comfort. I wanted him to think of me, if only for a second or two, each time he sat in that wing-back chair."

She let herself out the door.

"Are you sure I look all right?" Phila stood in front of the mirrored wall of Nick's bedroom and examined her image for the hundredth time. "I feel weird in black. Like I'm supposed to be going to a funeral or something." The dress was close fitting, accenting Phila's small waist. It was cut in an exquisitely simple style.

Nick stood behind her, tying his bow tie with practiced ease. "I'll admit it's not your best color."

"I *do* look terrible," Phila wailed, her worst fears confirmed. "I knew it. I tried to tell Vicky, but she insisted I buy it."

Nick grinned at her in the mirror. "I'm just teasing. You look terrific. Vicky was right. The dress is very sophisticated. I'm going to be proud as hell to walk into that room tonight with you on my arm."

"What's the bottom line here?" Phila demanded suspiciously.

"The bottom line is that I'm used to seeing you in shocking pink or Day-Glo orange, and somehow black just looks a little quiet on you, that's all."

"Meaning I'm not the sophisticated type?"

"You really are looking for trouble tonight, aren't you?"

"I told you I didn't want to go with you to this thing." She turned away from the mirror, knowing she was fussing too much. She should just accept the inevitable. She was going to go to Darren's fund-raiser because Nick had insisted she be there.

Phila was learning that when Nicodemus Lightfoot put his foot down about something, that foot was anything but light.

She collected the tiny black-and-silver purse Victoria had decreed was appropriate for the dress and stepped into the black evening pumps.

She had her reasons for being irritable and out of sorts tonight, and when the fund-raiser was over she would share the news with Nick. He would, no doubt, be vastly relieved. In the meantime, she had all she could do to deal with it herself.

"Ready?" Nick picked up his black tuxedo jacket.

"As ready as I'll ever be." She turned around and found herself staring at him. "Very impressive," she said at last.

The formal black-and-white evening clothes accentuated his powerful shoulders and the solidly built lines of his body. It made him appear deliciously dangerous, she thought.

"You look like you're seeing a whole new side of me," Nick murmured.

Phila grinned. "Actually, you look like a gangster. All you need is a red rose in your lapel and a bulge under your arm where your shoulder holster is supposed to be."

"And you look like a sexy little vamp." Nick tilted her chin with his forefinger and kissed the tip of her nose. "Let's go before I change my mind and decide to let you jump me."

"I didn't even know you were weighing a decision in that regard. I thought we had to go to this thing."

"Stop whining. We do have to go to this thing." Nick turned off the bedroom lights. "We'll save the jumping for later."

Phila grumbled and then automatically inhaled the magnificent view as they walked through the living room. The late summer sun was disappearing slowly, bathing Elliott Bay and the islands in a warm, yellow glow.

"Heck of a view," Phila said. "You must have missed this place while you were living in California."

"I did miss it. I don't think I realized just how much until now."

"This is certainly a fancy condominium. Great location, great view, all the amenities. First-class urban design. I wonder how many low-income housing units were demolished so the developers could build this sucker."

Nick chuckled. "Save your energy. I'm not going to let you make me feel guilty about living here. I earned every square inch of this place. Just for your information, however, the building that used to be on this site was an old, abandoned warehouse. A real eyesore. Does that make you feel better?"

"Much." She took one last look around at the refined collection of polished antique furniture. "Have the Lightfoots and Castletons always gone for the Early Constitution look?"

"You don't like the interior design of this place?"

Phila shrugged. "Kind of dark. Needs some color."

Nick glanced around as he turned off the lights. He smiled. "I wondered about that myself."

By the time Nick and Phila arrived, a well-heeled, well-dressed crowd had already gathered in the large reception room at the top of the sleek downtown high-rise. Phila looked around warily as she walked through the door on Nick's arm. The room was full, she noted. Darren must be pleased. The lively hum of voices was interrupted here and there by an occasional laugh and the clink of ice in glasses.

A formally dressed trio of musicians played Mozart in one corner, and waiters carrying trays of hors d'oeuvres and drinks circulated through the crowd. The panorama of Seattle and its bay was spread out far below, magnificently showcased through huge windows. The last gleam of sunlight glanced off the Olympics.

But the view, the food, the drinks and Mozart all took second place to the main attraction of the evening. There was no doubt about it, Darren Castleton was the primary focus of attention. Lean, elegant, dynamic, he held center stage wherever he moved in the crowd. He did so easily, naturally, as if it were second nature to him. He came alive in a crowd like this the way a brilliant actor came alive on the screen. Beside him, Victoria looked just as beautifully at ease, just as much in control. The ideal American couple.

"Charisma," Phila murmured, snagging a glass of champagne off a passing tray.

Nick crunched an oyster wrapped in bacon. "Yeah, he's got it in spades, doesn't he? You sort of have to see him working a crowd like this to realize the effect he has on people."

"It's a rare form of power," Phila said slowly.

"Uh huh. I always knew Darren had something going for him, something I couldn't quite define, but as long as

Burke was alive, it was subdued. As if whatever it was hadn't had a chance really to blossom. Now it's starting to shine. Jesus. The man really might be the next governor of this state."

"I think you're right," Phila said softly. "And look at Vicky. She'd make a perfect governor's lady. Heck, she'd make a perfect president's lady. She's so poised and charming and lovely."

"And when they bring out little Jordan for the photographers, they're going to get the front page in tomorrow's *Seattle Times*," Nick concluded.

"Be interesting to see if Jordan tries to display his self-destructing seaweed collection for the photographers." Phila glanced around and saw Eleanor moving toward them.

"There you are," Eleanor said grandly as she stopped in front of them. Her face was aglow with maternal pride. "Thank you for coming tonight, Nick."

"I said we'd be here." Nick took a glass from a passing tray. "Looks like everything's going well. Where's Dad?"

"Over there with Hilary, talking to some business friends." Eleanor glanced at Phila. "I see you decided to attend after all?"

"I couldn't get out of it." Phila smiled brilliantly. "I'll try not to embarrass the families."

"That would be much appreciated." Eleanor moved away with a nod to Nick.

"In our baiting mode tonight, are we?" Nick observed quietly, his eyes on the crowd.

"She started it."

"Eleanor didn't start anything. You're just edgy this evening. Why?"

"I am not edgy. It's Eleanor who's edgy, not me. If you want to calm her down, tell her you've decided to give full support to Darren in his bid for the governor's job."

"I'm here tonight, aren't I? Doesn't that show support?"

"It's a step in the right direction, but Darren requires more than that and you know it. He needs your help behind the scenes, not just at public functions like this."

"Philadelphia Fox, the political mastermind."

"That's me." Phila realized she was still feeling irritable and a little depressed. She reached for another glass of champagne.

"Has it escaped your notice that Darren is hardly a liberal Democrat?"

"No, but I have hopes for him."

"You think he'll convert?"

Phila smiled ruefully. "I don't have that much hope for him, but I think he can be made to see reason, which puts him several notches above the average Republican. He's educable."

"I'm sure he'll be delighted to hear that."

Phila grinned briefly. "I already told him." She glanced around again and spotted a familiar figure. "Hilary certainly looks gorgeous tonight."

"Hilary always looks gorgeous." Nick did not seem particularly interested. "Come on, we'd better mingle. This is business."

"Think of it as Family Unity night. The Castletons and the Lightfoots—just one big happy family."

Nick started into the crowd, towing Phila behind him. He nodded at several pepple, stopped to talk briefly with others and finally halted near a man and a woman who were standing near the windows. The woman, an attractive brunette in her early forties, glanced up and then smiled warmly.

"Nick! Good to see you again. It's been awhile. Are you just visiting, or are you home to stay?"

"I plan to stay this time. Phila, this is Barbara Appleton and her husband, Norm. They're old friends. Barbara, Norm, this is Philadelphia Fox."

"How do you do?" Phila said politely. "Don't I know your name from somewhere, Mrs. Appleton?"

"I make the papers once in a while, when there's nothing else of great importance occurring in the world." Barbara laughed.

Phila thought quickly, made the connection and brightened immediately. "Now I remember. You're one of the people working to get funding for day-care facilities for the children of homeless people. We've heard about your efforts all the way over in eastern Washington. I'm thrilled to meet you."

Barbara Appleton smiled, looking faintly bemused. "Most people run the other way when they're introduced to me. They're afraid I'll ask for money. Do you have an interest in the matter of day care for homeless kids?"

"I am—*was*—a social worker. Until recently I've been working with the foster-home program. I'm very aware of the homeless problem here in Seattle."

"The parents are under such stress, and the children suffer so. They desperately need a structured, safe environment. You can't raise children in cars and buses and shelters."

"If you're a parent, you can't very well hunt for a job or get training or deal with the bureaucracy of the welfare system if you've got a couple of kids in your arms. I think the day-care idea for those kids is great. How's the project going?"

"We're supporting two centers now and hope to get a third started this fall."

"Have you talked to Darren and Vicky about this?" Phila asked.

Barbara's eyes narrowed thoughtfully. "No, as a matter of fact, I haven't. I assumed Darren would not be particularly supportive."

Phila tossed that assumption aside with a flick of her hand. "Oh, don't worry about Darren, he's not a reactionary, ultraconservative, right-wing turkey like the rest of the Castletons and Lightfoots. He's much more flexible, much more open to information. What's more, he's married to a woman who is very interested in children's issues."

"Is that right?" Barbara's gaze drifted toward the center of the room, where Darren and Vicky stood talking to a circle of people. "I hadn't realized that. Perhaps I'll just have a word or two with Victoria Castleton. Norm, go ahead and get out the checkbook. It looks as though we may be making a contribution tonight, after all. Nice to have met you, Phila. Good to see you again, Nick. Let's get together for dinner soon."

"Yeah, we'll do that," said Nick, his eyes amused as he nodded at the other two. When the Appletons were out of earshot, he looked down at Phila. "Congratulations. You just got money out of the tightest checkbook in the room."

Phila was astonished. "Why are they here, if they're not strong supporters?"

"According to Vicky, you don't dare not invite Barbara and Norm to an affair like this. They wield a lot of clout in this town. But no one actually expected to get their financial support tonight. Barbara's notorious about only backing a few selected pols. When she does back them, however, they generally do well. She can bring money out of the woodwork. Lots of it. Let's hope you didn't oversell Darren's support for children's issues."

"I didn't. Darren will listen to children's advocates. I know he will. If he doesn't, Vicky will make him listen." Phila was sure of herself. She looked thoughtfully around the room. "You know, a person could do a lot with a roomful of money like this."

"That's the whole idea." Nick's voice was bland. "What's that funny expression on your face? You thinking of getting into politics?"

"Who, me?"

"Don't look so damned innocent."

"Heavens, I'd make a lousy politician."

"That's true. You're too mouthy. You'd be much better at the fund-raising end of things."

"You think so?"

"Sure. You're the type who'd be happy to beat up on people until they forked over a contribution. It takes nerve to be an arm-twister at an event like this."

Phila looked around. "This could be fun. Let's go practice."

Nick groaned. "Give the woman a taste of power and she goes wild."

Phila spent the rest of the evening listening, observing and asking questions. It took her mind off her other problems. Reed gravitated toward her at one point, a drink in his hand, and asked how she was getting along.

"Well, no one's tried to throw me out yet."

Reed nodded, pleased. "A good sign. You must be keeping your mouth under control."

"I'm getting sick and tired of comments on my mouthiness. Where's Hilary?"

"Talking to some business acquaintances. Where's Nick?"

"Over there with that heavyset man in the corner."

Reed glanced in that direction and nodded. "That's Graveston. Owns a couple of restaurants here in town."

Eleanor spotted them and left a small group of women to come over to Reed.

"There you are, Reed, I've been looking for you. Have you seen the Brands yet?"

"Over near the buffet table," Reed said. "Why?"

"I want to make sure they meet Darren and Vicky. Everything is going very well, don't you think?"

"It's going great," Phila said, even though she hadn't been asked. "Darren's a natural, isn't he?"

Eleanor looked at her. "Yes, he is."

"Nick and I were talking earlier about how this political business definitely seems to be Darren's proper niche. Be a shame to waste all that charisma. Lord knows we need more decent men in office."

Eleanor's gaze sharpened. "You and Nick were discussing this?"

Phila nodded, sipping at her champagne. "Nick's seen the light, you know, Eleanor."

"What light have I seen?" Nick asked from directly behind Phila.

Phila jumped in surprise and then smiled meaningfully. "The light about Darren's future in politics. I was just telling Eleanor that you've decided it's the right thing for him."

Nick looked at his father. "With her around, I don't even need to open my own mouth. She's starting to do all my talking for me."

Reed's grin came and went. "I've noticed."

Eleanor was staring at Nick. "Do you mean it?"

"Ask Phila. She seems to be doing all my thinking for me tonight." Nick glanced across the top of Eleanor's head. "There goes Howard Compton. I'd better say hello." He started to excuse himself and then spotted the full glass in Phila's hand. "How much champagne have you had already?"

"This is only my second glass. I think. Maybe it's my third. I'm not sure. Don't be such a grouch."

"Keep an eye on her," Nick said to Reed. "She's a bit testy this evening. In this mood she gets into trouble easily."

"I don't know what you expect me to do with her. Want some more food, Phila?"

"Yes, please." She smiled widely at Reed. "Don't pay any attention to Nick. He never wants me to have any fun."

Half an hour later Phila found herself standing alone conveniently near the hall that led to the rest rooms. She decided she'd better take advantage of the opportunity. She went down the carpeted hallway and pushed open the appropriate door.

She stood staring in amazement at the plush facilities. The room had been done in soft turquoise and rose and featured a couple of graceful velvet sofas, a wall of mirrors lit with makeup lights and marble trim on all the stalls.

But it was the view from the window in each stall that captivated Phila. The scenic panorama would have graced any upscale condominium, and here it was wasted on a rest room. Real class. Phila started opening stall doors to see which cubicle had the best view.

She was watching the lights of the city from the middle stall when she heard the outer door of the lounge open and close. Phila hurried out to wash her hands, embarrassed that someone might discover her enthralled with the view from a rest-room stall.

She stopped short, her insides twisting with sudden, sick tension as she saw Hilary standing by the long row of marble sinks. Phila's pleasantly lightheaded feeling died when she saw the anger twisting the other woman's beautiful face. It was obvious Hilary had psyched herself up for a confrontation.

She looked like a savage queen, Phila thought, awed by the threat of the uncontrolled emotion in Hilary's eyes.

"Hello, Hilary," Phila said cautiously.

"God, you have a talent for looking innocent, you little bitch."

Phila sucked in her breath as a cold, anguished chill shot through her. "I know how you must be feeling—"

"You know nothing of how I feel. *Nothing*. You really think you're going to win, don't you?" Hilary asked. "Oh, I've seen the way they're starting to pay attention to you—believe in you, listen to you. And because of you, they're all starting to believe in Nick again. An interesting process. But you won't win, Phila. I can't let you. I've put too much time, too much of myself into this game, to lose it all now."

Phila mentally fought the onslaught of Hilary's fury. "Nick told me all about Traynor and your plans to ruin the company. But I can't let you do that to the families. They don't deserve it."

The lounge door opened again, and Nick strolled into the room with as much aplomb as if he were walking into a boardroom. He stood there, raw and masculine-looking, amid the luxurious, ultrafeminine surroundings. He looked at Phila.

"I saw you head for the ladies' room and I saw Hilary follow. Something told me I'd like to be included in a high-level meeting like this. What don't we deserve, Phila?" he asked.

"She wants to punish all of you for what happened three years ago," Phila said softly, her eyes on Hilary's rigid features. "But it isn't fair. You're all innocent. Except Burke, of course."

"You're right, you know." Hilary folded her arms under her breasts and watched Phila. "I intend to take C&L apart bit by bit and make a fortune for myself in the process."

Hilary turned her eyes on Nick. "I'm going to destroy everything any of you care about."

"It's taken you nearly three years to set it up but you're about ready to pull it off, aren't you?" Nick asked mildly.

"Yes," Hilary said proudly, "and I will pull it off. When I'm finished I'll have everything I want, everything I need, and the Castletons and Lightfoots will just have to watch their precious family firm go into the hands of strangers."

"There was no rape, was there, Hilary?" Phila asked. "It was a seduction. You seduced Burke out of desperation when you realized Nick was going to leave the firm and go through with the divorce if you refused to follow him. You knew you had no chance of seducing Reed. He would never have touched you. Neither would Darren. But Burke was a different breed of cat."

"You're wrong. There was a rape. It was a rape in almost every sense of the word except the physical as far as I was concerned. Everything I had been promised was taken from me. I had made a bargain with the Lightfoots. I had married one of them, and in return I was supposed to get what I wanted."

Phila nodded slowly as the rest of the puzzle fell into place at last. "But when you realized you were going to lose all of it, you turned to Burke, didn't you? It had to have been Burke. He was the weak one. You knew he was the only one left you could use."

"He wanted me so badly he could taste it. He had wanted me ever since I'd walked in the front door as Nick's wife."

"Probably because you fell into the category of forbidden fruit," Phila said. "You played on that, didn't you? You thought if you controlled Burke he would support you after you lost your status as a Lightfoot wife. You were terrified of losing that status. It was all you cared about. It was the reason you had married Nick in the first place."

"True." Hilary smiled. "You think you know me so well, don't you? Because of Crissie, I suppose?"

"That's part of it. You were right, Hilary. You did have a lot in common with Crissie. You need an enormous amount of financial security the same way Crissie needed it. You're pathological about it. It's the single most important thing in the world to you."

"A woman has to take care of herself in this world."

"With your marriage falling apart and with no possibility of getting your hooks into Reed or Darren, Burke was your only chance of hanging on to some security. How far did your fantasies take you, Hilary? Did you actually think he might divorce Eleanor and marry you?"

"It was always a possibility," Hilary agreed. "But there was no need to go that route after I accidentally got pregnant. I hadn't even thought of that approach. But when I realized I was going to have the baby, I suddenly saw how much simpler everything would be if I said the baby was Nick's. As the mother of a Lightfoot baby, my status would be inviolate for the rest of my life."

"But why set out to take apart the company, Hilary?" Nick asked softly. "Why not just be satisfied with taking control of it?"

Hilary slid a cold glance in his direction. "Because after I lost Burke's baby, I realized I was in constant jeopardy. I knew that, sooner or later, you would probably come back like a king returning to claim the throne. You always considered C&L your birthright."

"But you were Reed's wife. You were safe," Phila pointed out.

"Just how long do you think I would have remained Reed's wife if everyone discovered the truth? I couldn't take the chance. I saw my opportunity to take over when Reed began losing interest in the company. I realized that if I handled things right, I could gradually acquire enough power to sell off the company and make myself safe and secure for the rest of my life. I wouldn't need Lightfoots or Castletons at all. I would be free. *And that's exactly what's going to happen.*"

"It isn't going to go down that way, Hilary," Nick said. "I'm back."

Hilary smiled. "You came back too late, Nick. Or perhaps too soon. Either way you don't have the power to take over now. Even with Crissie's shares, you can't get enough family backing by August to pull it off. I'll still be CEO after the annual meeting."

"Don't count on it."

"You think the families will believe any of this? You can shout yourself hoarse trying to tell them what's going on. They won't buy it. I've had three years to work on all of them. By now they all have reasons for wanting me to stay in charge. You're the renegade as far as they're concerned, not me."

"I know."

Hilary's beautiful face became tight with sudden fury. "None of it had to happen this way. It's all your fault, damn you. We had a business deal, you and I. You violated our agreement."

"It was supposed to be a marriage, not a business arrangement. I wanted a wife, not a business partner."

"A wife? You wanted a fool of a woman who would follow you barefoot through the burning sand anywhere you chose to lead." Hilary's lovely mouth twisted with sarcasm. "What kind of an idiot did you think I was? I married you because you were the heir apparent to C&L. Not for any other reason. What other reason could there have been?"

"Good question. Certainly not because you loved me?"

"You bastard. Love had nothing to do with it. It was business on both sides. You wanted me for what I could bring to the family: beauty, background and breeding."

"You wanted me because your family fortunes were on the skids. You wanted to marry money."

"It's the way it's done in our world, Nick. Remember? I was brought up to understand these things, just as Eleanor understood them forty years ago."

"You don't have a glimmer of understanding, Hilary." Nick propped one shoulder against the wall.

"That's not true. I was prepared to hold up my end of the deal. I would have made you a good wife as long as you were head of C&L. But within eighteen months of our wedding you were getting ready to walk away from the firm just because Reed and Burke wouldn't let you do what you wanted with the company. *And you expected me to go with you.*"

"Yeah. Real dumb on my part. Somewhere along the line I got the idea that a wife is supposed to stick with her husband regardless of what kind of job he holds."

"That's an outdated, chauvinistic, stupid thing to say."

"Depends on the wife," Nick said. "My mother would have followed my father into a swamp."

Hilary gave a sharp exclamation of disgust and turned back to Phila. "Crissie understood. She knew what I wanted, what I needed. She would have helped me."

"She understood, but she didn't turn the shares over to you and she never bothered to change her will, did she?" Phila shook her head. "Some part of her could never have let you destroy C&L, Hilary."

"You're wrong. She would have backed me all the way."

"No, I don't think so. The thing is, Hilary, no matter what happened, no matter how much she sympathized with you, she could never have allowed you to hurt the Castletons that badly. You see, in the end, when the chips were down, Crissie considered herself family."

CHAPTER SEVENTEEN

~~~~~~

"I need a drink." Phila walked through the door of Nick's condominium and headed straight for the kitchen.

"You've already had enough champagne to float a tanker. It's a wonder you can still stand up. What is it with you tonight? I've never seen you like this." Nick shot the bolt on the door and followed her.

Along the way, he managed to leave behind his bow tie, black jacket and gold cuff links. By the time he reached the kitchen he looked thoroughly disreputable and dangerously sexy as far as Phila was concerned. She decided it wasn't fair.

"I'm celebrating." Phila jerked open the cupboard and removed the half-empty bottle of scotch. She had a little trouble getting a glass off the next shelf. It almost slipped out of her grasp.

"What are you celebrating?" Nick reached out casually and took the bottle from her hand. Then he reached for the glass.

Phila ignored the question and sighed softly. "It was very sad, wasn't it, Nick?" She looked at him as he splashed a minuscule amount of scotch into her glass and handed it to her.

"What was sad? That little scene with Hilary in the

women's room? It wasn't sad. It was inevitable. She's beginning to feel the pressure. Tonight she realized she's losing."

"How did you happen to walk in when you did?"

"I've learned that it's best to keep an eye on you. You do have a way of getting into trouble."

"Totally untrue. I resent that." She tasted the scotch and realized she really didn't want any more to drink after all. She put the glass down on the counter.

"When did you realize the baby was Burke's?" Nick asked quietly.

"It all came together tonight when Hilary started talking about how she had been cheated. It's obvious when you stop and think about it, though. Everyone should have realized it a long time ago. After all, there's no way you could have done it and then walked out. You're just not the type. And Darren is a little too wary of Hilary to be comfortable going to bed with her. Besides, he loves Vicky. But the real clue was the way Eleanor acted."

"Eleanor? How did she act?"

Phila shrugged. "She was always so protective, so adamant about supporting and defending Hilary. After a while it became obvious she suspected the truth or at least part of it. She still believed there had been a rape. But deep down I think she believed it was Burke who had raped Hilary, not you. Hilary probably planted that fear herself, and played on it to her own advantage."

"Christ."

"Whatever the reason, Eleanor felt she had a responsibility toward Hilary. After all, she was the one who had brought Hilary into the families. Then, too, she feels a kind of kinship with her because they both married into the families for similar reasons."

"Kinship or not, the last thing she would want is for the truth to come out. That would tarnish old Burke's image as well as the image of family unity beyond repair."

"Right. In this case, poor Eleanor was forced to choose which family to protect. She stuck with the Castletons, naturally, although she could never really turn completely on your family, either. She's very fond of you and Reed. So she tried to ignore everything, as usual, and did her best to keep the image intact. She's an expert on living the image."

"For the past three years she was the one who kept me posted on what was happening in the families. Why did she bother?"

"She felt guilty about the way you had been forced to take the rap. But there had to be a bad guy, and you were the logical choice for the job. She could not admit it was Burke."

"And there was my father, conveniently offering marriage to atone for my behavior."

"And as a means of keeping his grandchild. Don't forget that part. He really did believe the baby was yours."

Nick frowned. "Why was Hilary so certain Crissie would have backed her with the shares? How did those two get to be so close?"

"Crissie and Hilary were lovers."

"They were *what?*" Nick stared at her, dumbfounded.

"You heard me."

"Hilary prefers women?"

"Yes. So did Crissie. Don't look so shocked, Nick. Fact of life, you know. Some women do."

He looked a little dazed. "I know. I realize that. But I never thought Hilary might be like that. It just never occurred to me. Damn. It explains a lot. Maybe that's why we . . . she and I . . . Maybe that's why I could never get her to . . ."

"Could be," Phila agreed.

"And Crissie?"

"Uh huh. She hated men because she had been badly abused by a couple of her mother's live-in boyfriends. Knowing her father had deserted her before she was even born didn't help matters, either."

Nick's expression was stark. "What about you and Crissie?"

Phila shook her head, a small smile playing around the corners of her mouth. "No. We were friends, Crissie and I, but not lovers. Frankly, I wasn't sure I was cut out for sex of any persuasion until I met you."

Nick grinned slowly, his eyes revealing his satisfaction. "Aw shucks, ma'am, t'weren't nothin'. Just glad to be able to help out."

"Sometimes the redneck in your soul is not far below the surface."

"I told you in the beginning I come from a long line of shitkickers."

"So you did."

Nick paused and then said gently, "You didn't tell me what you were celebrating."

She looked at him. "I just found out today I'm not pregnant."

"I see." He watched her with one of his inscrutable expressions.

Phila was annoyed by his lack of reaction. "Well? Aren't you relieved?"

"Not particularly. What about you? Are you relieved?"

"Of course I'm relieved. Why shouldn't I be relieved?" She began to pace the kitchen. "This makes everything much simpler all the way around."

"You think so?"

"Don't be dense. It certainly does."

"I guess I don't have to worry about you coming after me with a gun," Nick observed thoughtfully. "But I can't help thinking that a miniature Philadelphia would have been sort of cute."

"It's not a joking matter, Nick."

"No, ma'am."

"This way we both have all our options open."

"Right. Nothing like having options."

"Are you going to take this seriously or not?" she raged, swinging to a halt in front of him.

"That depends."

"On what?"

"On the answer to my next question." Nick braced his hands on the counter and leaned back. He studied Phila carefully. "Do you think," he said, "that it's just barely possible you might be a little in love with me?"

The room spun around Phila. She reached out and grasped two fistfuls of Nick's pleated white shirt and scowled fiercely up at him. "Are you making fun of me?"

"Absolutely not."

"You're laughing."

"No. It's just a nervous reaction, I think."

"You are never nervous. You're always cool as a glacier. Besides, what have you got to be nervous about?" She tightened her hold on his shirtfront.

"Well, I'm in love with you, and it stands to reason I'm a tad anxious in case you might not be in love with me."

"Nick." She released his shirt to clamp her hands behind his head. Then she stood on tiptoe and pulled his face down to hers. Her mouth crushed his until she felt his teeth grind against hers.

"Does this mean yes?" Nick lifted his head and grinned down at her.

She clung to him, burying her nose against his pristine white shirt. "I love you. I've been falling in love with you for ages. I was so disappointed at first today when I discovered I wasn't pregnant. Then I told myself it was for the best. It *is* for the best. Only it would have given me a good excuse to hang around you and I did want to hang around. Oh, Nick, I was so scared you wouldn't be able to love me back."

He propped up her chin with his finger, his eyes gleaming behind the lenses of his glasses. "To tell you the truth, I was sort of hoping you'd gotten knocked up that first time. I realized it the next morning when you threatened to come after me with the gun. I found myself thinking that wouldn't be such a bad fate."

"Knocked up? Is that any way to talk? Show some respect, Lightfoot."

He looked down at her with eyes full of laughter. "I'll try. But I think I could do a much better job of it in bed."

A rush of excitement went through her, and then she remembered exactly why she was celebrating. Phila sighed and leaned her head back against his chest. "Soon," she promised.

"Yeah, like two minutes from now. Let's go, honey. I can't wait for you to start ripping off my clothes."

"Nick, for heaven's sake, weren't you listening? I said I was celebrating the fact that I wasn't pregnant, remember?"

"How could I forget?"

Phila grew exasperated. "Well, how do you think I first realized I wasn't knocked up, as you so delicately put it, you big idiot?"

"Uh, the usual way, I guess?"

"Yes, the usual way. Now do you get the point?"

"About not going to bed? I fail to see the problem."

"Nick, for pete's sake, can't you demonstrate a modicum of sensitivity here?"

"I get it. You're embarrassed at the idea of throwing yourself at me during this particular time of the month. How's that for sensitivity?"

Phila collapsed against his chest. "Good lord, what brain power. Must be all of two watts. Hard to believe they let you run a zillion-dollar-a-year corporation."

He nuzzled the place behind her ear and wrapped his hands around her waist. "I've got news for you, sweetheart, a good executive never lets petty details get in the way."

"But, Nick . . ."

"I don't mind, if you don't."

"Well, I certainly do mind. It doesn't sound like a respectable idea at all."

"Are you uncomfortable? Got cramps?"

"No." Her voice was muffled against his shirt. "This is getting embarrassing."

"Are you flowing very heavily?"

"*No*. Just spotting. I told you, I barely started today, but . . ."

"Then let's go fool around, huh?"

"Nick, I can't. I'm too embarrassed by the whole idea, and that's that." She pushed herself away from him and started to stalk out of the kitchen. Nick caught up with her at the door.

"Take it easy, love," he said with a smile and scooped her up into his arms. He started down the hall to the bedroom.

"Where are we going? What are you doing?"

"You are obviously too embarrassed to make your usual assertive moves on me tonight, so maybe the time has come to try it another way."

"What other way?"

"Trust me."

"Hah. Why are you carrying me?"

"Because I feel like it. Do you mind?"

She thought about it carefully. "No, I guess not."

"Good, because it's too late to argue."

He strode into the bedroom and stood her carefully on her feet while he turned back the covers on the bed. Then he smiled at her as he removed his glasses and set them on the bedside table. There was love and laughter and a rapidly kindling desire in his normally cool eyes.

"Okay," he said. "Sit down."

Phila sat down abruptly on the edge of the bed. She watched with more curiosity than anything else as Nick went down on one knee in front of her and began removing her high-heeled evening shoes. "What are you doing now?"

"What does it look like I'm doing? I'm undressing you."

"You're doing a good job of it."

"I've been learning from you," he said. He eased her out of the black gown and then went to work on her pantyhose and bra. She closed her eyes, savoring the feel of his hands.

"Go take care of things in the bathroom, honey. When you come out, I'll be ready."

Phila nodded agreeably and opened her eyes just far enough to find the bathroom door. When she emerged a few minutes later she saw Nick waiting for her. He was naked and fully aroused. She stood staring at him, thinking about how magnificent he looked.

"Hi," she said.

"Hi, yourself."

"I used to think you were too big, you know," she said.

"Did you?"

"I don't like big men."

"Maybe I'll shrink with time."

"I doubt it." Then she giggled as her eyes went lower to his heavy, thrusting manhood. "On second thought, maybe parts of you will shrink from time to time."

"But probably not for long. Not with you around." He came forward and took her hand to draw her over to the bed.

Phila sank down onto the sheets with a vast sense of relief. "Do you really love me, Nick?" She gazed up at him with dreamy eyes.

"I really love you."

"I've never been in love before. Not really. It's nice, isn't it?" she asked.

"Very nice. And for the record, I haven't ever really been in love before, either. Not like this. Nothing has ever felt the way it does with you."

He ran his fingers slowly along the inside of her thigh. She squirmed a little beneath the sensual stroking and somehow his palm slid over her, cupping her intimately. A familiar liquid heat began to build between her legs.

"Nick?"

"Hmm?"

"You're going to do this your way tonight, aren't you?"

"Yes." He kissed her breast and then raised his head to look down at her. His eyes were intent. "I want you to learn to trust me in every way there is."

"Yes."

"Will that be so hard for you?" he asked gently.

"No." It was the truth, Phila thought in growing wonder. She was floating. His hands felt good—strong and sure and safe. His mouth drifted lightly, lazily over her whole body. He tasted her as if she were a rare delicacy, sampling the curve of her shoulder, the underside of her breasts, the insides of her ankles and every place in between.

It had never been quite like this before, she reflected in a fleeting moment of rationality. She had never just lain flat on her back and given herself up to the erotic sensations. Always before she had been too busy exploring him, learning her own power, delighting in the thrill of being able to make him explode beneath her touch. Too busy feeling safe and in command of everything.

For the first time since she had met him their lovemaking position was reversed. She waited for the familiar sense of panic. But nothing happened. Everything was happening so slowly and she was feeling so relaxed that she could not manage to work up any real alarm.

This was Nick, and with Nick she would always be safe.

His hands continued their infinitely patient movements. Time ceased to have any meaning for Phila. She felt heavy and warm, filled with a languid sensuality that made her begin to twist and turn on the sheets. Her legs parted.

When Nick's finger strayed into the crisp strands of silk at the apex of her thighs Phila moaned and pulled a pillow over her mouth. His finger stroked lower, separating the soft folds and circling her gently.

"Nick, Nick." Phila tossed aside the pillow but did not open her eyes. She lifted herself against his hand and he slid a second finger into her moist heat. "Oh, my God, *Nick.*"

"Does that feel good, sweetheart?"

"Yes, yes, yes."

"How about this?"

She trembled and clutched at the pillow again as he flicked the small, swelling nub of sensation between her thighs. Simultaneously he plunged his fingers back into her and Phila was suddenly flying into a million sparkling pieces.

"Come here." Instinctively she released the pillow and grabbed at him. In that moment it didn't matter who was on top and who was on the bottom. She just wanted to feel all of him. She had to have him close to her.

Nick allowed her to pull him down on top of her. He entered her heavily as the last tremors of her release began to fade. He plunged quickly, withdrew himself almost completely and then, when she cried out in frustration, drove forward again.

Nick was the focus of her whole world. He was over her, in her, enfolding her, confining her within the sensual prison of his arms. Phila was aware of his weight along every inch of her body. She was also aware of feeling safe and cherished as she never had before in her life.

She felt as if she had finally come home.

Before Phila could grasp the fact that her first climax was nearly over, another one was upon her. This one was slow, deep and seemed to last forever. She called Nick's name and held him closer, wrapping her legs around his hips.

"Sweetheart. Oh, *Phila*. Love me, Love me."

"I love you, Nick."

Nick went rigid in her arms, arching over her, filling her, crushing her beneath him as he lost himself in her warmth. Phila was dimly aware of his shuddering release and she held on to him more tightly than she had ever held on to anything or anyone in her life.

When it was over he collapsed along the length of her, his legs pinning hers, his hands holding her wrists gently captive. His solid weight pressed her deep into the bedding.

Phila came slowly back to her senses. The first thing she was fully aware of was the musky, sexy scent of the man lying on top of her. The next thing she focused on was the fact that she was trapped beneath Nick's full weight. She waited again for the panic, but it did not come.

When the old fear did not materialize, she began drawing an interesting pattern on Nick's strongly contoured back.

"You all right?" He shifted drowsily, lifting himself up on his elbows. His eyes glittered with the age-old expression of the fully satiated male, but there was a tenderness in his gaze that made Phila catch her breath.

"I think so." She smiled up at him. "You're on top."

"I told you I decided it was time to experiment with a new position."

She grinned. "I think the basic missionary position is considered a classic."

"You've got to admit that, for us, it's definitely a change of pace."

"True. Very wicked."

He waited a few seconds and then made an observation. "I can't help noticing that you're not clawing and kicking and trying to push me off onto the floor."

"No." She moved one leg experimentally. Nick let her slide it out from under his. She curved her foot and drew it up along the back of his calf. The hair on his leg tickled the sole of her foot, and she smiled.

"Do you like it better this way?" Phila asked softly, searching his face.

"I like it any way I can get it with you." He kissed her throat. "Believe me, there's nothing on this earth like the feel of you throwing yourself on top of me. But I've been wondering when you'd trust me enough to let me return the favor."

Phila narrowed her eyes. "It was a matter of trust, in a way, wasn't it?"

Nick nodded, his gaze serious. "I sensed that much right from the beginning. I figured the day you could let me make love to you like this would be the day I'd know for sure we were making real progress in this relationship."

"Typical of a man to look for progress in terms of a physical relationship," she said with mocking scorn.

"Yeah." He kissed her thoroughly and moved reluctantly off to the side. "Not, you understand, that I ever want you to give up your patented flying assault tactics." He yawned.

"You're a greedy man." She punched him lightly on the shoulder and slid out of bed. "Be right back." She headed for the bathroom.

When she returned a few minutes later she thought he had gone to sleep. But his arm curved around her as she crawled back into bed beside him.

"I've been thinking," Nick said.

"What about?"

"Getting married."

Phila froze. "Married! Who? Us? You and me?"

"You've got to admit there's a certain logic to it."

Phila sat up, holding the sheet to her breasts. "Good grief, Nick, we can't possibly get married." She swallowed nervously. "But thank you very much for asking," she added lamely.

He didn't move, but his eyes pinned her in the shadows. "You've got a problem with the idea of marrying me?"

She took a steadying breath. "Be reasonable, Nick. Anyone who marries a Lightfoot or a Castleton marries into a lot of family. It would be miserable for everyone concerned if you married someone the other members of the families didn't like. Let's be honest here. If there's one thing we can say with absolute certainty, it's that I'm not Miss Popularity as far as the rest of the Lightfoots and Castletons are concerned."

"Phila, I'm asking you to marry *me*, not the other people in the families."

"They could never accept me, Nick, and you know it."

"I don't give a damn if they accept you. I'm the one you're marrying. We don't have to deal with any of the rest of them except at the annual meetings."

"And Fourth of July celebrations and Christmas and summer holidays and Darren's political functions and Eleanor's dinner parties and a hundred other events during the year."

"You're exaggerating. We won't go to any of those things if you're uncomfortable."

"I told you I would be uncomfortable at that fund-raiser tonight, and you insisted on dragging me to it."

"That was different," he bit out.

"Was it? I don't think so."

"I thought you'd find it interesting once you got there, and I was right. Just as I was right about you enjoying a new position in bed tonight."

"Don't try to draw any parallels between going to a political fund-raiser and going to bed, for heaven's sake."

"Hell, if you feel that strongly about family events, we'll avoid them. I've skipped them for the past three years, haven't I?"

"Use your head, Nick. You can't possibly run the company and avoid socializing with the families. Besides, look at it from my point of view. Do you think I want to be the reason you don't take part in all the family traditions? I'd always feel guilty about coming between you and the rest of them."

"That's a damn fool notion."

"Is it?" Phila used the back of her hand to brush away the dampness that had gathered behind her eyelids. "Nick, I don't want to be another Crissie."

"Shit." He reached up and pulled her down beside him, folding her close. "So that's what this is all about."

"I know what that rejection did to her. I'm not sure I could take it day after day. You don't know what that kind of thing does to someone, Nick."

"Don't I?" His voice was soft and harsh. "I spent three years living with it."

Phila was silent as the reality of his words sank in. "Yes, you did, didn't you?"

"Phila, no one is going to say one word out of line to you. If anyone tries it, he or she will answer to me. That will be understood right from the beginning."

"I don't think it will work, Nick."

"Trust me."

"It's not a question of trust. It's a question of emotional reality. The Castletons and Lightfoots do not like me or approve of me. I've been able to handle that because right now I'm in an adversarial position with them. We all know I'm on the opposite side of the fence. We're natural enemies, and we can all deal together on that basis. But if I marry you, I'll become family and that will create a real mess, believe me."

"You're overanalyzing the situation. Probably comes from your training as a social worker."

"This is not funny, Nick."

"I know. I'm just trying to get you to see the situation from a different perspective. You're looking at it from your usual antiestablishment point of view. Things will work out if you'll just settle down and give everyone a chance."

"That's a totally unrealistic approach to a complex, highly charged situation. Leave it to a man to think things will be that simple."

Nick propped himself on his elbow and leaned over her menacingly. "I don't care what label you put on it, it happens to be my approach, and I will damn well guarantee you it will work."

Phila heard the implacability in his words and heaved a small sigh. "I don't think so, Nick. I'll tell you what, we'll compromise."

"I am not in the mood for any wimpy compromises. Lightfoots don't do that kind of thing."

"Stop acting like the king of the jungle and listen to me, will you?" She looked at him, pleading with him to understand. "Let's just go on as we have been for a while. We'll try living together. I'll attend a few more family functions. We'll see if any of the rest of them get to the point where they can accept me. Maybe in a few months or a year or so things will be different. Then, if you're still interested, we can talk about marriage."

"We'll talk about it now, damn it."

Phila bit her lip. "Don't be too quick to assume that marriage is what you want."

"Why should I change my mind?" he asked. "I never change my mind. That's another thing Lightfoots don't do very often."

"Is that right? Well, you may change your mind about marrying me when I tell you I'm going to give my C&L shares back to Darren tomorrow."

Nick was stunned into silence. When he finally spoke, his voice was cold and brutally soft.

"Like hell you are," he said.

CHAPTER EIGHTEEN

Nick shoved back the covers with a violent motion, climbed out of bed and stalked to the window. He stood looking out at the darkened waters of Elliott Bay. "I need those shares."

"No you don't."

"You're an ex-social worker, not an MBA. What the hell do you know about it?" he asked savagely.

"I may not know business, but I know people. This is a golden chance for the families to unite behind you. Darren will back you. Your father, too. I think."

"You think?" Nick darted a furious look at her over his shoulder. "What do you mean, you *think* they'll back me? I'm not playing games with C&L's future based on your emotional assessment of the situation, lady. There's too much at stake to take that kind of risk. I want to know your shares are in my corner, and I want everyone else to know it, too. I've explained all that. My best chance of getting one of the others to back me is for everyone to know you're backing me."

"Yes, I know, but it would be better all the way around if I gave them back to Darren and let him vote them," Phila said quietly.

"Better for whom? For what?"

"Family unity."

"Don't give me that crap about family unity. What do you care about the family unity of the Castletons or the Lightfoots?"

It was a good question, but Phila could not think of a way to answer it. She was following her instincts, and her instincts told her that she was doing the right thing. She gathered her legs close to her chest and hugged them. With her chin propped on her knees she watched Nick with the wary attention any intelligent being gives to a predator that has finally been aroused. She tried to speak calmly.

"It will be better for everyone, including you, if you take control of the company with the consent of as many of the members of the families as you can get," she said. "I'm fairly certain your father will back you, and I think Darren will. If Darren does, that means you've got Vicky's vote, too. With any luck Eleanor will fall into line if she sees the others backing you. You'll have a united front. The only nonparticipant will be Hilary."

"You know nothing about running a company. We're not playing psychological games here."

"Yes we are. You've been playing them all along. You just pin a different label on it. What do you call using me to convince the others it's safe to back you, if not a mind game?"

Nick paced back to the bed. He leaned over her, and she inched back onto the pillows. He planted his hands on either side of her head, caging her. "Listen to me, my smart-mouthed, troublemaking little do-gooder. I'm walking a very tricky line trying to save Castleton & Lightfoot. I won't have you jeopardizing everything at this point. The whole idea was for you to hang on to those shares until after the annual meeting. Once I have C&L back from Hilary, you can do what you damn well please."

"Nick, I really think it would be better if I got out of the picture."

"It's too late for you to get out of the picture. You've been in it since I found you in Holloway, and you're going to stay in it until I say otherwise."

She was getting nervous. He wasn't touching her, but she was starting to feel some of the panic she had once felt when he used his physical size to pin her to the bed. Phila tried to ease herself farther back against the headboard. "Nick, please listen to me. I know what I'm doing."

"No, you don't."

"It will be better this way. I'm sure of it. I have a feeling about it. You need to know the families are behind you. They need to feel they picked you freely as their next CEO. This is a family matter, and I'm an outsider."

"You've been happy enough to get involved up until this point."

"That was different. That was because of Crissie and then, later, because you asked me to stay involved. But now I want out. Besides, I'm tired of being used and manipulated."

"Is that what you think has been happening?"

"Of course. You've been doing it from the beginning. I love you and I think you love me, but I'm not completely blind. You used me to get back into the family nest, and now you're trying to use me to get back the company itself. Swell. Go right ahead and take back the company. I agree with you; it's for the best. But do it without me."

"Damn it, Phila." Nick straightened, plowing his fingers impatiently through his hair. "What's happening here? You won't marry me; you won't back me with those shares. You expect me to believe you really love me?"

"I do love you, Nick." She pushed aside the sheet and stood up slowly. "I'm doing this for your own good."

"Don't give me that crap."

"Trust me." Her smile was wobbly. "Wasn't that what you were saying to me a little while ago when you made love to me?"

He scowled. "It's not exactly the same thing."

"You don't think I'm having to go on trust, too? After the way you've used me right from the beginning? You don't think falling in love with you after everything that's happened requires a major chunk of trust?"

"Stop saying I've used you."

"Why? It's the truth, isn't it?"

"I can't believe I'm standing here arguing with you like this. It wasn't more than twenty minutes ago that you were going wild under me."

She touched his arm. "It will be better this way. Believe me. The families need to settle family business together. They need to know they're not being pushed around by an outsider. I'm not family, Nick. I don't have any right to interfere."

"You already have interfered, damn it."

Her mouth tightened. "That's true, isn't it? But I'm getting out now. You don't need me any longer. I'm almost sure you'll get what you want at the annual meeting. Everything's changed since you came back. You'll see."

"I'm not so sure about that. The risk is just too great, Phila. Everything is too delicately balanced. If everyone knows you're out of the picture I'm not sure what will happen."

"They'll back you. The thing is, Nick, they all want to back you. All except Hilary, of course. But deep down they all want to believe in you again and they sense that you're the one who should be running things. I can tell."

"You going to give me a written guarantee?"

Phila shook her head. "You don't need one."

"You're a hundred percent sure of your analysis?" he asked, eyes scathing.

"Well, no. There's no way to be a hundred percent sure. Not when you're dealing with human beings."

"That's the whole point. That's why I want your shares in my corner."

"I have to do what I think is best."

Nick dropped down onto the bed and lay looking up at her with a grim, watchful expression. "You're right, you know."

"About the families backing you?"

"No. About my having used you."

Phila didn't say anything. She just looked at him.

"It all came together when I found you. I knew right away that with you I had the missing piece I needed to get back into the game. But you weren't what I expected. I wasn't always sure *how* to use you."

"Thanks a lot."

"Half the time you surprised me by going off on a totally different tangent than the one I had anticipated. Like the first morning you played golf with my father."

Phila reached for her robe and drew it around herself. "What about it?"

"I thought it would be interesting to throw the two of you together. I thought Dad would get a kick out of arguing with you and you might be able to draw him out of his shell, maybe get him to take more of an interest in what was going on around him and with the company. I thought I could work with that. I didn't realize you were going to start out by lecturing him on my terrific sense of responsibility."

"Oh."

"I was more astonished than he was. During the past three years I'd forgotten what it was like to have someone believe in me without any hard evidence."

"People rarely get hard evidence to believe in, not when it comes to judging other human beings. You almost always have to go on instinct and trust."

"Yeah. Well, the way you handled my father wasn't the only thing that threw me. There was the totally unexpected way you got Vicky and Darren to take another look at their own pasts and what Burke had done to them. You also realized what was motivating Hilary before I did. You even understand Eleanor and her compulsive need to protect the family image. Every time I turn around lately, you're dabbling in family business."

"I'm through dabbling."

"No, you're not, but we'll go into that later. I've got enough to deal with at the moment."

"I'm not going to change my mind, Nick. Tomorrow I'm phoning Darren and I'm going to tell him the shares are his to do with as he pleases."

"Yeah. I believe you." He didn't take his eyes off her.

"Screw the shares. There's a part of you that still doesn't trust me, isn't there?"

She frowned. "This has nothing to do with trust. I'm doing what I think is right."

"I'm not talking about your decision to give the shares back to Darren. I'm talking about us—you and me. You don't trust me completely."

"Should I? After you've just admitted you used me?"

"That worked both ways. You were using me, too."

"Yes."

"Tell me, Phila," he said, his voice growing rough and low and beguiling.

"Tell you what?"

"Whatever it is you need to tell me."

"I don't know what you're talking about."

He exhaled slowly. "You're lying."

"So?" Phila challenged. "What are you going to do about it?"

"The only thing I can do." He caught her hand and tumbled her down on top of him. "Make wild, passionate love to me, sweetheart."

"I thought you were angry at me."

"I'm definitely pissed. As usual, you're not following the rules. But I don't want to argue about it right now."

"You think if we make love again I'll become sweet and compliant and change my mind about the shares?"

"I think if we make love again I'll become a lot less pissed. Isn't that a worthy goal in and of itself?"

Phila smiled very brilliantly. "It certainly is."

Victoria stood with her tennis racket in one hand, watching anxiously as Darren hung up the court phone. "Did I hear that correctly? She's giving the shares back to you? Just like that?"

"Just like that." Darren absently tossed a tennis ball into the air, caught it and tossed it again.

"What about Nick?"

"What about him?"

"Well, what did he have to say about all this?" Victoria frowned impatiently. "Is he going along with the idea?"

"It didn't sound to me as if he had much choice. Phila made her decision all by herself. She says she's answered her personal questions about what went on around here while Crissie was in our lives, and now she's taking herself out of the picture."

Victoria twirled her racket slowly between her fingers. "She acts as if she just dropped in, asked a few questions and decided to leave. So casual. The truth is, she changed everything. She put doubts in everyone's minds about things we've all assumed were true for three years. She shook up both families pretty thoroughly. Now she's just going to walk away?"

Darren scratched his jaw. "So she says. I don't see Nick letting it happen that way, though."

"All right, maybe she won't be able to walk away from him, but she's apparently walking away from her slice of C&L." Victoria paused. "*Our* slice."

"Apparently."

"You think there's something more involved?"

"Not exactly. She acts as if she no longer cares what happens to C&L, but I don't believe that. As long as Nick is involved with the company, she'll care about it."

"She's in love with him." It was a statement. Victoria was sure of herself on that score.

"But she's not going to back him at the annual meeting even though that's what he probably intended her to do all along."

"Which means that Nick will need your help and his father's if he wants to assume control of C&L." Victoria thought for a minute. "What are you going to do, Darren?"

"I'm going to give the entire matter my closest attention." He grinned. "That's what politicians are supposed to say when they get caught flat-footed by a surprising turn of events, isn't it?"

"Eleanor will back Hilary all the way."

"Probably. But I no longer even know that for certain.

Everything seems to have become slightly bent out of shape since Phila and Nick landed."

"You've always voted with your mother."

"I generally voted the way my father voted, too. But not out of blind loyalty to him. It was because all of us usually wanted the same things for the company."

"Burke always wanted what was best for the company. I'll give him credit for that much. It was all he really cared about." A slight morning breeze ruffled the hem of Victoria's short white skirt as she stood momentarily lost in thought. "Crissie used to say things about the two of you."

"What kind of things?"

"The wrong things. They're not important any longer." She stood on tiptoe and kissed him. "You're not at all like your father, thank God. A part of me knew that all along, and that's the real reason I didn't go through with the divorce three years ago when the future looked darkest."

Darren reached out and pulled her into his arms. His eyes were very clear and serious. "The world of politics can get rough, Vicky. There may come a time when I'll get sick and tired of it and want to walk away from it."

"It doesn't matter. I'll walk away from it with you if that's what you want. All I care about is you and me and Jordan."

He nodded, stroking her hair. "You and Jordan are the most important things in my world."

Victoria smiled tremulously and stepped back. Her eyes were shining. "That's settled. Your serve, I believe."

"She gave the shares back to Darren today." Eleanor finished pouring tea from the silver Crossley pot and busied herself with the spoons. She did not look at Hilary. "Such an odd, unpredictable girl."

"Perhaps she's decided she's caused enough trouble." Hilary sipped her tea with an outer calm she did not feel. Frantically she tried to assess the new information. This was the last move she had expected from Phila after their confrontation. Maybe it was all going to work out, after all. "I'm surprised Nick allowed her to do it."

"Darren thinks she made the decision on her own and that Nick probably is not at all happy with it."

Hilary considered that, cautious of her feeling of vast relief. Perhaps Phila's loyalty to Crissie and therefore to Crissie's lover had won out. She might not have felt right about turning the shares over to Hilary directly, but she would know that giving them back to Darren was almost the same thing.

Hilary wondered if Nick would get rid of Phila now that she was no longer of use to him. It seemed likely. He was a businessman, after all. He knew when to cut his losses.

"I imagine that will be the end of the relationship between Phila and Nick," Hilary observed aloud. "Nick is too smart to keep a liability around for long."

Eleanor nodded slowly. "She's certainly not his type."

"It would have been a bit awkward having her in the families."

"Extremely awkward. But I don't suppose there was ever any real possibility that he would have actually married her. There was no need, unless that was the only way he could have gotten hold of the shares."

"Well, this certainly simplifies things," Hilary said, hoping she was right. "You and Darren will be able to make your own decisions now."

"Yes, of course, dear. Darren and I only want what is best for C&L."

"And for Darren's career," Hilary added pointedly.

"Naturally." Eleanor smiled with vague satisfaction. "The fund-raiser went off rather well the other night, didn't it?"

"It was definitely a success." Hilary recalled the scene in the women's rest room and wanted to throw the bone china teacup against the wall.

"I heard that even Barbara Appleton and her husband wrote out a sizable check." Eleanor frowned. "Strange, isn't it? I've always found Barbara so distressingly liberal in her views. I'm surprised she was interested in contributing to a Republican campaign. Vicky said it had something to do with her interest in child-welfare issues."

"A contribution is a contribution. It doesn't matter where it comes from, does it?"

"Very true, dear. Perhaps Barbara has seen the light at last. After all, my son is going to make a real change in this state, and everyone wants to back a winner. Who knows how far Darren will rise in public office or what he'll accomplish in the future?"

"Provided he has family backing and family money behind him."

"That goes without saying, dear. More tea?"

"Goddamn it, what the hell does that mouthy little gal think she's doing now?" Reed's voice was so loud that Nick had to hold the phone five inches away from his ear.

"Disobeying my explicit instructions, for one thing." Nick munched a cracker with some cheese on it. Phila had just returned from her daily trek to the Pike Place Market. Every time she went she discovered a new and more exotic cheese. He didn't know the name of this particular specimen, but it held strong overtones of goat.

"Well, what in hell are you going to do at the annual meeting if you can't control her shares?"

"Same thing I've been planning to do all along. I'm going to try to get myself elected chief executive officer of C&L."

"Christ almighty, she's a real little maverick, isn't she?"

"Only in some things." Nick looked up as Phila came into the room carrying two glasses of wine. "In other ways she's quite predictable."

"She's going to run you ragged."

"Yeah, I know. It's probably my karma." Nick took a glass from Phila's hand. She sat down beside him and curled her legs under herself. He smiled at her magenta top and turquoise pants.

"What are you going to do if you don't beat Hilary at the meeting?" Reed asked in a more subdued voice.

"I've still got another job to go back to, remember?"

"I remember. What about Phila? Will she be going back to that other job with you?"

"Definitely. That's not open to debate the way the future of Castleton & Lightfoot is. Got to go now, Dad. I'll see you at the meeting. If you've got half the brains I've always assumed you have, you'll vote for me." Nick hung up the phone before his father could respond.

"The wine," Phila announced, "is supposed to complement the cheese perfectly. Brings out all the subtle nuances."

"Is that what they told you at the wine shop?"

"Yep."

"I've got news for you, Phila. There is nothing subtle about goat. You don't want to draw out the nuances, you want to drown them. This wimpy Riesling isn't going to do the trick. It would take a gallon jug of dollar-ninety-eight red to get the job done."

She smiled serenely. "I'm still learning the fine points of trendy cuisine."

"I've noticed." He crunched another cracker with cheese on it. "You do realize the families are in chaos?"

"Are they?"

"Hilary must be going nuts trying to figure out what you're up to now."

"What about you?"

"Me? I've given up trying to figure you out. I'm just going to ride the roller coaster to the end of the line."

"And if it doesn't stop where it should?"

"Then you and I leave for California the day after the annual meeting," Nick said without any hesitation.

Phila eyed him cautiously. "Are you sure you'll still want me around if what I'm doing keeps you from saving C&L?"

Nick smiled deliberately. "Yeah, Phila, I'll definitely want you around if you cause me to lose the company. I'll want to work out all my frustrations on your sweet ass."

"That sounds like fun."

Much later, in bed that night, Nick lay awake thinking about his own words. After having come this far, it was more than a little disconcerting to lie there seriously contemplating losing C&L at this stage.

But it wouldn't be so bad, he realized. It would be a damned shame if C&L got broken up into bits and pieces and run by outsiders, but sometimes that was the way things went. Everyone would survive.

As long as he had Phila, Nick decided, losing C&L wouldn't be the end of the world. She talked blithely about this being a golden chance for the families to reunite but the truth was, she was his golden chance in more ways than one. But damned if he was going to tell her that at this juncture. He knew that deep inside she was worried she might be wrong about the outcome of the annual meeting and that was just fine with him.

If he was going to sweat it out, she might as well sweat, too.

Reed looked up from his evening paper as Tec mixed martinis at the small bar. "Mariners won."

Tec dropped a toothpick loaded with giant green olives into a glass. "Yes, sir, I heard. That's the kinda thing that can make a man contemplate returning to his religious roots, ain't it?" He carried the drink over to Reed.

"I suppose you also heard the shares are back in Darren's hands?"

"Yes, sir. That little Phila is just one big surprise after another, ain't she?"

"Goddamn right." Reed munched an olive and went to stand in front of the window to watch a sleek yacht glide through the waters of Puget Sound. The Bainbridge Island homes had been built with an expansive view of the water, just as the summer cottages in Port Claxton had. "I wonder what that son of mine thinks he's going to do now?"

"Anybody's guess, sir. Nick always did play 'em close to the chest."

"I'll say one thing. I was dead wrong three years ago when I told him he didn't have any guts. He's got 'em, all right."

"Beggin' your pardon, sir, but it takes more'n guts to walk back in here after what happened three years ago and try to take over the company. Takes a pair of stainless-steel balls." Tec broke off as Hilary appeared in the doorway. "Evenin' ma'am. Can I fix you a martini?"

"Yes, please, Tec." Hilary smiled wearily as she walked into the room. She sat down gracefully in the green silk damask–upholstered Chippendale chair. "Hello, Reed. How was your day?"

"Fine. Played eighteen holes with Sweeney over in Bellevue. Won twenty bucks."

"Congratulations." Hilary took the drink from Tec. "Thank you, Tec. That will be all for now." She dismissed him with a nod and waited until he had left the room before she spoke again. "Well, it will all be over one way or the other tomorrow, won't it?"

Reed didn't turn away from the view. "You make it sound like Judgment Day."

"Probably because that's the way I see it. The families will be sitting in judgment on me and on everything I've done for Castleton & Lightfoot during the past three years." Hilary smiled again, briefly. "I hope I'm not found wanting."

"You've done a hell of a job with the company, Hilary."

"Thank you, Reed. Your approval means a great deal to me. C&L is more important to me than anything else in the world. It's my life. I wonder if you and the others will remember that when it comes time to vote for the next CEO."

"Hard thing to forget." He ate another olive.

"A lot of things can be forgotten when the prodigal son returns home. That's understandable."

"It's been three years, Hilary."

"Yes, but has anything really changed? Once before, Nick walked out on all of us, not just me and the baby, but the company, too. What is there to say he wouldn't do it again if he regained control of C&L?" She got up and moved over to stand beside her husband. "The thing we all have to ask ourselves is, what does Nick really want?"

"What do you think he wants?"

Hilary took a deep breath. "Revenge. I think he wants control of C&L so that he can turn around and destroy it.

He's never forgiven any of us for what happened three years ago. He was the heir apparent, the man with the golden touch. He saw C&L as his future personal kingdom. When you and Burke refused to let him take the company in the direction he wanted, he lost his temper. He took out his rage on me first, and then on all the rest of you. I don't think he'll be satisfied until he's destroyed the company."

Reed stirred his martini with the spear that had held the olives.

Hilary waited a moment longer before she said, "There's only one thing I really regret."

"What's that?"

"I'm sorry I lost the baby. I would have liked to have given you the grandchild you've always wanted, Reed."

Of course the baby had not been Nick's, Reed thought. He wondered how he could have been so blind three years ago. Phila was right. Nick was his son, and no son of his would walk out on his child.

CHAPTER NINETEEN

Nick walked into the plain, unpretentious office that C&L had used as a boardroom since before he was born. This was the room in which all the major decisions regarding C&L's future had been made. Today it would witness the one that would determine the company's survival.

Tradition. C&L had long since reached the point where its annual meetings could have been held in plush, modern, corporate-style surroundings complete with paneled walls and thick carpets, but it clung to tradition. Even Hilary had not dared mess with this particular ritual, Nick thought as he examined the familiar surroundings.

"There you are, Nick." Reed, dressed in a pair of golfing slacks and a polo shirt, was sitting at the round table in the center of the room. "We're all ready and waitin'. Let's get on with it. Got a one o'clock starting time at the course."

"Wouldn't want to delay you," Nick said.

Eleanor, Darren and Vicky were already seated at the table. Hilary, looking serene and elegant in a white silk suit, was just drawing up her own chair. She arranged a stack of folders neatly in front of her and glanced up without speaking as Nick sat down beside his father. The others murmured their greetings.

"Coffee," Tec announced, carrying a pot into the room.

"Thank you, Tec. You may go now," Hilary said.

"Yes, ma'am."

Hilary looked around the table. "I believe we're ready to begin."

Phila, loaded down with two huge bags full of fruit, vegetables, cheese, pesto and wine made her way up First Avenue from the Market and hoped she had not made a very serious mistake.

Perhaps she should have hung on to those shares. She might have been wrong about Nick already having all the support he needed within the families. What if Hilary had done some major damage during the past few days?

Phila tried to tell herself that Darren was not a fool and neither was Reed. They could see for themselves that they had all misjudged Nick three years ago. She did not expect Eleanor to shift allegiance because the older woman had her own reasons for backing Hilary. But Darren was an independent thinker. He would not be swayed by his mother's vote. And Vicky would vote with Darren.

Phila tried to add up the various components of the situation in a variety of ways, but there was no getting around the fact that without her, Nick needed the support of at least two others on the board.

But he needed to take control of the company with as much family support as he could get, Phila reminded herself as she leaned a shoulder against the glass doors of the condominium lobby. It would be so much better for everyone concerned if the outsider stayed out. The Lightfoots and Castletons needed to settle the future fate of the firm among themselves.

Phila freed one finger to punch the elevator button and glanced at her watch. By now the meeting was in full swing. She wondered how long an annual C&L stockholders meeting lasted. She was going to go nuts waiting for Nick to walk back through the door this afternoon.

The elevator doors slid open on the top floor, and Phila

stepped out into the carpeted hall. She struggled with her keys and packages as she approached Nick's apartment.

She was wondering if she and Nick would be on their way to California in the morning as she opened the front door. She used her foot to nudge one grocery bag into the slate-tiled foyer. Holding the other bag in one arm, she closed the door behind her.

She was halfway to the kitchen when she realized she was not alone in the condominium. She opened her mouth, but the scream was trapped in her throat as a huge hand clamped over her lips.

"Did you think you could escape me, you lying little bitch?" Elijah Spalding hissed in her ear. The cold metal of a gun barrel pressed against her throat.

"Before we call for the vote," Hilary said calmly, "I would ask that all of you think very carefully about what each of you wants for Castleton & Lightfoot. You've asked Nick what he envisions for the future of the company, and he's told you he will take it in a new and unproven direction. Are you willing to turn your back on the successful track record C&L has established in the field of military instrumentation?"

"Don't overstate the case, Hilary." Nick looked expressionlessly at his ex-wife and wondered how he could ever have wanted to marry her. She wasn't his type at all. "I'm not going to make the transition all at once. We won't dump the government contracts until we have things working profitably in the commercial area."

Darren frowned. "What about your plans to expand the Pacific Rim markets? That's easier said than done, Nick. Those are tough markets to crack."

"I've spent the past three years developing contacts in those markets. When C&L is ready to move into them, the markets will be ready for us."

Reed poured himself a third cup of coffee. "C&L has done just fine working for the government all these years."

"Times change, Dad. There are other ways to grow and expand. C&L hasn't changed its basic mode of operation in nearly forty years. It needs some fresh conquests and some new direction. Nothing stays the same forever. The company is getting calcified."

"We just finished an excellent second quarter and things look fine for the third," Hilary interjected. "How can you say the company is calcified?"

"There are other factors besides the quarterly bottom line that have to be considered," Nick said quietly.

"Such as?" Hilary challenged.

"Such as management foresight. We should be planning for the next century, not just a year or three years from now."

"Government contracts aren't going anywhere. There'll always be a need for our kind of product," Reed said.

"We've always done so well in the past," Eleanor said. "I'd hate to see us change too quickly."

Nick looked at her. "It won't happen overnight, Eleanor. I'll make sure we keep everything balanced before we make commitments in any direction." This wasn't going to be easy. When it was all over, he was going to know he'd been in a fight. Castletons and Lightfoots were stubborn, hard-headed and opinionated. He wished he had Phila sitting beside him. He could have used a little moral support.

"You lied and they all believed you, didn't they? Did that give you a feeling of power, bitch? To have that whole courtroom believing your lies? Well, I hope you got a thrill out of it then, because I'm going to make you sorry you ever opened your mouth. I warned you I would punish you for the lies you told. I warned you, didn't I? Didn't I?"

He smelled. His huge body stank. Phila breathed quickly through her nose, feeling as if she were about to suffocate. She could not stand his hand over her mouth much longer. She was getting sick to her stomach. He was dragging her back out of the kitchen. In desperation, she let herself go limp.

When she sagged against him, Spalding released her mouth so that he could grab her more securely. The muzzle of the gun scraped her arm. "Lying bitch. Lying little tramp. You had no right to take those children away from me. They were mine. I was gonna raise 'em right. Teach 'em discipline and obedience."

"The way you did little Andy?" Phila asked, forcing herself to keep her voice low so that he wouldn't panic and put his hand back over her mouth.

Spalding's frightening blue eyes blazed. "Andy refused to obey me. And I made it real clear to all the children that they had to obey me. I had to make an example of him. I had no choice." He shook Phila so hard her head snapped back. "No *choice*. He was mine to do with as I wanted."

"Did you make the others watch? Is that why they were all so frightened the next day when I tried to talk to them?"

"I told you, I had to teach 'em discipline. They had to know what would happen if they didn't obey me. Discipline is the key. And a kid learns discipline best when he's scared shitless. That's the way I learned it from my Pa."

"I don't want to hear your crazy reasoning or your excuses. There are no excuses for what you've become and, deep inside, you know it. You're a murderer, Elijah Spalding. You're nothing but a child abuser and a child killer. The scum of the earth. Beating those children and killing poor little Andy wasn't all you did either, was it? You used some of them in other ways, too, didn't you? You raped some of them."

Spalding's heavy face turned red with his fury. "Those kids were given to me to do with as I saw fit. I was supposed to raise 'em. I had the responsibility to do it right. They were *mine*. I had a right to do whatever I wanted to them. I had to enforce discipline. I had to let them know I was in total control."

Nick looked around the circle of faces as Reed seconded the motion for a vote. In that moment he knew Phila had been right. Win or lose, it was better this way. This was family business. If he did win, he needed to know the families backed him. If he lost, the hell with it. California and Phila were waiting.

"All those in favor of appointing Nick CEO, say aye."

"Aye," said Reed.

A curious relief went through Nick. If nothing else, he now knew for certain that his father believed in him again.

"Aye," said Darren.

"Aye." Victoria looked at Nick and smiled faintly.

Eleanor hesitated, glancing once at Hilary, and then she nodded brusquely, "Aye."

Hilary put down the silver pen she had been toying with for the past few minutes. Her smile was as serene as ever, but her eyes were bottomless pools of bitterness. "That seems to settle the matter, doesn't it? Congratulations, Nick. You've won."

A taut silence followed that observation. It was broken by Reed, who reached out to slap Nick on the shoulder. His eyes were gleaming with satisfaction. "Better call Phila and tell her the news. She'll be on pins and needles, if I know her."

Nick's brows rose. "You think so?"

"Yep. Give her a call. That little gal will be a nervous wreck by now wondering what happened." He reached for the phone and shoved it over in front of Nick.

Nick picked up the receiver and dialed, aware of the others watching him. It was as if they all wanted Phila to be a part of this morning's decision, he suddenly realized. They were treating her like family.

In the condominium the phone rang for the third time. "That will be Nick," Phila said patiently. "He knows I'm here. If I don't answer, he'll be suspicious."

The phone rang a fourth time.

"All right, answer it, damn it, but don't say anything to make him think I'm here or so help me, I'll wait for him after I've finished with you and I'll kill him, too. I swear to God, I will."

With trembling fingers, Phila picked up the phone, trying to think clearly. She knew it would be Nick on the other end of the line. He was her only hope.

* * *

The phone rang four times before she answered. Nick knew instantly that something was wrong. Her voice was thin and breathless.

"Phila?"

"Oh, Nick. Nick I'm so glad you called." The false cheerfulness burned Nick's ears. "Everything's fine here, but do you know, after you left this morning I realized I had forgotten to thank you for that gift that you and Darren and Reed and Tec gave me. You remember the present I'm talking about?"

"What the hell *are* you talking about?" Nick demanded, hunching over the phone.

"Yes, that's it. That's the one. Well, I just want you to know I'm going to get a lot of use out of it starting right now. Can't wait to use it, in fact. I . . . Oh, dear. I've got to run. I'll talk to you later, Nick. *Hurry home.*"

Nick slammed down the receiver and surged to his feet. Everyone else at the table stared at him in astonishment.

"Something wrong?" Reed asked.

"I'm not sure, but I think so." Nick was already moving around the table, heading for the door.

Darren stood up. "What the hell's the matter, Nick?"

Nick paused briefly at the door. "What's the only thing any of us ever gave Phila?"

"We taught her how to use a gun," Darren responded instantly.

"Exactly. She just told me she had an immediate use for our gift. And she asked me to hurry home."

"Goddamn it," Reed breathed. "You think it's the guy she put in jail?"

"I don't know. I'm not taking any chances. Eleanor, call nine-one-one. Tell them we've got a suspicious situation and we'd appreciate having it checked out right away. If you don't get the feeling we're going to get help in a hurry, call the manager of my condominium building and ask him to go upstairs and check on Phila. Tell him I'm on my way."

Eleanor reached out immediately to pick up the phone. "Of course, Nick."

Nick went through the door. "Thanks," he called back over his shoulder.

"Hold on, a second," Reed announced, shoving back his chair. "I believe I'll go along for the ride. Tec will want to come, too, just in case."

"Count me in," Darren said, rising swiftly to his feet.

Victoria was out of her chair. "I'm going with the rest of you."

Thirty seconds later Hilary and Eleanor sat alone at the table. Hilary watched Eleanor punch out 911 and begin speaking in the imperious tones the older woman always used when she wanted instant results from the people she employed.

Just like Eleanor to think of the cops as her personal employees, Hilary thought fleetingly as she quietly gathered up her files.

Eleanor had finished speaking just as Hilary reached the door. She put down the receiver. "They're on their way," she announced.

Hilary nodded. "That doesn't surprise me. It's rather amusing, isn't it? The Lightfoots and Castletons are rushing to Philadelphia's rescue."

"Perhaps it's only simple justice, Hilary. She seems to have done her best recently to rush to C&L's rescue."

"That's one way of looking at it."

"Where will you go now, Hilary?" Eleanor asked. "What are you going to do?"

"Does it matter?"

"Yes, it matters. You're family, Hilary."

"No. Not any longer. I don't think I ever was. Not in any real sense. Not in the way Phila is going to be."

Hilary let herself out the door and closed it very quietly behind her.

Phila could have wept and she knew she probably would have if she hadn't been too scared and too busy trying to think clearly. Spalding still had her pinned against his bulk. He started to drag her toward the bedroom. She marshaled her thoughts. Once before she had manipulated this man. She knew how to push his buttons. She must do it again.

"You'd better leave me alone and get out of here while you can. The authorities will be looking for you."

"By the time they figure out where I've gone, I'll be out of here."

"How did you find me?"

"I made Ruth keep track of you. She went and hired somebody to find you and tell her where you were all the time."

Phila closed her eyes in silent anguish. She had never been safe, not even during the time she had spent in Port Claxton. Someone had been watching her. The realization was almost as horrifying as her present situation.

"What are you going to do, Elijah?" she asked, fighting to keep her voice calm.

"First, I have to punish you for the way you ruined everything. I'm going to hurt you for what you did. Hurt you bad, the way we used to hurt the women prisoners when I was workin' as a merc. And when you're crying and beggin' for mercy, I'm going to kill you."

"You're a fool. What will you do? Where will you run? You'll have to hide for the rest of your life because everyone will know for certain this time that you're a murderer. The man I'm living with will hunt you to the ends of the earth. He's a powerful man, Spalding. A lot more powerful than you are."

"You're only his whore, not his wife. Why should he care about you when you're gone? I'll be safe."

"Nothing will protect you from Nick Lightfoot. You'll be looking over your shoulder as long as you live."

"Shut your mouth, bitch. I can take care of myself."

"Not a chance, Spalding. I want you to know what you're risking by killing me. I put you in jail once before, remember? You'll be going back there because of me."

"I said *shut your mouth*, you bitch. You don't know what you're talking about." He dragged her as far as the bedroom door and then through it. He released her, took a step back and gave her such a violent slap with the back of his hand that Phila fell onto the bed.

Phila tasted blood from her cut lip. When she opened her eyes Spalding was towering over her with maniacal lust in every line of his face. She had seen that look on a man's face once before, the afternoon she had been attacked in the foster home. But this time there was no Crissie to save her. She watched in horror as Spalding began unzipping his dirty trousers.

"*No.*" She remembered the other time, remembered the lamp Crissie had used.

Without stopping to think she lashed out and caught the base of the bedside lamp. It flew from the table and crashed against Spalding's side.

"Bitch." Spalding leaped back in an instinctive movement as glass shattered. He raised his gun hand to shield his face from the fragments of the exploding light bulb.

Phila rolled to the side of the bed, yanking open the bedside table drawer. Her fingers closed around the familiar grip of the .38. *Just aim it and pull the trigger.*

Lying half on and half off the bed, she jerked the gun out of the drawer, whipped it around toward Spalding whose hands were just falling away from his eyes. She fired.

The roar of the revolver deafened her. Spalding shrieked, staggered back against the wall and then went down with a thud. Blood welled from his shoulder, staining his shirt and trousers. His hand twitched but he did not move.

Phila's ears were still ringing a few seconds later when Nick, followed by a lot of familiar faces, came through the bedroom door.

"Holy shit," said Tec Sherman.

Spalding groaned.

"He's alive," Reed observed. "She must still be rushing her shots."

"I'm working on the problem," Nick said as he gathered a trembling Phila into his arms and held her close.

* * *

"I'm glad he didn't die. He deserved it for what he did to those children, but I'm glad I don't have to live with the knowledge that I killed someone." Phila shuddered as she sat drinking brandy a long while later. The police interviews had been exhausting. The aftermath of a shooting, even one done in self-defense, was extensive, she had discovered.

But Castletons and Lightfoots had been everywhere, fixing tea for her, buffering her from the endless police questioning, dealing with the lab technicians, ushering the medical people in and out of the condominium. They had all hovered protectively over Phila during the long process, and Nick had never left her side.

"Might have been a goddamn sight simpler if you had punched his ticket for a one-way trip," Reed said. "The way the bleeding-heart liberal laws are in the country these days, the bastard'll probably be able to turn around and sue you from jail when he recovers."

"We can handle any lawsuit Spalding throws at us," Nick said as he poured another shot of brandy into Phila's glass. "After all, we can afford better lawyers than Spalding will ever be able to buy. And you know how it works, the one with the most expensive lawyer wins."

"Very reassuring." Phila smiled weakly as she looked around at the circle of faces in Nick's living room. Everyone was there except Hilary. Even Eleanor had grabbed a cab after making her phone call to the police.

Tec Sherman smiled contentedly. "Shot was a little wide on account of you rushed it, but under the circumstances you did damn good, ma'am. The creep'll live, but you made your mark, that's for dang sure."

"How are you feeling?" Victoria asked as she handed out cups and saucers. "Heart still pounding?"

"I think it's slowly returning to normal, thanks to all of you. I honestly don't know what I would have done if you hadn't been here. I could hardly think straight when the police arrived."

"The detective told me privately that the whole case looked real clean. For starters, Spalding is an escaped prisoner. The deck is stacked against him from the get-go," Reed said. "Shooting him was a clear case of self-defense."

"Speaking of which," Phila said softly, "I owe you gentlemen my thanks. I would not have known how to defend myself if you all hadn't nagged me into learning how to shoot that horrid gun."

"Always nice to be appreciated," Nick murmured. "Drink your brandy, Phila. It will help you sleep."

"I doubt it. I'm not going to sleep a wink tonight."

"You will," he promised.

But contrary to Nick's prediction, Phila was still lying wide awake at one o'clock in the morning. A variety of emotions were clamoring for attention in her mind. Her mood seemed to be very fragile. She ricocheted between peaks and valleys. For a while a sense of euphoric relief would prevail; a moment later she would find herself on the verge of tears.

"Take it easy, honey. It's going to be all right. You'll be fine after you've had some sleep. It's just nerves." Nick's voice was deep and soothing. He pulled her into his arms, cradling her carefully against him. "You're going to be okay."

"I hope so."

"Is it any worse this time than it was last time?"

She froze. "What are you talking about?"

"I'm talking about the last time you had to deal with Spalding on your own."

"Oh."

His fingers worked slowly through her hair in a gentling movement. "When are you going to trust me enough to tell me the full story about what happened that time, Phila?"

"I did tell you the full story. You even checked up on it yourself. I saw that copy of the newspaper article you got hold of while you were here in Seattle. Besides, why should I want to talk about the trial? It's the shooting that's upset me." Phila couldn't seem to marshal her thoughts in a straight line the way she always had to when she discussed the Spalding trial.

"Maybe you're trying to keep too much inside. You don't have to bottle it all up, you know. Not any more. You're not alone now. You've got me. I love you, Phila."

"I love you, too, Nick."

"So tell me the truth and get it out of your system."

She held herself very still in his arms. "It's not fair to put the burden on anyone else."

"It won't be a burden for me. I've got no problem handling a few perjuries committed in the name of putting away a guy like Spalding. I'm no bleeding-heart liberal, remember? I'm a Lightfoot."

Her eyes widened. "How did you know?"

"Know what? That there was more to that whole incident with Spalding than you had told me?" He shrugged. "Just had a hunch. It had something to do with the drug charges against him, didn't it?"

Phila nodded her head against his chest. "I planted the heroin on him during the struggle in the restaurant parking lot. I set him up for that arrest, Nick. I arranged everything. I couldn't think of anything else to do. He'd already killed one child. I was so afraid he would kill another. He was hurting all of them. Raping them. I had to stop him."

"I know."

The words rushed out of her in a torrent now. "I knew the cops took their morning coffee break every day at that restaurant. In a small town like Holloway, you get to know the routine. There were always a couple of patrol cars parked in front of the restaurant at ten-fifteen in the morning. People used to joke that if they ever decided to pull a bank robbery, they'd be sure to do it around ten-fifteen."

"So you knew the cops' schedule and timed everything accordingly?"

"I knew what time they would be pulling in, and I knew I could make Spalding explode. It was easy enough to goad him into a violent response. But I didn't think a simple assault charge would do the job. I needed a felony count. Something that would get him put in jail."

"So that he wouldn't be eligible to go on running a foster home?"

"Yes."

"Where did you get the heroin?" Nick asked.

"Good grief, Nick. You know as well as I do that it's easy enough to buy drugs these days. As a social worker I had all kinds of contacts and information, including information about people who could get me the heroin. When it was over, all I had to do was let the law take its natural course. All I had to do was lie on the stand and make damn sure I stuck with that lie. The fact that Spalding had been a mercenary who had worked in Southeast Asia and South America was in my favor."

"The jury was willing to believe he might have started using drugs in those places and had been continuing to use them here in the States," Nick concluded for her.

"Yes." Phila fell silent, aware that she was waiting for his response.

"Damn it to hell, Phila."

She tensed. "I'm sorry, Nick. It was a terrible thing to do, but I couldn't think of anything else. I had to stop him. I had to get the kids away from him."

"*Sorry.* For God's sake, don't apologize. The only thing to be sorry about is that we don't have a foolproof way to offer kids protection from creeps like Elijah Spalding. You should never have been forced into a situation where you had to take such an incredible risk to save those children."

She let out the breath she had been holding. "I didn't want to tell anyone, ever. I figured I had made the decision to do it in the first place and I would have to live with what I had done. I couldn't ask anyone else to help bear the burden of the truth."

"But you quit your job."

"I had to quit. I knew I couldn't go on working as a caseworker. This time I hadn't just bent a few rules. I'd gone past all the boundaries. Taken the law into my own hands. I was no longer a professional, I was a vigilante."

"You don't feel guilty, do you? Because you sure as hell shouldn't."

"No. It isn't guilt I feel. I'd do it again, if I had to. But it was hard, Nick. Hard to do. Hard to live with afterward. Just like the shooting today."

"Keep in mind that you're not living with it alone any longer." He kissed her, his eyes gleaming in the shadows. "I love you."

"What really made you think there was more to the story than I had told you?"

"There seemed to be a lot of convenient coincidences in the account. Coincidences that sounded like a lot of luck or some very clever planning. I knew how badly you had wanted to shut down the Spalding foster home. I also knew you well enough to know you'd do whatever you had to do if you thought it was right. Then there was that bit about Ruth Spalding adamantly claiming her husband had to be innocent of the dope charges. She was so convinced you'd lied. It all added up to a question mark."

Phila was awed. "Sometimes you're a little too smart, Nick. Too clever and too slick. It scares me."

"But sometimes I'm just an ordinary dumb macho male." He grinned. "As you have pointed out on numerous occasions."

Phila began to relax for the first time all day. "True. I'll try to comfort myself with that thought. Good heavens, I almost forgot. What happened at the annual meeting? Who's the new CEO of Castleton & Lightfoot?"

"Guess."

"They voted for you? All of them?"

"All except Hilary."

"Oh, Nick, that's wonderful. I knew you'd win." She threw her arms around him. "I just knew it."

Nick rolled over onto his back and looked up at her with laughing eyes. "I've got news for you, honey. I won before I even walked into that meeting this morning."

"What's that supposed to mean?"

"I had you, didn't I?"

"That would have been enough? Even without C&L?"

"More than enough."

She kissed him thoroughly. "Congratulations, Mr. Chief Executive Officer."

"Just call me boss."

"Never."

"Then," he said smoothly, "you can call me husband."

Phila raised her head to look down at him. "You still want to marry me?"

"Phila, we are definitely going to get married. There was never any doubt about that. I decided this morning that I was willing to give you a little time to get comfortable with the idea of marrying into the families."

"Oh, gee, thanks."

"I knew you weren't sure how they felt about you," Nick continued, unperturbed. "But after the way they all rushed over here to save you today and stayed to protect you from the cops and the reporters, you can't doubt any longer that they're on your side. Face it, honey. You're family now, whether you like it or not."

CHAPTER TWENTY

❦

The voluminous white satin skirts of Phila's wedding gown drifted down in gleaming, rippling waves from the railing where she had her ankles propped up on the boards of the Gilmarten porch. She sat in a comfortably decrepit wicker chair, a glass of champagne in one hand. Her veil was draped over the railing beside her crossed ankles. A light late-evening breeze ruffled the gossamer netting.

Her new husband was sitting beside her, his chair tipped back on two legs, his ankles propped up next to Phila's. Nick was still wearing his formal black-and-white wedding attire, but he had long since removed his jacket. His shirt was unbuttoned at the collar, and his tie hung loosely around his neck. He had a glass of scotch in his hand.

The wedding had been a traditional Castleton and Light-foot affair, according to Victoria. It had taken place on the lush green lawn in front of the Lightfoot beach house with most of the populace of Port Claxton in attendance.

The families, it seemed, liked weddings and made the most of them. Phila told herself she should be grateful somebody hadn't brought out fireworks. It had been bad enough having to fend off Cupcake and Fifi at the buffet table.

The last of the guests had, with obvious reluctance, finally left less than a half hour earlier. Nick had wasted no time whisking Phila away from the beach cottages to the privacy of the Gilmarten place. There he had poured himself a scotch and filled Phila's champagne glass. Then they had both gone out onto the porch to watch the evening close in around them.

"I've been thinking," Phila announced, feeling more content and happy than she could ever remember being before.

"I'm going to hate myself for asking this. What have you been thinking about?"

"Hilary."

"Of all the damn fool things to be thinking about at a time like this. Phila, this is our wedding day. The last thing you should be thinking about is my ex-wife." Nick swore under his breath. "Make that my father's ex-wife."

"Hilary's and Reed's divorce isn't final yet."

"It will be soon enough. There's sure as hell no need for you to be thinking about it right now."

"But I've come up with a really terrific idea, Nick."

"Yeah?" He eyed her suspiciously. "Like what?"

"Like why don't you sell Lightfoot Consulting Services to her?"

Nick's feet came down off the railing and hit the porch with a thud. "Sell her Lightfoot Consulting? Are you out of your mind? Why in hell would I want to do a thing like that?"

"Now, Nick, be reasonable. You said yourself just the other day that you won't be able to continue running Lightfoot Consulting as well as Castleton & Lightfoot. You can't spread yourself that thin."

"Yeah, but I sure as hell never meant to turn my company over to Hilary, of all people."

"I didn't say turn it over to her. I said sell it to her in exchange for her shares in C&L."

"The families will get those shares back after the divorce. It's in the prenuptial contract Hilary signed."

Phila was dumbfounded. "There was a contract?"

"Sure. It was decided years ago that anyone marrying

into the families would get a block of shares to vote but that those shares would revert back to the rest of us in the event of a divorce. All Castleton and Lightfoot brides sign wedding contracts. If we ever get any grooms from outside the families, they'll sign them, too. It's a tradition."

"I didn't sign anything!"

Nick grinned and sipped his scotch. "I know."

"Well? Why wasn't I asked to sign a contract?" Phila demanded.

"I decided to break with tradition in your case. Besides, I know damn good and well you're not going anywhere. You're stuck with me for life." Nick repropped his feet up on the railing alongside Phila's. His chair tilted back on its two back legs once again.

"Is that so?"

"Damn right. Where else are you going to find a man who will let you attack him every night with your special Patented Flying Assault?"

"Oh, Nick." She didn't know quite what to say. Then she smiled. "You're right, you know. I was extremely lucky to find you. There's probably not another male on the face of the earth like you."

"If there is and if he ever gets close to you, I'll personally remove him from the face of the earth."

Phila heard the cool certainty beneath the bantering tone. She slid a quick glance in his direction and saw the implacable expression on his face. She decided it would be best to go back to the original subject.

"About Hilary."

"Do we have to talk about this now?"

"Stop whining, Nick. I'm serious. Sell her Lightfoot Consulting. She'll thrive on the challenge of expanding that company. And it will be all hers."

"This," Nick announced, "is the dippiest idea you've come up with yet. Give me one good reason why I should sell Lightfoot Consulting to Hilary."

Phila smiled. "I could give you plenty of logical, practical, intelligent reasons but there's really only one that counts."

"Which is?"

"She's family."

Nick groaned and swallowed more scotch. "I knew you were going to be trouble the day I met you."

"The feeling was mutual," Phila said cheerfully.

A cool, soft darkness had enveloped the porch.

"I'll think about it," Nick finally muttered. "But not tonight."

"All right," Phila agreed. "Not tonight."

Nick glanced at his watch. "It's about that time."

"What time?"

"Time," he explained patiently, "for you to drag me off to bed."

Phila felt a warm, tingling sensation move through her, stirring all her nerve endings the way a summer breeze stirred leaves. She sighed happily. "I guess it is about that time."

She put her champagne glass down on the railing and leaned over to kiss Nick. The wicker chair tipped precariously and started to collapse. Phila tried to steady herself by clutching at the back of Nick's chair. As it was already balanced delicately on two legs, Phila's weight was more than sufficient to send it toppling over onto its back.

Nick grabbed Phila and flung out one arm to break their fall. They both landed harmlessly on the edge of an old sofa and rolled off onto the porch. When they came to rest they were entangled in the skirts of Phila's wedding gown.

Nick pushed aside a wave of satin and grinned up at his wife. "A new technique?"

"I'm not used to wearing long dresses," Phila explained, turning pink.

"Maybe it would be easier if I carried you off to bed this time. After all, it is our wedding night. Would you mind very much if we did this the traditional way tonight?"

She smiled down at him, her love in her eyes. "Not at all," she said graciously. "I know how big you Lightfoots are on tradition."

"Yeah. Something to be said for tradition." Nick got to his feet and helped Phila to hers. Then he picked her up, her long skirts falling in a snowy wave over his arm, and carried her inside the old beach house.

"I think," said Phila a short while later as she lay naked and gently crushed beneath her husband's weight, "that I could get to like it this way."

Several months later Nick and Reed took advantage of a rare sunny morning in winter to get in a round of golf on a private course that bordered Lake Washington.

"How come Phila was in such a prickly mood this morning?" Reed asked, shading his eyes with one hand as he watched Nick's fairway shot.

"You know Phila. She's often prickly in the mornings." Nick shoved the iron back in his golf bag.

"Not like she was this morning. You two been arguing?"

Nick swore. "A small disagreement, that's all."

"Goddamn it, Nick, don't you know any better than to argue with a pregnant lady?"

"I hate to disillusion you, Dad, but your precious Phila is not above using her delicate condition to get what she wants."

"So give her what she wants."

Nick smiled fleetingly. "You don't know what you're saying."

"Well?" Reed demanded as he climbed back into the golf cart. "What does she want?"

"More money from Castleton & Lightfoot for Barbara Appleton's day-care centers. This is the third time she's hit me up for cash for that project in the past six months."

"Big deal. She's worked hard with Barbara to keep those centers running. You coughed up the money the other two times with barely a whimper. Why dig in your heels now?"

"Because Phila doesn't show any signs of ever being satisfied," Nick said grimly. "Left to her own devices she's going to run amok giving away C&L money."

Reed chuckled. "Nick, I'm going to level with you. I'll be the first to admit you're doing a hell of a job with Castleton & Lightfoot, even if I don't agree with every move you've made since you've been in charge. But you've still got a lot to learn when it comes to handling women."

"Oh, yeah? You're an expert?"

"Let's just say I've had a little more experience dealing with Phila's type. Way I see it, you got no choice but to do what I finally did with Nora."

Nick glanced thoughtfully at his father. "You convinced everyone to let Mom handle most of the charitable contributions for Castleton & Lightfoot."

"Worked out just fine."

"The hell it did. You were always arguing with her over where the money was going."

"So do it more formally than I did. Set up a Castleton & Lightfoot Foundation. Put Phila in charge, and give her a budget. Make her stick to it."

Nick climbed out of the cart and stood in the middle of the fairway, staring at his father. "Have you gone soft in the head? Put Phila in charge of a foundation designed to give away C&L money?"

"Think of the tax write-offs."

Nick began to grin. The grin turned into a roar of laughter.

"What's so funny?" Reed demanded.

"All right, I'll do it. I'll let Phila set up a foundation and I'll put her in charge. But don't come squawking to me when she presents her list of worthy charities and institutions at the annual meeting."

Reed grinned, slightly abashed. "You think a few of the old standbys are going to get dropped?"

"Not only will some of your favorites get dropped, but I can personally guarantee you the first thing Phila will do is demand an increase in her foundation's budget. Don't look now, Dad, but C&L has acquired a conscience and her name is Philadelphia Fox Lightfoot."

"I reckon I can live with a conscience as long as I get my grandkid."

"Don't worry. You'll get your grandchild. Hell, you're going to get a whole bunch of grandchildren."

"Think you can talk Phila into having more than one?" Reed looked pleased at the prospect.

"Yeah," said Nick, already anticipating the way Phila would give herself to him in bed that night even though she had argued with him that morning. She would be all over him, hot, fiery and full of a boundless love. "I'm working on the problem."

Jayne Ann Krentz *writing as*
Jayne Castle

Amaryllis Lark is undeniable beautiful.
She's also one of the best psychic detectives on St.
Helen's, the earth colony recently cut off from the
mother planet, yet not so very different from
home — a place where love still defies the most
incredible odds. Lucas Trent, the rugged head of
Lodestar Exploration, isn't keen on the prim and
proper type, and Amaryllis is *excruciatingly* proper.

Amaryllis

Amaryllis may have psychic powers, but she can't
read minds — least of all her own. When a wild
murder investigation leads to a red-hot love affair,
Amaryllis is shocked, Lucas is delighted — and no
power on heaven, earth, or St. Helen's can keep
them apart!

Available from Pocket Books

POCKET
B O O K S

1238-01

New York Times bestselling author

JAYNE ANN KRENTZ

DEEP WATERS

"There is no finer exponent of
contemporary romance than the
immensely poplar Jayne Ann Krentz."
—*Romantic Times*

Available from Pocket Books

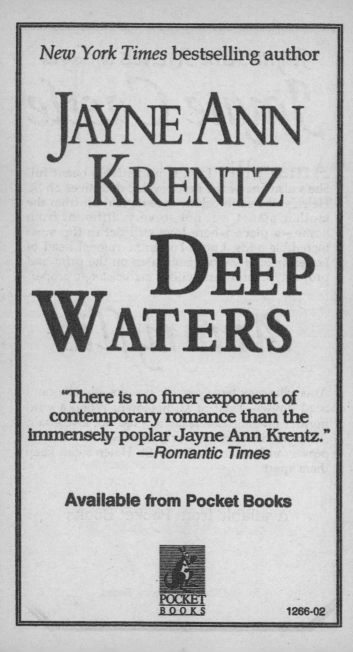

POCKET
BOOKS

1266-02